MW01131441

Let Me *Love* You

(The McClain Brothers: Book 1)

Alexandria House

Pink Cashmere Publishing, LLC
Arkansas, USA

Copyright © 2018 by Alexandria House
Cover image by **JAIDA A. PHOTOGRAPHY**

All rights reserved. This book or any portion thereof may not be reproduced or used in any manner whatsoever without the express written permission of the publisher except for the use of brief quotations in a book review.

This is a work of fiction. Names, characters, businesses, places, events and incidents are either the products of the author's imagination or used in a fictitious manner. Any resemblance to actual persons, living or dead, or actual events is purely coincidental.

Printed in the United States of America
First Printing 2018

Pink Cashmere Publishing, LLC
pinkcashmerepub@gmail.com
http://pinkcashmerepublishing.webs.com/

Let Me Love You

Trying to put past hurts behind you is hard when your ex is a fool, but buoyed by child support and alimony, Jo Walker is moving forward with her life, pursuing a career, raising her little girl, and trying to live in peace. She believes she has all the bases covered in her world. But what about her heart?

Rap legend Everett "Big South" McClain is divorced, too, knows all about failed relationships, and has relegated his love life to casual connections rather than pursuing something real. That is, until he lays eyes on Jo.

She's exactly what he never knew he needed.

He's what's been missing from her world.

Will she accept what he has to offer and let him love her?

For the love of hip hop.

1

I stumbled through the front doors of Bijou Park, hoping, wishing, and praying that the black coffee and plain bagel in my hands would serve to appease my boss. Peter Park was a horrible person. Temperamental, demanding, flippant, but talented and at the top of the custom jewelry game. An internship with him was an anxiety-ridden thrill ride and an opportunity most aspiring jewelers would kill for. I just happened to walk in on the right day—the day he and his assistant-slash-girlfriend received a beat down at the hands of his wife, Twyla. He was bloody and in need of a new assistant. I took advantage of his desperation by adding a little custom-jeweler training to the deal. I'd been assisting and training under him and his staff jewelers for a little under a year.

But today I was late.

Peter Park didn't do late—*ever*.

I nodded at Freda, the tall, ebony receptionist who could slay any fashionista even though she was in her sixties, and headed straight for the gold door with the silver lever handle that led into Mr. Park's office. I knocked, waited, and when the door swung open to reveal a livid Twyla, I thanked the heavens for my tardiness. Twyla was a certified fool and only showed up at Bijou Park when trouble was brewing between her and Mr. Park.

"Good morning, Mrs. Park," I offered.

Twyla flipped her forty-inch Remy hair extensions over her shoulder and clasped her hands to her wide hips. She was at least three inches taller and sixty pounds heavier than her Korean

American husband, and a damn pit bull. Mean, jealous, violent, and destructive. Peter Park might have reigned terror down on his employees, but his wife reigned terror down on him. Oddly enough though, she liked me, probably because she didn't see me as a threat since I didn't dress or act like I was trying to catch a man—specifically, *her* man. However, I still hated being around her. With her drama-filled reality show antics, she made black women as a whole look bad.

"Jo, honey, give us a minute. I'm in the middle of reminding my husband of a few things."

I glanced behind her to see Mr. Park at his desk, his silky black hair disheveled, tie crooked, glasses askew. The contents of the top of his desk were littering the floor around it. I almost felt sorry for him.

Almost.

But not quite.

"Uh…sure. I'll be in the back with Shirl."

"Mm-hmm." She shut the door in my face.

I scurried to the small office occupied by Shirlene Ramsey, the most tenured bench jeweler. Shirl's strength was making Peter Park's artistic visions a reality since he rarely got his hands dirty anymore, so to speak. She didn't design jewelry, but she was excellent at interpreting others' designs. My goal was to design *and* create, and I was fortunate to be able to see both sides of the process on a daily basis.

"She still on the warpath?" Shirl asked, when I dropped into a chair next to her work station.

"Yep. What'd he do this time? You know?"

Shirl glanced up from the piece she was working on and shook her head. "All I know is we had all barely made it through the front doors when she stormed in yelling and screaming, but I can guess what happened."

I could, too. Mr. Park loved black women, surrounded himself with us here at his company, and was a compulsive cheater despite the fact that Twyla always caught up with his infidelities. It was as if he refused to stop cheating on her and she refused to take their five daughters and leave him. He cheated; she beat his ass and tore up his office. Rinse and repeat. It was a wonder if the ridiculousness of it all didn't affect Bijou Park, but then again, half the clientele ordered custom pieces for their mistresses or side chicks. The relatability of Peter Park's life was probably what made the business so successful.

"You were late?" Shirl asked, her eyes on her diamond-drenched work again.

"Yeah...overslept. I didn't fall asleep until early this morning."

"Netflix or Hulu?"

I rolled my eyes at how predictably pathetic my life was. "Hulu. Watched a bunch of *Top Chef* episodes."

Her forehead creased as she carefully added another diamond to the eagle-shaped medallion. "I didn't know you liked to cook."

"I'm tryna learn how to cook."

"By watching *Top Chef?*"

I shrugged. "I've picked up some good tips from that show."

"Girl, you better be getting you a soul food cookbook, so you can cook your way to a husband."

"Had one of those. I'm good."

"Humph. Okay..."

I sighed as I pulled my cell from my purse to see if Mr. Park had summoned me via text as he usually did after he was able to calm his wife down and get rid of her.

"Shutting down on me?"

"Just checking my phone."

She looked up, rested her back against her chair, and gave me her full attention. "Jo, how old are you?"

Here we go. "You already know that."

"Humor me."

"Twenty-eight," came out on a sigh.

"Twenty-eight and all you do is work and watch TV at home—"

"That's not all I do, and you know it."

"You didn't let me finish. You—"

The door to her office burst open to reveal Peter Park and his wife's handiwork—a swollen eye, bruised cheek, and busted lip. "Jo, my office," was all he said before leaving, rubbing his jaw as he shut the door behind him.

I hopped up even though I was pretty sure this man was about to take his frustration with his situation out on me in some way, like having me drive all over the city for some elusive Korean dish or something. But at least I was avoiding this repetitive conversation with Shirl.

Once in his office, he nodded toward a black Bijou Park box on his desk. "I need you to deliver this to a client. I was supposed to, but I obviously can't now, and I'm late, so you need to leave immediately."

I opened my mouth to protest, because I wasn't about to deliver something to some side chick, and if it was a man I was delivering the piece to, I wasn't going anywhere looking like I jumped out of bed, threw on the first clothes I could find, and raced to work—which was actually what happened—but Peter Park cut me off.

"My driver will take you there, and Oba will accompany you since the piece is quite valuable."

I frowned slightly. "H-how valuable?"

"That's a thirty thousand-dollar piece."

My eyes widened as they fell on the box again. I barely noticed as he stood, grabbed it, and shoved it into my hand. Then I was being pushed out his door to Oba, one of the humongous security guards who carried holstered weapons and were an ominous presence at Bijou Park because of the nature of our work.

Minutes later, I was in the backseat of a black Denali with heavily-tinted windows and Oba was in the front seat chatting with the driver as we made our way to—

"Hey, uh...Oba, who are we delivering this to?" I asked.

Oba shrugged while glancing back at me. "He didn't tell me."

I didn't ask the driver, because his old ass creeped me out. He reminded me of Samuel L. Jackson's character in *Django Unchained*—gray and ornery. I did, however, lift the lid and peek inside the box at the piece, one I'd seen Todd, another bench jeweler, working on. A puffed heart made of what appeared to be zillions of tiny diamonds on a platinum chain. It was brilliant and gorgeous.

What felt like forever later, we stopped in front of a small boutique hotel, a really nice one, and I started feeling pissed about delivering this beautiful piece of jewelry to some skank. Nevertheless, I slid out of the vehicle after the driver opened the door for me. Oba checked his phone, said, "Fifth floor. Penthouse suite," and then motioned for me to walk ahead of him.

I clutched the box nervously, wishing I had a bag to put it in because I was afraid I'd drop it and its contents before we made it to our destination. As if reading my mind, Oba said, "Hold on," reached into the front seat of the SUV, and unearthed a shiny black Bijou Park sack. I took it from him, carefully sliding the box inside.

Oba walked closely behind me as I stepped through the elegant lobby toward the elevators. My legs felt like rubber as the weight of what I was doing settled on my shoulders. I was delivering an insanely expensive piece of jewelry to someone, someone obviously rich and probably famous. What if someone had followed us from Bijou Park and tried to rob us? Sure, Oba was huge and armed, but what if a group of huge, armed dudes tried to rob us? What if they kidnapped me and held me for ransom and—the elevator dinged, making me jump, snatching me from my thoughts and prompting me to step inside. Moments later, the doors opened, and after we exited the elevator, Oba had to give me a little nudge so I would start moving toward the only door in the hallway. A cavernous bassline grew louder and louder as I approached the door, and when I knocked timidly, I doubted it could be heard over the music.

Oba reached over my five-foot-two frame, which seemed even smaller in stature with his imposing one towering over me, and beat his fist against the door, startling me even though I saw him do it. I glanced up at him nervously. He gave me a shrug and a smirk.

The music was lowered, and the door swung open. A man that damn near matched Oba in height and girth appeared with a scowl on his face. He and Oba were on opposite ends of the skin tone spectrum. Where Oba was dark as night, this man was extremely light-skinned with orangey-colored hair. He frowned down at me, then let his eyes climb up to Oba. That's when a smile appeared on his face. As I stood there, he reached over my head and gave Oba dap. "'Sup, my nigga?!'"

Oba was just as animated as he said, "Sup, Dunn?! You know…same ole grind. Shit, Park didn't tell me we were coming to see your guy. Wish I'da known. I ain't know what I was getting into."

"Who dat?" This querying voice came from inside the suite.

"Tell Boss Man Peter Park's folks are here with that piece," Dunn said.

"A'ight," answered the voice.

"Y'all come in," Dunn offered, and then he smiled at me. "O, man? Who we got here?"

I rolled my eyes before I could stop myself. Because I was running late this morning, I'd thrown on a pair of jeans and a loose t-shirt, didn't bother to apply a stitch of makeup so the freckles that I'd always hated were prominent on my face, and my wild natural hair was pushed away from my face with a thick, cloth headband. I didn't look hideous, but I wasn't displaying anything that made me worthy of his leer.

Before Oba could introduce me to Dunn and vice versa, the voice returned and I found it was attached to another behemoth of a man—all height and muscles like Oba and Dunn with a skin tone somewhere in between theirs. "Aye, the boss said y'all can go on back there," he announced, nodding toward a door deeper in the suite.

"A'ight, Tommy," Oba said, looking from the voice to me. "Lead the way, Jo."

I swallowed and moved toward the door only to hear mumbling and snickering behind me, sure one or both of the two giants who evidently resided in that suite were looking at my ass. I rolled my eyes again.

Knocking on the door, I felt my heart begin to race. Who was this boss man of theirs? Was he rich and famous or just rich? Oba obviously knew who he was, because he was familiar with his security. I wished I had time to ask Oba who—

"Come in!" was yelled through the door.

I turned the knob and walked inside, stopping without giving Oba room to enter.

I recognized him instantly, but anyone would've since he was probably the most recognizable rapper on the planet. He wasn't old, only in his late thirties, but had been in the rap game for so long he was definitely considered one of the old heads at this point. Award-winning, multi-platinum-selling, world-renowned, skilled like no other, and fine as all hell. That's how I'd describe Big South. I was shocked, pleasantly stunned into silence and paralysis.

He was shirtless, and the swollen muscles of his chest and abdomen teased me as a sheet covered his lower body. He was sitting on the side of the bed, his dreads hanging loosely around his face. He wore a blank look on his face as I stood there unraveling in his presence.

His chocolate eyes raked over my body before shifting behind me to Oba. "Park too big to make deliveries now? Got his side pieces doing his work, huh?"

Side piece?

Negro, what?

That broke the I-cannot-believe-I'm-in-the-same-room-with-this-fine-as-hell-man spell. I blinked a couple of times to try to calm myself, and while Oba explained that Peter Park was "under the weather," I made quick strides across the room, got all in Everett "Big South" McClain's face, and hissed, "For your damn information, I ain't *nobody's* side piece!" I glared at him for a moment and then noticed the woman—actually, just her ass—in bed behind him.

Did this man really tell us to come in here while he has a naked woman in bed with him?

Was he naked, too, underneath that sheet?

What an asshole!

His eyes widened with surprise at my abrupt movements. "Shit, my bad, lil' mama."

My top lip involuntarily curled into a snarl as I dropped the sack in his lap. "And here's your damn necklace," I said, then turned and breezed past Oba, leaving the room, then the suite, without another word. Yeah, everyone knew of Park's reputation, but to assign the side chick role to me was presumptuous and totally disrespectful! Big South was a jackass, and a nasty one at that, nasty as hell. But the worst thing was how turned on I was from just being in the room with him. I didn't do rappers, especially not asshole ones.

But I'd be damned if I didn't want to do Big South's stupid ass at that moment.

2

"Aye, hold up!"

Oba's voice didn't slow my steps as I headed down the hall toward the elevator. While I loved hip hop music, I hated most rappers, especially conceited ones. Maybe I was in the wrong business. They were the main ones buying custom jewelry. Damn-it!

"Aye!" Oba's big hand stopped the elevator doors from closing and he slid inside. "You better hope he don't complain to Mr. Park."

I frowned. "Complain about what? He got his necklace, safe and sound. Not a scratch on it."

"Yeah, but you threw it at him."

"I didn't throw it. I kind of…dropped it in his lap."

"And you cursed him out."

I laughed. "You call that cursing him out? You need to get out more. I can do way worse than a couple of 'damns.'"

"I'm just saying, he's a client. You don't think you were out of line back there?"

"*Me* out of line? He let us in that room with a naked ass in there with him. He was probably naked, too! And he called me a damn side piece!"

"South is good people. He ain't mean nothing by that shit. Everybody know how Mr. Park get down. Plus, he used to send Keisha out to do stuff like this all the time. That's probably why South thought you were his girl."

Keisha was the assistant-slash-girlfriend I replaced, so I said, "Well, I ain't Keisha."

"That shit is obvious," Oba said, as the elevator doors opened.

We were halfway back to Bijou Park when it hit me that he was right, though. Since he was already dealing with a Twyla beat down, Mr. Park was probably about to act a whole fool with me for "disrespecting" one of his clients.

*****

The day was nearing its end, and I was manning the receptionist's desk since Freda left early for a doctor's appointment. Peter Park had been closed up in his office since Oba and I returned, opting to communicate with me via text, instructing me to spend the day training under the bench jewelers and then to take over for Freda. No yelling. No mention of Big South at all.

Maybe he didn't snitch on me after all.

Things were slow, so I had my face buried in my phone, perusing Facebook, when I heard his voice.

"Is Park in?"

My head jerked up to meet intense chocolate eyes. He towered over me and the desk, his free-falling dreads framing his impassive face. His thick, dark lips were relaxed. My eyes slowly descended over his plain black tee to the diamond letter "S" hanging from the chain around his neck. It was undoubtedly a Peter Park piece. I could recognize them from a mile away. Mr. Park definitely had his own style and was irrefutably the best at what he did. As a matter of fact, I could tell he'd created this piece with his own two hands.

My eyes rose in time to see him lift an eyebrow. Shit, now I was staring at him. I blinked a few times and finally said, "You have an appointment?"

He glanced behind himself at Dunn, who I hadn't noticed up until that point, and chuckled. "Much money as I spend up in this bitch? I don't need one, lil' mama. Just tell him South is here. He'll see me. He's here, right?"

There he was. The asshole. The smug asshole. That brought me out of my stupor. Forgetting I was sitting at Freda's desk and could simply use the intercom, I texted my boss to let him know Big South was there to see him. Two seconds later, the door to his office burst open and Peter Park stepped out wearing a huge pair of shades.

"South! Did you like the piece?"

"Yeah, yeah. Let me holla' at you for a minute."

Mr. Park nodded vigorously and led him into his office, leaving me and Dunn alone. I didn't realize I was staring at the door they'd closed behind them until Dunn said, "So…what's up with you?"

My eyes shifted from the door to him. "You talking to me?"

He grinned. "Ain't no one else in here, is it?"

I sighed. "Can I help you with something?"

"Shit, yeah…with your fine ass."

I shook my head. "Unh-uh. Nope. Not interested. At. All." Letting my eyes fall back to my phone, I added, "*Shit*, no."

"Come on now, ma. I can make you see Heaven."

I glanced up at his gigantic ass again. "HELL, no."

"You want the boss? I'ma tell you right now, you ain't his type."

I'd already gathered that from the size of the ass I saw in bed with him. I wasn't flat in the back, but I had nothing on ole girl. Not that I cared anyway. So I said, "Good thing I don't want his ass either then, isn't it?"

His eyebrows flew up. "Really? Then why were you drooling over him a minute ago?"

"I wasn't—"

Peter Park's door flew open again, startling me. Like, I actually jumped in my chair. Big South breezed past me without giving me a glance and Dunn quickly fell in step behind him, seemingly having dropped our little disturbing conversation. Talking about me drooling over that man. Was he craz—

"Jo, I need to see you in my office."

I was staring after Big South again. Had no idea Peter Park was standing right in front of me. What the hell was wrong with me?

I nodded, and as I followed him into his office, I thought about how Big South didn't acknowledge me when he left, noticed the stern look on Mr. Park's face as he fell into the high-backed chair behind his desk, and realized I was in trouble.

Shit. He'd actually told on me.

Snitching-ass mother—

"Jo, uh…I'm gonna head out for the day. Would you let everyone know Big South has invited us to his listening party Saturday night?"

"Um, okay. Sure. That's-uh-it?"

"Should there be something else?"

"Oh, no-no. Just wondering if you need me to do anything else before you go."

"No."

"Okay." I hesitated, then turned to leave.

"Oh, yeah. He told me to be sure you knew he's especially looking forward to seeing you there."

I spun around, confused. "He did?"

He nodded. "He did."

"Uh…okay. Th-thanks?"

I left his office feeling perplexed, and for some reason, thrilled.

*****

"So, let me get this straight. You acted a fool with Big South? *Big South?* Are you serious?!"

"He's an ass, Bridgette. I don't care how famous he is. He's a jerk."

"And you're not going to the party because of that? Who in LA is not an ass? And hell, who cares?! Ain't like you gotta date the man! Just go to the party and take me with you so I can meet him. Maybe he'll put me in his next video."

"I thought you just finished filming a movie. Wouldn't a video be a step backwards?"

"Not a Big South video! The man is a rap icon. He has a career other rappers would die to have just a piece of. He's had like ten platinum albums, toured the world several times, got a baby by a supermodel. Shit, he's a rap god! A spot in one of his videos would put me in high demand as an actress!"

"I'm not going, Bridge. Sorry—not sorry."

"You can't take one for the team just this one time? For real, Jo? Not even for your BFF?"

"Last time I took one for the team, I ended up hooking up with the man who eventually fucked up my life."

"All you were supposed to do was go to the party with me so I wouldn't be alone. I didn't put a gun to your head and make you talk to Sidney or date him or marry him. Damn!"

"True, but I'm still not going."

"Jo! Come on! The man personally invited you. You've *got* to go!"

"Okay, so he didn't personally invite my ass to nothing. He invited the staff through Peter Park and then assumed I would show up because I guess he assumes no one will turn him down. Well, he gon' learn better, because he could have invited me personally, had more than one opportunity to, but he didn't, so screw him. I'm not going."

"Maybe if you hadn't thrown a sack of jewelry at him, he would've personally invited you."

"Bridge—"

Saved by my doorbell. I was too happy to end this call, because I knew Bridgette wouldn't stop until I agreed to go and take her with me.

"That's my door, gotta go," I said, ending the call before she could respond. I made my way to my front door and smiled at the sight of the love of my life on the other side. Taking her from my neighbor, I said, "You could've used your key, Ms. Sherry."

She shook her head. "Thought you might've had some male company."

I gave her a smirk. *As if.*

She shrugged. "You never know."

"How was she today?" I asked, ignoring her statement. Turning my attention to my little girl, I kissed her chubby cheek, and cooed, "Did you have fun with Ms. Sherry today, Nat-Nat?"

She puckered her little two-year-old lips and kissed me on mine before saying, "Yeah," in her tiny voice.

"We went to story time at the library and she sat still like a big girl. We had a great day. Thanks for letting me take her to my friend's house this afternoon, too. Seeing this doll always lifts her spirits. I think being able to spend time with Nat is speeding up her healing process."

"You know it's cool. I knew you were gonna take good care of her. You always do."

"I love it. Always wanted kids. You moving next door to me and needing a babysitter was a blessing. Believe me."

I gave her a smile, and after she left, fixed me and my little girl some microwave meals. Then we settled down for an evening of *Top Chef*. Nat-Nat watched the TV with rapt attention until she fell asleep in my arms.

3

Bridgette's persistent ass called me every day up until the day of Big South's party, and when it finally sunk in with her that I was indeed not going, she stopped talking to me for a week. But that was just how she was, how she'd been when I met her at a group home back in middle school, years before I followed her from Alabama to LA. I was in that home because my mother had a nervous breakdown and had to be institutionalized for some months, but had no family willing to take me in. Bridgette had been in the system since she was nine or ten. Both her parents were cracked out. Hear her tell it, her whole family was strung out, including her grandparents. I was able to return home to my mother after four months; Bridgette stayed until she graduated from high school, but in those months we were there together, we developed a bond that endured despite her dramatics and were thick as thieves all the way through school. I knew how badly she wanted to succeed, how hard she worked, but she was just going to have to be mad at me for now. She'd get over it eventually. She always did. Unlike the acquaintances I'd made because of my association with my ex-husband, Bridgette was a real one. She'd had my back through my messy divorce, and I appreciated her for not abandoning me like them.

But the depth of our friendship wasn't enough for me to spend time in the same space as Big South's revolting, arrogant ass.

That wasn't happening.

As was the usual in my life, any remote thought of my ex-husband conjured him up. As I was heading back to Bijou Park with my boss's lunch that afternoon, he called. I fought the familiar urge to ignore him, reminding myself that we shared a child, and accepted the call.

"Hello?"

"Hey, Jo. Just calling to check on you and the baby. Y'all good?"

It irked me to no end that he still wouldn't speak her name.

"Yeah, we're good, Sid."

"Good. Good. I made the deposit for this month. Need anything else?"

I need your sorry behind to step up and be a father and stop thinking money will solve everything. "Nope."

"A'ight. I'll check on you two in a couple of weeks."

"Yeah, bye." I hung up before he could respond, parked my car, and headed back to work, hoping my coworkers would stop gushing over Big South's party. I was tired of hearing about it.

Everett

I was in the studio trying to come up with my contribution to this Rihanna track. I didn't like it, but had promised her I'd do a feature for her since she'd done one on my last album. The problem was that the beat wasn't moving me; plus, I was distracted as hell. Sitting my overgrown ass up there thinking about little mama from Peter Park's place, the short cutie with the caramel skin and dark brown freckles all over her nose and cheeks. I can't even say what was drawing me to her. I'd been with beautiful women, gorgeous women, famous women—women other men would die to be with, but none of them intrigued me like she did. She was all natural. Big, kinky, sandy-brown-reddish hair, no makeup. She was short as hell compared to my six-six body, and I couldn't remember the last time a woman under six feet tall caught my eye. She wasn't even pretty in a classic way, but still beautiful with those wide eyes and huge lips. Shit, I don't know. She was just different from any other woman I'd ever seen.

I meant what I told Park about looking forward to seeing her. Hell, I spent the entire party looking for her, had planned to apologize to her properly there, and was lowkey disappointed when she didn't show up. And now? I was kind of pissed about it. I mean, who stands me up? Me! But did she really stand me up? It wasn't like we were supposed to meet up for a date or something. I was confused as fuck. I was thirty-seven years old and had never felt this twisted up about a woman. Not even Esther, and the whole world knew I loved her ass.

I was going to have to shake this shit off. I had money to make. It was what I did best. So I sat there and listened to Rihanna sing about how some nigga would never get with her and let my frustration over little mama lead me in the booth.

4

Standing at the door in my pajamas, I stretched my eyes in surprise, dug my fingers in my hair and rubbed my scalp, then finally said, "Bridgette? What are you doing here?" It'd been two weeks since I'd spoken to her, and her way of taking me off punishment was to randomly show up at my door? Typical Bridgette Turner.

"Wench, I know you didn't forget!"

"Forget what?" I asked, genuinely confused. Then I felt little hands on my leg.

"Teetee Bijitt!" Nat squealed from below.

"Hey, Nat-Nat!" Bridgette chirped, then lowering her voice, said, "Jo Lena Walker, I promise before God, as sure as your mama's name was April, if you stand here and tell me you forgot about the premiere of my movie tonight, the first movie in which I have an actual speaking part, I am going to beat your complete ass in front of my godbaby."

"I didn't forget. You're early."

Yeah, I forgot.

"I know. We got a lot to do to get you red carpet ready." Then she turned and yelled, "Come on!" to someone behind her. Seconds later, she and Sage, her favorite makeup artist and a mutual friend of ours, entered my house. Since they both were loud and could get raunchy with their conversations, I knew I needed to get Nat to Ms. Sherry's place ASAP. I hoped she wasn't busy and could babysit on short notice. Otherwise, Bridgette was going to kill me, and I honestly wanted to be there for her, too.

As per usual, Ms. Sherry jumped at the chance to watch Nat, insisting that she spend the night. I hated my house and the neighborhood when Sid and I first moved there, but Ms. Sherry being next door had been a true blessing. I was glad I'd decided to stay after my divorce.

When I made it back from dropping Nat off, Sage was emptying her makeup case on my kitchen table and Bridgette was nowhere to be found. Before I could ask Sage where she was, Bridgette yelled, "You got any shoes to go with this little royal blue dress?!" She was in my closet.

"I don't think so!" I yelled back. "I was gonna wear the black maxi dress anyway."

Bridgette sauntered into the living room, which was a part of the huge open floor plan. My living room, kitchen, and dining room all flowed together. She had the royal blue mini draped over her arm while she held a pair of gold stilettos in her hand. I'd forgotten about those shoes.

"You're too short to wear maxi dresses. How many times I gotta tell you that? They make you look shorter," she said.

"What's wrong with being short?" I asked.

"Nothing, except you wanna be seen in the sea of Amazonian models that pop up everywhere in Hollywood, don't you? A maxi dress will make you disappear. You'll be looking like a damn hobbit under them."

I rolled my eyes. "Who said I was tryna be seen?"

"Girl, you too cute to be hiding," Sage chimed in.

I fell into a chair at the kitchen table and grabbed my Firestick remote. "Whatever, y'all. Ain't like I'm looking for a man or something."

"You should be. Sid ain't the end all be all, Jo. You need to get out there again," Bridgette said, pulling her own dress from the garment bag she'd arrived with and laying it over the back of my black leather sofa, the one Sidney just had to have. I really needed to buy new furniture. Everything in my house reminded me of my failed marriage.

"You don't date," I said.

"Because I'm focused on my career."

"Maybe I'm focused on mine."

"You don't even sound convinced of that yourself. That job with Peter Park is a hobby just like when you were training to be a makeup artist under Sage for like three seconds. The only thing you ever wanted to do was be a wife and a mother. It's all you talked about when we were younger, being a happy homemaker."

Yeah, I wasn't the most ambitious kid. "And we see how that turned out."

"Who knew Sid would turn out to be such a sorry ass? But you were a good wife, Jo, and you're still a good mother. Just gotta find you a better man this time."

"Yeah, girl. It's some good men out there," Sage offered.

"Where?" I asked, with lifted brows.

Sage seemed to think about that for a second, pursed her full lips, and then she shrugged her meaty shoulders. "Hell if I know."

I chuckled as I resumed the video I was watching before they arrived. As Sage motioned for me to sit in the chair closest to her, Bridgette asked, "You watching YouTube?"

I nodded. "Yeah. *4C Angie*. She and Ryan are doing that thing where they debate which artists are the best. They're talking about Frankie Beverly and Marvin Gaye right now. Ryan lost it when Angie picked Frankie Beverly."

"Remember that time they did Drake and Tupac? I died when Angie said Drake and Ryan just stared at her for like ten minutes and then the camera cut off," Sage said.

I chuckled. "Yeah, that was hilarious."

"Awww, he's holding their baby. He's so cute!" Sage gushed.

"Girrrl, that Ryan is fine as fuck! Shit!" Bridgette declared.

"And crazy about him some Angie. I met them at a beauty expo like a year ago, and he couldn't keep his hands and eyes off her," Sage informed us.

"Must be nice to have a man that crazy about you," I sighed.

"Yeah..." the two ladies agreed, sounding just as forlorn as me.

*****

The movie was so good! I mean, wow! Beautifully shot and directed with an all-black cast. It was the story of a group of college friends meeting up for their favorite professor's funeral, and in the process, catching up on each other's lives and learning that perceptions of others can be skewed and the trajectory of one's life can take surprising turns. Bridgette played the wife of one of the friends, a guy everyone had always assumed was gay. She only had three short lines, but got lots of time on-camera; her onscreen presence was huge. I was so proud of her! This had been her dream since she was a kid and she was making it happen.

Following the premiere, there was an after-party at a club called The Launch Pad. I drove us there in my car, and as I followed my leggy friend inside where we would be able to mix and mingle with the producers, her cast mates, and everyone else in attendance, I bobbed my head to Charlie Puth's funky, bass-driven tune, *Attention*.

The place was teeming with beautiful brown people smiling, dancing, chatting, and sipping drinks. I spotted a few minor celebrities as I stood at the bar with Bridgette, letting my eyes scan the place that was aglow with ambient yellow lighting. Whoever the DJ was, was on point with his R&B and hip hop selections, so the atmosphere was buzzing.

Bridgette handed me a shot of something, and I turned my nose up. "You know I don't drink real liquor. It's gotta be disguised by fruit or something for me to stomach it."

She flapped her manicured hand at me, her bejeweled nails reflecting the muted lighting. "This is a celebration. You about to get lit and then we hitting the dancefloor Reola, Alabama-style!"

I rolled my eyes as she tossed her shot back then shook her head, making her curly weave bounce. Bridgette was tall and lanky with gorgeous copper skin that she swore was the bane of her career, because dark-skinned, light-skinned, or Hispanic girls were on-trend.

She said being a regular, non-exotic-looking, brown-skinned black woman with a perm was killing her chances for success.

In her tight red tube dress, she planted a hand on her hip and lifted a brow expectantly. "Drink, bitch."

I shook my head. "Nope. Remember, I'm the driver. I'm not getting drunk and having to leave my car here, and you know straight liquor will have me straight tore up with the quickness."

"You never drink with me," she groaned, and then grabbed my drink, throwing it back, too. I was sure I'd be carrying her giraffe ass out of the place sloppy drunk by the night's end.

"Oh, there's the director! Let me introduce you!" She grabbed my hand, and I stumbled through the crowd behind her in my little blue dress, my big hair in full effect. Sage had beaten my face with precision, and judging from the winks and smiles I got from more than a few guys, I knew I was looking pretty good. No, I didn't want a man, but the attention was nice.

An hour later, my feet were calling me all kinds of bitches and hoes—and I think I heard a couple of motherfuckers, too—so I excused myself from a huddle of actresses in deep conversation about all of them vying to be in a Fenty Beauty commercial and set out to find myself a seat where I could ride out the night until Bridgette was ready to go. Ten minutes later, my fruitless search ended with me leaning against a wall, lifting one foot at a time to relieve the pain shooting through the balls of my feet in my unnaturally high heels. I was mentally deciding which fast food joint I was going to stop at after we left when someone tapped me on my shoulder. I looked up to see an older gentleman in a black suit wearing a smile and some really nice cologne.

"Excuse me, ma'am, but I've been asked to escort you to VIP."

"Huh? Who...what?"

His smile widened. "I've been asked to escort you to VIP. I'm George, the VIP concierge."

What the hell was a VIP concierge? "Um, why are you—why am I going to VIP?"

He dropped the smile.

I guess that was a dumb question. Who would be concerned about *why* they were going to VIP? Plus, hell…surely I could get a seat up there.

"I—my friend…I can't leave my friend."

"Of course not. Your guests may accompany you."

Well, technically, I was Bridgette's guest, but anyway. "Uh…let me go get her."

George followed me as I wove my way through the crowd, searching for Bridgette. Then my brain turned on and I thought to text her, hoping she'd see the message and meet me at the bar.

She did, her almond-shaped eyes wide with curiosity as she approached us. Her eyes darted from George, who stood at attention beside me, to my face. "What's going on? You getting kicked out? What happened?"

"No…he's taking us to VIP for some reason."

"VIP?! Sage is gonna wish she'd turned down that job tonight to do that stripper's makeup instead of coming with us when she hears this! Wait, you think it's Sidney? Is he here?"

The thought of it being my ex hadn't crossed my mind, but he was definitely someone who'd have access to the VIP section. "God, I hope not. If it's him, I'm getting the hell up out of here."

"Let's just see. Maybe it's not him," she said. I could tell she was itching to get to that VIP section.

As we followed George through the crowd toward the glass staircase, I realized it had to be Sidney. Who else could it be, and where the hell did he get off summoning me to VIP? I was pondering the cursing I was going to give him when I saw a face that made me stop in my tracks at the top of the stairs. Confirmation of what was really happening came when George approached the door the man was standing by.

"I can't believe this shit," I muttered.

Bridgette, who somehow heard me despite K. Michelle screaming through the speakers, said, "Fuck! It's Sid, isn't it? Damn, I really wanted to see what the VIP rooms up in here look like."

I shook my head. "It's not Sid. That's Big South's bodyguard. I'm not going in there."

Bridgette jerked me around to face her so fast, my head spun. "Let me tell you something. Jo, I love you like a sister, but if you don't take your ass in that room with that man, I'ma punch you in the back of your damn head. And I mean it. Move!"

"Bridge—"

Her eyes narrowed. "Unless that motherfucker sexually assaulted you, called you a bitch to your face, told you your pussy smelled like fish, or touched Nat, carry your ass on in that room!" she hissed.

"Why would he say my pussy smelled like fish? What you tryna say? I washed my ass, Bridge—"

"Jo, I'm not playing with you!"

"He called me a side piece!"

"Because you work for a ho' who's known for screwing his employees! And you said he said, 'my bad' after you told him you weren't one! Dayum!"

"You act like that's an adequate apolo—"

"Biiiitch, take your ass on in that room before I kick it!"

"Shit! Okay! I'm going!" I shrieked. "Damn!"

Once I made it to the door, I rolled my eyes at a smirking Dunn and followed George into the room. Like the interior of the main floor of the club, it was bathed in yellow lighting and included an entire wall of tinted windows that gave a view of the first level. There was a sectional of black leather couches in the center of the room with a huge glass coffee table in the middle and a small bar with its own bartender on the back wall. After George left, the room was empty save the bartender and me and Bridgette. I turned and looked at Bridgette, whose face bore confusion identical to what I was experiencing.

Then she shrugged. "Girl, whatever. I'ma get me another drink and enjoy being in here anyway."

As she did just that, I walked over to the window wall and peered down at the action, then decided to take my shoes off. I was sitting on the sofa while Bridgette chatted with the bartender when the door to the room opened and *he* entered, closely shadowed by his bodyguard. I froze, still leaning over clutching my right foot, cleavage smushed between my arms, mouth slightly agape.

If this man ain't fine…

He stepped further inside wearing black slacks and a burgundy dress shirt open at the collar, a thick platinum rope hanging around his neck, his dreads pulled back into a ponytail. He smiled as he moved closer to me.

"Hey," he said, like he knew me or something. He sat down beside me, not real close, but close enough to make me feel antsy as hell.

"Uh, hey," was my response.

"Jo, right?"

I frowned, glanced back at Bridgette, whose mouth was hanging wide open, and returned my attention to Big South. "How do you know my name?"

"Park told me."

"Oh…"

"You an actress?"

"Um…no, I'm here with my friend. She's in the movie." I gestured toward Bridgette with my head.

She took the cue and rushed over to sit on the other side of me.

"Word? I'm one of the producers," he said.

Bridgette gasped. "Really? How did I not know that?!"

"I don't want it known."

Bridgette thrust her hand in front of me toward him. "Oh…Bridgette Turner. It's amazing meeting you!"

As they chatted about how the screenwriter was an old friend of his, I stood and walked back over to the windows, tuning them out and gazing down at the crowd while my mind whirred with thoughts and my heart galloped in my chest. What the hell was going on? Why did he have me brought up there? What did he want from me? Sex? In a club? Hell, no! I wasn't some groupie ho'!

"It's packed down there, huh?"

He was right in my ear, and he scared the shit out of me. I flinched and turned to look at his tall frame as he moved from behind me to my side, his eyes shifting from the window to my face.

"Why'd you have me brought up here?" I asked.

He grinned, making his eyes crinkle in the corners. God, he was a gorgeous man. I'd always thought so, but standing there peering up at his face was overwhelming. "Straight to the point, huh? You don't like it up here?"

"You think I'm going to sleep with you?" I inquired, ignoring his question, because it was stupid. Of course I liked being in a VIP room. Who wouldn't?

He lifted his eyebrows and cocked his head to the side. "Damn, well...since you asked. *You* wanna sleep with *me,* lil' mama?"

"Can you stop calling me that?"

"Calling you what?"

"*Lil' mama.*"

"A'ight, what you want me to call you, then?"

"My name."

"Okay...Jo, you wanna sleep with me? If you do, I'm not gonna turn your ass down." His eyes skirted from my face, down my body, and back. "That's for *damn* sure."

"You must think I'm some loose groupie or something like that chick you had in your suite."

He frowned slightly like he was confused, then recognition lit in his dark eyes. "How you know she was a groupie or loose?"

It was my turn to frown. "You usually let complete strangers see your girlfriends' naked asses?"

"I didn't say she was my girlfriend, either."

"Whatever she is, your total and complete lack of respect for her is disgusting, and if you think I'm about to put myself in her position, you are dead-damn-wrong."

"That's why you didn't come to my party? Because you think I disrespect women?"

"Think? I *know* you do. If your music wasn't proof enough, Exhibit B was Miss Naked Ass. You let me and a gigantic man in that room while she was nude and exposed! Didn't even try to cover her up! You are a pig! A jerk! An asshole!"

He stared at me, his eyes burning into my face like a laser. A full minute passed of him just standing there staring at me before he finally said, "You think my music is disrespectful to women?"

"'South in your Mouth?' 'She be Babysitting?' 'Bitches and Hoes?' 'Butt Her Face?' 'Pussy and Coronas?' Do I need to run down your entire discography?"

"I made that shit close to twenty years ago when I was a kid who didn't think about nothing but fucking. You just gonna act like I haven't evolved at all?"

"Yeah, well, I saw that girl's ass like three weeks ago. Big evolution. Plus, you basically called me a Peter Park ho'."

He stared at me again, and the reality hit me that I was in a club, in VIP, arguing with a complete stranger who happened to be a bona fide superstar. I glanced around the room to see the amused eyes of Bridgette, Tommy-the-bodyguard, and the bartender on us.

I sighed and closed my eyes. "Look, all I'm saying is that was straight foul of you—"

I felt his body heat first, and when I opened my eyes, saw that he was in my face, so close his cologne was crowding my nose. With his eyes stapled to me, he murmured, "You're right. That was fucked up of me. I apologize to you for calling you a side piece and to her for doing that shit you just said I did."

"Um-uh…" I couldn't think for shit! "Um, you can't apologize to her here. That's-that's an indirect apology. Doesn't count."

"Can't apologize to her directly," he said, his face inching closer to mine.

"W-why not?" I asked, my eyes glued to his.

"Don't have her number. Never saw her again after that day. Don't plan on seeing her again. Shit, I can't even remember her name."

I frowned. "She—"

His lips met mine, cutting me off. Somewhere in the distance I heard a gasp that I think came from Bridgette. My mind was screaming at me, telling me to stop this, to stop *him*. I didn't even really know the man! But I didn't stop him. Maybe I couldn't, because his lips felt so good on mine. No tongue, just his thick lips covering mine. Then I felt his hand on my arm. Then he was backing away from me.

"I've wanted to do that ever since you threw that damn necklace at me," he said softly.

I lifted my hand and touched my lips. What was going on? Like, what the entire, total, and complete hell was happening? "Uh…what-why?"

"Just wanted to know if you'd taste as sweet as your mean ass looks. For the record, you do." He gave me a lopsided grin. "Maybe even sweeter than I thought."

"I didn't throw your necklace at you," was all I could think to say.

"Yes, you did, and that shit turned me on." His voice was husky, low, and his eyes were on my lips.

"Uh…" I didn't know what to do or say. I was feeling things in places that had lain dormant for a long time. Sensations were shooting through areas of my body I'd boarded up after my husband left me. My legs were weak, and the loudest thought in my mind was that I wanted him to kiss me again…and again…and again…and—

"You are sexy as hell, you know that?" he muttered, and moved in again, almost as if he'd read my mind. This time when his lips met mine, his tongue darted out. I quickly, eagerly—too damn eagerly—opened my mouth in response. I think I might have moaned or something when he grabbed the back of my dress and pulled me closer to him as he deepened the kiss, his tongue swiping nearly every inch of my mouth. Then *he* moaned, and my arms lifted on their own and wrapped around his neck. I had to fight not to wrap my legs around him, too. When we finally broke apart, we were both breathing heavily. He stood there, his eyes on me, a strange look on his face. I was so damn confused at this point, I was close to tears. What the fuck was going on?!

"Boss Man…" Tommy's voice cleared a little of the fog, and I backed away from Big South a bit.

"I gotta go. Got a flight to catch," Big South said, reaching up and rubbing a finger over his bottom lip. Then his eyes shifted away from me to Bridgette. "Nice meeting you."

Bridgette said something. I have no idea what.

His eyes found me again, and all I could do was stand there. Leaning in close, he inspected my face. Then he smiled at me, turned, and left. I stumbled to the sofa and clutched my head, feeling almost intoxicated with confusion and well...lust. Bridgette rushed over to me yelling and squealing, but I couldn't concentrate on her words, because my mind had left that room with the big, tall, fine, black man who was just as skilled at kissing as he was at rapping.

5

I have an obsessive personality. It's something I inherited from my mother, one of the hallmarks of her mental illness. I was just fortunate I hadn't inherited her other issues; the obsessive personality was more than enough of a burden. It makes you dissect and scrutinize the smallest of incidents, turn situations over in your head endlessly, analyze every syllable of an old conversation, ask interminable internal questions, and ponder the consequences of your actions fruitlessly. Hell, I've been known to ruminate over things I said years ago.

The premiere and after-party were on a Friday night. I spent all day Saturday and most of Sunday dodging Bridgette's phone calls and obsessing over my encounter with Big South, feeling shivers shimmy down my spine at the recollection of his lips touching mine, of his tongue invading my mouth, and by Sunday evening, I was seriously considering powering up my long-abandoned vibrator to ease the consequential sexual tension that was inundating every cell of my body.

I hadn't had sex in a couple of years, not since before Sid and I separated when I was six months pregnant. After I had Nat, I was too preoccupied with learning how to take care of her, since I had no one to show me, to even think about sex. My mom died a few years before I met Sid, so she couldn't teach me; therefore, the motherhood learning curve was steep for me and required too much brain power for me to be worried about a penis. Up until that night at the club, my pelvic region had been hibernating. Big South had awakened it, and now, everything down there was acutely alive and active like molecules colliding in the atmosphere. It felt as if someone was throwing a damn rave in my yoni.

I was never one to be star-struck, so my obsession had nothing to do with the fact that he was Big South, AKA Southy, AKA Big 12, AKA The National Champ of Rap. Yeah, he was a celebrity, a gorgeous one with strong, chiseled features, but what had my brain roaring was his effect on my body.

And none of this made sense.

So, I was horny *and* frustratingly perplexed.

I supposed he was attracted to my weird-looking ass for some reason. Maybe he had a thing for freckles, big lips, short slightly-bowed legs, and dusty-looking hair. He *did* say I was sexy. But why kiss me twice then leave without bothering to at least get my phone number? But then again, he knew where I worked. Maybe he planned to drop by Bijou Park to see me. Of course he wasn't going to do that. I was nobody to him, just some girl he kissed. He was a star. I was merely a game he was playing…wasn't I?

Shit.

If I kept this up, I was going to end up in a psych ward like my mother did.

My obsession led me to YouTube, where I watched countless Big South interviews, some so old he looked like a kid in them, chubby and baby-faced. His name originally came from his love of college football. Big South as well as Big 12, one of his other monikers, were NCAA conferences. The National Champ was another nod to his love of football. But one would think Big South was derived from the fact that he was from the south and was overweight when he first hit the rap scene. A big, tall, eighteen-year-old from Houston who spit witty rhymes with a distinct southern drawl. At twenty, he adopted a healthier lifestyle, eventually morphing into six feet, six inches of chiseled muscle, transforming him into a talented rapper who was also seen as a sex symbol. By twenty-two, he was in a relationship with British supermodel, Esther Reese, a gorgeous, six-foot, dark chocolate Barbie doll of a woman who was fifteen years his senior. The two were on serious couple goals status for anyone who saw them together, and as mismatched and unlikely as their pairing was, they married just four months into their relationship.

Less than a year later, their daughter was born. The whirlwind relationship lasted another five years, spawned South's acclaimed album, *E2*, a love letter to Esther, and ended after he cheated on her. As far as I knew, neither had ever married again, but both had been linked to several other celebrities in the tabloids and on the gossip blogs.

Big South was a documented womanizer who'd made misogynistic music and disrespected a woman in my presence. Hell, he'd even made assumptions about me! Yes, he apologized for it, but that still didn't explain why on Earth I let him kiss me, kissed him back, and was so completely and utterly turned on by him that I was sitting in my home overheating. Maybe I did need to find me a man so I could stop lusting after him. One thing was for sure: I needed to do *something* to get myself together.

Everett

I had to fly to NYC for some meetings after the movie premiere and was supposed to head to Houston, my hometown and the only place where I owned a home, afterwards. Instead, I headed back to LA, thinking I'd figured out a way to see Jo again.

Yeah, she was *still* on my mind.

I was standing at the window in VIP that night when I saw her—or actually, her hair—moving through the crowd. At first, I wasn't sure it was her. I mean, yeah, her hair was unique—never seen hair so big and full and bouncy and soft-looking before—but I still watched her for ten or fifteen minutes before I was sure.

The original plan was for me to contact Phil, the screenwriter I'd been knowing since back in the day, and kick it with him and his people that night, but after I saw her sexy ass in that tight little dress, my plans changed. I sent that butler dude for her, told him not to tell her or anyone else who was sending for her, and it took him so long, I thought her mean ass had refused to come up there. So I hit the toilet and was surprised and happy as hell when Dunn told me she was in the room. She looked so good up close, I kind of lost it in my head. The only thing that bothered me was that her makeup covered those freckles, but she still looked beautiful in the way that only she could. I found it hard not to touch her, which was crazy because I didn't even know her. And when I kissed her? I felt some shit I'd never felt before when I tasted those big, juicy lips of hers. Had those freckles been showing, my ass might've really lost it up in there right in front of Tommy and her friend. Those freckles turned me the hell on for real.

Anyway, on the flight back out to LA, I came up with a solid plan of how I'd get to see her again. As soon as we landed, I headed to my penthouse suite at Le Larousse to get the ball rolling. I always stayed in that suite when I was in LA since Esther got the house I once owned there in the divorce and that whole shitty mess made me not ever want to buy a house in LA again. The penthouse suite was expensive, but I never stayed long in the past. If something popped off with Jo, I'd have to rethink things, maybe get a little condo or something.

Damn, I was planning a future that involved a woman who openly talked shit about me to my face and turned me all the way on while doing it. I hadn't had the desire to do more than screw a woman in a long time, but Jo? For some unknown reason, I believed I could build something with her. And for the first time in a long time, that was what I wanted, to build something. Something real. And I wanted it with her. And as mean as she was, I could tell from the way she always looked at me and from what I felt from her when I kissed her that she was down for the same thing.

Or at least I hoped she was.

6

I couldn't believe it, didn't want to believe it. Was more confused than ever as I handed the valet my keys and stepped out of my car. This was what I'd been waiting for, training for, hoping for, but not like...*this*.

Wednesday morning, after I thought I had finally obsessed Big South out of my system and convinced myself that I'd imagined the whole club thing despite Bridgette circumventing me ignoring her phone calls and texting me about it like I was in a relationship with the man or something, Peter Park called me to his office to inform me that I was to meet with a client to discuss a new commission. My first emotion was elation. Me? Park was finally trusting *me* to discuss a piece with a client? He said I had free reign to conceptualize the piece, sketch out examples, and even create it. I would receive a portion of the total fee for it, too. I thanked him profusely for giving me the chance, for believing in me, to which he scoffed, "Oh, I *never* would have let you loose on your own so soon. You were requested."

Deep grooves formed in my forehead. "By who?"

"Big South, so don't mess this up."

As I walked through the hotel lobby to the elevator, my feet felt like lead. What did this man want with me, *from* me? Again, I hoped he wasn't summoning my ass to his suite expecting me to drop my panties for him. That was not happening. *Ever*. And I had a mind to curse him out for kissing me.

But you kissed him back.

And you liked it.

*And you **know** you want to have sex with him.*

As I stepped off the elevator, I squeezed my eyes shut and tried to ignore that stupid inner voice. Approaching the door, I took a deep breath and knocked. Dunn's ever-smirking ass opened it for me, swept his arm inside, and licked his lips somewhat seductively. "Nice to see you again," he said, amusement in his voice.

I rolled my eyes, stepped into the massive, but familiar, living area of the suite, and almost leaped out of my skin at the sight of Big South sitting on the sofa, his long legs stretched out before him. I don't know what I expected, for him to be in the bedroom or something?

And this motherfucker was wearing gray jogging pants.

Shit.

He looked like he always looked—good, good as hell—and because of that, the memories of him kissing me instantly sprinted to the forefront of my mind. All I could do was stand there. When the door slammed shut behind me, my ass jerked around to look at it like I didn't know a door could close. I was jittery as hell.

"Have a seat," he said, making me snatch my head back around to face him.

My eyes scanned the room and settled on an accent chair a couple of feet away from me. I plopped down in it and crossed my legs at my ankles, my eyes skimming the room again before settling on his face.

He smiled, exposing his big, straight teeth. Shit, even *they* were sexy. "Glad to see you again."

"Apparently, both you and Dunn," I mumbled.

"Come again?"

Since I was sure he really hadn't heard me, I said, "Don't have a choice but to be here if I want to keep my job."

"Been thinking about you," he replied, disregarding my statement.

"Obviously."

He chuckled. "You been thinking about me?"

Incessantly. "Nope."

"Aw, now. You mean to tell me I didn't make any type of impression on you at the party?" He cocked his head to the side and licked his lips. "At all?"

I uncrossed and re-crossed my ankles, ran my hand over my lap, glanced down at my tribal print maxi dress, then back up at him. "Uh...how did you know I was apprenticing under Peter Park?"

"I asked him what you did there the day I dropped by to invite him to the party you missed. He told me," he said.

"That's gotta be a privacy violation or something…" I mumbled.

Ignoring me, he mused, "I'm just wondering how long you been working there and how it is that I've never seen you there before. I been dealing with Park for years."

"I was probably busy *not* being his side piece when you came by there."

He chuckled again. "You a trip, you know that?"

This time, *I* ignored *his* statement and informed him, "I've never designed or created a piece before. He's never let me. You sure you want me to do this?"

"Positive."

I blew out a breath. "Okay—"

There was a light knock at the suite's door, and Big South said, "Hold up a second." Then he shouted, "Yeah, come in!"

The door opened and a woman in a short, excruciatingly tight pencil skirt and matching crop top entered the room looking uncertain.

Big South stood and beckoned her to him. I frowned, wondering what the hell this was. What was he trying to pull? Some ambush threesome? Well, he had me all the way fuc—

"Sheena, right?" he asked the woman.

She nodded, her eyes roving from him to me, and back.

"Jo, this is Sheena. I had my folks comb through every picture and IG post from the party I met her at the night before I first met you when you delivered my daughter's necklace. Evidently, she's the woman who left with me and ended up here. The shit's a blur because to be honest. I got halfway fucked up that night. I don't do that often—get fucked up, I mean—but I was celebrating a new business venture. But anyway, here she is." He turned to the woman. "Sheena, I owe you an apology. While you were sleep, I allowed Jo here and her bodyguard to come into the room and they saw you in my bed naked. It was disrespectful of me to do that to you. I'm sorry."

"O-okay?" Sheena said. "I mean, it's all good."

I eyed him and her, then said, "How do I even know if that's the right woman?"

His eyes widened as if he wasn't expecting for me to say what I said. Then he looked at her, leaned in and whispered something, and she turned around in response.

Yeah, it was her. Even in clothes, her ass was easily identifiable.

I shifted my eyes from her badonkadonk and rolled them at Big South.

He softly said something else to her and she left. A second later, he reclaimed his seat.

"You have to pay her to come here?" I asked.

He nodded. "And my lawyers had her sign some non-disclosure thing in case she decides to try to sue me or something."

My eyes were in my lap. "Why go to all that trouble?"

"Because, like I said before, you were right."

"You didn't have to do it in front of me, though."

"I wanted to, to show you I'm not as much of a jerk as your hostile ass thinks I am, because despite your attitude, I like you. A lot."

I fought not to roll my eyes again. "That necklace I brought was for your daughter?"

His eyebrows flew up. "Yeah. Who'd you think it was for?"

"Sheena."

He leaned forward and clasped his big hands together. "Sheena was someone I fucked. Nothing more and nothing less. I don't pay that kind of money for jewelry for women I merely fuck. Shit, the last time I bought a gift for a woman at all, I was married to her."

"And then you cheated on her, right?" I don't know why I said that. It was like I compulsively tried to antagonize this man because he seemed to like me.

And I liked him.

But why?

He reclined in his seat. "That's what they say."

"What is that supposed to mean?"

"Whatever you want it to mean."

I sighed and glanced at my lap, then reached down in my purse and pulled my phone out, navigating to the notes app. "Okay, how about we get started? What kind of piece are you thinking about now? Something else for your daughter?"

He observed me for a moment as he rubbed a finger across his bottom lip. Then he nodded. "Yeah."

"Um, birthday gift or just because? Do you have a deadline in mind?"

"Uh, yeah. I mean, no. I mean, how fast can you make it?"

"It'd depend on what you want, how elaborate it is, the kind of stones you want in it and if they're readily available to me."

"Diamonds."

"Okay. Um, did you have a design in mind? What are her favorite things? What does she like?"

"Hmm, besides Rihanna and Cardi B? Butterflies."

I smiled. "I like butterflies, too. So, maybe I can draw up a few designs for you and—how long will you be in town?"

He shrugged. "A week or so."

"Let's say I come back and show you the mock-ups in a couple of days? Here. Same time. Or you could come to Bijou Park?"

"A couple of days here is fine."

I tapped out of the app and slid my phone back into my purse. "Great!"

As I stood from my seat, he did the same and was right in front of me in seconds. His proximity made me feel a little woozy, so I grabbed the back of the chair I'd just vacated and looked up at him, afraid he was going to kiss me again, because I knew I couldn't be responsible for my reaction. I might've ended up involuntarily naked.

Instead, he raised his hand and dragged a finger from one of my cheeks, over my nose, to the other cheek. "I missed these Friday night."

It took me a moment to realize he was referring to my freckles. I had asked Sage to mask them the night of the premiere. "What?" I asked.

"You have any idea how sexy you are?"

In this? An oversized maxi dress, denim jacket, and flip-flops? "What?" I repeated.

"I wanna see you again."

Huh? "Uh-um, you'll see me in a couple of days, right?" *Didn't we just say that?* As usual when I was in this man's presence, I was confused as hell.

He shook his head. "I don't wanna wait that long. Can I see you tonight?"

"Tonight? Here?" *If I come here tonight, I'ma definitely have sex with you. No doubt. And that wouldn't be good...would it?*

He shook his head again. "Dinner. At a restaurant."

He was so close that his warm breath was grazing the skin of my face. It smelled nice and minty. "A-a date? With you? You and me? Us? On a date? Together?"

"Yes."

"How do you know I'm available?"

"That's what I'm trying to find out."

"No...I mean, how do you know I'm not—that I'm single?"

Alarm clouded his handsome face. "Are you? You are, right?" The man was damn near pleading.

"I am, but—"

His shoulders dropped. "Shit! Good," he breathed, and then he leaned in and slowly kissed his way across the path of my freckles. "So, will you go out with me?"

"Mr. South—"

"Everett."

"Ev-Everett, I don't date rappers."

He tilted his head to the side. "But you kiss them?"

"*You* kissed *me*."

"You kissed me back...and you moaned."

"You moaned, too!"

"Because you tasted like cotton candy. Tell me, Jo, would you melt in my mouth?"

Damn! "Uh...um..."

"Have dinner with me."

"I-I don't want to be listed as your newest jump-off on any of those gossip blogs. I live a quiet life. I'd like to keep it that way."

"We can go someplace where I know they practice discretion, dine in a private room. I promise not to put you out there like that. I'd just like to get to know the sexy little angry but obviously very smart woman who won't leave my thoughts." He cupped my face in his big hands, looked me directly in the eye, and added, "*Please*."

Well, shit. What else could I say to that but, "Okay."

7

"Hey." I sounded as sheepish as I felt after ignoring her calls for days, but I knew she'd want to gush about Everett kissing me and I was confused enough without her gassing me up, making me believe something like him actually being interested in me was possible. But now? Hell, it was more than possible. It was happening.

And I was still confused, but also kind of...I don't know. Excited?

"Oh, now your ass wanna talk to me?" she responded.

I decided to take that deserved jab and keep going. "You work this evening?" Bridgette did what every other struggling actress did for a living. She was a waitress.

"Nope. Called in sick."

"What's wrong with you? Is it contagious, because I need you to come help me with something, but I'm not trying to get sick."

"Only thing I'm sick of is that job. What you need me for? I mean, I don't know if I wanna help your ass since you been—"

"I need you to help me get ready for this date with Ever—Big South. And can you call Sage because I need her, too. I'm supposed to meet him at eight."

The call ended so abruptly, I first thought my phone dropped the signal or something. I tried calling her back three times but got no answer. I sighed and looked around my place, feeling lost. I wasn't a fashionista. If it were up to me, I'd throw on some jeans and a t-shirt but felt like I needed to step things up for this man.

So I decided to go ahead and call Ms. Sherry to impose on her again by asking her to watch Nat, and of course she readily agreed. I had dropped Nat off at her house and was on my way to dig through my closet when my doorbell rang. After checking the peephole, I flung the door open. "Why'd you hang up on me?"

"Shit, this is an emergency. I hung up so I could get over here ASAP! Sage is on her way." Bridgette stumbled into my house out of breath.

"Did you drive or run?" I asked, as she collapsed onto my sofa.

"Drove, then ran from my car. Spill the tea. How'd this happen?"

"I had to meet with him for work, and he asked me to go out with him tonight and I don't know why I said yes. This is stupid, right? I mean, what am I doing going out with someone like him?" I shook my head and fell onto the sofa beside her.

"Uh, are you crazy? Let it be me and Big-motherfucking-South asked me out. Girl, what's the problem? He's fine as hell and he's...*him!* Shit, if you ask me, you hit the jackpot. And I bet he can fuck, too. Lord!"

"I'm not sleeping with that man, Bridgette!"

"And why the hell not? You know you need some maintenance."

"Maintenance? What you trying to say?"

"I'm saying you ain't had no sex in years. You probably on the precipice of giving Sid some at this point."

"Shiiiit, wanna bet?"

"Yeah, I don't guess you're that desperate."

"I'm not. Listen, what if Big—Everett is just trying to use me for sex or something?"

"Don't let him, or *do* let him. I'd let him..."

"Bridgette! I'm serious!"

"Hell, so am I."

I sighed.

"Okay...look, I don't think he's about that. He seems to really like you from what I saw at the club. You should've seen the look on his face when you were talking shit to him. I think his ass was turned on."

"He likes my freckles. He-he kissed them today."

"He kissed you again?!?!"

I nodded.

A slow smile spread across my friend's face. "You like him. That's the real issue here, isn't it?"

I sighed and lied, "No. It's just weird for him to be so...aggressively interested in me. Haven't ever had a man pursue me like this, and he's damn famous. I just don't get it."

"Why not? You're beautiful!"

"I'm funny-looking, and you know it. But thanks anyway."

"Your ass ain't funny-looking to him, obviously."

I shrugged.

"Where is he taking you?"

"Uh, Ilbert's? Never heard of it before he mentioned it. He said they cater to celebrities, have a strict privacy policy. I told him I'm not trying to be on those gossip blogs..."

"Ilbert's? That's like one of the most exclusive places in the whole damn state! Not many people can afford to eat there, and I hear the food's crazy good."

"I'm scared, Bridge. No, I'm fucking *petrified*. What if this actually leads to something? What if he just ropes me in and then let's me down? What if I end up being hurt? I couldn't survive that shit again."

Bridgette reached for my hand, squeezing it in hers. "I knew that was where your mind was going. Jo, Sid was-*is* indisputably a total and complete asshole who wronged you. He deserves to have his dick cut off and stuck in his mouth, and if you recall, I offered to do just that for you. But this man is not your ex. It's just a date, something that could be fun if you get out of your head. Maybe it'll lead to love and marriage, or maybe it'll just lead to sex—which, like I said before, your ass needs—or maybe you'll have this one date and never see him again. It doesn't matter. What matters is you need to do something other than hide from the world because your ex-husband is a piece of shit and you had a rough childhood. You deserve to live, sis. So...*live*. Starting tonight. Enjoy being in the presence of a man half the world's female population would kill to have one conversation with."

I blinked back tears. "Okay…okay."

"Now, let's see what you got in your closet. Hopefully, we can put something together before Sage gets here, but look, if you're gonna keep seeing him, we're gonna have to do some shopping."

I smiled and followed her to my bedroom, thinking to myself that I needed to go shopping anyway. I'd shut down after Sid left and focused solely on taking care of Nat, hadn't really done anything for myself in a while. Maybe Bridgette was right. Maybe it was time to begin living again, starting with doing some things for myself, including spending some time with a man who seemed nice, was handsome, and if I was honest with myself, a man I was once a fan of and was very attracted to.

8

Everett

She was late.

I wasn't big on punctuality, but she was *really* late, thirty minutes late to be exact, and I didn't have her phone number. That was a dumb move on my part, but I had a feeling she wasn't ready to give it to me yet. Jo was cagey as hell. I could tell she liked me but didn't want to like me. I probably needed to slow my roll with her, but shit, I couldn't. She stayed on my mind and I had no idea why. It was like all these years since breaking up with Esther, something had been missing and whatever it was, was hidden inside of Jo. I was drawn to her like a motherfucker.

When she finally arrived, Tommy escorted her into the private room I'd reserved. I stood and pulled out her chair for her, licking my lips as I got a good look at the short black dress she wore that gave me a nice view of those bowed legs of hers. Her hair was big and wild, and although she wore makeup, including bright red lipstick on her big, soft lips that made them look even bigger, I could see her freckles. Whether she realized it or not, and I really don't think she did, Jo oozed sex appeal.

"I'm so sorry I'm late," she said, as she sat down.

After I'd reclaimed my seat, I said, "Traffic?"

She grabbed the water glass sitting before her and took a sip before giving me an embarrassed look, and saying, "Got lost."

I raised an eyebrow. "Really? Don't you have a GPS?"

She nodded. "Yeah, but I rarely use it because it distracts me, which makes me almost as nervous as LA traffic does, but I found my way and made it. Just…late."

"How long have you lived here?"

"Uh, about nine years. Since I was nineteen. I followed my friend, Bridgette, the one you met at the after-party, here. We're both from Alabama."

I grinned. "I thought I heard a hint of an accent. Southern girl, huh?"

She smiled and shrugged. "Yeah."

"Where in Alabama are you from? I got people there."

"Reola. A small town, so small if you blink, you'll miss it when you drive through there. I loved it as a kid, but don't think I could live there now. Shit, I'm rambling. Sorry. I'm so nervous."

"Nervous? Why?"

Her eyes met mine and expanded. "Um, because you're *you*, and I guess I don't get your interest in me."

"I like you, Jo."

"I know that, but why? I've seen the pics of you with other women, none of which look like me. Models and actresses. I'm a regular chick just trying to make it. I'm not from your world."

"I think maybe that's why I'm drawn to you. You're different, you speak your mind, you're beautiful...or maybe I just like women who curse me out."

Her mouth dropped open. "I didn't curse you out."

"Yeah, you did. And you were sexy as hell when you did it."

She rolled her eyes. "So what's good here?" she asked, picking up the menu sitting before her.

I shrugged. "I have no idea."

She looked up at me. "You've never eaten here before?"

I shook my head. "No, but I hear their seafood is good."

Frowning slightly, she asked, "Why would you bring me here if you've never eaten here before?"

"Trying to impress you."

I could see her cheeks flush.

"You look gorgeous, by the way," I said.

"Thanks. Uh...so do you. I mean...shit, I mean, *so do you*," she stammered, ending with, "Fine ass."

I chuckled. "Thanks."

The waiter arrived, took our orders, returned shortly with our drinks—ginger ale for Jo and wine for me—and then we sat there in silence for a few moments.

Finally, I asked, "What is a woman like you doing single, Jo?"

Her eyes widened. "Uh, I was married. I'm divorced now."

That was a surprise to me, made me wonder what type of fool would let himself lose a woman like her, despite the fact that I barely knew her. "Were you married long?"

"Three years. We were together for four. Things ended badly. Don't really like to talk about it. It's over and I'm glad."

"I am, too."

She gave me a little smile. "So, tell me something about you that I can't find out by doing a Big South Google search."

I leaned back in my chair and thought for a moment, sat up, and said, "I'm lactose intolerant."

Her mouth fell open and she covered it, stifling a giggle. "Seriously?"

I nodded. "Like a motherfucker. Milk, ice cream, and cream cheese tear my stomach up. It ain't pretty."

She laughed for another minute or so, cleared her throat, and said, "Okay, I wasn't expecting that."

"I bet you weren't. Anything else you wanna know?"

"Who's your best friend?"

"Keith Coleman. Been my best friend since fifth grade."

"You still in touch with him?"

I shook my head. "Not like I should be. Been busy, haven't talked to him in years."

"You should reach out to him."

"I know, but I got my brothers, too. They're probably my closest friends right now. Who's yours?"

"Bridgette."

"I figured that."

She dropped her eyes and then peered up at me. "Um...does your girlfriend know you're here with me?"

"If I had a girlfriend, I wouldn't be here."

She gave me a smirk. "If you say so…"

I looked her in the eye. "I didn't cheat on my wife, if that's what you're getting at."

"Why didn't you deny it when I brought it up before, then?"

"Because I usually like letting people think what they wanna think, but you ain't just…people. The truth is, we didn't split because I cheated."

"My husband did. I mean, he cheated on me."

"He's a damn fool, then. Why would anyone want to cheat on you?"

"You wouldn't?"

"Hell, no."

Our conversation was interrupted by the waiter bringing our salads, and we ate in silence. Then our entrees were delivered, so more silence. It was Jo who broke it.

"Um…Big—Everett?"

I looked up from my ribeye. "Yeah?"

"I have a daughter."

I laid my fork down. Wasn't expecting that, either. Had no clue she was a mother, not that it mattered. "You do?"

She nodded. "Yeah. She's two. Um, I don't know what your intentions are, but I wanted to give you full disclosure, so you can…" Her voice trailed off.

I stared at her for a second. She was nervous again, and I had no idea why. "So I can what?"

She shrugged. "Just thought you should know."

"What's her name?"

"Natalie."

"That's a pretty name. Classic. Like my daughter's name."

"Ella…"

"Yeah. Hey, can I see a picture of your daughter? You got one on you?"

She sat there for a moment before reaching for the cell phone she'd placed face down on the table, tapping on it for a few seconds then handing it across the table to me. Her little girl was smiling in the picture, little white teeth gleaming. I tried to find Jo in her face, but other than the lips and the gap between her two top front teeth, she looked nothing like her. She was beautiful, though, and a shade or two darker than her mother with curly, black hair.

"She doesn't look that much like you," I said, "but she's still beautiful."

"Thank you," she replied, as I handed the phone back to her.

"So, what am I supposed to do now that you've told me about her? Change my mind? Break and run?" I asked, as I relaxed against the back of my chair.

Her eyes went to the curtain-covered window to the left of the table. "That's what her father did, came home one day when I was six months pregnant and told me he didn't want a family anymore, that he'd never really wanted kids. Left me, filed for divorce, didn't even come to the hospital when I had her, has probably seen her ten times in her whole life. He won't even say her name."

I frowned as I leaned forward, my eyes on her. I knew she was guarded and mean as hell. Now I knew why. Some idiot had hurt her in the worst fucking way. "Then he wasn't a fool like I said before. That motherfucker is a moron. For a man to treat the mother of his child like that? Not treat that little girl like a princess? He don't deserve to be above ground. Stupid ass..." I might have done my dirt, lots of it, but I didn't believe in mistreating women. I was always up front with everyone I dealt with.

Her eyes darted around the room. "I like you, too," she confessed out of the blue.

"I'm glad you do."

"And this food is good. Thank you for inviting me here. I-uh-don't get out much."

"Then I'll have to change that."

*****

I practically had to beg her to let me follow her home, but since she got lost on her way to the restaurant, I wasn't taking no for an answer. I wanted to be sure she made it safely. She almost looked like she was going to cry when she finally agreed, and that made me wonder if she was ashamed of where she lived. Hell, she could've lived in a rat trap and I wouldn't have cared. I'd buy her a better place if she'd let me, because Jo just made me want to take care of her.

When she pulled up to the guard shack in what I knew was a very exclusive gated community, I had to wonder if she was leading me to a friend's house or something. Maybe her actress friend?

I sat in the backseat as Tommy followed her little Lexus into the driveway of a house I recognized, one I had looked at shortly after I left Esther. At the time, I was thinking of buying it but changed my mind, deciding I didn't want to live in LA full time anymore. I was trying to wipe my marriage out of my mind and believed living in LA would make that impossible. I remembered that the house was just as nice on the inside as it looked on the outside. Who the hell lived there? As Jo climbed out of her car and walked toward my truck, I hopped out, taking her arm gently. "Let me walk you to the door."

She nodded and led the way.

Once we were at the door, I asked, "Whose house is this?"

Her eyebrows rose as we stood in the well-lit doorway. "Mine."

"Word? Peter Park paying you like that?"

She shook her head. "Got it in the divorce along with great child support," she said, almost as if she was ashamed.

Who the hell was her ex? Fucking Michael Jordan? I should've asked, but I was afraid to. My ass was feeling threatened like a motherfucker. Her used-to-be man was obviously rolling. What the hell could I give her that he probably hadn't already? Shit. This revelation really messed me up. "Oh, okay," I said, playing it cool. "Did you enjoy yourself tonight?" I asked, as I rubbed her freckles with my fingertip.

"I did. You are surprisingly much less of an asshole than I

originally thought."

I threw my head back and laughed. "Glad to know I improved your impression of me." I dragged my finger over her nose and smiled down at her.

"You really like my freckles, huh?"

"Yeah. Don't you?"

"No. Always hated them. My lips, too. Got teased mercilessly about both when I was a kid."

Speaking of lips…I leaned in and softly kissed hers. "You mean, *these* lips?"

Her mouth hung slightly open as she nodded.

"Well, I'm fond of them, too."

I could see a little smile playing at the corners of her mouth as she reached up and touched my top lip. "I like yours, too."

I don't know what about her touch got to me, but the next thing I knew, I was leaning in kissing her again. This time she instantly opened her mouth to mine, and my tongue found hers the moment it slid inside. We kissed for what felt like hours, her arms around me, her small hands rubbing my back as I held her face in mine.

When we broke apart, I whispered, "Can I see you tomorrow?"

Through heaving breaths, she replied, "Tomorrow night? Dinner again? I'll have to check with my babysitter…"

"Dinner, lunch, breakfast—shit, a snack. Whatever. I just wanna see you." I rubbed the back of my hand over her cheek.

Closing her eyes, she said, "L-lunch would be better."

"I know you don't wanna be photographed, so we can eat in my suite, or at the hotel's restaurant, or wherever you want."

"Um, your suite is fine as long as you promise not to—"

"I won't do anything you don't want me to do."

Her eyes met mine as she licked her lips. "That's the problem. I want you to do a whole lot of stuff to me."

My damn chest tightened. "I—shit, for real?"

"Yeah. For real."

"Damn, Jo. You're messing with my head," I murmured.

"Don't mean to. It's the truth. What's your number?"

"Huh?" My ass was mesmerized, caught up in thoughts of just what I could and would do to her given the chance. My shit was rock hard. The things this woman made me feel...

"Give me your number so I can text you what time we can meet for lunch. I don't have a set lunchtime. It always depends on Mr. Park's moods."

"Okay. Um, all right..."

We exchanged numbers, then I kissed her one more time and reluctantly left.

In the truck, Tommy asked, "You really feeling her, huh, Boss?"

As he backed out of her driveway, I smiled, and said, "Yeah, I really am."

9

I spent the night after our date obsessing, of course. But it was a good kind of obsessing. I kept mentally rehashing every word he said, the way he looked at me, the way he seemed to unravel when I basically told him I wanted to have sex with him, how he kissed me, his smile, his touch. The look in his eyes right before he left me on my doorstep, like the last thing he wanted was to have to leave me. Everett "Big South" McClain made me feel…special, desirable, sexy as hell, and powerful, *very* powerful.

I didn't get much sleep, but energized from thoughts of Everett and the excitement of getting to do what I'd been dreaming of doing since I stepped foot in Bijou Park, I hopped out of bed and managed to make it to work early. Had to stand outside the double doors and wait for Freda to unlock them for me. Peter Park was already there, but we all knew not to bother him about unlocking the doors. Once inside, I glided to his office to see if there was anything he needed me to do before heading to Shirl's office where I occupied a corner, quietly making mock-ups of the piece I was to create for Everett's daughter.

"Here early, huh?" Shirl said, when she arrived.

I looked up at her, smiled, and nodded. "Yep. Got work to do."

"I heard Mr. Park finally let you loose. I know you're gonna do a great job. You've got a good eye."

My smile grew wider. "Thanks, I'm excited but scared to death. I hope you won't mind me calling on you to help me."

"Of course not! You know…you look different today. You

wearing makeup?"

"A little."

"You look cute."

"Thanks."

A second after Shirl left to get the piece she'd been working on from the onsite vault, a text from Bridgette popped up on my screen: *So is your ass ever gonna tell me about your date?*

Me: *Damn! It was just last night!*

Bridgette: *And that's when your ass should've spilled the tea! How was it?*

Me: *Good. Great. Wonderful. He's nice. Really sweet.*

Bridgette: *Awwww* (Heart eyes emoji) *Did he kiss you again?*

Me: *Yep. Got another date with him today, too. Lunch.*

Bridgette: *What?!?!?!?!?!?! Damn, Jo! He's really feeling you! I hope y'all fall in love and get married and shit. That'd kill Sid's dumb ass.*

Me: *You stupid. Gotta get to work. Call you later.*

Bridgette: *You better!*

I shook my head, stuck my cell in my purse, and buried my face in my sketchpad for the next hour. I wasn't the best artist, but I was decent, and I was feeling the butterfly designs I was coming up with off the top of my head. So deep was I into my work that I barely noticed when Shirl returned, and the sound of her filing away at something didn't bother me. When a knock came at the door, I didn't even flinch.

"Come in!" Shirl shouted.

"There she is." I recognized Freda's voice but didn't look up until I heard her say, "Jo, these fellows have a delivery for you."

Tearing my eyes away from my work, I frowned when I saw only Freda in the doorway. Before I could ask her who she was talking about, a man walked in and handed me a huge vase of what looked to be two dozen red roses. My mouth dropped open when another man entered the small office and placed another vase, this one holding yellow roses, at my feet. The third guy brought pink roses that Shirl quickly made room on her work station for. The three guys left and came back with more roses until Shirl's office was nearly overtaken with twenty huge vases full of the flowers, the last of which held a card that read:

Thanks for sharing your time with me last night. Can't wait to see you at lunch. - Everett

I was staring at the card, my heart beating furiously, when Shirl said, "So, I take it you have an admirer?"

I looked up at her, feeling my cheeks heat up. "It would seem so. I'm so sorry about this. You can barely move around in here."

She grinned. "Girl, I'm fine. Just happy for you. I hope you're going to give whoever he is a chance."

"Oh, I am. I'm meeting him for lunch."

"Good!"

"Yeah, but what am I going to do with all these flowers?" I sighed. I was flattered, but also a little overwhelmed.

"I'll help you load your car up this evening. You don't need to be worrying about that. Just get your mind right for this lunch date so my old man-less ass can live through you."

I shook my head, wondered if I should text Everett to thank him, then decided to do so in person.

*****

Dunn met me at the door, as expected. No smirk on his face this time, but rather a look of irritation. I didn't know what that was about and didn't care. I wasn't there to see him, I was there to see his boss. I stepped into the suite to see a table set up with cloche-covered plates, glasses of water, and a beautiful centerpiece of assorted flowers at the far end of the massive space. Glancing around the empty room, I wondered if it would be appropriate to call his name or if I should just wait. Or maybe I could text him and let him know I was there...or I could knock on the suite's bedroom door. Or—

The bedroom door opened, and out he walked wearing jeans and a plain white t-shirt along with a pair of his own *South* sneakers. His dreads were loose, his molded features just as beautiful as ever; a bright smile was on his face that made me feel like I was the answer to his prayers. It probably only took him four steps to cross the room and wrap me in a hug that was so warm and snuggly, all I could do was close my eyes and inhale his scent. He smelled so good, too good. What was this? How could I be so drawn to a man I barely knew outside of his public persona?

"Jo," he breathed in my ear.

I leaned into him and smiled, sighing lightly.

He held me tightly for another moment or two and then backed away a bit. I had to fight not to grab him and pull him back to me.

"You smell good," he murmured, his smile replaced by a smoldering look as his gaze rose from my lips to my eyes.

"Thank you, and thanks for the roses...all of them."

The smile reappeared. "You got them? Good. You like them?"

"Yes, I really do. That was so sweet of you."

"You're welcome. I know it was a lot of them, but I couldn't decide on a color, and the more I thought about you, the more I decided you deserved all the colors, then I was like...you deserve all the roses they had in the place. So I bought all of them."

"All of them? Really? Wow, that's...you know, I've never been given flowers before. Ever."

He gestured toward one of the chairs at the table, and said, "I can't believe that. Are you serious?"

I nodded as he pulled the chair out for me. "I am."

"Wow."

He watched me sit and get settled in my seat then took the chair across from me. "So, I just ordered a couple of club sandwiches and fries. Something light. Then I thought, shit, I should've let you order your own food. So if that's not okay with you, I can order up something else. It's whatever you want."

I lifted the cloche, and my eyes grew wide at the sight of the quadruple-decker, loaded sandwich cut in quarters. It looked and smelled delicious. "No, I think I'm good."

He gave me what seemed to be a relieved smile. "Great. Hey, I'm glad to see you again. I was almost scared you wouldn't show up."

He was...scared? "Why wouldn't I?"

"Oh, you know. The whole Sheena thing, you hating my music, the fact that you are the most beautiful woman I have ever laid eyes on, and then I'm so much older than you. When you were telling me how long you've been in LA, and I started doing the math in my head, I realized we're like nine years apart. I thought you might've been older than you are. Not that you look older, but you know...you can never tell with a black woman. Y'all are age-defying and...damn, now my ass is rambling. Guess I'm the one who's nervous today."

I nearly choked on my sandwich, coughed so hard that he jumped up and almost broke my spine hitting me on my back. I grabbed his arm, coughed a few more times, and said, "I'm good. You're gonna paralyze me if you keep trying to help me. You're heavy-handed as hell!"

He gave me a sheepish grin as he reclaimed his seat. "My bad. You good, though?"

"Yeah, yeah...I'm just sitting here wondering if you're out of your mind."

His eyebrows nearly met. "Huh?"

"I was a fan of yours, Everett. I have followed you for years. I follow you on Instagram, see the way you live, the places you get to visit, and like I said before, the women you've been with. And you're nervous about being around a girl from Alabama who ain't got nothing going for her but alimony and child support? I don't even have a real career. I'm in training!"

"*Was* a fan?"

I rolled my eyes. "That's all you got from what I just said? Really? You truly are just a regular guy."

"I never said otherwise."

I shook my head and looked down at the gargantuan sandwich I knew I wouldn't be able to finish. Then I took another bite of it.

"Look, I've been with…a few women. I have, but I didn't pursue anything serious with them. They were just something to do. I know that sounds fucked up, but it's true. And honestly, I was the same thing to them. I want more than that with you. And as far as you not having anything going for you…shit, all I see is a woman who speaks her mind, is fearless, and is pursuing a dream all while being a single mother. You got a lot going for you, Jo, *and* you are attractive as hell, intimidatingly attractive."

"Well…thanks."

"You have trouble accepting compliments, huh?"

I shrugged. He was making me feel…hell, I don't know. Tingly?

"Back to you *used* to be a fan?"

"Oh, yeah. You lost me with that conceptual album. What was it called? The one with the cover art you could only see under a black light?"

"You talking about *Southbound*?"

"Yeah, that one. Too far, bruh. The music was totally off the wall and the beats were whack. That shit made no sense. It was like you were just saying whatever was on your mind, some strange stream-of-consciousness stuff."

He scoffed. "Are you serious? That's some of my best work!"

I shook my head. "No, you were bored and tried something different. I mean, I get it. You've been in the business forever, so I can understand you getting bored. Hell, I have a touch of ADD, so I can get bored in a second. You tried it, but it was bad, Everett. Baaaaad."

"Bad? That motherfucker went double platinum!" He was actually getting upset, and it was kind of hot.

"Oh, that was the Beyoncé effect."

"The what? Now you gon' hate on Bey?!"

"No, I'm not hating on anyone! I'm saying, Beyoncé's so good and beloved, an album of her whistling would go diamond at this point. Same with you. Your fans love you no matter what."

"But not you, huh?"

"I love your old stuff. *Stop and Frisk* was my shit back in the day, old man! I stayed jamming to that song!"

"Ooooh, shit! Old man? So my age *is* gonna be an issue for you?"

I couldn't help but laugh. "Look at you. I got you shook! No, Everett...your age is not an issue. At all. You ain't *that* old. You're still in your thirties. I mean, everything is in working order, right? Isn't it?"

"I can show your ass better than I can tell you."

Well, now I was wet, drenched, shit...*flooded.*

Instantly.

Then I glanced around the room as a thought occurred to me. "Is *my* age a problem for *you?*"

He leaned forward, his eyes glued to me. "Hell, no. It just makes me a lucky man if I can hold on to you."

There I went blushing again. I could get used to hearing things like that. It was a welcome change from my past. Not that Sid was mean or anything, he was just not the most affectionate man. He was kind of neglectful when it came to romance even before we got married. I believe he loved me at one point, he just wasn't the most mature when it came to expressing himself. His proposal consisted of him driving to City Hall and asking me, "You wanna do this shit? I don't think I want nobody else."

Yeah, and my dumb ass married him.

"I wanna see you again, but I don't want to take you away from your little girl too much. Plus, I'm trying to get some time on my daughter's busy schedule tonight," he said.

"We can do lunch tomorrow, if you want." Damn, I was sounding eager as hell.

He smiled. "Yeah. That'd be good. Wait...shit, I forgot I'll be in the studio tomorrow. Don't know how long I'll be there."

I couldn't hide my disappointment as I mumbled, "Oh."

"But you can come kick it with me there. I can have Tommy or Dunn get us some food and everything."

"Would that be okay? I mean, for me to come there?"

He chuckled. "Yeah, it's *my* studio, Jo."

"Oh...okay. Where is it?"

"How about I send Tommy for you when you're ready? He can pick you up from work and drop you back off after lunch."

I gave him a smirk. "Why? You think I'ma get lost again."

"Yep."

I faked an annoyed eye-roll. "Fine. Send Tommy."

"Will do."

A few minutes later, after he'd sent Dunn to find a to-go tray for my sandwich, he was walking me through the lobby of the hotel. Stopping just inside the revolving doors, he pulled me into his arms and kissed my cheek. "Text me when you get back to work. Wanna make sure you make it back safely."

I smiled up at him. "I will. See you tomorrow."

"Looking forward to it."

10

Everett

Coming back to this house, the first one I ever bought, always messed with my head. There were too many memories that came rushing back just from pulling into the driveway, both good and bad. But like most things in life, the bad seemed to overshadow the good. It was hard for me to be there, but I'd do anything for Ella, and she'd asked me to come there to spend time with her rather than us meeting up somewhere else.

When she opened the door and fell into my arms, all the negative shit left my mind. This was my baby, my princess, and even though she was fifteen and only a few inches shorter than me, she'd always be my little girl.

"Daddy!" she squealed, as she squeezed her arms around me. "So glad to see you!"

I kissed the top of her head. "You could've seen me every day since I've been here, but you're too busy for me, huh?"

She backed out of my arms and sucked her teeth. "Daddeeee! You know I've got all this stuff I have to do for school and cheerleading and the show. Just got a lot going on!"

The show she was referring to was *Go-See*, a reality show chronicling the private lives of Esther and three other supermodels who were past their prime but still living extravagant lives. It'd been on the air for years. Ella had basically grown up on that show.

And I hated that shit.

I fought with Esther about it for months until Ella, who was seven or eight at the time, called and begged me to okay her being on the show. I knew Esther was behind that shit, because she knew I couldn't say no to our daughter. So I went along with it with the understanding that her camera time would be limited. Since the show came after our divorce, I was never on it and never would be. That reality stuff ruined lives. I hoped it wouldn't ruin Ella's.

As I followed her deeper into the house, I said, "Yeah, I guess I should just feel lucky to get a few minutes of your time."

"Daddy, stop! I'm sorry, okay?" she whined.

"It's all good. What are we watching?" I asked, as I sat on the sofa. Esther refurnished the house every year or so, because she was a professional money-waster. I can't lie, though; I kind of liked the new white couch she had in the family room.

Grabbing the remote and sitting down beside me, Ella said, "*Blair Witch*. Been wanting to watch it, but you know I can't watch scary stuff without you."

I grinned as she started the movie and burrowed close to me. Yeah, she was still my little girl, the one who had coloring and thick hair like me, but instead of the hard edges and angles of my face, she had her mother's soft but exotic features.

We chatted on and off through the movie, and by the time it was over, I was all caught up on her life, including her crush on some boy I threatened to kill if she went near him. I had to remind Ella's ass that she wasn't allowed to date until she was thirty. And I meant that shit.

We had finished *Blair Witch*—which sucked in comparison to the first movie in that franchise—and had watched half of one of those *Saw* movies before she started yawning. It was getting late and I knew I needed to get to bed myself, so I called for Tommy to come pick me up. He'd just texted letting me know he was pulling into the driveway when *she* came in through the door that connected the kitchen to the garage, and my only thought was...*shit*. I had really hoped I wouldn't run into her ass. As a matter of fact, I'd only agreed to visit Ella at home because I knew Esther had some event to attend and wouldn't be back until late. Well, my ass had miscalculated, because there she was in a beaded black gown looking just as beautiful as she always had, even now at fifty-two years old.

I hugged Ella, made her promise to call me in the morning, said goodbye, watched her head to her bedroom, nodded at Esther, and moved toward the front door. I was almost home free when I heard the clicking of her heels against the marble floor in the foyer and her heavily accented voice echoing against the vaulted ceiling. "Everett, wait!"

I kept walking and had grabbed the doorknob when I felt her hand on my arm. With a frown, I looked from her hand to her face. "The hell you want?" I said, keeping my voice low.

"My God! It's been years! Are you really still going to behave like this with me?"

I guess since I'd managed not to be in her presence for a couple of years, she thought my attitude toward her might have softened. She thought wrong. Esther was always on some bullshit. It was just her nature, and I was never in the mood for it.

"Look, I don't have time for this. I came to see Ella, meant to be gone before you made it home. Leaving now."

"Everett...I still miss you, you know? God, you look good. I was thinking that maybe you could drop by while Ella is at school and we could...talk?"

Talking in Esther speak meant fucking. And to that, I said, "*Hell*, no. Ain't shit changed between us. Just like I told you all those years ago when I left, I wouldn't fuck you with my worst enemy's dick, and you *still* disgust me. I will speak to you, and I will never disrespect you in front of Ella, but I honestly don't care if your ass falls off the face of the earth."

"So you're still angry about what happened all those years ago? That's petty, Everett."

I opened the door, and as I stepped outside, said, "Call it what you want, but I don't want shit to do with you and I never will. Bye, Esther."

"Everett!" she shouted.

I ignored her as I made my way to my truck, climbed into the back of it, and closed my eyes as Tommy pulled off the property.

I'd just crawled into bed when a text from Everett came through: *Hey, about to lay it down. Wanted to say good night to you.*

Me: *Awww, you really are sweet. Have a good visit with your daughter?*

Him: *Yeah. Always a good time when I get to see her and I can't wait to see you tomorrow.*

I grinned.

Me: *Can't wait to see you, either. Good night, Everett.*

Him: *Good night, Jo.*

11

Peter Park's ass was really on one.

The morning started with him sending me out for his favorite coffee—a coconut latte—from this obscure café that I always had a hard time finding. Then I had to go to his favorite bakery and get him two chocolate croissants. The two establishments were nowhere near each other, and when you factor in the morning traffic, it took me two damn hours to complete this task. As soon as I made it back, he had me drop an envelope off at an apartment in a really nice complex. One look at the hood-rat who answered the door, and I knew she was his mistress—one of many. That realization pissed me completely off. I made it back and was finally getting to sit down and work on the mock-ups for Everett's piece when Peter Park texted me, letting me know he wanted to eat lunch early and for me to take my ass over to Koreatown to pick him up some beef bulgogi, whatever the hell that was. I did what he asked, had to sit and wait for them to make it since he didn't have the decency to call and order ahead, and took the shit back to him only for him to go off on me about it being neobiani and not bulgogi. Well, shit. I'm a black woman from rural Alabama. Korean cuisine wasn't exactly a staple in my hometown. How in the hell was I supposed to know it wasn't the right food? He had the nerve to ask if I checked it before I left the restaurant and my reply was to ask what difference would that have made? I had no idea how it was supposed to look anyway.

So then, I had to carry my ass back to Koreatown to get the damn bulgogi, and this time, they got it right. After I looked at it, I could see the difference and promised myself I'd check Google for a pic of whatever he had me pick up from then on.

After all that Peter Park bullshit, it was two in the afternoon before I was able to text Everett so that Tommy could pick me up, and I was half-starved, tired as hell, and pissed. Totally pissed. But my mood instantly lifted after I followed Tommy into a building, down a hall, and into the studio to see Everett sitting at the humongous mixing board. The bright smile that adorned his face had me smiling right back at him.

No sooner than I'd crossed the threshold, he had crossed the room and was in my face, pulling me to him. "Damn, it's good to see you," he whispered in my ear.

I grinned as I leaned into his big, broad body. "You just saw me yesterday."

"More than twenty-four hours. Too long." He leaned in, planted a kiss on my lips, and grabbed my hand, kissing it, too.

Damn, this man is too good to be true!

My eyes roamed the room, noting Dunn sitting on a sofa on the opposite wall from the door and another man occupying a chair at the mixing board.

"You know Dunn, and this is Heath, the sound engineer. We were just wrapping up."

"Aw, man. I was hoping I'd get to watch you work. You're done?" I said.

He nodded. "Wanna hear what we got?"

"Yeah. Is this something for another album? You just released one, right?"

He led me to his seat and leaned over the board, pushing some buttons. "Yeah, got a tour coming up in a couple of weeks. But this is just a feature I'm doing for another artist."

As I settled in the chair, I said, "Oh, okay. So…someone else is going to come in here and do their part?"

He shook his head. "No, I'm just sending my part to the producer and he'll put everything together."

"Okay." I knew a little bit about the music business but not much. It was interesting, though. "What's the song supposed to be about?"

As a track began to play, he said, "Uh, just some braggadocios shit. Me and Bugz are supposed to be dropping verses about some girl that's hard to get, telling her what she's missing out on."

"Oh...so the other artist is Bugz-NYC? I didn't know you two were that tight."

"We're not. We're label mates. I honestly don't think our styles are compatible, but the label pushed for this collabo, so here we go..."

Everett's voice began to pour through the speakers, the rhythm and cadence familiar. He spoke with a slight southern accent in everyday conversation but amplified it when he rapped. He sounded good, but I'd heard him sound better, and I told him so after his portion of the track ended.

"What? I mean, you don't like it?" he asked incredulously.

"I did. It was cool, but like...is that all you got?" I asked.

His mouth hung open as Heath murmured, "Damn..."

"Is that all I got? What the hell you mean? That shit was lit!"

"I'm just saying, if you're supposed to be impressing a woman, that did nothing for me. And I'm definitely a woman."

"Jo, are you serious right now?"

"Yeah...I mean, you used better lines on me, and I'm here, aren't I? You need to be real with it. Bugz-NYC is raw. Have you heard his verses yet? I bet he's yelling and growling and making all those crazy noises, being his own hype man like he always does. Your verses are going to sound weak compared to all that. I know you have a different style. You're more of a story-teller and all of your words are intelligible, but that doesn't mean you can't make folks *feel* you. You know? You need to take a more visceral approach to this, find your edge again."

"Shit," Heath mumbled.

"Would you shut up with the damn commentary, man?" Everett shot at him.

Heath, a short, brown-skinned brother, raised his hands and

scooted back from the board a little. "I'm just saying, man. She does have a point. Shit, a few points."

"Damn, man! You agree with her?" Everett asked.

Heath shrugged in response.

I glanced over at Dunn, who had his face in his phone, then shifted my gaze back to Everett. "You wanted my honest opinion, right? That's what I'm giving you."

He stood there next to me, his eyes on mine for a good three or four minutes before saying, "Run it back, Heath," and then opening a door and heading into the booth.

I can't lie, I felt an adrenaline rush when I saw him put the headphones on and begin bobbing his head to the beat. I was about to see *the* Big South in action! And when he opened his mouth and words began flying out, delivered with such force that I could feel them in my chest, I was left speechless.

You say you ain't got no time for a nigga
But the way you looking at me got me asking, "How you figure?"
Shit, you know who I am, what I'm known to do
I bring the heat, don't need no muthafuckin' crew
You told me "Stop and Frisk" was your shit and how you used to vibe to it
I bet you touched yourself the first time you heard me spit
I know you laid in your bed at night wishing I would hit
I know you wet right now just thinking about some Big
I'll make you cream, baby girl, with just one swipe at your clit
Make you feel every inch of me before I even take out my shit
I know you like what you see...South got your ass hungry
I'll have you climbing the walls, screaming from A to Z
You might be fine as hell, slim thick with them juicy-ass lips
You might have a nigga sprung just from the way you wiggle them hips
Big ass afro, nice little ass, perfect titties...shit!
Open them thighs, lil' mama...let me see if I fit
I might want you bad. Fuck it, I might even beg.

But I'll have your bow-legged ass yelling, "Daaaaamn, Big South!" once I get you in my bed.

They don't call me Big 12 for nothing, baby.

That last line ended with his signature chuckle that could be heard on many of his songs.

He pulled the headphones off, strode out of the booth, and stood beside me. "How was that?"

I squeezed my thighs together and swallowed. "Uh…better."

He gave me a smirk. "Uh-huh." Looking down at his phone, he said, "Tommy just made it back with our food. You hungry?"

I nodded. "Starving."

"We done in here, South?" Heath asked.

Everett turned to me with raised eyebrows. "Am I done, Jo?"

Licking my lips, I said, "Uh, yeah. I would say so."

"You heard the lady."

12

We had a good lunch together, and that evening, we talked on the phone until the wee hours of the night, then met again the next day so I could show him the mock-ups. He was impressed with all of them but chose my favorite design—a capital E for Ella with a butterfly wing attached to the leg of the E. I told him it would take me a while to complete it since this was my first time creating a piece, and he told me to take my time.

I didn't see him face to face again before he left town that Sunday morning, but he called every day and right before he boarded the plane. As he ran down his busy promo schedule with me and promised to call as much as he could, I already began to miss him. I'd only been getting to know him for a short period of time, but Everett was growing on me something bad, so bad that I spent that Sunday morning enveloped in sadness, the familiarity of the loneliness I'd endured since my divorce lurking in every corner of my home again. But when you have a child, you can't afford to lie around in a depressed stupor. So I dragged myself out of bed, went grocery shopping, and as I pulled back into my driveway, saw a red Bentley Continental GT sitting there.

I parked beside it, sighed, closed my eyes, and then looked back at Nat in her car seat. "Your daddy's here, Nat."

She kind of just looked at me as if to say, "Who?"

A tapping at my window made me snatch my head around. There he stood in all his asshole glory wearing a track suit and too much jewelry, looking like an adult male version of my only child. I opened the door, climbed out the car, and said, "Sid…didn't know you were coming by."

Without answering me, he climbed inside the front seat and reached into the back, freeing Nat from her car seat. Lifting out of the car with her in his arms, he smiled at her, and said, "Hey, baby."

Nat's little eyes shifted from him to me as if she was trying to see if this was okay with me. I smiled at her, and said, "Say hi to Daddy, Nat-Nat."

"Hi," she said with uncertainty.

"You want your mama, huh?" he asked, displaying an unusual amount of common sense.

I was relieved when he handed her to me. I hated that I had to explain who the hell he was to her whenever he decided to come around. It'd been six months since he last saw her. Poor Nat had no idea who the hell he was. But I wanted her to know him, because I'd never known my father. I just wanted better for Nat, and as stupid as Sid was, I believed he could be a decent father if he tried. He was never abusive toward me, just selfish as hell.

Balancing Nat on my hip, I nodded toward the front door. "You wanna come in for a minute?" I was thinking maybe if he spent more than two seconds around her, Nat would become more familiar with him.

He seemed to think about that for a moment. "Yeah."

As he followed me inside, I said, "Let me set her up at the table with a snack. You can have a seat if you want. Or you can check out her room. I finally finished decorating it."

"Damn, who died?" was his response.

I sat Nat in her booster seat at the table. "What?"

"You got all these flowers. Who died?"

I'd forgotten about the millions of roses Everett sent me that I'd had to find room for even in this spacious house. He really went overboard, but I loved it. "No one," I answered.

"Then what you doing with all these flowers?"

I glanced up to see him staring at the coral bouquet, the one with the card in it. I hurriedly opened a snack-sized container of applesauce for Nat and handed her a spoon before heading into the living room to try and get the card before he saw it.

I was a second too slow.

"Who is Everett?"

I snatched the card from him. "None of your business."

He glanced toward the kitchen and lowered his voice. "You fucking him?"

I frowned. "That's even less of your business."

He shook his head. "You better not be fucking another nigga in my house, Jo. That ain't what I pay you for. I pay you to take care of my baby, not fuck niggas."

"Pay me? I'm not your damn babysitter," I hissed softly. "I am Natalie's mother. You are her father. You pay for the support of your child, you fucktard! And this ain't *your* house. I got it in the divorce; hence, it's mine!"

"You need to watch that damn name-calling, Jo," he rumbled, barely above a whisper. "All I know is I told your ass when I left not to be fucking a lot of dudes. You ain't fucking none of my friends, are you? I might want your ass back one day and that shit can't happen if you been fucking my friends."

"Okay, so you can get the fuck out," I whisper-shouted.

"So I can't see my little girl, now? You gon' keep her from me? That's what you doing, Jo?"

"You didn't come here to see her. You came here to aggravate me and try to exercise some control you do not possess. What I do and who I do it with is none of your business."

"You fucking him in my bed?" he rasped.

"Leave, Sid. *Now*. Go on home to the woman your I-don't-want-to-be-married-anymore ass married after you left me. Ain't she pregnant? Don't you need to go rub her big-ass feet or something? Or do what you do best, go sell some crack?"

"I don't do that shit no more and you know it. And Sonya ain't got shit to do with this."

"Just like *you* ain't got shit to do with *me…and* I'm tired of whisper-arguing with you. Go!"

"A'ight. I'ma leave, but I'm not playing with your ass. Keep your nigga out my house."

After I'd shut the door behind him, I took a deep breath and almost, but not quite, yelled, "Ugh!"

Nat giggled and yelled, "Rawr!" Applesauce marred her little cheeks as she grinned at me, showing me all her tiny white teeth. Nat had a thing for lions and would roar at any moment.

I couldn't help but laugh and think to myself, *I need to move out of this damn house since this fool doesn't understand that it's no longer his.* Then I headed outside to get my groceries out of my trunk.

13

"What you doing?!" Bridgette's voice blared through my phone, piercing my ear as she shouted over the shaking bassline of some song.

"Shit, what are *you* doing? Where you at?" I asked.

"At Vault with Sage, where your ass needs to be!" she hollered.

I pulled the phone from my ear, put her on speakerphone, and lowered the volume. "Y'all crazy. I am never going back in there. It's too tiny and the cover charge is so cheap, it's always full of broke, touchy-feely niggas. No, thanks."

"Shiiiit, ain't nobody fucking with me and Sage! We'll tag team an ass-whooping on 'em! Hell!" Bridgette yelled.

"You damn right!" Sage screamed in agreement.

Yeah, they were both drunk, which would explain why they were calling me from a loud-ass club.

"I hope neither of you drunk fools is planning to drive home. Be done killed someone."

"Naw, girl. We rode with Viv."

"Viv? Since when you start hanging with her again? I thought she was mad at you about something. Didn't you promise to cover her shift and then bail on her?"

"Girl, she stay high so much, she don't even remember that shit."

"So you letting her drive and she's high?"

"No, she's not high right now…I don't think. Anyway, you didn't answer me. What you doing? Watching *Iron Chef* or something?"

"No. *Best Baker in America*."

"That's just damn sad. You are a healthy young woman with a sexy, rich-as-hell boyfriend and you laying up at home watching fucking Gordon Ramsey?!" Damn, I'd turned the phone down and she was steady getting louder, about to bust the speakers on the thing.

"First of all, Gordon Ramsey is not on this show, or at least I don't think he is. Second, Everett is not my boyfriend. Third, what's he got to do with anything?"

"Well, he may as well be your boyfriend. And he's got *everything* to do with *everything*. Shit, instead of you laying up there watching folks bake cookies, you need to be getting your cardio in on this dancefloor so you'll be ready when that man gets back."

I sighed. "Be ready for what, Bridgette?"

"That dick! He been taking it slow, but it's only a matter of time. Shoot, I'da been done gave him some by now!"

"Shiiiiiit, I woulda fucked him on sight!" Sage interjected.

"I know that's right!" Bridgette shrieked. "He'd have to peel me off that thang!"

I could almost see them sloppily high-fiving each other.

"Whatever, y'all. We're nowhere near that. We're just getting to know each other. I mean, I just met him a few weeks ago."

"Uh-huh. Make sure to eat plenty of yogurt and pineapples so your coochie'll taste scrumptious to him when he decides to eat it, 'cause I know he gon' slurp it up!" Bridgette shouted. "He looks like a damn cunnilinguist!"

I shook my head as I stared open-mouthed at the phone. This girl... "You need help, Bridge. Like, therapy."

"Your ass better listen to me. Look, I'ma leave you to your cake watching. It's lit up in here!"

"Okay—wait! Uh...do the pineapples need to be fresh? I already have some pineapple fruit cups. Will that work?"

"Yeah, I'm sure that'll be fine...you freak. Bye!"

"Bye, nut."

No sooner than I'd hung up with Bridgette, my phone lit up again and Everett's name popped up on the screen. I was grinning like a fool as I accepted the call. "Hello?"

"Jo…" I loved the way he said my name, like seeing me or hearing my voice made his day.

"Hey…how's it going?"

"Good, tiring. I miss you."

I closed my eyes and sighed internally. He just made me feel so good. "Already? You've only been gone a few days."

"I missed you the moment I stepped on the plane. Hey, I didn't wake you, did I? Or your little girl?"

"No, I was up watching TV. Just got off the phone with Bridgette's crazy ass. Nat's still sleep or else she'd be in here by now."

"Good. Your friend okay?"

"Yeah, just drunk at the club wanting me to be there with her."

"You didn't wanna go?"

"Wasn't in the mood tonight."

"You hit the club often?"

"Every now and then. but I get tired of dudes trying to feel on me and stuff. Some of those guys are relentless. Like, they think you gotta be looking for a man just because you're in a club. Rubbing all on your booty with their junk. Half the time, you have to yell at them to get them to back off."

"Damn, really? That's fucked up."

"Yeah…"

A loud silence settled over the phone line, an odd occurrence for us. Our conversations always flowed well. It felt super awkward.

"Uh, Everett, is everything okay?"

"Yeah, I mean, I don't know…I was just thinking about you going to clubs and—shit. Look, you wanna be my lady? Like my girlfriend? I know we haven't known each other that long, but I'd like for what we have to be exclusive."

I didn't even think before I said, "Yes."

I could hear him blow out a breath. "All right. It's official, then. Uh, I got a ton of promo to do for this album. I'm shooting a video with Bugz in a couple of days. Then rehearsals start for my tour. And then my tour starts. It might be a month before I get back out there to see you since I did all my LA promo before I left and my Cali shows are a ways down the road, at the end of the US leg of the tour. And even then, it might only be for a few hours. A day at the most."

"I know you have to work, so it's all right. You really don't owe me an explanation of how you spend your time, Everett."

"I thought we just established that I was your man."

"You are…"

"Then I do owe you an explanation. I just want you to know this is work and I gotta do it, but what we're building together is important to me. *You're* important to me."

"I-I am?"

"Yeah…and I really do miss you."

"I miss you, too, and I'll be glad to see you whenever you can see me. I'm a patient woman."

"You're too good to be true, baby. You know that?"

I smiled. "That just means you gotta work hard to keep me."

"Shit, that's what I'm tryna do. Talk to you later, Jo."

"'Night, Everett."

14

I was sitting on my sofa watching Nat play with a little tea set Ms. Sherry bought her and damn near fell off of it when my phone rang, because I was sure it was Everett calling. He had made a habit of calling me before I left for work in the morning and before he hit the stage in the evenings. I wasn't trying to miss his call.

"Hello!" I answered excitedly.

"Hey, what you up to?" His voice sounded so good in my ear, I came close to melting right then and there.

"Nothing, really. Watching Nat play with some new toys."

"Oh, you not watching *Top Chef, Master Chef, Iron Chef, the Real Chef-wives of Atlanta, Love and Chef Hop, The Chef Ink Crew, The Chefdashians*..."

I smirked. "You see me a few times, talk to me on the phone every day for a couple of weeks, and you think you know me, huh?"

"You saying I don't?"

"Tell me about myself then since you're a Jo Walker expert now."

"A'ight. Your favorite color is blue, you love hip hop but you're a hater when it comes to my music, you like food and cooking shows but can't boil water, you're a homebody and rarely go out, you don't drink, Nat is the love of your life, and you try to play hard, but you like me."

"I actually *can* boil water, negro."

He chuckled into the phone. "Oh, for real? My bad."

"Mm-hmm, and I'm not playing hard. I told you I liked you."

"I know. Just wanted to hear you say it again."

I rolled my eyes. "So spoiled."

"I know."

"Well, I know you, too, Big South."

"A'ight, shoot."

"You like hip hop and you're your own biggest fan, you like dressing up and going out, you love the spotlight, you love your daughter, you're not particularly fond of the paparazzi but see their value as far as your career goes, you don't give even half a damn what folks think about you and prefer to let them guess, you can't cook, either, you do like to drink, you like—no, scratch that. You LOVE women, and have been with lots of them, tons of them, shit...scads of them, heaps of them, buckets of—"

"I ain't never told you I've been with tons of women."

"You didn't have to. I've got eyes and ears. Seen the pics, the naked-assed evidence..."

"So you tryna call me a ho'? I ain't no ho', Jo."

"If you say so..."

"This is about the Sheena thing? Look, I haven't been with another woman since then. Been too busy trying to get you to act right."

"So I'm supposed to believe you met me and the player in you just bowed down?"

"No, you're supposed to understand that I've never been a player. I've been with some women, yeah, but I never played anyone. They were mutual arrangements, just like ours. I give the respect that's demanded of me. Some women are good with casual sex; some won't settle for anything less than a commitment of some sort. I figured out from jump you weren't someone who would be down for a purely physical relationship, and to be honest, I knew from the start that I wanted more than that with you anyway."

"You did? I mean, really?"

"Yes, Jo. I pursued you with the intention of us having a future together, and that's still my intention."

"Wow, I don't know what to say."

"Say you'll let me keep pursuing you."

"But aren't we a couple now? I mean, if you're my man, why would you need to keep pursuing me? You can't pursue something that's already yours."

Silence from Everett.

"Did I say something wrong?" I asked.

"No…you said—shit, Jo, what you just said makes me want to hop on a plane and fly to LA just to stand in front of you and hear you say it to my face."

"Say what?"

"That you're already mine."

"I am, and you're more than welcome to hop on a plane and come see me whenever you want to. I'm not going anywhere."

"Damn, girl. You messing my head completely up right now. I hate I have to leave for the venue, because I could stay on this phone and listen to you say this stuff all night. Man…thank you, Jo."

"For what?"

"For confirming what I knew from the moment you chucked that necklace at me."

I leaned forward on the sofa. "I didn't chuck anything at you!"

"Shiiiiiid! I was like, does this woman play softball or something? You hit me right on my dick with it!"

"Everett! No, I didn't!"

His laughter through the phone was so infectious, I was soon joining him. Nat gave me a curious look before laughing herself, even though she had no idea what was going on.

"Whatever, Everett. What did I confirm?"

"That you are the one thing I've been needing for a long time, and I don't think I even realized I needed it until I met you. Gotta go. Talk to you later."

"Bye, Everett."

I ended the call and joined Nat on the floor, sipping imaginary tea and grinning from ear to ear.

*****

I was tired and frustrated and aggravated as hell. Nothing seemed to be going my way. After having to miss a couple of days of work because Nat was sick—and so was Ms. Sherry, and I didn't have sense enough to have a backup babysitter—I was faced with Peter Park's wrath. He sent me from one corner of LA to the other on errands for a full week, crowding my time at work with foolishness and making it nearly impossible to work on Everett's piece, and I was having a hard enough time with it without his bullshit making it even more difficult.

Making jewelry by hand is complicated and tedious as hell, especially with the concept I'd conceived. It was taking me forever just to get the platinum casing to look like a damn E, let alone the butterfly wing. It had become painfully clear that my ass wasn't an artist. By the third week of me working on it in the little snatches of time I could get when Peter Park wasn't pulling me away, I was ready to give up, surrender, and admit that this career, like being a makeup artist, wasn't for me.

And besides my professional failures, after nearly three weeks of him being gone, I missed the hell out of Everett. Sure, we talked on the phone literally every day—sometimes for hours, other times for mere seconds—but I still missed him, his smile, his laugh, his kisses. It was like I was having withdrawals from a drug I'd only tried a couple of times. Everett was that potent. I was almost afraid to have sex with him if I was already this attached to him.

It was a Tuesday, and I was feeling particularly down as I grabbed the sack holding Peter Park's meat-only burrito and headed back into work. Just thinking about how much I missed Everett and how jacked up work was had me near tears, and to top it all off, before I could close my car door good, my phone rang with a call from the fool of the century. I stood next to my car for a second, took a deep breath, and answered it. "Hello?"

"Hey, I just thought about something," was his greeting.

"What, Sid? And make it quick. I'm at work."

"You be fucking niggas in front of my baby, Jo?"

I shook my head as I shut my car door with force and began

stomping toward the building. "I don't have time for this today."

"Answer me, Jo. Do you?"

"Do *you*?"

"Do I what?"

"Do *you* be fucking niggas?"

"Okay, you wanna play today, huh? Let me find out, Jo. Let me find—"

I hung up on his stupid ass and tucked my phone in my purse, ignoring its buzzing as I made my way to what was becoming my own personal hell hole. Oba, who was guarding the door, gave me this weird look as I breezed past him, and I almost dropped Peter Park's burrito when I stepped into the lobby. Standing just on the inside of Bijou Park leaning against the wall with his head tilted to the side and his eyes on me was Everett.

I fell into him so fast I think I startled him. He chuckled as he wrapped his arms around me and said, "I missed you, too, baby." Squeezing me closer to him, he added, "Yeah...I really missed you."

"You have no idea how much I missed you," I said into his chest.

He released me and gazed down at me with concern in his eyes. "What's wrong?"

I shook my head. "Just feels like I have nothing good going on in my life but Nat. Things are...never mind. I'm just glad you're here. Wait—what are you doing here? Shouldn't you be in Indianapolis? Don't you have a show there tonight?"

"I'm here because I missed you."

"But your show...was it cancelled or something?"

"No. I gotta be on a plane in two hours so I can make my show."

I frowned. "You flew here just to see me?"

"Yeah. You had lunch?"

I shook my head. "Of course not. Been too busy... *not* side-piecing."

"You're never gonna let me live that down, are you?"

"Nope."

"So damn mean," he murmured, and then leaned in close to my ear, and said, "and sexy."

I whispered, "Really? How sexy?"

"Keep playing." Before I could process it, his lips were on mine, he was pulling my body against his, and his tongue had invaded my mouth. I moaned softly and heard someone clear their throat.

Breaking away from Everett, I gave Freda and Tommy, who was sitting in front of her desk, a sheepish look. Hell, I'd forgotten we weren't alone and that we were at my job just that quickly.

"Hey, why don't you go let Park know you're going to lunch?" Everett suggested, pulling my attention back to him.

"If he'll let me," I mumbled.

"What?"

"Nothing...be back."

I walked across the lobby, past the huge tank full of exotic fish that served as the focal point of the decor, and knocked on Mr. Park's door.

"Yeah!" he barked, the tone of his voice instantly telling me he was in a worse mood than when I left him.

I eased the door open, and before I could utter a word, he lit into me.

"About damn time, and it better not be cold! If it is, you're gonna take your ass right back there and get me another one because I don't eat microwaved shit!"

I squeezed my eyes shut. It was a daily internal battle for me not to curse his ass completely out. Taking a deep breath, I opted not to speak, and instead, moved toward him, handing him the sack.

He pulled the burrito out and placed it on his desk. "No cheese dip? You brought me a burrito with no cheese dip? Damn-it, Jo!"

"Uh...you never mentioned cheese dip," I said.

"Do I have to tell you everything? Who the fuck eats a burrito without cheese dip?!"

Shit, I do. "Mr.—"

"Park!"

I jumped at the sound of Everett's voice. I'd closed the door behind me, but I was sure anyone within a ten-mile radius had heard Peter Park screaming at me.

Mr. Park hopped up and rounded his desk, bumping into me on his way to Everett, extending a hand to him that he ignored. "South! I didn't know you were here!" He cut his accusatory eyes at me. "What can I do for you?"

I could see Everett clenching his jaw. "Stop screaming at my lady so I can take her to lunch."

Peter Park whipped around and looked at me with wide eyes, returned his attention to Everett, and uttered, "Uh…your—Jo?"

Everett nodded.

Mr. Park checked his watch and looked back at me again. "You haven't been to lunch?"

For real, motherfucker? "Um, no. I haven't."

"Go! Go!" he said, stepping towards me and grabbing my arm. "Go—"

"Hey, you need to chill with touching her like that. Matter of fact, don't ever fucking touch her again. At all."

My eyes skirted over to Everett as Peter Park quickly dropped his hand.

"Oh…sorry. Jo, go on to lunch. Uh, you know what? You can have the rest of the day off. With pay."

What? "But I need to work on Ev-Big…*his* piece," I protested.

"Don't worry about it. I'm not in a hurry for you to finish it. Come on, let me feed you," Everett said.

I nodded and took his outstretched hand. When I thanked Peter Park for letting me leave early, Everett almost squeezed my hand to death.

The walk to his car was silent, and the tension was palpable. Everett was obviously pissed about what he had heard, and I was beyond embarrassed. We were well on our way to…somewhere when he asked, "That motherfucker talk to you like that all the time?"

I shook my head. "Only when he's in a mood." *Which is eighty percent of the time.*

"Why don't you quit?"

I frowned as my eyes met his, which were trained on me as his arm rested on the windowsill of the car door, his finger on his bottom lip. "I-uh-working for him is a good opportunity. I've learned a lot. And I—shit, I don't know, Everett. He's mean, I hate him. I hate the job. I'm struggling to make your piece. I don't even think this is the career I want anymore." I basically vomited my words. I guess I needed to share my pent-up frustrations with someone, and since he'd asked, he was my victim of choice. "I honestly don't know what I wanna do with my life. Well, that's a lie. The only thing I've ever wanted to do was be a wife and mother, to have what I never had before—a real family. But that didn't work, so I've gotta do *something*."

"But this? That motherfucker almost got dealt with back there. Jo, I've gotta work. Too many people depend on me for me to start missing shows, but my mind can't settle the fact that Park treats you like this and I feel some kind of way about leaving you knowing you work for his ass. I mean, is that as bad as it gets?"

I shook my head. "No. It gets worse."

"Worse than him yelling at you?! He touch you? Hit you? Try to fuck you?" He looked like he was about to jump out of the moving SUV.

"No—no! I mean, he can yell louder, use more foul language. Today is the first time he's ever put a finger on me, and that was because you had him frazzled."

"He don't wanna lose my business. His ass is scared now. Jo...why would you think it was okay to stay there and take that abuse? Is it that you need the money that bad? Baby, I'll help you. I'd be glad to. I can't deal with you being mistreated like this."

I didn't need money. The child support and alimony Sid was court-ordered to pay covered me and Nat's expenses and then some. Plus, the lump sum I received from the divorce was still sitting in the bank untouched. So, I honestly didn't need money. I needed a purpose. I had hoped it was making jewelry, but I now realized that wasn't it. I shared these thoughts with Everett.

"Then quit," he said.

"And do what? Live off my ex's money? He already—" I cut

myself off. I'd dumped enough of my sad existence on him.

"He already what? He bothering you?"

"He's just…being him. Look, before I got a job, I was losing it sitting around the house all the time."

"Okay, but who said you had to sit around the house? You could do stuff with your little girl, get to spend more time with her. I know you said you wanted to do that. We talked about that the other night. And you could take a class or something. Jo, you're in a unique position a lot of women wish they were in. You're financially able to do what you want. Shit, you could hit the road with me if you wanted to. Bring Nat with you."

I smiled as my heart swelled in my chest. "I don't know if Nat is ready for the road, and I'm not quite ready to give up on my job yet. I want to at least finish your piece, but I appreciate what you're saying."

"Jo, I don't care if you never finish that piece. Shit, at this point, I don't feel right giving Park any more of my money. I care about your wellbeing. That's what's important to me right now."

"I wish I understood why…why I mean so much to you, what your fascination is with me."

"You're special, Jo, and if I have to keep telling you that from now to the end of time for you to get it, I will."

"You're just too good. You know that?"

He gave me a huge grin, holding his tongue between his teeth. "Yeah, I know."

I rolled my eyes.

*****

We had lunch in the back room of a soul food restaurant I'd never heard of before—Miss Hattie's—and were greeted by Miss Hattie herself, who was also from Houston and a good friend of Everett's late mom. The food was good, and I was enjoying hearing about how his tour was going but felt a little sad knowing he had to fly back out that same afternoon.

Once we were back in his truck, on our way to Bijou Park so I could pick up my car, Everett grabbed my hand and brought it to his lips, kissing the palm, wrist, and up my arm to my shoulder. Then he found my lips, planting a soft kiss there, and murmuring, "I wish I could stay or that you could come with me."

I reached up and slid my finger over his lips. "Me, too."

"Hey, my annual charity event is coming up in a couple of weeks. We usually do it in Houston, but since my label is co-sponsoring it, we're doing it here this year. I know you're concerned about being photographed with me, and I'm not going to lie, I can only control that to a certain extent with so many guests there, but I'd like you to go as my date."

"I'd love to go. I don't care about pictures or gossip blogs anymore." At that point, I didn't care about much else other than taking care of my baby and spending as much time as I could get with him. Damn the blogs.

"You sure?"

"Yeah! Never been to anything like that. It'll be fun to dress up and get out of the house for a night—oh, Lord! I gotta find a dress!" I was excited more because I knew I'd be with him than anything, but the thought of going to something like a charity event really did appeal to me.

"You don't have to worry about that. I'll have my assistant get in touch with some designers and set up some fittings for you. She can also set up hair and makeup if you want."

"She? Assistant? I didn't know you had an assistant." Who was this ho'?

"Yeah, Courtney. She's also my play cousin, been knowing her since we were kids. She lives in Houston but travels with me from time to time. I'll get with her and give her your number."

"Okay."

"It'll be a late night, so be sure to let your sitter know ahead of time after Courtney gives you the details."

"I will."

He walked me to my car, kissed me so deeply that I feared I would actually pass out, and just like that, my knight in shining armor was gone again.

15

This was his first time in my house, and although we weren't alone—Sage, Bridgette, his assistant, Courtney, a stylist, and the dress designer were all present—it still felt strange to know that while I was in my bedroom shimmying into another dress, he was sitting in my living room, waiting to give his feedback on the look. This was the second round of fittings, because I hated everything I tried on the first time. This time, Everett flew in on a rare day where he didn't have a show, a tiny break in his tour, to help me pick something out. So far, we had both unanimously vetoed five dresses. I was trying to adhere to Bridgette's sound advice and only consider shorter dresses, but it was hard to find something that flattered my body without making me look like a THOT.

Bridgette had been giving good input, but Sage, who I invited so she could come up with a makeup look to complement whatever I chose, spent nearly every second she was in Everett's presence gawking at him. I had to knock her phone out of her hand to keep her from sneaking a picture of him, and if she told me fifty times how extra fine he was in person, she told me a hundred times. Hell, I knew the man was fine. As a matter of fact, Everett was so fine, I had to make myself not stare at him when we were alone together. I didn't want to seem obsessed with him, but shit, he was obsessively fine.

Bridgette zipped me into the dress and winked at me. "I think this is the one. You look super hot but in a respectable way, and it fits really well. Won't need much altering. South is gonna love this one; I just know he is!"

As I inspected myself in the mirror, I had to admit the dress looked good on me. It was covered in gold sequins with a plunging neckline, bare back, and stopped just above my knees. It showed a lot of skin, but still left a little something to the imagination. As Sage helped me into the red—or as the stylist described them, Flamenco—Douce Du Desert Louboutin's the stylist insisted would complement the dress perfectly, she mumbled, "Big South is in your living room," for the tenth time.

"I know, Sage. And guess what? He's just a regular guy. Please, chill."

"Uh, Jo...that's a Gia Smalls original, one of many you've tried on today. Those dresses run at least five grand. Not to mention that fucking Gia Smalls is in your living room, too, along with Carlita Frost, who happens to have styled half of Hollywood. And these are Louboutin's, which I'll never in my wildest dreams be able to afford without risking being homeless. Oh, yeah, and the motherfucker offered to pay me a thousand dollars to do your makeup for one event. That ain't no regular dude."

"He is to me. And stop calling him a motherfucker." I checked my image in the mirror again, smiled, and said, "I like it. Let's see what Everett thinks."

The girls followed me into the living room where Everett was eating a pineapple fruit cup. Upon seeing me, he set the fruit cup on an end table, stood and quickly crossed the room, stopping in front of me, then walking around my body before pulling me into a deep kiss. Behind me, I could hear Bridgette mumble, "I guess he likes it."

When he broke our connection, making me want to yank his head back down to mine, he kept his eyes on me as he asked Gia, "How much?"

"Five thousand-fifty," she answered.

"Is it one of a kind?"

"Uh, no. It's going up on my website as a limited run of fifty dresses. You guys are the first to see it."

"How much will it cost to make it one of a kind?"

"W-what?" Gia, an obviously mixed race young woman, sputtered.

"I want Jo to be the only woman to ever wear this. How much I gotta pay to make that happen?" He leaned in and buried his nose in my neck, inhaling deeply. I nearly fell, would've had his hands not been gripping my arms.

Sage muttered, "Damn, Jo."

"Um, I don't know, Mr. South. If I actually sold all fifty dresses, I'd make a little over two hundred and fifty thousand dollars?"

He lifted his head, dragged his finger over the path of my freckles, and asked, "How about two hundred even? Plus, we'll plug the shit out of you on Instagram."

Did he mean two hundred thousand dollars? My mouth dropped open. "Everett, you can't—"

Before I could finish that statement, his mouth was on mine again, then his tongue was sliding against mine, his big hands splayed on my bare back. I relaxed against his body in seconds, allowing my tongue to play with his. Everyone in that room seemed to disappear as I closed my eyes and moaned into his mouth. I was so damn horny, I was two seconds from stripping out of that dress, throwing Everett's big ass on the floor, and riding him into the sunset. It'd been a long time, and Everett wasn't making it any easier for me being fine and sweet and all.

I think I heard Gia say it was a deal or something like that. My mind was in a fog as Everett's hand slid down my back to my ass and he squeezed it a little. It was the ringing of my doorbell that finally brought us back to reality, tearing us apart.

"That-that's probably Ms. Sherry bringing Nat home." It was a Saturday, but I'd asked Ms. Sherry to watch her so we could get the fitting done in peace.

Everett nodded and headed over to Gia while I headed to the door. It wasn't Ms. Sherry but Tommy, who'd dropped Everett off earlier. Since I lived in a very secure gated community, he hadn't felt the need for his bodyguards to stay with him. My first thought was to panic. Had Everett called Tommy because he was leaving already? He had mentioned us having dinner together before he left, and I'd been looking forward to it. I also wanted him to meet Nat for the first time.

"Hey, Boss Man left his phone. I just noticed it. Will you give it to him?" Tommy asked.

Taking the phone, I said, "Yeah, thanks."

Tommy nodded and left. Seconds later, I'd handed Everett his phone and was in my bedroom again as Gia pinned the dress in a few places that needed to be taken in to properly fit me. Less than an hour later, my house had cleared out with the exception of Everett and we were perusing Postmates, having decided to have something delivered to my house and eat in.

"Courtney is so sweet. I really like her," I said, as I tried to decide between Mexican and Italian.

"That's good. She's the main point of contact if you can't get me on occasions like today, when I forget my phone, but that only happened because I was so excited to be seeing you."

I leaned in and kissed him. "I'm always excited to see you, but I can't believe you paid that much for that dress. That was outrageous, Everett!"

He took my laptop from me, placing it on the coffee table, then pulled me into his lap, leaning forward to kiss the hollow of my neck before sliding the spaghetti strap of my tank top to the side and kissing my shoulder. "You don't think you're worth it?"

As he easily positioned me to straddle him and reached around to grab a handful of my ass, I stammered, "Uh-um-I…yes? I do."

He reached under my top, gently grabbing my left breast through my bra, his eyes locking with mine. "Then what's the problem?"

"I-I, it just…shit, I can't think."

Licking his lips, he asked, "Can I touch you, Jo?"

"Um, aren't you already doing that?" I asked, as I closed my eyes and tried to recall how to breathe.

"Yeah, but not like I wanna touch you. Can I touch you like I wanna touch you, baby?"

Hellllll, yeah! "Yes," I whispered, opening my eyes to meet his. "Please."

He smiled before capturing my mouth while squeezing my breast. When I felt him easing his other hand from my butt into the front of my sweat pants, I gasped into his mouth. Then his huge hand was inside my panties, stroking me, and all I could do was grab his shoulders and involuntarily grind against his hand as he slipped a finger inside me.

His mouth left mine. "Damn, Jo. You wetter than water."

He stared at me, his fingers adroit and smooth as he watched my reaction. I leaned in to kiss him again, but he shook his head. "I wanna see you come for me, baby."

Well, shit. That did it. Not even a second later, the frenzied pressure that had been growing inside of me bubbled to the surface and popped. I threw my head back, howling, "Evvvveeerrreeetttttt!" like a crazy woman as the pleasure washed over me. Then I collapsed against his chest, wondering how we'd gone from A to Z so quickly. All these weeks, we hadn't even really addressed sex. Okay, so he'd hinted at it and I damn sure had thought about it, but I still found it shocking that there I was, melting all over his hand while his very noticeable bulge poked me from underneath. But that might have had more to do with who he was. Yeah, I'd tried to play it cool with Sage earlier, but a part of me still found it hard to believe I was in a relationship with *this* man.

"Damn, Jo. You always come that quick?" he asked, eyelids low as he licked his lips again.

My cheeks flushed as I bit my bottom lip, tried to catch my breath, and shook my head. "No…it's-it's been a while for me."

The next thing I knew, he was on his feet with me in his arms, carrying me to my bedroom. He had just laid me on the bed when the doorbell rang. This time I was sure it was Ms. Sherry, because she'd texted me to let me know they were on their way from her friend's house. In my heated Everett lust haze, I'd forgotten.

"That's Nat?" he asked, as he stood over my limp body.

I scurried from my back to my feet, taking a moment to steady myself. "Probably," I said, giving him a regretful look.

"It's all right, baby. Let me wash my hands right quick so I can meet her." His voice was steady, calm, understanding, words I'd never attribute to the man I was once married to.

"Okay."

I went to open the door on shaky legs, my panties in ruination and my yoni pulsating. I wanted the real deal so bad I was aching, but there was nothing I could do about it at that moment. Sniffing the air, I was glad everything was so open in that part of my house. I could smell no evidence of Everett fondling me.

"Nat-Nat!" I squealed, as I took my little girl from Ms. Sherry. "Did you have a good day?"

My tired little droopy-eyed girl nodded and rested her head on my shoulder.

I smiled at Ms. Sherry. "Thanks so much for watching her today."

"How many times I gotta tell you that the pleasure is all mine? Did you pick a dress—oh my God! It's really him! I know you said it was him, but it's him!" she shrieked, alerting me that Everett must have entered the room.

Then I saw his big hand as he stepped beside me and offered it to Ms. Sherry. "Hi. I'm Ev—"

"You're Big South! And I'm Sherry Sykes! Oh, my goodness! Aren't you just as handsome as you always are?! Jo, you came off the bench and hit a home run!"

I stretched my eyes wide. "Wow."

Everett chuckled, and Nat's little head popped up, eyes alert with confusion, so I said, "Nat, this is Mr. Everett, a very special friend of mine."

"She can just call me Everett," he amended.

She eyed him for a moment before giving him the biggest smile. "Hi, Ebbwitt."

Everett returned her smile with a beautiful one of his own. "Hey, Nat. Did you know you're pretty just like your mom?"

She nodded. "Uh-huh. I got a lion. Wanna see it?"

"Yeah! I love lions!"

As she wiggled out of my arms and toddle-ran to her room, Ms. Sherry gushed over Everett a couple more seconds and left.

Nat soon returned with two of her stuffed lions—she had at least fifty of them—and handed one to Everett with a "Rawr!"

Everett gasped. "Oh, man! That was scary!"

Nat giggled. "You do it!"

Everett crouched down, beat his chest, and let out a less-than-fierce roar of his own, sending Nat into a fit of giggles that showcased the gap between her two front teeth that mirrored mine. "Rawr!" she shouted.

Everett fell onto his back, his big body stretched out on my living room floor as he roared right back at her.

Nat giggled and fell on her back, roaring again.

This went on until our dinner arrived. I don't think I'd smiled so much in my life.

*****

I was nauseatingly nervous as I sat on my sofa flanked by a twittering Sage and Bridgette, waiting for Everett to pick me up for his charity event. I mean, my stomach was bubbling and churning and everything. As I glanced down at myself, their chatter sounded hollow and distant. Gold and red...did I look too festive? Like I was going to a Christmas party? It was barely August. And maybe I should've let Bridgette put my hair up in a bun like she wanted to instead of wearing my usual unruly afro. But Everett liked my afro, had told me so on more than one occasion. Was my lipstick too bright? And these damn freckles. Everett loved them. Hell, it was almost like he fetishized them the way he made a point to ask Sage not to conceal them, but I wasn't trying to get stared at all night because of them...unless he was doing the staring. What if I looked crazy in pictures because I wasn't wearing enough makeup? Oh, and speaking of pictures, I had tried to prepare myself for the possibility of my face being splashed all over the gossip blogs as his latest fuck buddy—one blog actually described a model he was seen with that way—if some guest leaked a shot of us, but I was still feeling paranoid about it. And the damn dress was showing too much side boob. My legs looked too oily. Why didn't I get the gap between my teeth fixed years ago? Why did I agree to go to this thing with Everett? What the fuck was I doing being Big South's girlfriend? How did I get to this place in my life? What—

When the doorbell rang, I jumped straight to my feet and nearly toppled over in the four-inch heels that still only put me at Everett's shoulders.

"I'll get it!" Sage eagerly offered, scurrying her ultra-curvy, only-a-couple-of-inches-taller-than-me body to my front door.

I swatted Bridgette's hand away as she picked at my hair with her fingers. I was too nervous for that shit. "Stop," I hissed.

"You stop! All tensed up. You act like this is a blind date or something. The man is your *boyfriend*," she rebutted.

Before I could explain that he'd only been my boyfriend a matter of weeks and that this was our first public date and would likely be my introduction to his world and the world in general as his woman, he stepped into my living room, six feet, six inches of Heaven covered in a sleek black tuxedo, his dreadlocks free-falling to his shoulders.

My mouth dropped open as I was rendered speechless, and as far as I could tell, so was he. He just stood there, a hand in his pant pocket as a smile inched across his face. When he finally said, "Jo…" in the way only he did, I was able to return his smile.

"Everett," I said.

"You look…damn, Jo. You look absolutely beautiful. I mean…" His eyes scanned the room and then lit with recognition, as if at just that moment, he realized we were not alone despite the fact that Sage had opened the door for him. "You ladies did a great job. I'll have to pay y'all a bonus."

"Really?!" Sage squealed.

Everett nodded. "I don't play about money." He moved closer to me, stood in front of me, and slid a finger over my freckles. "I've got something for you, baby."

"You do?"

"Yeah, you look gorgeous, but something is missing."

I glanced down at myself. "What?"

"Turn around."

"Huh?"

"Turn around, Jo."

I did, and a second or so later, felt him place something cool around my neck, heard Bridgette yell, "Damn!" and watched as Sage's eyes ballooned.

"What?!" I shrieked, as I reached up and caressed the choker.

"Yellow diamonds to match your dress," he said, with a smile in his voice.

"Yellow—This is mine? To keep? Or to borrow, or—"

"It's a gift. From me to you."

Bridgette rushed to my bedroom and returned with my hand mirror. It was a lovely choker. Stunning. I lowered the mirror and turned to Everett. "But you already paid way too much money for this dress, and—"

"Girl, if you don't take the man's gift and hush! Damn!" Bridgette fussed.

I shot her a look, let my eyes fall on Everett again, and said, "Thank you, but you didn't have to do this."

"I wanted to. You ready to go?" he asked, leaning in to kiss my neck.

Closing my eyes and shuddering a little at his touch, I whispered, "Yeah." Hell, he could've been taking me to the damn electric chair and my ass probably would've followed him at this point, skipping the whole way there. I was just that happy to be with him.

The event was held at Second Avenue, a very exclusive nightclub co-owned by Everett and his brother, Leland. Yeah, *that* Leland—Leland McClain, the NBA star. I'd forgotten there were two famous McClain brothers until Everett mentioned Leland's name. A third brother, Nolan, managed the club. Apparently, I would get to meet all of the McClain siblings that night, including Nolan's twin, Neil, and their only sister, Kathryn.

We rode there in his SUV, him sitting close to me holding my hand but silent, seemingly deep in thought. I didn't mind the quiet, because I was nervous, on edge—shit, *petrified*. I wasn't ready for what was to come: the pictures, the celebrities, standing in Everett's huge spotlight with him, but this was his life and I wanted to be in it, so I had to suck it up and try to smile through it so I could have him in private again. I had pretty much psyched myself up, ready to fake it through the night and pretend I belonged on his arm until we pulled up to the three-story club and I saw the red carpet, the cameras flashing, and the gorgeous people making their way into the building.

Panic struck me like a bolt of lightning. I hadn't considered there'd be a red carpet. Everett hadn't mentioned it, either. I grew so anxious, my hands started trembling, and then the itching started. I always itched under circumstances of extreme anxiety, but this was especially bad, because I was itching *everywhere*, including the soles of my feet, and since my shoes were tied in a big satin bow at my ankles, I couldn't kick them off to scratch them. I moaned as I wiggled in my seat, tears pooling in my eyes. I was losing it in the back of this man's limited-edition Escalade.

Releasing Everett's hand, I palmed my cheeks to keep from scratching my makeup off. I was damn near gasping for air, and I could feel heat covering my body.

"Jo? Jo, what's wrong?" He looked and sounded so concerned. I was ruining his night, and that made me want to cry even more.

"Y-y-you didn't mention a red carpet. You-I-oh…I'm-I'm scared."

He grabbed my trembling hands, his eyes locked with mine. "Of what, baby? The cameras? You said you were okay with pictures now."

I shook my head. "I don't know. All I know is I'm terrified. I'm so sorry. You didn't sign up for this. I'm ruining everything."

His eyes rounded the inside of the truck before landing on me again. "No, I…I'm sorry I didn't mention the red carpet. I guess I thought you'd know there'd be one. There's not much I attend that doesn't have one. I…you wanna be let out around back? I can do the carpet alone. That's what I had planned to do if you still wanted to avoid your picture being taken. Then you said you didn't care, but this is a lot. I realize that."

I gazed out the window and then back at him. I didn't want to go in there alone, either. I didn't know anyone. "No, just…it'll be okay, right? I don't want to—I want to stay with you, if that's okay."

"Of course it is." He released my hands and placed his on my cheeks. "Just pretend we're alone, that there's nobody here but us. You can do this."

I nodded and took a deep breath, tried not to throw up when Dunn opened the back door and Everett climbed out, reaching for my hand. I took it, holding my clutch in the other hand and praying I didn't lose my balance as I stepped out of the truck.

Everett instantly pulled me to him, planting a kiss on my lips that muted the shuttering of cameras and screaming voices of the reporters and fans. I was glad Sage applied long-lasting lipstick or else he would've definitely been wearing it, too. When he backed away from me and gave me a smile, it really did feel like we were alone, and that served to slow my racing heart down.

He tightly gripped my hand as we crept along the red carpet with him stopping to talk to reporter after reporter, folks representing a wide variety of outlets from the E! network to The Shade Room. I stood mutely by his side with a smile on my face, praying none of them would address me and none of them did, but they did ask him who his "lovely companion" was, to which he answered, "My girlfriend, Jo." That would rev them up, but he just kept it moving before they could pry any further.

Once we were finally inside the huge club that was bathed in soft red lighting for the occasion, my nerves settled a bit. There were considerably less camera flashes as there was only one official photographer and one videographer commemorating the occasion, a fundraiser for the Juanita McClain foundation, an organization Everett created in his late mother's honor. He'd told me during one of our many conversations that she'd died at a relatively young age, when Leland, his youngest sibling, was just eleven years old and Everett was about twenty-two and newly married. Ella hadn't even been born when complications from a stroke she'd suffered took the widow away from her family when she was only forty-five. His dad had died years earlier, making my heart further ache for him. Money raised by the foundation was funneled into stroke prevention research, education, and rehab benefits for other stroke sufferers. It was truly a noble effort.

We'd barely followed Dunn inside with Tommy bringing up our rear before Everett was approached by some woman he introduced me to, some woman who was carrying a champagne flute and seemed very familiar with him, so familiar that when he introduced me to her, she snatched me into a hug, bathing me in her great-smelling perfume.

As we moved further into the club, Everett said, "That was Samantha Streeter, my former manager and still a good friend of mine."

I nodded, as I did when I met record execs, other recording artists, actors, and actresses, most of whom were bona fied superstars. It was overwhelming to say the least, especially since I wasn't just in some club spotting them from afar, as I'd often done when out with Bridgette or Sage or both. I was actually meeting these people, shaking their hands. It was surreal, but no more surreal than being on Everett's arm.

As we perused our way to our table, I thought about Bridgette and how being here would probably change her life and boost her career. She was super talented; she just needed a chance. I hated that the event was sold out when Everett invited me to it.

When we finally made it to our table, I smiled. Our table mates were obviously his siblings and their dates, because the men all looked like variations of Everett—the oldest of the clan—dressed in tuxedoes. One by one, they stood wearing Everett's smile and welcomed me to the table, but it somehow felt like they were welcoming me to their family. Leland seemed even taller than Everett while Nolan and Neil were much shorter—yet, still taller than me. All of them were handsome, and their dates were gorgeous. None of the McClain men were married. Bridgette was going to kill me for not sneaking her in through the back or something. Sage, too.

His sister, Kathryn, was tall, statuesque, beautiful, and the only McClain sibling who was lawfully wed. And her husband? He was hot as hell! I had to make myself stop staring at him. As I took my seat and listened to the siblings banter back and forth, I began to relax even more. I could already tell this was going to be a great night.

"Wow, Ev. She's like, a real woman. And she's cute. And I can tell that's her real hair. What happened? You ran out of models?" Kathryn asked.

"Shut up, Kat," was Everett's response.

"Hell, she's just saying what the rest of us are thinking," Leland chimed in. "I see you're tryna be like me, now. I love me a real woman." He emphasized his statement by wrapping his arm around his date's shoulder, his noticeably older date. Leland couldn't have been any more than twenty-five, maybe twenty-six. The chick by his side could've been forty, possibly even forty-five, beautiful, and super curvy. Leland evidently liked his women thick, and yes, real.

"Nah, you copying off me, man," Everett said, echoing my thoughts since Esther was quite a bit older than him when they got together.

"Ev's got a point," Nolan said, with a smirk. His date was pale and blond, the only non-melanated person at the table.

Neil rolled his eyes. "Nole, man. Just..." He sighed, obviously irritated with his twin about something.

"Just what?" Nolan asked.

Neil threw up his hands. "Nothing. Hey, Ev…glad you sticking with women that look like our earth, unlike some folks. She'd be proud."

"Don't start with me, Neil," Nolan shot back.

Everett whispered in my ear, "Neil is hotep as hell, can't stand Nolan dating all these white girls."

"Oh," I said with wide eyes, but I had gathered that when he referred to their mother as their earth. I'd only ever heard hotep folks use that term. And as I thought about it, I'd never heard of Everett dating anything but black women. I had to wonder about *his* opinion of Nolan's dating practices.

"I ain't starting shit. But you need to stop. It's getting ridiculous. What are you doing? Flying them over from the Ukraine or something? They fucking you for freedom?" Neil asked, then took a sip of wine. "All these sisters floating around here and your ass over there with Svetlana."

Nolan's date grinned as he chuckled, obviously oblivious to Neil's insult. "You know what, Neil? At least I got a woman. Hell, I *keep* one. I ain't stuck in the past like you. Shit, your ex done got married and you still sitting around waiting on her. You need to find *you* one of them sisters you keep talking about."

"Fuck you," Neil spat. "Whitewashed ass…"

With a satisfied grin on his face, Nolan said, "Truth hurts, huh?" He leaned in and kissed his delighted date on the cheek. "And her name is Danya, for your information."

Neil shrugged. "Danya, Svetlana, whatever."

"Hey, when's the last time you talked to Emery, anyway? Or is she still ignoring your phone calls?" Nolan asked Neil.

"You a bitch for that, Nolan. A real bitch," Neil said, then left the table, returning a few minutes later with a glass of something that was most definitely stronger than wine. By then, Nolan's attention was solely on Danya.

As the conversation lightened with Kathryn talking about her online boutique, *Quintessence,* a site full of t-shirts with quirky sayings and gorgeous black art that I'd patronized without realizing it belonged to her, I felt Everett rest his warm hand on my thigh. I placed my hand on top of his and smiled at him, giving him my attention.

"Did I tell you how gorgeous you look tonight?" he asked.

I nodded. "A few times."

"Just making sure you know."

"Well, I *should* look good. You paid enough for this dress."

"Stop that. I'da paid twice as much to see you in this, because…*damn*." He kissed me and once we parted, my eyes swung around the table to see that everyone was staring at us, of course.

I cleared my throat and as the thought occurred to me, leaned in close to Everett, and asked, "Is Ella at another table?"

He sighed lightly. "Her mom said they had some important event to go to. Something they're filming for their show." It sounded like the whole reality show thing was a sore subject for him, so I didn't pry any further. I merely nodded in response.

I let my eyes scan the filling room as the McClains talked amongst themselves. About ten minutes later, I asked Everett where the restrooms were. Though I was attempting to whisper, Kathryn heard me and offered to go with me since she was, of course, familiar with the club's layout. So after Everett planted a soft kiss on my lips, we were on our way, navigating the sea of people to the ladies room.

"Girl, I haven't seen my brother this happy in a long time," Kathryn said. "You must be something special."

I smiled at her. "Well, he seems to think so."

"He—"

Kathryn's words morphed into a yelp when I was grabbed from the other side and yanked toward a wall in the dim corridor that led to the restrooms.

"I thought that was you. The fuck you doing here with Big South?" he asked, his nostrils flaring as he tightly gripped my arms.

"Sid, let me go!" I hissed. "Don't start this right now! Please! Just let me go!"

"You fucking that nigga, Jo? That's who you been fucking? Huh? Tell me!"

"Sid! Let me the hell go!"

"Is South that nigga Eric?"

"What—who?"

"The nigga who sent them flowers to you! That was South?"

Out of the corner of my eye, I saw Kathryn hurriedly leaving, and I knew she was going to get her brother. I also knew the shit was about to hit the fan.

Everett

"Can't believe I'm sitting here with a Trump supporter at this table. Nole, man, you gotta stop this shit," Neil said, shaking his head.

"She's not even from here. She's Russian, Neil," Nolan said through gritted teeth.

"Exactly."

Neil had tried to stop himself, but now that he was juiced, he was back to shading the hell out of Nolan about the model he'd brought to the benefit, and it was all I could do not to crack all the way up. Ole girl could barely speak English, but her smile was on point. She looked happy as hell to be there with Nolan and ignorant of the fact that Neil's ass was about to lose it. Those two were identical with totally different personalities.

I was happy Jo had relaxed and felt bad for not preparing her properly for the evening, but I guess I forgot she wasn't from my world even though that's what I liked most about her. I'd honestly not dated a woman who wasn't in the industry somehow since high school. Being around someone who hadn't been ruined by fame or the desire for it was a nice change. Hell, it was a needed change.

Scanning the room, I smiled at the people who caught my eye. It was a great turnout, and at ten grand a ticket, I knew we'd raised a good amount of money for the foundation. I was feeling proud, content, and happy to be spending the evening with Jo, so when Kathryn came rushing back to the table without her, I frowned, and when I saw the frantic look on her face, I jumped to my feet. What the hell was going on?

"Ev, where's your security?" she asked, as soon as she reached me.

"Why? Where's Jo? The fuck is going on?" My ass was seriously panicking.

"Some guy just grabbed her."

"Grabbed her?!" I virtually shouted. "He took her? She's gone? Jo is gone?" My mind was racing, turning corners, and about to skid out of control with crazy thoughts. I'd told several reporters she was my girlfriend. I was rich, rich as hell. Had someone kidnapped her for money?

I should've had security follow her and Kat to the restroom.
Shit.

"No—no...I don't know. He just grabbed her and started talking to her. I couldn't hear what he was saying, but she looked, I don't know...startled? Like she knew him but wasn't expecting to see him here?"

"Ev, you need us?" Leland asked, nodding toward Neil and then Nolan.

I shook my head. "Nah, y'all stay here."

I caught Tommy's eye across the room and signaled for him to follow me while all at the same time wondering if someone had snuck into the club. I mean, I wasn't associated with anyone who'd pull some shit like this, was I? Tommy must've alerted Dunn, because he was on my heels, too, as I followed my sister to where I hoped Jo still was. When I got to her, I was confused as hell. This nigga had her hemmed up, basically pinned against the wall. She looked like a caged animal. And that shit pissed me completely off.

"Yo, what is this?" Tommy asked.

"The hell is going on? Nigga, if you don't get your hands off—" I started, but was cut off by this fool.

"Man, South...you need to get the fuck on while I talk to my wife. I don't know what she told you, but this pussy right here is off limits."

My eyes shot from the dude to Jo. "Wife?"

She shook her head. "*Ex*-wife. Sid, you need to stop this shit!"

"This is your ex? Bugz-NYC is your ex?" I asked.

"Daaaamn," Dunn said.

"Ain't shit ex about us. We just taking a break," Bugz said. "She ain't supposed to be fucking nobody else!"

"How in the shit are we taking a break when you're married with a baby on the way, you damn fool?!" Jo shrieked.

"You know I'm just with her for my career. Your impatient ass supposed to be waiting on me!"

"Huh? Are you the-fuck insane? You left me pregnant and alone, married another woman, and I'm just supposed to be sitting at home waiting for your sorry ass? For real?"

"Hell, yeah! That pussy—wait, that shit you spit on my song was about her? You was talking about my muh-fucking wife on my damn song?!" He was out of Jo's face, approaching me now.

"Whoa, pardna', you don't want the shit you gon' get if you step to him," Dunn said, tapping the gun holstered under his tuxedo jacket.

While he handled Bugz, I stepped over to Jo, grabbing her hand and feeling her tremble. "You all right?" I asked.

She nodded hesitantly, and whispered, "I-I'm so sorry. He's-he's out of his mind. We are divorced, and I want nothing to do with him. I can't stand his ass. I'm sorry he's Nat's father. Worst decision of my life was marrying him."

"Yo, South! You need to take your hands off her, my nigga! And your ass better not've been touching my baby, either! Disrespecting me on my damn track, talking about how you gon' fuck my woman!"

I turned and gave him a smirk. "Look, man, it's not my fault you couldn't hold on to her. She's moved on to better. You just gon' have to deal with it." I kissed her just to fuck with him.

This fool tried to jump over Dunn and Tommy to get to me. Bugz was maybe a couple of inches shorter than me and was one of those Snoop Dogg-built niggas; he didn't have nothing on them. Those dudes were giants.

"You got your goons on me, but I'ma get your ass! You lucky I ain't got my security with me!"

"Didn't they all quit because they were tired of getting your no-fighting ass out of fights?" Jo spat at him.

"Bitch—"

"That's it. Get his ass out of here before I show him what a bitch looks like. Now!" I said, my eyes on Tommy.

"I paid into your whack-ass charity to be here!" Bugz shouted, as Tommy began pushing him toward the back door just beyond the restrooms.

"You'll get a refund. I don't want your damn money," I replied.

He screamed all the way out the door. The DJ was still spinning records so I knew no one could hear him, and I was glad that the actual presentations hadn't started yet. At the same time, I was pissed at Jo; I just wasn't going to let Bugz's ass know it.

Her eyes were all over the place. I could tell she wanted to cry but was fighting it hard. "Everett—"

I shook my head. "Jo, ain't shit you can say right now that I'm tryna hear. Did you even make it to the restroom?"

Her shoulders fell. "No, I…"

"Go. Get yourself together. Do what you need to do. I'll wait here for you."

She nodded, and I waited, gave Tommy and Dunn a nod when they returned, and when she finally emerged from the restroom, escorted Jo back to our table before quickly being summoned to the stage with my siblings. I must have been right about the music drowning out the confrontation, because it didn't seem that anyone other than the folks at my table knew something had gone down, so that was good.

This was one occasion for which I was happy Nolan's long-winded ass was taking the lead, explaining what our foundation was about and making the presentations, because all that was on my mind was that bullshit with Jo and her ex. Hell, *was* he her ex? Had my ass been running in behind a married woman? She said they were divorced, and Jo didn't seem like the type to lie, but did I really know her? Had I been moving too fast with her? Shit, probably so, but I honestly couldn't help it. I couldn't stop myself when it came to Jo, and I couldn't explain why. That's why Bugz saying that shit messed with my head.

Damn, I should have had a background check done on her. The hell was I thinking?

After my brothers and sister and I finished our hosting duties, dinner was served, and after that, the entertainment—our mom's favorite group, The Whispers—started their performance. When I got back to the table, Jo refused to look at me, barely said another word all night, and I had to wonder if she was guilty or just embarrassed. Hell, I didn't have much to say either, but I did introduce her to the folks that visited our table, and when I asked her to dance, she didn't protest.

By the end of the night, I was tired as hell from thinking about this shit between us, and although I had planned to take her home with me, thought it was best to put some space between us for now.

16

What should have been one of the best nights of my life turned out to be one of the worst. After the whole Sid thing, I wanted to disappear, somehow blink my eyes and be back at home on my sofa wrapped up in a blanket with the AC blasting and curled up with Nat, because that was where I belonged anyway. This was never meant to be my world. I wasn't supposed to dress up and go to parties with rich people on a famous man's arm. Sid had proven that by dumping me as soon as the paychecks started rolling in. We were still together when he got his record deal and his star started rising, but he rarely took me out, said it was better for his image if no one knew he was married. Me getting pregnant with Nat just fueled that claim. He definitely didn't want anyone to know he was married with a kid on the way. With Sid, I was good enough to be in the shadows of his life, but he made sure I never shared the spotlight. He was right to make that decision. Me being in the spotlight was a horrible idea.

Everett was different after Sid was kicked out—quiet, inattentive, nothing like he usually was with me, and it made my stomach toil with anxiety. I couldn't eat my dinner, couldn't focus on the music, was barely able to smile and engage with his siblings because I knew this was the end of us. We'd ended before we even really started. I thought I'd finally found something good, something—*someone*— for me, but I'd messed that up by not being up front with him about my delusional ex-husband. I didn't give him full disclosure for fear of losing him if I did, and I'd lost him anyway. Confirmation of that was him introducing me as just "Jo" to the people that approached our table instead of "my girlfriend, Jo," like he did out on the red carpet.

My heart was heavy when I climbed into his SUV at the end of the night. It splintered when he didn't grab my hand or smile at me or even look at me when he climbed in beside me. And I had to fight not to bawl my eyes out as the thick silence between us nearly smothered me on the way to my house. When the truck stopped in my driveway, I hopped out without waiting for him to open my door, as I was sure he wouldn't now anyway. I hurried to my door, fumbling with the magnetic closure of my clutch as I tried to open it. If I'd been thinking more clearly, I would've dug my key out while in the truck and had it ready. As it was, I was such a wreck, I dropped the damn purse, and as I bent over to get it, the tears came. Sniffling and gasping for air, I finally got ahold of my key and stuck it in the lock.

"Damn, you weren't gonna let me walk you to your door?"

I looked up to see Everett standing behind me with a half-hearted grin on his face. "I d-didn't think you'd want to."

At seeing my face drenched in tears, he dropped the grin. "Why wouldn't I?"

"Be-because you believed my ex. I-I can tell. But-but it's okay. I understand. Thank you for tonight. I…" That was it. I dropped my purse and covered my face with my hands and cried like I'd lost my best friend.

"Jo…"

I shook my head and turned to the door again. "Go. I'll be fine."

He didn't say a word, just reached around me, turned the key in the lock, and opened the door, taking me by the elbow and guiding me inside. I was still crying, in mourning of what could have been, what *should* have been, but like everything I saw as good in my life besides Nat, including the dignity I worked hard to build within myself despite my upbringing, Sid ripped it away from me.

Everett closed the door behind us, and there we stood in my living room in silence.

My bleary eyes roamed the room as a thought hit me. "Can you stay for a minute? I need to show you something."

He hesitantly nodded, and I took off toward my room, digging through a dresser drawer, quickly locating what I was trying to find. He was still standing by the door when I returned and thrusted the packet of papers at him.

"My divorce papers. I'm not his wife or his woman. I'm not shit to him, never was, not even when we were married. I didn't lie to you, and I never said I'd wait for him. *Ever.* He probably just assumed I would because it was so easy for him to make a fool of me in the past. What he fails to realize for some reason is that I don't want his ass. *At all.*"

He stared down at the papers, then let his eyes land on me. "But you didn't tell me who he was. You let me spit all that shit on his track, knowing I was referring to you. Knowing he…shit, dude is a fool anyway. The whole industry knows it. But he's a super fool over you. He proved that tonight."

"If you were married to someone like that, would you not be embarrassed? His own family barely claims him, or at least that's how it was when we were together. Hell, I'm ashamed to admit I even know him, let alone exchanged vows with him, but I wanted a family *so bad*, never had a normal one. My mom was out of it most of the time, and then she died and left me when I was only eighteen, and I've never even laid eyes on my father. That fool seemed like a good thing at the time. And I didn't know you were gonna say what you said on his song. I was just tryna help. Your verse was too soft at first, soft as hell."

"Soft as hell? Damn, Jo. Look, all I'm saying is you could've told me who he is to you after you heard what I said. He's an idiot, but he had every right to be fucked up about me saying what I said about you on his song."

"Why? Why does he have a right to be upset about that? The man dated me, courted me, married me, made me believe in his talent so much that I actually worked three damn jobs to support us so he could stop selling dope and concentrate on his music. I paid for his studio time. I bought his clothes, paid for the beats he used for the tracks on his mix tape, paid for his website, was at every show he did when he was walking around calling himself Thumper instead of Bugz-NYC—"

"Thumper? That nigga got a thing for rabbits or something?"

"Who knows? Anyway, I did all that stuff for him, thinking I was helping him build *our* future, and you know what he did? He hid me. Even when he did take me places after he started making money, he never told people I was his wife, just let me blend into the background as a part of his entourage. Was actually pissed when I got pregnant. Left me because 'being married was gonna kill his career' and then married his fucking manager, who he'd been screwing the whole time. For some reason, his ass thinks alimony and child support is supposed to fix the fact that he shat all over my heart! And now...now *this*." I threw my hands up. "You were supposed to be my good thing, the only good thing I had besides Nat and my few friends, and he took *that* away from me, too. You know, all that shit he said tonight about me still being his? I guess he proved it's true. I guess I should stop fighting him and just be his ex-wife/side chick. He bought this house, my car, and he thinks he owns me, so I should just go ahead and start screwing him again. What's the point in refusing him? He won't let me move on. Maybe this is what I deserve for ever being with him in the first place. Maybe me and him—"

His lips were on mine so fast, I couldn't really think through what was happening. So I stood there, stiff as a board as his tongue pushed against the seam of my mouth until it occurred to me to open it for him. He pulled me closer as his tongue explored mine, caressing it as he slid a hand up from my waist to the back of my head, pushing my mouth into his and making me frantic with desire for him. I grabbed at his arms, ended up clutching his tuxedo jacket as we explored each other's mouths. As the one hand clutched my head, the other slid down to my ass, and he squeezed a handful, saying something into my mouth that I couldn't make out. And then we were moving backward. He was steering me...somewhere. I couldn't open my eyes as our kiss seemed to intensify with every step we made. I didn't care where we were going just as long as he didn't leave me.

I bumped into something, and then I was being lifted from the floor. It took me a second to realize I was being placed on my dining room table, and that realization drove me completely wild. I wrapped my arms around his neck and my legs around his waist and kissed him hungrily, moaning, "Yesssss!" into his mouth.

He finally broke away from me, his breathing labored as he asked, "You gotta get Nat tonight?"

"No. Ms. Sherry said she could stay all weekend if I want her to, but I'll probably get her tomorrow," I responded, my own breathing loud and laborious.

He stared at me for a moment. My chest heaved as I watched him watch me, afraid he was going to change his mind and leave after all. Instead, he reached into his pants pocket, pulled out his phone, and made a call. I observed him with a throbbing core and knitted brows as he said, "Yeah. Y'all can leave. I'll call when I'm ready to go...probably tomorrow."

He ended the call, and his phone hit the floor. "Lay back, baby," he nearly growled.

I fell back on the expensive-ass mahogany table, sucked in a breath when he pulled my panties down my legs, and closed my eyes in anticipation of what he would do next. I heard a chair scrape across the hardwood floor, felt his big hands grasp my hips and pull my butt to the edge of the table. A second later, his mouth was on me, his tongue dragging over my clit.

I sat up a little, jolted into action by the sudden pleasure, but he reached up and gently pushed me back down. Fastening my eyes to the chandelier above us, I tried to remember to breathe, because it felt so good it almost felt...bad. Like nothing I'd ever felt in all the days of my life. He licked and slurped and then pulled my clit into his mouth, and I screamed, grabbing his dreadlocks as I thrusted my sex at his face.

"Shiiiiiiit! Everett! Damn!"

He let up for a second, murmured, "You taste so motherfucking good!" and then resumed his wonderful torture.

I didn't explode as fast as I did the first time he touched me in that way, but it wasn't long before his skillful tongue caused the sensations building inside me to boil out of control and I burst in his mouth. I jerked and writhed on the table, and my legs trembled as I screamed his name over and over again, but he kept going as if he couldn't tell I'd already met my bliss. He gripped my hips and held me in place as he feasted on me, moaning against my sensitized flesh.

"Ev—Everett...please," I begged. I was going to lose it if he didn't stop, and by *it*, I mean any semblance of sanity I possessed.

I raised up and looked down in time to see him shake his head.

"Are you...are you trying to make me...I can't do it twice. I can barely come once, so—" I cut my own words off as he sucked harder and I felt the pressure begin to build again. Sweat popped up all over me. Every muscle in my body tightened. What the hell was he doing and how was he doing it? What was he? A damn clit magician? I could count the number of times I climaxed with Sid on my hands and we were together for four years. But this shit Everett was doing was freaking mystical or something. I almost felt like a puppet under his control, like if he said the word "come," I'd melt all over him on command.

And I did melt again...and again. I had four orgasms before he relented, rising from the chair and lifting my wilted, sweat-slickened body to sit up on the table. I watched him undress with a smile on his face, the handsome face smeared with my essence. I was weak, tired, but I still wanted him, and as he undressed, revealing his chiseled pecs, carved abs, and sculpted thighs, I wanted to pinch myself. I was in such a fog, high on orgasms, that I didn't see where the condom came from, but watching him sheath himself, I thought about the line he delivered with such confidence that day in the studio: *They don't call be Big 12 for nothing, baby*. That wasn't nothing but the truth.

Because...shit!

My eyes scurried from his groin to his face.

He reached for me, kissed me so deeply I was sure he tasted my tonsils, and backed away just as abruptly. "Take that dress off," he basically ordered.

I eagerly obliged, removing both the dress and adhesive bra, covering my breasts with my hands once I was completely bare.

Moving my hands, he asked, "What you hiding? You breastfed Nat?"

Damn, he read me that easily. I dropped my eyes and nodded. They were droopy as hell. Not pancakes, per se, but they weren't standing at attention, either. I'd been thinking about getting them fixed so they'd be perky again, but—

He inhaled my right breast, sucking it like he expected gold to spring forth. I forgot to be self-conscious about them after that, because once he was done with breast number one, he ravished breast number two. Then he lifted his head and grabbed his shaft.

"Um, Everett?"

The nimble fingers of his free hand found my core, two of them pushing inside me at once. "Hmm, baby?"

"Oooooo, shit! Uh, I-I-I don't think that'll fit in me. I've never seen—"

"It will. As wet as you are right now? It'll definitely fit."

"Are you sure?"

"Yeah...you wanna stop? We can stop if you wanna stop." He was squinting at me, one hand still holding his shaft while the fingers of his other hand kept working my flooded playground, turning me on and confusing me at the same time.

"No," I said.

"Are *you* sure?"

"Yes."

"Okay."

In a series of moves that I barely perceived, I was pushed onto my back, pulled to the edge of the table again, and he was inside me—*deep inside me*. I arched my back, and screamed, "Ohhhhhh!"

"See," he moaned, "it—oh, shit! It fits, and damn, Jo!"

As he eased out and slid back inside me, I raised up and grabbed his face, kissing him, moaning into his mouth, clawing at his shoulders. He lifted me from the table and moved us to a wall where he plunged deeper inside me, taking his lips from mine and staring into my eyes. "You feel so…fucking…good!"

I frowned as he knocked me against the wall. Closing my eyes, I whimpered, "So…do…you…"

"Baby, shit! Shit! Damn!" he yelled. Everett had to be the most vocal lover I'd ever encountered. I had to wonder if he always made that much noise or if I actually felt that good to him. One thing was for damn sure: *he* felt freaking wonderful. If I thought I was obsessed with the idea of him before, my ass was going to go full stalker after this.

Lost in a feeling I can't even describe, I reached around and grabbed a handful of his dreads, yanked his head back, and sank my teeth into his neck.

He growled, "Hellllll, yeah!" and then his lips met mine again as he continued to plunge inside me to an aching fullness and glide out, repeating the process at a pace that was somehow both steady and frenetic at the same time. We kissed, moaned, screamed, and by some miracle, as my body began to pulse with yet another orgasm, he peaked, roaring into my neck with a final thrust and a final, "Shit!"

*****

I woke up just before the sun rose, lying on my side with his heavy body encasing mine, his breath on my neck. A smile crept across my face. It wasn't a dream. He was there with me, in my bed, holding me tightly. All I could do was sigh and close my eyes and bask in his warmth.

"Jo…you up?" he asked softly.

I nodded.

"You good? I mean…I didn't hurt you, did I?"

I shook my head.

"Good. Uh…" The arm that had been wrapped around my body moved, and the hand attached to it slid to my yoni. I opened my legs through no will of my own and shuddered when his finger found its way inside me. "You sore?"

Was I? Shit, I was…but I didn't care, so I lied, "No."

He repositioned us so that I was on my back and his long body was stretched over me. His mouth hovered over mine as he opened my legs wider and rested between them. "You have any idea how good you taste—" He kissed me softly. "—and feel?"

Before I could formulate an answer, he was inside of me again. My mouth fell open as I grabbed his arms to anchor myself. Then I lifted up enough to slide my hands to his tight ass and push him in deeper.

He closed his eyes, mumbled, "Got-damn, Jo…" and slid out of me with a moan.

"Oh!" I whined.

He plunged deeper, faster, and harder, sending me over the edge twice before he released, collapsed onto my body, and said, "Damn, Jo…what're you doing to me?"

17

Everett

She wasn't in bed when I woke up, which made me wonder if I'd imagined what happened between us. I had almost convinced myself that was what happened, that nothing on this side of Heaven could possibly feel so good, when she walked into the bedroom with this shy look on her face. Jo was so damn beautiful to me, like the most beautiful woman I had ever laid eyes on. Beautiful and sexy as hell, and the way it felt to be inside her? There weren't enough words in the English language to describe that shit.

I'd had a lot of sex with a lot of women, but Jo was just…different. The kind of different that made me want to pick her little ass up and fly her to Vegas to make this thing official, scoop her up before she actually decided to give her ex another chance. At that point, I'd do just about anything for her, and that shit scared the hell out of me.

"Is that my shirt?" I asked, observing the oversized dress shirt hanging from her petite frame.

She nodded, pulling her bottom lip between her teeth. "Yeah. You hungry?"

I sat up on the side of the bed. "Why? You cooked? I ain't see nothing but pineapples in your fridge the other day…and yogurt, but mostly pineapples. It's like five whole pineapples in there and a bunch of those pineapple fruit cups. You really like pineapples, huh?"

I swear she was blushing as she replied, "Yeah, I do. Um, I can't really cook, but I could make some instant oatmeal or some of Nat's Eggos or some cold cereal. Or I could order us something."

I stood, crossing the room and pulling her into my arms. "Or I can text Dunn, have him bring us something."

She leaned into me. "I'm fine with that, just don't want you to leave yet."

Smiling down at her, I cupped her face in my hands. "You got me today and most of tomorrow if you want me. Then I have to hit the road again."

"Oh, I want you," she said, as she wrapped her arms around me. "Everett?"

"Yeah, baby?"

"Am I still your girlfriend?"

I frowned, stepped back a little, and said, "Of course you are. Why you ask that?"

"Because last night, you stopped telling people I was your girlfriend after the whole situation with Sidney."

"Who?"

"My ex. And I'm sorry about that again. I—"

"Jo, look…I was pissed and confused about all that shit he said. You already explained and apologized. The only thing I'm concerned about is that stuff you said about fucking him again. Now, that shit—"

"I was sad and out of my mind. I despise his ass, wouldn't let him touch me if he was the last man on Earth. I just hate that he acted a fool at your event."

"It's all right, Jo. It's all good. We're fine, but let me make this plain. You're my girlfriend, my woman, my lady. You and no one else. I'ma need to be your only man, too."

"You are!"

"Okay. So it's settled. Bugz or Sidney or whatever? *Fuck him*, but don't actually…fuck him."

She rolled her eyes.

"Look, he ain't changed nothing. We're still us, and after last night and this morning, your ass might never get rid of me."

She grinned. "Good."

*****

We spent most of the day in bed after breakfast, and I'll be damned if she didn't feel just as good as the first time, every time. She tasted good, too, sweet like she was made of fruit or sugar or something. I'd never tasted anything like it and had to wonder what the hell made her taste like that. Well, whatever it was, it made her addictive. I sat up in her living room trying to watch some cooking show with her thinking about eating her pussy the whole time, despite spending most of the morning licking on her. My tongue was twitching and shit just from the idea of tasting her again. When I couldn't take anymore, I buried my face between her legs until she screamed my name then dove back in that good pussy of hers again and again. By the time the babysitter brought Nat home, I'd lost count of how many times we did it. Little Nat was the only thing that saved Jo from yet another tongue-lashing.

I had Dunn bring my duffel bag with him when he delivered our breakfast, so I changed and proposed that we go out for dinner and take Nat with us. Since our faces were already splashed across social media because of the benefit, Jo didn't have a problem with going out. We still ate in a private room at the pizza joint, but we went in through the front with Tommy and Dunn in the front and rear of us as she carried Nat on her hip. We had a great time. Jo was probably more relaxed than I'd ever seen her, and Nat was a funny kid with her random giggling and roaring. And she had my name down,
asking me for my drink and my pizza. She liked me, which put my mind at ease, because if this thing with Jo was going to work, I needed Nat on my side since her father was obviously going to be a problem. He'd already had his people email my people to let me know he wouldn't be using my verse for his track and that they were cutting me out of the video, not that I gave half a damn. The label wanted me on the track to expand *his* audience, not mine. He'd have to deal with the fallout from them. I truly wasn't fucked up about it.

As a matter of fact, I decided I'd take that verse and build my own track around it. Make it available on an updated version of the digital album or something. I was even thinking of naming it "Jo" just to fuck with Bugz. The prospect of it alone had me grinning.

When we left the pizza joint, there was a whole crowd of paparazzi waiting outside. Jo had already told me little Nat liked taking pictures, and she proved it by smiling brightly and waving at the photographers. It was cute, but I also knew the whole scene—me with Jo and Nat—was going to set Bugz's ass off again. I could handle it. I just hoped Jo could, too.

18

Everett

I bunked in Jo's guest bedroom that night, so we wouldn't confuse Nat if she woke up in the middle of the night and found me in her mom's bed. I was cool with it, because at least I was there with Jo. I just wasn't ready to be away from her. Not yet. Not when I had to leave her the next night to continue a tour I regretted booking. This thing between us was new, and I felt like I needed to spend more time with her in order to grow closer to her, and honestly, to protect her from her ex. Not that I thought she couldn't handle him. I just...there was more to Jo that I couldn't put my finger on. Something that I thought made her vulnerable to him, so leaving for another month to finish the North American leg of the tour bothered the shit out of me. It bothered me so much that I couldn't sleep. Well, that and the fact that I wanted to be wrapped around her body. We hadn't done anything since Nat made it home, and I was horny as hell, but I was a father and I understood the responsible thing was to wait until we were alone again. Jo had offered to see if the babysitter could watch her tonight, but I didn't want Nat to associate me with her having to be away from her mom. So I laid there in the dark with my dick hard as hell, thinking about Jo's soft body, the way she smelled, those juicy lips, those freckles, and those damn bowed legs. I was torturing myself. My ass probably should've gone to my suite and spent the night there. At least then I could've handled my hard dick with dignity. Couldn't do that with little Nat down the hall.

I almost jumped out of the bed when my phone's text message

alert chimed.

Jo: *You sleep?*

Me: *No. What u doin up?*

Jo: *Thinking about you.*

Me: *What u thinking bout?*

Jo: *I'm horny.*

Shit!

Me: *Don't say that.*

Jo: *Why? It's the truth.*

Me: *Because we can't do nothing about it right now.*

Jo: *I know. You're too loud.*

Me: What?! I ain't that loud!

Jo: *You yell the whole time. You're loud as hell.*

Me: *What if I promise to be quiet?*

Jo: *Don't know if I can trust you.*

Me: *Let me come in there and prove it to u.*

Jo: *No.*

Me: *What if I beg? I'm harder than a motherfucker right now.*

Jo: *You are?*

Me: *Yeah. U gonna let me come take care of this? Ima die.*

Jo: *LOL!!! No you won't.*

Me: *I'll lick it and stick it real good.*

Jo: *LOL!!!! Goodnight, Everett. Go to sleep.*

Me: *How Ima sleep with a hard dick?*

Jo: *Count sheep.*

Me: *That's messed up. Good night, Jo.*

Jo: *Night*

I laid my phone on my chest, smiled into the darkness, and somehow managed to fall asleep.

I'm not sure how long I was out before I felt soft hands inside my underwear, kisses on my chest, and heard, "Everett, wake up."

My eyes popped open in time to see her pull my dick out. "What—Jo?"

"Help me take these off." She was tugging at the waistband of my underwear.

Almost mechanically, I lifted my ass for her. She worked my briefs down my legs, then straddled me. That's when I noticed she was butt-ass naked. "Jo, baby. What you doing?" I asked.

Leaning in, she suckled on my neck, and whispered, "What does it look like?" She grabbed me, sliding her hand up and down my erection.

"Damn, baby. Shit…uh, I thought you said—"

"I can't sleep, because I can't stop thinking about this." She nodded toward my dick. "Just don't yell, okay?"

"I—shit, Jo! Uh…I won't," I said, as she kept stroking me.

"You're already getting loud," she whispered.

Lifting my head, I said, "I'm not trying to, baby."

"Hold on." She jumped out of the bed, grabbed a robe from the floor, covered herself, and left the room. I fell back on the bed, hard as hell and frustrated as fuck, wondering how long I was supposed to *hold on*. She had me ready to go.

She popped back into the room a minute later, closed and locked the door, then handed me a scarf as she let the robe fall to the floor.

"Damn, you fine," I almost whined.

"Put that scarf in your mouth," she said.

"Huh? You want me to gag myself? I ain't—"

She climbed on top of me, sat right on my dick, and said, "If you want this pussy, put that scarf in your mouth. *Now*."

So I put the damn scarf in my mouth, waited for her to ride me, and almost lost my shit when she slid down my body and wrapped her mouth around me.

"Ooooh, got-damn!" I said into the scarf.

She slid me out of her mouth. "Shh!"

I nodded, my eyes on her as she Hoovered the hell out of me. I mean…damn! Jo had skills like a motherfucker! There was something about seeing those lips of hers around me and seeing her take me deep into her mouth, slide me out, and pull me back in again that made me come unglued. I needed to stop watching her, because I was gonna start growling and roaring and shit, and not the cute little roaring I did for Nat. I was about to go beast-mode because it just felt too good, but I couldn't stop watching her. Seeing her do it made it that much better. So I stared at her, moaned into the scarf, and when I knew I was gonna lose control, I reached down and dragged her up my body until her face met mine. I yanked the scarf out of my mouth and kissed her until we were both out of breath, then I asked, "You gonna ride it, baby?" My words came out in almost a croak, like I was in pain or something. I was damn sure aching for her.

"I don't know if I can," she replied, eyes heavy with lust.

I knew she probably couldn't. Not many women could, so I didn't push her. "Get on your knees," I groaned.

"Scarf, Everett."

"Shit, okay."

While she got on all fours, I kissed her soft skin from the back of her neck to her ass, then shoved the damn scarf back in my mouth and positioned myself behind her, pushed on her upper back until her chest met the bed and slid a finger inside her, causing her to moan softly. Jo stayed wet as hell, like there was a fountain in her pussy. I had to close my eyes and calm myself before I glided inside her, felt her knees buckle a little as she moaned again, and I yelled into the scarf. She was so hot and wet and tight, I wasn't sure how long I could go this time. I watched her clutch the sheet as I thrusted in and slid out, my heart hammering in my chest. I bit down on the gag, groaning and whimpering. I wanted to talk to her, tell her how much I loved her pussy, how much I'd miss it when I left, how I was gonna make her mine forever, how if I even thought another man was going to touch her I was going to lose it, and how special she was to me, but I couldn't because she was right. I couldn't control the volume of my voice when I was inside of her. So I made all kinds of animalistic sounds into the scarf, and when I felt her walls squeeze and shudder around me, I lost all composure, hitting my peak with a muffled roar before rolling onto my back and pulling her onto my chest.

"I thought you were gonna *lick* it and stick it," Jo said, as she tried to catch her breath.

I grinned and rubbed my hand down her back to her ass. "Who said I was finished?"

*****

"How was your flight?" she asked.

"Good, I guess. Slept the whole time. You wore me out."

"You liked it."

"Sure did."

After a moment or two of silence, Jo said, "I miss you already."

"I miss you, too. Hey, you can come to any of my shows. I'll fly you out. You can bring Nat, too."

"I have a job, Everett."

I sighed into the phone. "You need to quit it before I have to kick Park's ass. And you know I'm not messed up about that piece you're working on. Ella doesn't need it. I just commissioned it to get close to you."

"I figured that, but I wanna finish it, and I'm not ready to quit. Thanks to you, Mr. Park treats me like a human now, but it's messed up that he couldn't be nice to me on his own."

"That's why you should quit."

"I know. Maybe I'm just a glutton for punishment. You see who I married."

"Don't do that."

"What?"

"Talk down about yourself. You deserve better. *I'm* your better."

"Yeah, you are definitely that."

"I'm glad you know it. Hey, I gotta go, baby. Got Skype meetings and sound check and shit."

"I know. You're a busy man in high demand, Big South."

"I'd rather be with you, though. I'll call you later."

"Okay, bye."

I turned my attention to Courtney, who'd traveled to Montreal with me to coordinate the business I had to conduct while trying to get ready for my show that night. We were heading to Toronto the next day, then down to NYC for a show that weekend. I was tired, irritable because I had to leave Jo, and just kind of out of it as Courtney ran down my schedule.

"Got it?" she asked.

I nodded. "Yeah. Be glad when this tour is over. Don't know if I'll ever do one like this again. I'm getting old."

Never taking her eyes off her tablet, she replied, "Well, I've been telling you to slow down for years. You've got your hands in so many things, Ella's grandchildren will be able to comfortably live off your money. You need to spend more time living than working. You've earned the right to do that, Ev."

"Yeah, you're right. Speaking of Ella...I got time to call her before this next meeting? I think it's her lunchtime now. She texted me this morning wanting to know how I got a girlfriend she knows nothing about. She saw us on Instagram or something."

"You didn't tell her because you didn't want Esther to know or because of what happened with Jo's ex at the benefit?"

"Kat told you?"

"It's my business to know all of *your* business."

"Yeah, Kat told you. I don't know, Court. No, I don't want Esther to know, but I also think i wasn't sure where things were going with Jo at first. I liked her, but now? Man..."

"You *really* like her, huh? Not letting the thing with her ex stop you?"

"To be honest, I don't think anything could stop me from being with her. She's special."

Courtney looked up from her tablet and smiled. "I can tell she's different from the other women you've dealt with. She's genuine and really sweet, not tainted by this industry. You deserve to be happy, and I can tell being around her makes you happy. Plus, she's nothing like Esther."

"And that's the best part about her."

"Yeah, so hurry with your call to Ella. Meeting's in twenty minutes."

"Yes, ma'am, cap'n."

19

"What are you doing?" Bridgette's voice filled the interior of my car.

"Headed back to work with Mr. Park's lunch," I replied, as I navigated my way from Koreatown with some dish I couldn't pronounce sitting in a sack on my passenger seat.

"You're at work?!"

"Yeah, it's Monday, right? I work Monday through Friday, which reminds me. I thought I had it bad being Mr. Park's assistant, but Everett's assistant works twenty-four-seven!"

"Yeah, but South isn't an ass cookie like your boss, letting his wife punk him and acting a fool with you."

"Not anymore."

"Because of South. And I'm tryna figure out how you get your coochie filleted by a fucking billionaire over the weekend and report to work on Monday? You're all over the internet and stuff. Girl, I woulda hopped my ass on a plane with him with Nat strapped to my back."

"I don't think he's a billionaire, is he?"

"Damn near. And how you don't know for sure? I did the research the moment he started trying to get with you. Didn't you?"

I knew he was wealthy, as that was more than obvious. He'd maintained a highly successful career for his entire adult life, wrote all his own songs, and owned his masters. While he'd never started his own label or produced other artists, he had a ton of endorsement deals. So yeah, he was rich, but I, more than anyone, knew money didn't make a man a man, so I said, "No! I'm not looking up the man's net worth. It doesn't matter. All that matters is he's good to me, kind to Nat, and—"

"Got your short ass walking sideways."

"Yep. That, too."

Bridgette sighed wistfully into the phone. "He's like my dream man. Rich with a big dick."

"Wow."

"He is!"

"Well, stay your ass away from him."

"Hell, if I was the type to betray my friends and try to break folks up, I'd have no chance with him anyway. His eyes never leave you when you're in the room. It's actually really beautiful."

That made my heart beat faster. "Really? You think he's that crazy about me?"

"I know he is! Anyway, I'ma try to get that sexy-ass Leland."

"Girl, I think he likes older women."

"I'm older. He's like twenty-six, and I'm twenty-eight."

"*Much* older."

"Damn, I can't win."

"Maybe Neil will work for you. He's one of the twins."

"Shit, I'll take him."

I laughed. "Okay, I'll figure out a way to get you two in the same room. Oh, he's shorter than Leland and Everett, though."

"Hell, I don't care."

I shook my head. "Bye, Bridgette. Let me get off this phone before your silly ass makes me have a wreck."

"Bye!"

Fifteen minutes later, I'd made it back to work and was about to climb out of my car when my text alert buzzed.

Everett: *I miss u and TBPITW.*

I had a big goofy smile on my face as I replied: *What's TBPITW?*

Everett: *The best pussy in the world.*

Now I was giggling.

Me: *Wow. That's a long name.*

Everett: *It was either that or wet-wet because u stay wet as hell.*

Me: *You make me wet. It's not like I walk around like that all the time.*

Everett: *Jo?*

Me: *Yeah?*

Everett: *Come see me in NYC this weekend.*

Me: *You really miss me that much?*

Everett: *Yeah. Come see me, baby.*

Speaking of being wet. Damn! He was turning me on in a text message.

I was tapping out my response when a loud thud almost made me drop my phone. Looking up, I saw Sid with his fist pressed against the driver side window.

Shit.

I closed my eyes, rolled them to the back of my head, and sighed. *Here we go.* "Go away!" I shouted through the closed window. I had half-expected him to be waiting at my house after the benefit. When I didn't hear from him all weekend, I thought maybe he'd grown some sense. I thought wrong.

"I need to talk to you!" he shouted back. "Get out the damn car!"

"No! Leave!"

"Talk to me and I will!"

I slapped my hand against the steering wheel. "Fuck!" I snatched the door open, hitting him with it as I got out of the car and in his face. "What the hell do you want?!"

He rubbed the back of his neck and shook his head dramatically. Sid was handsome in a rugged way. Tall, medium brown skin, decent body. Not as chiseled as Everett, but he was fine with hooded eyes and thick hair he almost always wore in cornrows. The full, dark lips he possessed as a result of his marijuana habit made him even more alluring. It was a shame he was a damn loon.

"I'm tryna figure out how you thought it was okay to start fucking Big South? How you gonna mess with his old ass when I'm sitting over here waiting for you? If you wanted to fuck, all you had to do was say the word, Jo."

I threw up my hands. "I don't even know what to say at this point.

I mean, you cheated, left…there was a divorce with a settlement and a custody agreement. You are married to another woman whom you obviously screw, because she is now pregnant with another one of those kids you told me you didn't want when you left me. Remember that? And you got the nerve to be upset about who I'm fucking?"

His mouth dropped open. "So you *are* fucking him?! Y'all ain't just dating? For real, Jo?! You screwing Big South?!"

Evil Jo, a part of me I fought hard to keep at bay, reared her ugly head, and said, "Well, actually, *he's* screwing *me*. Screwing the shit out of me. Got me all sore. And you know what? I can't wait for him to screw me again."

His eyes narrowed. "I'ma kill him. I'ma kill that mother—"

"Yeah, yeah, yeah." I reached into my car, grabbing my purse and Mr. Park's food. "I gotta get back to work. Go home to your ugly-ass wife and leave me alone. Shit, I didn't even know they made ugly Puerto Ricans until I met her."

As I slammed my car door shut, he said, "You can't dismiss me, Jo. We got a kid together."

"Mm-hmm, and that reminds me. You need to call ahead instead of just showing up when you wanna see her. Never know when I might be *screwing*."

"You better not be fucking that nigga in my house while my baby's in there! I'm not playing!"

He was still yelling when I entered the building. After delivering Mr. Park's food to him, I finally replied to Everett's last text: *I'll think about it.*

Everett

"Gullfriend? She's your gullfriend? Why was I not aware of this,

Everett? Why did I have to see it on the internet and hear if from our daughter? I saw those pictures of you out with her, and was that a child I saw her carrying?" Esther's ass had been living in the states for over thirty years, since she was a teenager, and sounded like she'd just arrived that day. She was holding onto that British accent for dear life.

"Why you calling me from Ella's phone?" I asked, ignoring her stupid interrogation.

"Because you won't answer when I call you from mine, haven't in years."

"Then that should show your ass I don't want to talk to you." It never failed. I'd had a good show in Toronto, was high off of that despite the fact that I missed Jo, and here comes Esther ruining what was left of my night.

"Well, we need to talk if you plan on having this woman around our daughter."

I sighed. "Esther, Ella is fifteen, a second from being grown. When it's time for her to meet Jo, I'll discuss it with her."

"Jo? That's her name? What is she, one of those new-age models? She's odd-looking to me. Not at all your type."

"And what's my type, cheating-ass British models?"

She huffed into the phone. "I can't believe you still haven't forgiven me after all these years."

"When did you ask for my forgiveness, Esther?"

"I'm asking now. Forgive me, Everett, and stop this charade with that little homely woman."

"And do what? Get back with you? Hell. Fucking. No."

"Everett—"

"And I don't care what you think of my woman. She's mine, not yours. Or is that it? You want her for yourself?"

"That was low even for you."

"How? Did I not catch you with your head between Ella's nanny's legs while your bodyguard had his head between yours? Was that not why I left you?"

"You are such an ass."

"It's hard to hear the truth, huh? Don't worry, I'll keep up my end of our agreement. I won't tell Ella or anyone else the truth about your nasty ass, and I'll keep letting folks think I was the one who messed us up, but you better keep your mouth off of Jo—literally and figuratively. What I do and who I do it with is not, never has been, and never will be your business. Stay in your damn place."

"And what place is that? The ex-wife you love to hate and disrespect?"

"I'ma try not to laugh at you talking about disrespect. And no, your place is out of my life and as far away from me as possible. You fucked our marriage up, so you gonna have to keep dealing with it. You got no right to say anything about what I do, and I don't care what you do. Don't call me with anymore bullshit, Esther." I ended the call before she could respond, glanced at the clock, and seeing it was too late to call or text Jo, rolled over in the bed in my hotel room and clicked on the TV, hoping it would lull me to sleep. Damn, I missed my woman.

20

Taking full advantage of the fact that Peter Park was scared of Everett, or at least scared of losing his business, I took that Friday off to have my hair braided. Yeah, I know taking off work to get your hair done is ratchet as hell, but I was tired of dealing with my hair, and as I did once or twice a year, paid someone else to tame it. I bought hair that came close to mine in color, and after five hours of my butt being numb from sitting on Hera Carter's floor while she worked her magic, I was looking too cute with my waist-length box braids. I grabbed a bite to eat, picked Nat up from Ms. Sherry's, and was about to give her a bath when a knock came at the door. My stomach instantly dropped, because I knew it was Sidney. I was sure of it. Could *feel* it. I was in such a good mood when I made it home, and here he came to ruin it.

No, he won't.

I made up in my mind that no matter that he was Nat's father, I wasn't going to let him keep badgering me about Everett.

With Nat on my hip, I opened the door, and before he could speak, I said, "Sidney, I thought I told you to call before you come over here. I'm telling the guys at the guard shack not to let you in the gate without notifying me first. I have a right not to be harassed."

"My bad. Look, I'm about to go on the road. Just wanted to see my baby first."

I lifted a brow. "That's it? That's all you're here for? No threats? Yelling? Cursing?"

He licked his lips and shook his head. "I just wanna see my little girl."

I hesitated, then backed out of the doorway, allowing him inside. "You wanna hold her?"

He shook his head. "Nah, I know she don't know me like that. She always looks...uncomfortable when I hold her." Wow, he noticed?

"Wanna have a seat then?" I asked. Nat was sleepy and heavy. I needed to sit down even if he didn't want to.

"Uh, yeah."

So we sat in silence. It was almost eerie being in his presence without him saying something dumb or offensive to me. That thought led me to think about Peter Park. Why did I keep gravitating to such asshole men and holding on to them even when I knew it was bad for me? Sid was Nat's father, so that kept me connected to him, but Peter Park? Why was I refusing to quit that job? Everett was the exception in all this, but because he was so kind to me, I had no idea what to do with him or how to handle being with him. Being respected by a man, *any* man, was foreign as hell to me. I missed him but couldn't make myself go to his show in NYC. I thought about it, decided against it, gave him a lame excuse that he probably didn't believe, and I had no idea why. Maybe I had a hard time believing I deserved someone as good and normal as him. Or maybe I was just batshit crazy like my mother.

I tore myself from my thoughts and looked up to see Sid staring at me. With a frown on my face, I asked, "You okay, Sid?"

"Yeah. Uh, I should go. Thanks."

And just like that, he was gone. It was the weirdest encounter I'd ever had with my ex-husband.

Everett

The NYC show was a good show, one of my best for this tour. I gave it my all, laid out nearly twenty years of music for the crowd, ending with my biggest hit, *Stop and Frisk*. Felt their energy, gave them mine, and was sweaty and exhausted when it was over, two hours after the first beat dropped. The last thing I wanted to do was meet and greet a passel of motherfuckers, but I took the black towel from Courtney and followed her to the little reception area backstage, took pictures with a few fans who had VIP access, was actually glad to see a few industry friends, especially John Legend who was there with his wife. He invited me to a private show he was doing the next night and I told him I'd be there, although I wasn't in the mood and probably wouldn't show up.

I was pissed at Jo. She said she couldn't come to this show because she didn't what to disrupt Nat's schedule or something like that. It was bullshit. I felt that in my damn soul. I also felt her pushing me away. And that bothered the hell out of me. She had me feeling like some regular nigga off the streets.

It was almost an hour after the end of the show by the time I made it to the dressing room where I could be alone to decompress for a minute. That was all I needed, time to come down from the high of the concert and maybe clear my head of thoughts of Jo.

Courtney and Dunn followed me to the door, but I entered the room by myself, wondered who turned the lights off and if that meant my damn stuff had been removed, especially my water. I'd sipped some during the meet and greet, but I was still thirsty. I fumbled until I hit the light switch, and jumped when I saw movement. My mouth flew open and my heart jumped in my chest. She looked different with her hair like that, sexier in a tight pair of jeans and one of my new *Mic Drop* tour t-shirts.

"Jo?" I said, as if I was making sure she was real. Damn, I was crazy about her. I don't think I realized how much until that moment. My heart was about to bust out my chest just because she was there.

Those thick lips spread into a smile. She had on some dark lipstick, kind of purple. She looked so good. "You don't recognize me with this new hair, Big South? You like it?" Moving from the wall she was leaning on, she stepped closer to me.

I grabbed the ends of the towel that was hanging around my neck with both hands. "Yeah. Looks good. Uh, what you doing here?"

She lifted her eyebrows, finally reaching me, smelling just as sweet as I knew she tasted. "Damn, I thought you missed me."

"I did, but you said—"

"I know what I said. Changed my mind."

"Why?"

"Because I missed you, too." She lifted her head and kissed me, making my head spin and shit. I was too old to be feeling what I was feeling, but I was feeling it nonetheless. I kissed her back, pulling her closer to me and forgetting I was tired, thirsty, and irritable. The world disappeared when I was with this woman.

"Where's Nat?" I asked, when we finally broke apart.

"At the hotel with Ms. Sherry," she answered, as she kissed my neck.

"You brought Ms. Sherry, too?"

She nodded. "I didn't feel right leaving Nat behind, and when I told Ms. Sherry I was coming to see you, she quickly agreed to come with us to watch Nat because she has a crush on you. That, and I'm paying her a grip."

I gave her a smirk. "That lady ain't got no crush on me."

"Shiiiiiddd. Yes, she does."

I grinned down at her. "You crazy."

Her hand slid down my chest to my crotch. "I know. You glad to see me?"

I cocked my head to the side. "Does that feel like I'm glad to see you?"

She answered me by squatting in front of me and unfastening my pants.

I fell against the door, fumbling behind myself to lock it. "What you doing, baby?"

"About to put South in my mouth, if that's all right with you."

"Hell yeah it is."

I could get used to this, lying in bed with him spooned behind me, his heavy, corded arm flung across me, his heart beating against my back. I was so nervous when I made the decision to surprise him, afraid he'd be with another woman even though Courtney, who helped me coordinate the trip and got me into his dressing room, assured me he had been spending all his nights during this tour alone. But as soon as he stepped into that dressing room and gave me that look only he had ever given me, all my fears fled from my mind. There was a peace attached to me being with this man that I couldn't adequately describe and didn't really understand. I just knew I'd never felt it before, not with Sidney or the handful of guys I dated before him. Not even as a child did I feel this kind of peace and comfort and security. It was a foreign but welcoming feeling.

My mother was never emotionally stable enough to make me feel secure, and Sid wasn't mature enough even though we were the same age, but Everett? It was in the way he looked at me, the things he said to me, the way he made me feel needed; all of that just saturated me with warmth and goodness.

I had to pee, but hated to move, not wanting to be away from him for even a moment. When I did attempt to ease out of the bed, he pulled my naked body closer to him and basically whined, "Nooooo."

"I gotta pee, baby," I whispered.

He groaned and let me go, smacking my cellulite-riddled butt when I stood from the bed, making my grown ass giggle. After I did my business and climbed back in beside him, he pulled me to his body and groggily whispered in my ear, "What took you so long?"

"I was only gone for like three minutes."

"Too long."

I placed my hand on his arm and smiled. "You're so spoiled."

"Yeah. Hey, how long you staying in town?"

"Till Monday, I guess. Why?"

He moved, causing me to roll over onto my back while he opened my legs and lay between them. "I got a break. A whole week. Something happened to the venue in Jersey, a fire or something, so that show's been rescheduled. I was thinking you could take the week off and you and Nat could stay here with me. We could take Nat to see *The Lion King* musical. I could take you for some authentic New York food—pizza, gyros, and I know this fire Jamaican place. Plus…John Legend invited me to a private show tomorrow night, so we can go to that. Anything you want. I just need you here with me."

My heart raced as his face hovered over mine. I was excited and just…happy. So I said, "I'll need to talk to Ms. Sherry and call Mr. Park, but I'd love to stay here and explore the city with you. Never been here before."

"For real? Ain't Bugz from here? Them New York niggas be claiming the shit out of him."

"Yeah, he was born here, but his family moved to Long Beach when he was like two or three. He claims the city but doesn't really know anything about it firsthand. And we never traveled outside of LA while we were together."

His lips met mine for a brief moment before he said, "Well, I'ma show you the world, baby. You want that?"

"I want you and anything that comes along with you."

He blinked, his dark eyes less drowsy but soft, almost dreamy in appearance as he leaned in to kiss me again. "And I damn sure want you."

21

Everett

I got so loud in my dressing room the night Jo surprised me, Dunn knocked on the door and asked if I was okay. After I lied and said I was, I shoved my sweaty towel in my mouth, dug my hands in Jo's hair, and blasted off in no time. I swear I was so weak I thought I was gonna have to leave the arena on a stretcher. When we got to the hotel and she actually tried to go to her own room, I looked at her like she'd lost her mind, took her up to mine, and sexed her all over my suite until we passed out in the bed. The next morning, I had her check out of her room, and Tommy brought her luggage up to mine. I didn't understand why she thought she needed her own room anyway. I also had her check Ms. Sherry out of her regular room and put her and Nat in a suite down the hall from ours, making sure all four of us had breakfast together in my room.

Ms. Sherry was cool as hell, a nice-looking older woman you could tell was probably fine in her day, and maybe Jo was right about her having a crush on me, but I could tell she was fond of Jo and Nat and wouldn't try anything with me. I was so glad when she agreed to stay for the week after Jo took off work to be with me that I offered to pay her fee plus a bonus. She talked almost nonstop during breakfast, telling me about how she ran a daycare years ago before meeting and marrying a really popular session drummer— Lonny Sykes. Shit, the man was a legend. Anyone who cared about music had heard of him.

"Wow," I said. "He was one of the best."

She smiled brightly while at the same time, I could see her eyes filling with tears. "He was an excellent musician and the best husband a woman could ask for. He took such good care of me. I never wanted for anything except children, but that just wasn't in the cards for us. That's why I'm so grateful to Jo for letting me watch Nat-Nat for her. She's just a little dream come true."

Grinning at her, I glanced at Nat sitting in her mother's lap inspecting an orange, and nodded. "Yeah, she's special. Reminds me of my daughter at that age. Smart."

"Yes! Too smart!" Ms. Sherry gushed. "And she really likes you. Keeps telling me about how Ebbwitt can roar really loud. You've impressed her."

I chuckled. "For real? I like her, too, and I *really* like her mama."

I looked over at Jo who blushed up at me, heard Ms. Sherry clap her hands together and say, "Awwwww."

Little Nat slid out of her mom's lap, walked the few steps to my chair, and held the orange out to me. "Open it, Ebbwitt."

I looked down at her face and thought my damn heart was going to explode. I missed Ella being that little and innocent, almost forgot what it felt like to be around a child so young. Giving her a smile, I took the orange from her, pulling her into my lap. After I peeled it for her and handed her a wedge, she turned around and hugged me, then squealed, "Thank you!" as if I'd just wrestled a bear and saved her life or something. That was the moment I knew she had my heart just as much as her mom did.

After breakfast, we split up. I took Jo shopping for something to wear to Legend's show while Nat and Ms. Sherry went to a children's museum in Manhattan. We also split up my security with Dunn staying with me and Jo and Tommy accompanying Nat and Ms. Sherry. We met back up for lunch, during which Nat asked to sit next to me and ended up eating more of my food than hers. It was a good day, one of the best I'd had while on tour in a long time. It was so good that I gave Courtney a well-deserved week off.

*****

Legend's concert was held in the ballroom of The Lyon Hotel, which made me think of Nat. But thoughts of Nat faded into thoughts of Jo every time I glimpsed in her direction and saw how she looked in that little black dress I bought her. She looked so good, all I could think about was getting her back to our suite and out of the dress.

The show was part of a birthday celebration for fashion designer Claude DuMont, and the room was packed with celebrities, many of whom dropped by our table before the show started. We were in the middle of the room, so we had a good view of everything. I was people-watching when I heard Jo say, "Wow." She was staring at her phone.

With raised eyebrows, I asked, "What?"

Glancing up at me, she said, "Bridgette told me I was all over the internet, but I had no idea it was like this, because I haven't been on social media in a while. I'm all over Instagram. They know my full name and that I was married to Sid. They even mentioned my daughter being his. I mean, this is crazy."

I frowned a little, hoping she wasn't going to panic and leave my ass. Jo never wanted to be in the spotlight. She'd made that clear from jump, but I thought maybe she was over it since she didn't seem to mind us being in public together. Hell, we'd been running into the paparazzi all day. "What they saying about you? Something bad?" I asked.

"Um...I don't know yet. I'm looking at a post on the Tea Steepers page titled, 'Big South's new lady is Bugz-NYC's ex. Looks like sis upgraded in a major way.'"

I shrugged and gave her a grin. "Did they lie?"

She rolled her eyes. "Anyway, folks are commenting in agreement, talking crazy about Bugz, saying he can't rap and has no talent."

"Again, did they lie?"

Shaking her head at me, she continued, "A few are calling me a rap-ho', saying I must be a gold digger to be with two different rappers and have a baby by one. Oh, here's a comment saying I'm actually on *platinum* gold digger status and that I must be a stripper since all rappers date are strippers and Kardashian-Jenners. And another says I'ma probably be pregnant by you soon if I'm not already. This one girl said I upgraded but you downgraded and how you gonna go from Esther Reese to me? Below that one, a guy said no doubt you're gonna cheat on me if you cheated on Esther. I read one comment that said they don't get it, because I'm not even that cute. One guy said I must give good head and have some bomb puss—"

"Okay," I said, taking the phone from her. "Let's turn this off. Ms. Sherry has my number." I powered it off and placed it on the table.

"You think I'm upset about what they're saying?" she asked.

"Are you?"

She shrugged. "I thought I would be, but they don't know me or Sid or you, so…I honestly don't care."

"You worried about how Bugz is gonna react?"

Her eyes narrowed. "He's a fool. He'll probably always be a fool. Nothing's gonna change that. So is he gonna act a fool over this? Yeah, but I don't care. And they didn't lie. He is talentless as hell compared to you. I can't believe I ever supported him or his stupid career."

I nodded. "So you're fine with the gossip, the blogs, the shit that follows me? You're not gonna run away from it? From us?"

Looking me in the eye, she softly said, "No, baby."

I grabbed her chair, pulled her closer to me, kissed her, and said, "Good, but you still not getting this phone back. Maybe I'm spoiled, but I want your undivided attention tonight."

She grinned at me and leaned against me. "So I can't pay attention to John Legend?"

"I guess."

She giggled as she reached up and kissed my cheek. "So I got two babies, now? You and Nat?"

I wrapped my arm around her shoulders. "Yep. And Jo?"

"Hmm?"

"They were right about you having some bomb pussy."

"Really, now? It's that good?"

"Helllll, yeah…that motherfucker is nuclear. I can't wait to dive back in it, and your head game? Daaaamn."

She gave me this look that told me she wanted me as badly as I wanted her, whispered, "You are so nasty," and was leaning in to kiss me when a piano began playing. John Legend had just kept me from getting busy right at that table.

The night was magical, beautiful, and dang near perfect. Everett looked tasty in his slacks and dress shirt, and if I had any doubt that I looked good in my dress, he quickly cleared that up for me.

And the show? OMG! John Legend sounded so good, and his voice coupled with the intimate atmosphere had me feeling all kinds of things—lust and adoration for Everett and a profound giddiness. I swayed to the music in my chair for the first half of the show, and then Everett stood and offered me his hand, leading me in a dance right there at the table. We were the first to do this with several other couples soon following suit. He held me close and I closed my eyes, relaxing against him as we danced through a couple of songs before reclaiming our seats. I was all up in his face, grinning, kissing on him, and all kinds of horny after John Legend wrapped up his abbreviated performance, when I heard her voice.

"Everett? I thought that was you." I guess it was no surprise that she was there. After all, it was a birthday party for a fashion designer and she was once a supermodel. Esther Reese towered over our table, her makeup and hair flawless as her slanted eyes inspected me, making me regret not flying Sage out to do my makeup. I'd done a good job of it myself, but still felt common as hell under this woman's glare. She was absolutely gorgeous, overwhelmingly so.

"Yeah, it's me," was Everett's curt reply.

Esther stood there, mute with her eyes on me, and the shit felt weird, awkward as hell, so I extended my hand to her, and said, "Um, hi. I'm Jo," since Everett obviously wasn't going to make any introductions.

She turned her nose up at my hand, said, "Yes, I know," and shifted her gaze from me to Everett. "A word, please?"

"Why? Something wrong with Ella? Where is she, anyway? She here with you?"

"No, she's staying with her friend, Jessica, and she's fine."

"Then we ain't got shit to have a word about."

My eyes shot over to him and widened. Esther looked just as shocked as I did.

"Ev-Everett," she stammered.

"Did I stutter?" he asked, with raised eyebrows.

"My God, you're going to behave like this in front of *her*?"

He leaned forward. "Esther, I know you. You came over here to disrespect her, didn't even shake her hand when she offered it to you. Now she knows you don't mean shit to me, because you don't. That's something she needed to know anyway, so thanks for expediting it by bringing your thirsty ass over here. Now you can go, or I can tell her *why* you don't mean shit to me."

Her mouth dropped open before she glanced at me and left.

Everett stood from the table and reached for my hand. "Come on. Let's go before she comes back and I really have to embarrass her ass."

"Uh...okay," was all I could say.

"I caught her cheating on me," he said into the darkness of the suite. We were in bed, and I was exhausted, because he ravished me before we could get in the door good.

"Esther?" I asked, then felt dumb for asking. Who else would he be referring to? I'd never known him to be in a relationship after his marriage other than with me. Yeah, he slept with lots of women. That was common knowledge, but none of them had ever claimed to be his woman, and I was the first one he'd referred to as his girlfriend in public since Esther.

"Yeah. I was on tour. Seems like my ass is always on tour. But anyway, Ella was like four then, and she had a full-time nanny. I was missing my family and decided to fly back home to LA since I had a couple of days between shows. Was gonna surprise them. Got there and found Esther in bed with the damn nanny, some real porn scene shit."

I gasped and lifted my head from his chest, searching the darkness for his face. "What?! She's a lesbian?"

He sighed. "I don't know. I think she's bi, because her bodyguard was in there with them. A damn threesome. In my fucking bed. In my damn house. And you know what? I don't care about her sexuality; I care about the fact that she disrespected me like that. I never cheated on her, *ever*, and believe me, I could've."

"Everett, I…wow."

"Yeah, and she did that shit after I took care of her. Esther was broke as hell when we got together. She was booking modeling gigs here and there, but she had a spending problem. Still does. So from the second we became a thing, I took care of her, because that's what being a man is to me. That house was the first one I'd ever bought, and she took it from me, not that I wanted it after catching her into her shit in there. She…she hurt me, Jo, and I still wasn't over losing my mom at the time. That shit cut deep, and it took a long time for me to get over it. Never thought I'd ever want to be with another woman in that way again until you. And she can see it. She can tell this thing between us is real, and she doesn't like it. That's why she came to our table."

"She still wants you?"

"Yeah."

"Has she said something to you about me? About us?"

I could feel him nod. "Yeah. Been calling me talking shit."

"Like what?"

"Nothing important, baby. I just wanted to explain what happened between us so you wouldn't think I was just being an asshole to her for no reason."

"Okay...but you're not like that with her all the time, are you? Like around Ella?"

"No, no. I'm as cordial as I can be. I don't curse her out around Ella or anything like that, but Ella knows we aren't best friends or buddies. I've honestly spent the last ten or eleven years trying to stay as far away from her as possible. Should've known she'd be there tonight. I just hate she ruined the evening for you."

"She didn't ruin anything."

"Good."

"Everett?"

"Yeah?"

"I know she hurt you, but it was a long time ago."

"I know. I was more pissed at the shade she was trying to throw at you. I'm not still hung up on her, if that's what you're thinking. I just know her. Esther won't understand me being nice to her. She'll take that as an opening for us to get back together, and that shit ain't never happening."

"I believe you, and thanks for tonight. It was beautiful despite her coming to our table."

"So are you, baby."

22

I quit my job.

Woke up the last morning of that week in New York and realized I didn't want to be away from this man. So I called Peter Park and resigned, and it felt like the heaviest weight had been lifted from my shoulders. When I gave Everett the news after he returned to our suite from the hotel's gym that morning, I thought he'd crush me when he grabbed me and lifted me from the floor, hugging me tightly. And Ms. Sherry? She was elated. I think she saw it as an adventure, a good departure from the quiet life she lived in LA. I saw it that way, too. Plus, I was falling hard for Everett "Big South" McClain, but who wouldn't? Especially after the life I'd lived before him. He was good to me and Nat, and hell, Ms. Sherry, too. He even bought her a whole wardrobe when she agreed to travel with us through the end of the US leg of his tour.

I got the chance to attend his shows in several states. Met tons of his fans and a bunch of celebrities during meet-and-greets, frolicked with him on a private beach in Miami. Made love in countless hotels, met some of his cousins while we were in his hometown of Houston for a show, met Ella when she flew out to Virginia to see him. She was nice, not altogether friendly, but respectful, and I couldn't ask for much more than that. By the time we made it back to LA for his final US show, I'd been on the road with him for a little over a month, and as exhausting as all the travel was, I knew I'd miss it, but I was also glad to get back to my house and be still for a moment.

Sid had been quiet, no phone calls, no comments on social media about me and Everett, but then again, he was on the road, too. And it honestly wasn't uncharacteristic of him to go silent on me and Nat, anyway. I guess I just expected him to act a complete fool with me since folks talked so much shit about him—that had finally died down, thank goodness—and because my relationship with Everett was now very public with pictures of us splashed all over social media. We'd even been mentioned on Wendy Williams' *Hot Topics*. Of course she was throwing shade, saying we weren't going to work, because everybody knew he hadn't had a real relationship since Esther Reese, but she did give me props for holding on to him longer than most. Whatever. When I decided to quit my job and follow him around the country, I made up in my mind that whether what we had was transient or eternal, I wanted it, *needed* it, and would enjoy it for as long as it lasted.

*****

The way you shakin' it make me wanna stop and frisk
Change your last name
And freeze your wrists
Smack you on the ass
And then give it a kiss
Slide inside and make you moan and hiss

Stop, stop, stop and frisk!
Stop, stop, stop and frisk!
Stop, stop, stop and frisk!

Keep shaking that ass and you'll be running a risk...

I was sweaty, having spent the entire show on my feet jamming to the beats and my man's bars. Shit, I even vibed to those *Southbound* songs included on the set list. After attending so many shows and having heard those songs numerous times, they'd grown on me. And armed with the truth of what ended his marriage and realizing *Southbound* was the first album he released after the divorce, I understood the songs better. Had a clearer idea of where his head was. Everett was hurting, and those songs were his therapy. Some seemed disorganized and random, but it was art, *his* art, and I loved it just like I loved everything else about him. But I was glad he took my advice and removed that one song with the damn shrieking in the background from the set list. That one freaked me completely out and honestly killed the vibe of the entire show.

"Aye! Aye! Ayeeeee!" Bridgette shouted with raised arms as she shook her booty to the beat of my man's biggest hit.

I grinned at her as I pumped my fist, and yelled, "South! South! South!" with the crowd as Everett moved from one side of the stage to the other, holding the mic with one hand and shading his eyes with the other.

"I see y'all out there shaking them asses! Which one of y'all want me to come frisk your ass right now?"

The women in the crowd filled the arena with squeals, including Sage's simple ass. I glared at her and she shrugged.

"Come on, y'all! Let me see you shake it like you getting paid to! Go! Go! Go!" Everett urged.

The crowd went wild. Hell, I even saw some dudes twerking. It was insane!

As the music was lowered, Everett stood in the middle of the stage with a big smile on his face. "LA, I gotta say, this is the best show of the best tour of my life. Y'all showed my ass all kinds of love. Almost twenty years in this business and y'all still buying tickets, buying my music, still rolling with my old ass, and I appreciate it!"

Some chick behind me yelled, "Big South! You so damn fine! Shit!"

We were in a special section, surrounded by celebrities—Sage's ass had pointed every last one of them out to us by shouting stuff like, "Bitch, is that Luke James?" or "Ho', I know that ain't LeBron!" or "Nigguuuuuuh, that's Amber Rose!" So that meant the heifer was probably a star. I didn't turn around to see, though, because that big fine negro onstage was mine. I had no doubts about that. He made sure I didn't.

"Uh! Uh! Uh! Oh—" I was cut off as his mouth found mind. His tongue, the one he used to smoothly convey his lyrics, moved crudely in my mouth as he grasped the front of my neck with one hand, squeezed my breast with the other, and pummeled my sex relentlessly, sliding in and out of me at a frantic pace. It all felt so…wonderful.

"Motherfucking pussy so good! Damn, Jo!" he yelled, once his mouth left mine. Then he kissed my freckles, my forehead, and my mouth again.

"Everett! Ohhhh!!" I was perched on a table in his dressing room at the Staples Center because he evidently couldn't wait until we got to my house to attack me.

"I love you! You know that? I love you, Jo!"

I heard him, heard every syllable he spoke, but everything was so foggy due to the surge of pressure in my core. Shit, I couldn't think to respond, could barely remember to breathe. I slammed my hands behind me on the table, bracing myself as I released a groan from the pit of my soul when my orgasm crested, muting all sounds and numbing every part of my body except my yoni.

My back hit the table, and I felt his big hands grab my legs and position them on his shoulders as he deepened his thrusts, shouting my name with each plunge, deep grooves in his forehead as he stared down at me like I was a wonder or something that was too good to be true. When he began to explode, he picked me up like I was a doll or one of Nat's stuffed animals, held me to him, and whimpered into my ear.

When things had quieted down and I'd almost caught my breath, I said, "I'll never understand how you can have enough energy to do that after spending two hours on that stage. You're a machine." Wrapping my arms around his sweaty neck, I laid my head against his.

He chuckled. "Never had stamina like this before. Must be the pussy."

"Humph. I'm beginning to think that's all you like about me. I bet if you could detach it from my body, you would and just leave me behind."

This time he threw his head back and laughed. "Naw, baby. I love all of you. But this thang I'm in right now is one of my favorite parts."

"Mm-hmm. You got me weak now, though. Legs shaking and stuff. You might have to carry me out of here."

"You know I will. I'll carry you to the end of the earth, baby."

And he did. After we got ourselves together, he let me ride piggyback all the way through the arena to our waiting car with both of us giggling like a couple of kids.

23

"You 'bout to run out of pineapples."

I looked up from the papers I'd been studying to see Everett standing in front of the open refrigerator door. "I am?"

"Yeah, you got like two fruit cups and one container of the fresh one you cut up the other day left."

"That's because you keep eating them up."

He shrugged and pulled the container of fresh pineapples out. "I like 'em, too."

"That's obvious." I returned my attention to the menus littering the kitchen counter. "What does Ella like? Chinese, Indian, Mexican, burgers?"

I could hear him rummage in the silverware drawer, yank the top off the container, and move closer to me. Seconds later, a pineapple chunk speared on a fork was held before my face. As I opened my mouth to accept it, Everett replied, "Pizza, like every other teenager in America."

"Any special kind?"

"Don't worry about it. I told you I'd take care of it."

"But it's my house. I'm hosting this little dinner. Shouldn't I contribute somehow? I wish I could cook…"

He set the container down. "You contribute by making her daddy happy, and when I'm happy, she's happy. Stop worrying. It's gonna be a good night. And you don't need to know how to cook when your man is rich," he said, before covering my lips with his.

I backed away a bit, separating my mouth from his. "She doesn't like me, probably because her mother doesn't. I could tell when she flew out to your concert that time, even though she tried to be nice. It was like she didn't want me there," I rambled, ignoring his reassurances.

"She's territorial and spoiled as hell, has never known me to have a real girlfriend and is not familiar with having to share me with anyone, but that doesn't mean she doesn't like you. She just doesn't know you, Jo, but once she does, she'll love you as much as I do."

I sighed. "I guess you're right."

He leaned in and kissed my neck, wrapping his arms around me. "You know I am. Hey, why don't you take your panties off right quick?"

"Uh, no."

"Why? Nat's taking a nap, right? I won't be loud. You can gag me if you want. Stuff your panties in my mouth after you take them off."

"Do you realize you've been asking me to do that since that one time I did it a few weeks ago? I think your freaky ass liked it. I only did it because I couldn't find anything else to use and you were gonna get us kicked out of that hotel."

He grinned down at me with raised eyebrows. "Yeah, but that shit was sexy as hell. The way you shimmied out of them motherfuckers and put them in my mouth? Damn! Look what thinking about that did to me." Grabbing my hand, he placed it on his groin.

"Everett, I'm on my period. You know that."

"And *you* know I give no fucks about that."

I had opened my mouth to reply when the doorbell rang.

"Unh-uh. They can leave a message," he said, refusing to release me.

"It's the door, not the phone."

"I know."

I rolled my eyes. "Let me go, old man."

He loosened his grip on me, and as he followed me to the door, said, "I guess you don't want no more of this old dick then, huh?"

Giving him a smirk, I said, "You tripping."

I checked the peephole, opened the door, and jumped when Bridgette shouted, "You're pregnant?!"

"You are?! I thought you just said you were on your period?!" Everett yelled from behind me. His big super-sized ass was panicking. It'd been his idea for us to get tested while we were in North Carolina, or was it South Carolina? Shit, we traveled to so many places while I was on tour with him, I can't remember. But anyway, he suggested we get tested so we could stop using condoms since I was on birth control, and now he looked like he was about to lose it thinking I was somehow pregnant.

"You didn't tell South, either?! That's foul, Jo!" Bridgette shrieked.

"It sure in the hell is!" Everett agreed. "How you gonna keep this from me?"

"From us!" Bridgette yelled.

"Hey! Would y'all calm the hell down before you wake Nat up? I am *not* pregnant. I have a damn IUD. Bridgette, you of all people know I don't do slip-ups. Nat was planned; Sid and I made a conscious decision to conceive her. He just changed his mind later. Furthermore, I'm bleeding like two stuck pigs right now. Ev, you are welcome to check if you think I'm lying."

"You know I will," he replied.

"Eww, that's just nasty," Bridgette groaned.

Everett shrugged with a sheepish grin on his face.

"And you think I'd actually keep something like this from you? Really, Ev?"

"Naw—I mean, she's your best friend. I thought she was a reliable source. You-you mad at me now, baby?"

"Yes."

"Shit. Thanks, Bridgette, for getting me cut off," Everett said.

"And for starting shit up in here," I added.

"My bad," Bridgette said, with a crazy look on her face.

I sighed. "Look, we'll talk about this later, Everett."

Leaning in so that only I could hear him, he whispered, "You could punish me by gagging me with your panties and doing that thing you do with your tongue."

"You wish, with your broken record ass." I didn't bother to whisper.

Kissing me on the cheek, he said, "I'ma go take a nap. Feel free to join me."

"No thank you," I retorted.

"Your loss. Dunn is supposed to be bringing me something. Wake me up when he gets here."

"Okay."

When he was out of earshot, Bridgette asked, "Damn, his ass live here now, don't he? Sid okay with that?"

I glared at her. "Yes, he lives here now and fuck Sid."

She raised her hands. "My bad. Sorry for mentioning him."

"Mm-hmm, and where did you get the false information that I was pregnant?"

"Girl, all the blogs are on Instagram talking about it."

"Well, they don't know what they're talking about. My uterus is vacant, and like I said, you should know me better than that. Me and Everett haven't been together that long, and I'ma have to have a ring and some vows exchanged before I have any more babies."

Following me to the living room sofa, she said, "Yeah, I forgot about your little rules: no sex on the first date, no babies outside of marriage. But y'all sho' up in here screwing up a storm outside of marriage."

"I'm not going to pretend I don't have needs, so I don't have a rule against that."

"Hell, neither do I, and yet I remain dick-less."

"That's on you. You're the one who won't date."

"Yeah, whatever. What happened to you fixing me up with South's brother?"

"Ev won't let me. Says his brother's a militant alcoholic gambler and he ain't gon' have me mad at him if Neil be asking you for money and stuff."

"Huh? A militant alcoholic gambler? That shit don't even go

together."

"That's what I told him."

She fell against the back of the sofa and sighed. "Well, I'm happy for you. You got it going on. Got Big South wrapped around your little finger."

I sucked my teeth. "No, I don't."

"Girl, please. That man is gone over you, and you are gone over him, too. Talking marriage and stuff. I remember after Sid left, you said you'd probably never get married again."

"I'm not talking marriage, I just said I'll have to be married before I have another baby."

"Which means you see it as a possibility now."

The doorbell rang again. And the next thing I knew, Everett was rushing past us to the door.

"I thought you were taking a nap," I said.

"Couldn't sleep without you in there with me."

"Awwww," Bridgette crooned.

I fought not to smile and failed.

Unsurprisingly, Nat appeared in the living room rubbing her eyes, her little yellow dress twisted on her body. Her eyes lit up when she saw Bridgette, and she quickly climbed into her lap, leaning against her chest.

"Man, she's getting bigger and prettier every time I see her," Bridgette observed.

I nodded. "Yeah, she's growing up fast."

"Hey, baby. Come out here a second." Everett was outside but peeking in the door. I gave Bridgette an amused look as Nat scrambled out of her lap and ran to him, yelling his name the whole way.

"Dang," Bridgette said.

"Don't feel bad. She puts me down for him, too. She is crazy about her some *Ebbwitt*."

Bridgette laughed as Everett picked Nat up and kissed her forehead. "Looks like he's crazy about her, too."

"Oh, he is."

"Nat, tell your mama to come on," Everett said.

Holding on to his neck, she replied, "No. I want Ebbwitt! Let's go!"

"But your mama gotta come, too, Nat."

She shook her head. "No. I wanna go with Ebbwitt."

As I met them at the door with a nosy-ass Bridgette right behind me, I wrinkled my nose up at Nat, and mumbled, "Traitor."

As soon as I stepped outside, I gasped and clasped a hand over my mouth.

Bridgette shrieked, "Oh my God!!"

Nat roared and giggled for no apparent reason.

And Everett asked, "You like it?"

I stepped closer to it, my eyes lifting from the customized license plate on the front that read: *Jo's*, to the big red bow on the hood, to the rest of the SUV—a brand new, black Mercedes AMG G65.

I turned to face him with wide eyes. "Everett, uh…what did you do?"

"I bought you a truck," he said, as if he'd just gone out and bought me an ice cream cone.

"But why? I didn't need a car."

"Jo, you said just the other day you wished you had a bigger car and how hard it is getting Nat in and out of her car seat because that Lexus is so small and only has two doors."

"Yeah, but I coulda bought myself one. You didn't need to do it for me."

"I wanted to," he said, then asked Nat, "You like your mama's new car?"

"New car!" Nat parroted him.

"It's too much. You went overboard. You always go overboard and—"

"Jo, I know if Ms. April Curry didn't teach you nothing else, she taught you to say thank you. So say thank you," Bridgette chastised me.

I knew I was being difficult and that the price of this vehicle, even at more than two hundred thousand dollars, didn't hurt Everett's pockets; it was just hard for me to accept gifts *period*, let alone something this big. But he knew that about me. That was why he was standing there waiting patiently for me to think through it, to process what he'd done.

So I finally walked over to him, slid under his free arm while he held Nat with the other, and said, "Thank you."

He kissed my forehead. "You're welcome, baby. It's customized just for you. Even got adjustable peddles for your short legs."

"You making fun of my legs?"

"No, I love your legs. You know I do. But they *are* short as hell."

"Short as hell!" Nat screamed. Those words were clearer than anything I'd ever heard her say.

I shook my head. "See what you did? Got my baby cursing."

He looked so embarrassed. "I'm sorry. I forgot. Don't say that, Nat. That's a bad word."

"Short as hell! Short as hell! Short as hell!" she gleefully repeated as Everett turned and walked back in the house, begging her to stop.

Everett

Dinner was a damn disaster.

Ella was fine when I picked her up from her mom's but was full of attitude from the moment we stepped into Jo's house. She barely spoke to her, turned her nose up at her house, and nibbled at her food in silence, basically ignoring Jo's attempts to make conversation with her. I was pissed but could deal with all of that. It was when she rolled her eyes at Nat when she tried to share her pizza with her that I almost lost it. That was when I realized just how much like her mother she really was and knew I should've fought for joint custody when she was smaller. At the time, I was working like a madman and thought Esther could provide a more stable environment for her and that visitation would work better for me. Now I could see letting Esther take the lead on raising her had been a huge mistake.

And I could tell the whole scene was breaking Jo's heart, making her feel bad, and it wasn't her fault. If it was anyone's, it was mine. So I took Ella home in Jo's truck with my security following us in mine. "You wanna tell me what your problem is?" I asked, cutting through the silence filling the vehicle.

"Nothing," she mumbled.

"Oh, it's something wrong with you to act like you did tonight. You don't like Jo?"

I glanced at her in time to see her roll her eyes.

"Ella, let me tell you something, unless you having a seizure, don't roll them eyes at me no more. You got a mouth. Tell me what's wrong with you."

"She's a gold digger, Daddy. Everybody knows that except for you." Her eyes were on the street ahead of us.

"Where you get that from? *Tea Steepers, The Hip-Hop Scoop, Wendy Williams?*"

"I got it from this car I'm sitting in that you posted all over your Instagram, telling everyone you bought it for her with her standing beside it. You haven't even bought *me* a car!"

"You can't drive, Ella."

"I know, and anyway, she lives in that neighborhood in that house and got a baby by Bugz. Now she's with you. Two rich rappers? That's got 'gold digger' written all over it. She's gonna hurt you, Daddy."

I sighed. "She was with Bugz before he got famous. She basically took care of him, helped him start his career."

She looked over at me. "That's what she told you?"

"It's the truth, common knowledge if you look at when they got married."

Shifting her eyes back to the street, she asked, "Why'd you get her this car?"

"Because I wanted to. Because she deserves it."

"How? With sex?"

"Hold up now!"

"That must be it since you're yelling at me now."

I blew out a breath. "Look, I'm trying to talk to you, hear you out and find out why you felt the need to embarrass me tonight, but let's not forget that I'm the adult here, Ella. I don't answer to you, and you don't get to just talk to me any kinda way. I see how you talk to your mom on that show. Your relationship with her is one thing. I ain't her by a long shot. You gonna respect me if nothing else."

"Sorry," she muttered.

"And I don't care how you feel about Jo, you gon' respect her, too. And you better not ever be mean to her little girl again. She's innocent. You were wrong to treat her like that."

"I know...just feels like you're replacing me with her."

I almost ran into the car in front of me. "What? Babygirl, you're always gonna be my princess. I care about Nat, but no one can take your place in my heart."

She glanced over at me with softened eyes. "Really, Daddy?"

"Yeah! Hey, I just want you to be comfortable with Jo...because she ain't going nowhere if I can help it."

"Are you living with her, Daddy?"

"Right now, yeah. But I'm looking for another place."

"For you and her?"

"And Nat and you, when you wanna visit."

"You gonna marry her?"

"Maybe."

"Does Mom know?"

"It's not her business to know, Ella."

"You know, she still thinks you two will get back together. I mean, I've always known better, but she just...she's gonna have a hard time with you marrying someone else."

I sighed. "I never did or said anything to make her believe we'd get back together."

"I know."

"I can't change the way she feels, and I can't give up my

happiness for her, either."

"Yeah, I can tell you're happy."

"Then can you be happy for me, and be nice to Jo the next time you see her? She's really nice, and believe me, she's no gold digger. I'd know."

"Okay, I'll try."

"Try?"

"Okaaaaay! I'll be nicer to her."

"Thanks, princess."

*****

Music greeted me at the door when I made it back to Jo's house. DeBarge's *All this Love* blasted from the speakers of her stereo system as she and Nat danced around the living room. Closing the door, I stood there for a moment and watched, thought about how much I loved her and Nat, how different my life was now with them in it, how lonely I had been before without even realizing it.

If I was to tell the truth, I'd admit I was culpable in my marriage ending because I was always working, always in the studio or on the road, and I never even slowed down to properly raise Ella, but I should've. I could clearly see that now. I lost one family, but would do anything in my power not to lose this one and to try to be more present in Ella's life.

When Jo looked up and saw me, she jumped and slapped her hand to her chest. "You scared me!" she yelled over the music.

I smiled when Nat realized I was there and ran to me. Picking her up, I closed my eyes for a second as she wrapped her little arms around my neck. Then I opened them, and asked Jo, "What you know about DeBarge, youngin'?"

Lowering the music, she said, "They were my mom's favorite, along with Diana Ross and Dolly Parton."

I walked over to the couch and plopped down. Nat slid out of my lap. "Be right back!" she said, and then grabbed one of her lions from the floor before returning to me.

"Wow, your mom had eclectic taste in music," I observed.

Jo sat down next to me, placing her hand on the thigh Nat wasn't occupying. "Is that a nice way of saying she was all over the place?"

"No. Just means she had a good ear and didn't discriminate about her music. She liked what sounded good to her. It's the same for me."

"Yeah. Did I tell you I'm named after that Dolly Parton song, 'Jolene?' She just split it up, made my first name Jo and my middle name Lena instead of Lene."

"For real?"

She nodded and shifted her eyes from my face to the floor in front of her. "She was...my mom was so pretty, beautiful. She was a little taller than me with smooth brown skin. No freckles, no gap in her teeth, no weird-colored hair. She was perfection. She believed in fairy tales, loved to laugh, thought women should have great affairs like Liz Taylor and marry ten times if that's what it took to get it right. She only wore dresses and heels no matter where she went. Never left the house without a full face of makeup. She was fun when she was happy, the best mom in the world who couldn't cook or clean and would let me have cake for breakfast and candy for dinner.

"But as fun as she was, it was like being raised by a kid. I didn't have any boundaries, and if she had a boyfriend, she'd tell me about them, *everything* about them. She couldn't hold a job, because if she didn't feel like going, she just wouldn't. And the depression? When that would hit her, I'd go from having a child for a parent to no parent at all."

She stood from the sofa and walked over to the stereo, turning to face me. "There was this one time she told me I was finally going to meet my father. She'd called him, and he was coming to town from wherever he lived. See, I was the product of a summer fling between the two of them, and he'd disappeared before she was out of her first trimester, so that's why I didn't know him. I was in middle school when she told me about the upcoming visit, and I was so excited, almost as excited as she was. She told me about how my father was the great love of her life and that they were going to get back together. She was convinced of it, that we'd finally be a family. Shoot, she convinced me, too.

"Ev, I lied when I said I've never seen him. When I got home from school that day, my mom was in her bedroom with the door locked, so I went to my room to do my homework. When I came out to get a snack, I saw him walking out the front door. I said, 'Daddy?' and he stopped for a second before walking out the door
without even saying a word to me or looking at me. So I saw the back of him. One time in my twenty-eight years, I saw the back of my father's body. I have his hair. I guess...I guess he was ashamed to look at me, or ashamed *of* me? I don't know. I haven't figured that part out yet."

"Jo, baby—"

"After that, she didn't leave her bedroom for weeks, wouldn't talk to me, didn't go to work. We ran out of food first, but our neighbor was nice enough to start feeding me dinner every day when she caught me trying to steal food from the little neighborhood grocery store. Then our lights got cut off. Then my teacher called child services because I was going to school with dirty clothes on. Mama got committed, and I had to go to a group home because no one in her family would take me in. I mean, that wasn't really a surprise since I'd never even met my mom's family. It was always just us, because from what I was told, they washed their hands of her after she got pregnant with me. She embarrassed them by getting knocked up by the young preacher my preacher grandfather had taken under his wing. They blamed her, although she was only eighteen and he was in his thirties.

"Anyway, I guess they saw me as an extension of their embarrassment, so I had to stay in that group home for four months. It was where I met Bridgette, and I'm thankful for that, because she taught me how to survive. After my mom got out and they let her have me again, she wasn't the same. She was never happy again.

The medicine just seemed to numb her, but at least she could function, and we had money because she started getting what folks back home called a 'crazy check.' I was young, but I put two and two together pretty easily. She and my father were in that room doing what grown folks do, and when it was over, he must've told her the family fantasy she had would never be a reality. She wasn't a whole person ever again after that, but she was a better mother in some ways. There was real food there, at least. But she tended to obsess over things, and she never stopped obsessing over what could've been with my father. She talked about it all the time until the day she died."

"How'd she die? Was she sick?" I asked softly, trying not to wake up Nat, who'd fallen asleep in my lap.

"She took an overdose of her sleeping pills the night of my high school graduation. I was out partying with Bridgette, who was in the same graduating class as me, and when I made it home late that night, I found my mother and a note telling me that I was grown now and didn't need her anymore, so she decided to kill herself. But I did need her. I really did. She was...she was all I had. All I'd ever had besides Bridgette. She was my world."

I watched as the first tear fell, gently laid Nat on the sofa, and walked over to Jo, pulling her into my arms. "Baby, I'm so sorry."

"It's okay. I just...it was hard. It was a lot to deal with at eighteen. Our neighbor helped me plan her funeral. There really wasn't any money, but the funeral home director felt sorry for me and put me on a payment plan. I had to get a job, but wasn't even able to get her a headstone. She still doesn't have one, because I just...can't. Do you know I met my grandparents and aunt for the first time at her funeral? They were so cold, didn't try to start a relationship with me or anything. They just showed up and left when it was over. I was in such a bad place back then...I probably would've lost my mind if I hadn't eventually come out here and stayed with Bridgette."

"Baby..."

She looked up at me with a wet face. "I said all that to say this: if you need to end this for Ella, I'll understand. She doesn't like me. I know she doesn't, and I don't expect you to choose me over her. Family is something I never really had, but I know it's everything. That's why I have taken so much crap off of Sid. I want Nat to at least have some kind of family. Look, if you have to let me go for Ella, I won't hold it against you. I mean, what good am I to you anyway? There'll always be people talking about me because of my past with Sid, and you obviously don't want any kids by me and—"

I held her damp face in my hands and looked into her eyes. "Jo, what I tell you about talking down on yourself?"

"I-I'm sorry, but it's the truth. What purpose am I serving you? It's not like you need me."

"Are you outta your damn mind? Of course I need you! You think I'ma let you go? Ella will be fine. She'll grow to love you as much as I do. It'll just take time. She's only seen you twice."

"But what if she doesn't? What if she never likes me?"

"Then she'll just have to respect you and my decision to be with you. I love you from the depths of my fucking soul, never felt anything like this before. You and Nat are as much a part of my heart as Ella; you just occupy different compartments. We'll work through all of this. I talked to her, heard her out, and let her know disrespecting you and Nat won't be tolerated."

"Everett, you didn't—"

"Yeah, I did. She was wrong for acting like that, and I've been wrong to let Esther handle raising her damn near alone. It's a lot of shit I gotta fix. But the bottom line is I love my daughter and I love you. Neither one of you is going anywhere."

"Everett, I—"

"And earlier, about the whole pregnancy thing? I was upset because I thought you were keeping it from me. Jo, I got a kid by a motherfucker I despise; you think I wouldn't want one by a woman I love?"

"But you loved Esther, didn't you?"

"Shit, I don't even know anymore. I used to think I did, but I couldn't have, because I didn't feel for her what I feel for you. I was young and she was *Esther Reese*. A damn icon. Everybody wanted her and *she* wanted *me*. I mean, I cared about her, but this? Nothing compares to this. I'm not letting you go no matter what, okay?"

She leaned into me and nodded. "Okay."

"And Jo?"

"Yeah?"

"Fuck your father and your mother's family. You got Bridgette and the makeup chick and Nat and Ms. Sherry, and me. We're your family, and I, for one, love the shit outta you."

She squeezed her arms around me, and said, "I love you, too."

24

"Trick or treat!" Everett and I yelled for the fiftieth time, while Nat backed us up with a "Rawr!"

She was dressed as Simba from *The Lion King*. I was Timon, and Everett was supposed to be Scar, but since he was wearing a white track suit and a random lion mask with a squiggle of a beard drawn on it with a permanent marker, no one could tell. He had insisted on going trick-or-treating with us, was more excited than Nat, and even though Tommy was trailing us around my neighborhood making us look out of place, we were having a good time and garnered only a few stares. This was my first year taking her trick-or-treating, and everyone in my neighborhood had been super nice and Nat had scored a boatload of candy.

"You settle on a dress for the NHHAs yet?" he asked, as he carried Nat to the next house. He was referring to the National Hip Hop Awards show we were supposed to be attending in a couple of weeks. While I searched for a dress for the show, I also had to get prepared to travel with him to Texas for Thanksgiving. Things were growing more and more hectic, but I was happy and enjoying this journey I was taking with Everett.

Our days were spent together either around my house or out and about. Occasionally, he'd leave for a meeting or something else business related, to go to work in the studio, or to spend one-on-one time with Ella. But for the most part, we were always together and I loved it.

"Not yet," I finally answered him. "You decide what songs you're gonna do at the awards show?"

"Since I'm getting the Lifetime Achievement honor, I'm thinking I should do a medley of my biggest hits, maybe throw something new in there. I don't know. I'll figure it out."

"Trick or treat!" we both yelled on cue at the next house.

"Rawr!" Nat offered.

The lady dropped the candy into Nat's bucket, and Nat yelled, "Thank you!"

As we moved on, Everett said, "Dang, they gave you a whole Butterfinger. You gonna share with me, Nat?"

She just grinned at him and nodded. I didn't bother asking her for fear of being rejected since she was totally and completely Team Everett. I'd just steal some after she fell asleep.

By the time we made it home, Nat was knocked out, so I decided to skip her bath and just eased her costume off her before tucking her in. I took my own costume off, threw on a t-shirt, and headed back to the living room to find Everett sifting through Nat's candy which he'd spread out on the coffee table next to his discarded lion mask.

"I'ma tell Nat you're robbing her," I said, as I sat down beside him.

"She ain't gonna believe you. That's my buddy. You just mad because you ain't in the Nat and Everett club. Anyway, she said she was sharing with me, so stop hating."

"She don't know what the word *share* means. She just heard you ask a question and nodded. Hey, let me have those Milk Duds."

He handed the tiny package to me. "Here. Me and Nat don't want that nasty shit anyway."

Ripping the package open, I rebutted, "Milk Duds are the bomb. You and Nat don't know what y'all are missing."

As he tore a mini Snickers open and popped it in his mouth, he said, "You crazy as hell."

We sat in silence, shamelessly eating my baby's candy until Everett said, "Jo, would you—can we—I want us to move in together."

I stopped chewing. "What? I mean, don't you basically live here already?"

"I do, but I mean, *officially*."

"Um, you spend every night and most days here. You even sleep in my bed instead of in the guest room now. What's not official about that?"

"What I mean is, our own house."

"This is my house, and I'm saying it can be yours, too."

"But it has memories of your old life with Bugz attached to it. I want something that was never his and isn't just yours. Something that'll be ours."

"Oh...okay. Um..."

"I already bought a house."

"You what? Where?"

"In Calabasas. It's empty right now. I wanna show it to you once I get it furnished. Or do you wanna help with that?"

"Ev, I don't...I don't think I'm ready for that. I don't think I'm ready to leave here. This is the only home Nat has ever known. I'm comfortable here. Just...I need some time. You're moving really fast."

My heart shattered at seeing the disappointed look on his face. "I know I am, I just...I love you, Jo, feels like I've known you my whole life. I love being here with you and Nat, but you said yourself that Bugz thinks this is still his house. It's hard for me not to think about that. But, uh...I won't pressure you. Just wanted you to know that's the next move I wanna make."

I nodded. "I understand."

*****

Another damn red carpet.

At least this time I knew this would be a part of everything, but that did little to calm my nerves because things were different from when I went to that benefit with Everett. I was very publicly his woman, the subject of all kinds of conjecture, and definitely would not be ignored by the interviewers this go 'round. As our limo inched up to the venue in New York, all was quiet as I mentally reminded myself of my dress's designer's name and told myself not to do that weird smile I do when I'm uncomfortable, and I guess Everett was preparing to receive his honor and perform. He was always quiet and in his own head right before a show. I'd seen it tons of times before when he was on tour, so I wasn't surprised about that. He was holding my hand, a sure sign that we were good, plus, there was no reason for me to think his silence was anything to be concerned about with the way he sexed me before we left the hotel. I mean, shit!

Right before we arrived, a text came through from my former Bijou Park coworker, Shirl: *I know I wanted you to get you a man, but did you have to quit your job and forget about me? Call me sometimes!*

I replied: *Sorry! Been busy but I promise to call.*

Shirl: *You better, Mrs. South.*

That made me giggle. I was always amused when people referred to Everett as Mr. South. Would they really refer to me as Mrs. South like Shirl did if we ever got married? That thought led to another: would Everett marry me one day? Would I want him to?

Before I could slip all the way down the obsession rabbit hole, the limo stopped, and a back door flew open. As Everett climbed out and the clamor outside grew louder, I slid my phone into my clutch and took his outstretched hand, emerging from the limo to cameras flashing and ear-piercing screams. With Tommy and Dunn nearby, Everett placed his hand on the small of my back, which was exposed in the Alexander McQueen dress that was short, sexy, and inappropriate for the cooling November New York weather, and led me down the red carpet. We paused, posed, answered questions, smiled, and halfway through the ritual, I stopped feeling like a total imposter and began sounding and looking like a pro, almost as if I belonged there on his arm. The main question I got was about my dress. A few asked things like how did we meet, was I proud of him, pretty benign stuff, but most of the questions were fielded by Everett.

Once inside, we were guided to our front-row seats in the humongous theater. "You good? You didn't even seem nervous out there," he said, as he settled in his seat next to me.

I nodded, looking around as people filed in. "I wasn't, really."

"See, it was that sex I put on you, and you were talking all that shit, tryna act like you didn't wanna do it."

I cocked an eyebrow up at him. "I *always* wanna do it. You know that. I just didn't wanna be weak and stumbling down the damn red carpet, Everett. Hey, I wonder how far back Bridgette and Sage are gonna be?" I craned my neck to see if I could locate them behind us.

"Not far. I got them some good seats."

"Thank you for that. They were so happy to get to come. And you paid for their rooms, too. I'm almost a fan again."

"Almost? Damn, what I gotta do to get back in?"

Before I could answer, J Cole walked up and congratulated Everett.

J-motherfucking-Cole!

I had to stop myself from yelling, "Cole World!" like a fool.

He was followed by everyone from Nas to Jay-Z to Drake. We were sitting mere inches away from Jay and Bey and right in front of Common. My eyes were about to pop out my head at the reality of it all. If I had caught a glimpse of André 3000 anywhere near us, I would've really lost it. I'd always been crazy about me some 3 Stacks!

"You do know I'm famous, too, right? Sitting your ass up here geeked about these other niggas." His spoiled behind actually looked and sounded irritated.

"Aww, come here," I said, leaning in to kiss him. "You know I love you, but these are my favorite rappers, baby."

"Got-damn, Jo. Really? I ain't nowhere on the list?"

I gave him a smile and a wink. "Of course! You're like in my top one hundred!"

He shook his head. "Ain't that some shit…"

I gave him a kiss on the cheek before turning just in time to see Bridgette and Sage take their seats a few rows behind us. I grinned and waved at them and turned back around to see Sid and his wife, Sonya, who'd recently had their little boy, take their seats on the front row, directly across the aisle from us. I snatched around to look at Everett in complete and utter horror.

He took my hand and squeezed it, leaning in and whispering, "The messy-ass producers did this. Just ignore him. Wanna trade seats so I'm on the outside?"

I inspected Everett in his dress shirt and slacks and almost forgot what the issue at hand was. Dang, he was fine! When I finally pulled my mind out of the gutter, I said, "No. If I move now, it'll look like he's bothering me."

"Is he?"

"No," I lied. The truth was, the fact that Sid even existed bothered the living shit out of me.

"Good. I love you."

"I love you, too."

I felt my phone vibrate, pulled it out of my purse, and saw that Sid had texted me: *U look good enough 2 eat, baby.*

I sighed, deleted the text, and turned my whole body to face Everett, who was now talking to either Offset, Quavo, or Takeoff. Those dudes all looked the same to me.

*****

The show was fun, and with Kevin Hart as the host, the laughs were abundant. He made fun of everything and everyone, including himself. Couple that with the performances, especially one from my fav, Cardi B, and I barely noticed Sid. I was too busy jamming to the music, hopping up from my seat and dancing while Everett stood next to me cool as hell with his hands in his pockets, bobbing his head to the beats to think about him.

It was such a good night with only one cringe-worthy moment when Kevin said, "All the women in the world and y'all rappers passing around the same ones. Look at Bugz and South. The hell y'all doing?"

Everett yelled, "That shit ain't funny, lil' nigga."

The audience laughed, and Kevin said, "Let me shut the hell up before South's big ass come up here. Or shit, Bugz's homicidal ass."

I didn't bother looking at Sid. I was glad when Kevin moved on to DJ Khaled.

Everett received the Grinder of the Year award but lost album of the year to Kendrick Lamar. When he accepted the Grinder award, he thanked tons of people but not me. I kind of felt slighted, but told myself we'd only been together a short while. It wasn't like I had really contributed anything to his career, and I was still happy for him. So I got over my little hurt feelings.

He had explained to me that when they honored him toward the end of the show, a video chronicling his career that would include interviews with various people in his life would play. He'd be escorted backstage before that in order to prepare to perform a few of his biggest hits, and afterwards, accept his award. He kissed me before following his handler backstage. I was watching another award be presented when the same handler came for me. Confused, I followed her backstage to a tiny room. Everett was inside sitting in a chair, his head lowered. Once the handler left, closing the door behind her and leaving Tommy outside to guard it, I asked, "Is something wrong?"

He looked up at me with knitted brows. "I'm nervouser than a motherfucker, Jo."

"What? You never get nervous before going onstage. What's going on?"

He shook his head. "A concert is one thing. This shit is a live TV show. Millions of people are watching. I always get nervous about doing stuff like this."

"Well, just pretend it's a concert, baby."

"That won't work."

"Then, what?"

"I'ma need some pussy right quick to calm my nerves."

"Uh, what?"

"I'ma need some pussy," he said, like it made perfect sense for us to screw in this broom closet for a dressing room with a zillion people running around outside the door.

"That's what you had me brought back here for?"

"Yeah."

"Where we supposed to do it? In here?"

"Yeah."

"Hell no!"

Alarm covered his face. "You not gonna give me none?"

"No!"

"Come on, Jo. Please?" he whined.

"Everett! I'm not gonna sit through the rest of the show with you leaking out of me."

Reaching into his pant pocket, he unearthed a condom. "I'll use this."

I moved closer to him. "What the *hell* are you doing with a condom when we don't use them anymore?"

"Aw, shit. I got it from Tommy, baby. I am not messing with anyone else."

"Tommy knows we supposed to be in here fucking?!"

"You know how many times Tommy and Dunn have heard us fucking in dressing rooms, Jo?"

I sighed. "We just did it before we left the hotel! You can't seriously want to do it again!"

"I *need* to do it again, baby."

"Everett…"

"Come on. We gotta make this quick. Just pull your dress up and bend over and grab this chair."

He vacated the chair, and I shook my head before snatching my panties off and shoving them in his mouth. "Fine," I finally agreed. "I think your ass just likes screwing in dressing rooms."

He was inside me so fast, my knees threatened to give out as I gasped and clutched the bottom of the chair. "Oooo, shit!" I whimpered softly.

"Biss pussfy fo' mubafuffing bood!" he garbled into the panty gag as he gripped my hips and plowed into me like he was running a race.

"Ah! Ah! Ah!" was my response, as I quickly hit my climax. I was trying not to scream since the gag wasn't doing much to mute Everett. He was making enough noise for both of us. Had it not been for Migos' performance, we would've definitely been found out. But then again, this was a hip hop awards show, so there was no telling how much freaky stuff was happening behind closed doors.

Through the orgasmic static in my head, I heard him clearly say, "You milking the shit out of me, Jo!"

"G-gag, Ev-Everett," I stuttered.

"But I'm—shit! Whew! I'm finished, baby." He spun me around and buried his face in my neck, sucking on it.

"Time for my walk of shame back out there, huh?" I asked, after I caught my breath.

"You ashamed of having sex with me?" he murmured into my neck.

"No, but I don't wanna fuel the nasty rap-ho' rumors."

"Fuck rumors. We love each other and I'm your damn man. Us having sex is natural."

"Yeah, you're right. You good now, Big South?"

"Yep, 'bout to go out there and murder this performance."

Since I had this extra lubrication issue, I still felt sticky and wet down there so I had the handler show me to a restroom where I tried to clean myself up. But I was panty-less because my thong underwear was ruined from being in Everett's mouth. So yeah, I was hella uncomfortable when I returned to my seat to find Sonya sitting alone. Sid was to close out the show with *Stop Playing*, the song that was originally supposed to be a collabo with Everett, but became a big hit for him and rapper, Talent the Prodigal One, instead. So I suppose he was backstage somewhere getting ready for his performance.

I smiled as the tribute began with everyone from Everett's high school music teacher to his daughter lauding his talent and the breadth of his success. The announcer ran down the records he'd broken by performing to sell-out crowds around the world, selling a total of over one hundred million albums, and scoring tons of number one hits. I flinched a little but maintained my smile when Esther popped up on the screen, and said, "South is one of the greats. I knew that when I met him all those years ago. I fell for his talent first. Married him for the gentle soul he was. Everett is truly a good man. I'd marry him again in a heartbeat, you know?" She ended her statement with a coquettish giggle.

Bitch.

She wasn't marrying *shit* again if I could help it.

I wasn't famous for anything but screwing two rappers, so of course they didn't interview me. I was his girlfriend, not his wife, but did they have to interview *her*? They'd been divorced forever.

I snapped out of my thoughts when I heard, "All right, y'all! It's the man of the hour himself, the national champ! Biiiiiiiig Soooouuuuth!"

Yes! He came out to *Stop and Frisk* like I'd told him to, and the crowd exploded. My sticky coochie ass even jumped up on my feet and danced, yelling the lyrics out in time with him. Without looking back, I knew Bridgette and Sage were doing the same thing.

Stop and Frisk seamlessly flowed into *She be Babysitting*, an older song of his about oral sex with lines about a woman "swallowing his babies." It was lewd but was a clever metaphor and the beat was banging. I had suggested that one, too. Then he went into newer, less suggestive songs like *The Truth*, *Hoodies Up*, and *My Girl*, a song he wrote for Ella. I'd suggested those as well. Everett was performing the entire set list I'd run down for him. That made me so proud!

Then a familiar interpolation began to play, one I easily recognized because I heard it a million times as a kid. It was the instrumental intro to DeBarge's *All this Love* repeating over a crazy drum beat. The song had been sampled before by other artists, but not quite in this manner. I stood still with a little frown on my face. I'd never heard whatever this was until that moment, but I already liked it.

"Y'all all right with me spitting something new right quick?!" Everett yelled into the microphone.

The crowd roared.

"All right, listen:

I ain't the type to slow it down no more, although I did this shit a time or two before

I'm going eighties with an LL vibe, cause I'm feeling this, Ma, deep down in my core

You got me thinking 'bout some crazy shit, when I thought I'd been done closed that door

And the harder I try to walk away, I just end up wanting you more and more

You young and been through so much shit, some shit that made you cry

But you too beautiful for that, special and real, so now I'm more than willing to try

To be a better man for you and to give you what you truly deserve

A love that's from the heart, and to make you my life, the center of my world

Unh, you're the answer to my prayers, the x to my equation, the solution to what I need

I love you, girl; you're my soul, my heart, my mean-as-hell black queen..."

Trey Songz appeared on stage singing the hook, an altered version of the original song's chorus.

People were raising their hands and swaying to the relaxed beat, which was out of character for Big South but fit Everett to a tee. I held myself as I continued listening to the song, wondering if it was about me. It was, wasn't it? It had to be...right?

My questions were answered when he descended the steps to the side of the stage and made his way over to me. He grabbed my hand while still holding the mic and delivered the final lines of the song with finesse:

"I love the way you love, how you put my ass in check, how you ain't afraid to speak your mind but always got my back

I love to see your smile and them love faces you make, how you look when you sleep at night when I'm wide awake

Special don't describe you, you a treasure, you a jewel

Guess that's why I found you where I found you at Bijou

What I'm trying to say is baby, I'll never let you go

You took my heart, fixed what was ripped, and for that I love you from my soul."

He hugged me amid wild cheers and applause. I was crying at this point, so I barely heard him say directly in my ear, "I know I move fast, but I've been ready for this for a long time, just needed to find you to make it happen. I love you, and I wanna love you forever. We don't have to do it right now, but I hope you're willing to do it sooner than later."

Then the man dropped to one knee, pulling a ring out of his pocket, and I think he asked me to marry him. I can't be sure, because I was crying so hard and the crowd was so loud, and then I felt someone shaking me, looking up to see Bridgette and Sage had left their seats and were yelling something at me. Other rappers rushed Everett, hitting him on his shoulders and yelling stuff at him with big grins on their faces, but he never took his eyes off me.

Through the haze of utter shock came a warmth that only radiated from Everett, from the way he treated me, from the way he touched me, from the way he loved me.

And I loved him, too.

Immensely.

So I held my hand out to him, and whimpered, "Yes!"

He slid the heavy ring on my finger and grabbed me, hugging me tightly and whispering, "Thank you," in my ear and kissing me on the cheek. A moment later, he was heading back to the stage to accept his Lifetime Achievement trophy.

I clutched my chest and watched him as Bridgette and Sage flanked me.

"All right, now that I done locked my Jo down, I wanna thank her for being here with me and for not making me look stupid by refusing to marry me. I never know with her disagreeable ass."

The crowd roared in laughter.

"I also wanna thank my daughter, Ella, who is pissed at me for not letting her come hear all the cursing we been doing on this stage tonight. I wanna thank my fans, my management, my family…"

I closed my eyes and listened, my heart full and my soul happier than it had been since the day Nat entered the world.

25

My hands were shaking, I could barely breathe, and I was itching all over. The TV was on, but the screen was a blur and the sound of it coupled with the chatter around me was cacophonous and irritating. I needed quiet so I could think straight, because as it was, my thoughts were muddled and tangled like a bowl of spaghetti pasta. Things in my head were so loud and confusing, I couldn't even obsess over how it got to this point.

I lifted my eyes toward the door and wondered if I should leave, just go back to my house in LA. Grab Nat, who was fast asleep in Ms. Sherry's suite, and catch the first flight out, but that would be so wrong. How could I justifiably run when everything that happened was my fault? Had it not been for me, or at least Everett's association with me, he'd be in that room at that moment, probably stripping some other woman naked and glorifying her body, loving her like he loved me. And he'd be better off. He was so kind to me, great with Nat. He cared about us, and look where that got him.

I jumped and looked down at the phone I held in my hand when it began to buzz. *His* phone. It was Esther...again, calling because she obviously knew what had happened, which made me wonder why in the hell she was marathon calling him when common sense should have told her he couldn't answer.

There were calls from his family members, too, and I wondered the same thing about them. Why call when there was no way he could answer? Closing my eyes, I placed the phone on the bed beside me and laid back. My head was throbbing, and my stomach was protesting its emptiness. I should've been at some after-party. *We* should've been at some after-party laughing, drinking, and dancing.

We should have been celebrating.

"You need anything?" Bridgette's voice was soft, almost apprehensive.

Opening my eyes, I gazed up at her concerned face as she stood over me. "Everett."

"I know. I know, and I'm sorry things are like this."

"What are *you* sorry about? This is *my* fault. All of it is my fault."

Bridgette wore a frown as she asked, "How? You had no control over what happened."

I sat up and sighed. "Yes, I did. I came into Everett's life with all this baggage. I knew better. I should've just kept living like I was living—alone. It's what I deserve. Everett is the innocent party in all this, and the shittiness of my life has just..." I broke down, tears racing down my face as I hung my head and sobbed. I felt Bridgette wrap her arms around me and squeeze as I leaned into her. I heard Sage, who had been staring at Everett's laptop since we made it back to the hotel, say something, but couldn't make it out over the sound of my own crying and the action on the TV.

"Did you hear Sage?" Bridgette asked.

I shook my head, but before either Sage or Bridgette could repeat whatever was said, a knock sounded at the door. I moved to answer it, but Sage was already opening it before I could get to my feet.

Dunn walked in, let his eyes sweep over the room, then settled them on me with an unreadable, but definitely unfriendly, expression on his face. "Got the call to go pick the boss up. He wants you in the car when I get him."

"That's what I was trying to tell you, that they were letting him go," Sage said.

I nodded and asked Dunn, "Can you give me a sec to get myself together?"

He shrugged. "I'll be outside the door."

Sage and Bridgette helped me collect myself. I declined getting my makeup refreshed, put on some lip gloss and a pair of shades, and left the suite in sweats with both my phone and Everett's in my purse as I followed Dunn to the waiting car, ignoring the paparazzi that were crowded outside the hotel's entrance. Once in the back seat of the rented SUV, I sighed and closed my eyes, relieved I would be seeing Everett but still on edge about the night's events.

"You're poison, you know that? Chicks like you? You kill shit."

My eyes popped open, and for a second, I thought I'd imagined Dunn's words. "What?" I replied.

"You're poison. South is a good guy. You come along and just fuck his world up. And I thought you didn't want him anyway. Why you out here messing up his life?"

"Excuse me? Are you seriously talking to me like this when I'm engaged to your boss?"

"I don't know how you pulled that one off, either. You ain't even the type to be wifed. You the type to be fucked and left alone."

I knew Dunn had never been a fan of mine, but he hadn't overtly disrespected me from the moment Everett and I became a thing. So it was shocking as hell to hear him say what he said. My state of being shocked left room for Evil Jo to appear, and she said, "You know what? I know you tried to get with me awhile back, but I swear you sound like you wanna fuck my man right now. Is that it? You jealous because he happens to enjoy fucking me? You want him for yourself? You been fantasizing about it or something?"

"Fuck you, bitch! You think you special? You ain't the first bitch he ever fucked in a dressing room. Shit, you ain't even the *last* bitch he fucked in a dressing room."

That jab stung, but Evil Jo quickly recovered. "You be listening to us, Dunn? That shit turn you on or something? Well, I got that dick on lock. Sucks for you."

"You ain't shit."

"I beg to differ. I'm *the* shit. And soon, I'll be Mrs. *The* Shit. AKA, your boss's wife."

"He's not just my boss, he's my friend, and—"

"No, he is your employer, and as soon as I tell him about this little conversation, he'll be your *former* employer."

"Bitch, if your temporary ass gets me fired, you gon' deal with some permanent consequences, but I ain't worried about that, because I know he wanted you in this car so he can dump your ho' ass. Shoulda done that months ago."

He finished his statement as he pulled up to the police station. I flung the back door open and tried to thread my way through a new throng of paparazzi, but found myself lost in a sea of cameras and bodies and loud voices. I started panicking, and was near tears when I felt someone grab my arm. My first thought was to snatch away, then I realized it was Everett and threw my arms around his neck. He pulled me close and apologized in my ear before leading me to the waiting SUV.

26

Everett

Six hours earlier...

I accepted my award, did the backstage press thing, and made it back to my seat before the end of the show. There was one award left to give and a final performance on the schedule, and then me and Jo could bounce up out of there. I couldn't wait, either, because we had some celebrating to do, some champagne to pop at the after-party, and some love to make once we made it back to the hotel if I could hold out that long.

I was happy as hell she accepted my proposal. After thinking about it virtually since the day I first laid eyes on her, I finally got up the nerve and seriously doubted she'd say yes, because she had to be the most argumentative woman I'd ever met. But she said yes without even questioning me. I half-expected her to have thought about it and changed her mind by the time I returned to my seat. Thought maybe she'd been swept up in the high of my proposal at the time but didn't really mean to accept, because the truth of the matter is, I really was moving fast, but I also really did love her. I was sure of that, so when I sat down beside her and she leaned in to kiss me with this big grin on her face, I was relieved.

"I loved the song," she said.

I faked a shocked look. "Damn, really? You liked a Big South song?"

She rolled her eyes. "Whatever."

While they announced the nominees for best collabo, a category I was not nominated in, I grabbed her left hand and rubbed my thumb across the fifteen-carat diamond ring on her finger. She grinned at me, and asked, "You get this from Peter Park?"

I smiled. "Hell, no. Ben Baller got that money."

"It's beautiful; thank you."

"You're welcome, baby, but it's not as beautiful as you."

As Blac Chyna announced Bugz-NYC and The Guerrilla Hittas as the winners for their song, *Spit It*, Jo said, "You trying to get in my panties later tonight or something?"

"Baby, I got your panties right here." I patted my pant pocket.

"Damn, that's right."

I chuckled and kissed her, then grabbed her hand again and squeezed it.

"...I wanna thank the fans. Y'all been holding me the fuck down since day one. I also wanna thank my label, my family, especially my kids—Little Natalie and my new baby boy, Junior. I wanna thank my current wife and apologize to my ex-wife. I heard some shit went down when I was backstage, so I see that I really fucked up with you, baby. I see that shit clearly now, Jo. I still love you, though. No disrespect to wifey."

As Bugz left the stage amongst applause and folks shouting and shit, I glanced at Jo, who looked like she wanted to crawl out of her skin. Then my eyes made their way across the aisle to Bugz's wife, who looked like someone had just slapped her.

"The hell?" Jo said softly.

"You all right?" I asked. Shit, I wasn't, because like Jo said, the hell? Was this dude out of his mind? Who says that type of stuff in front of their wife?

"I'm fine, but seriously, what the hell?"

I shrugged. "That motherfucker can declare his love all he wants, but he better not touch you. I know that much."

"He won't. I won't let him."

"Yeah...so you ready to celebrate?"

She nodded, lifted a brow, and licked her lips. "I can't wait."

I rubbed a finger across her freckles. "I can't believe you said yes.

You don't think I'm moving too fast?"

"You are, but I'm used to it. It's your thing, and of course I said yes. I love you and I might have made some dumb decisions in the past, but I ain't stupid. I'd have to be stupid *not* to marry you."

As I grabbed the back of her head, threading my fingers through her new braids and kissing her deeply, she clutched my wrist, returning the kiss. Music filled the theater, and I could hear Bugz's harsh voice as his show-closing performance began. We stayed like that, locked into each other, lost in each other as people yelled and rapped along with him. I knew folks were dancing to the the song, because the track was dope as hell. I could admit that, but all I could think about was Jo, how much I loved her, how much I needed her, and how blessed I was to have found her. She might not have thought she contributed much to my world, but she added so much to me with her honesty, loyalty, and a level of realness I had been missing. Jo gave me things my money could never buy.

When she snatched her mouth away from mine, I didn't know what was going on but looked up to see that Bugz was right in front of us, still performing. Shit, I was so lost in her, I hadn't noticed his loud, growling, unintelligible ass. She looked back at me, and I looked at her. We were stuck sitting there like a motherfucker, his eyes on Jo and a camera man behind him capturing the moment. Now I was thinking I should've either just scooped Jo up and left or kept her backstage with me and left right after accepting my award, because this fool was asking to get his ass kicked on national TV all up in her face like that.

I had no idea what he was saying, but his eyes remained clamped to Jo, which told me his mumbling was directed toward her. He was straight disrespecting me! I grabbed her hand and leaned in to say something. Shit, I don't even know what, but I needed to take her attention off him, because she was visibly upset at that point. Once she was looking at me, I felt something pull on her and her head shot up to look at Bugz again. Before I could realize what was going on, this nigga had yanked my damn woman to her feet and was trying to pull her into his arms, but she was fighting it, pushing him away. By this time, he wasn't rapping anymore. Talent was doing his verses since they were performing their new song to close the show.

I jumped up and pushed Bugz, making him lose his balance a little, but he still had ahold of her. "Nigga, back the fuck up!" I yelled.

He smiled, leaning in like he was going to kiss her while she squirmed and fought against him, and that's when my ass lost it. I shoved him so hard, he almost fell, had to let Jo go to catch his balance. I was all the way in his face in a second flat, my chest puffed out as I blocked him from her.

"Nigga, *you* back up!" he yelled. "I'ont give a shit about you fucking her or putting rings on her finger. She mine!"

"You out your damn mind! I guarantee I got that on lock! Your slow ass needs to move the fuck on! Ain't you got a got-damn wife?!"

Behind me, I felt familiar hands on my shoulders, heard Jo's pleading voice. "Ev, let's just go. You're on TV. Come on, let's go."

Never taking my eyes off her ex, I said, "Baby, back up. Back up."

"Call her baby one more damn time!" Bugz screamed.

I shook my head. "Man, you a bitch, all up in my *baby's* face and shit asking for an ass-whooping."

"Bet I'll be fucking her tonight, because she ain't leaving here with your ass. On life, she ain't leaving here with you! That's facts, my nigga!"

I scoffed. "Right." By now, we were surrounded by people, including Tommy, who was probably waiting for me to give him the word to jump in. Folks were yelling all kinds of shit I couldn't make out, and the damn camera man was front and center to catch the action, but I didn't care. I took her hand from my shoulder, and said, "*Watch* her leave with me."

Bugz stood there for a second as I pulled Jo beside me. Then he grabbed her arm. "Jo, bring your ass on."

She screamed, "Sid, stop this!" and grabbed my arm, pulling me away from him. I was walking backward just in case he tried to sucker-punch me in the back of the head or something, so I got a clear view of this sum-bitch grabbing her ass, and that was all she wrote. I don't know if it was because I really, *really* just wanted to kick his ass anyway or what. All I know is I saw the smirk on his face and knew there was no way I could let that ride, not with millions of people witnessing it.

So I yelled, "Motherfucker!" and punched the shit out of him.

The crowd parted as he stumbled backward, and I punched him again…and again…and again. Security had to pull me off him, and I was detained, then arrested, but I didn't give half a damn. I knew I had enough money and a good enough attorney to get little more than a slap on the wrist since I'd never been arrested before, but when I was being taken out in handcuffs and saw the tears streaming down Jo's face, I felt my heart break. That's when I realized my only child would see this shit, too. Her father being arrested. That really messed me up. What the hell was I doing? I'd lost my mind over Jo.

27

Now...

Everett opened the door for me and helped me inside the SUV, then climbed into the backseat beside me. I glanced at him as Dunn pulled away from the police station to see him staring out the window in deep thought. I wanted to say something but wasn't sure what the appropriate thing to say was in this instance. "I'm sorry my ex is a damn lunatic," just didn't seem like it would be enough.

My stomach was in knots, and I could feel that familiar burning of my skin which told me an anxiety-induced itching fit was on the horizon. So I closed my eyes and took a few deep breaths, because I knew this was not the time for me to have a breakdown. Not now. Fixing my eyes on my side of the vehicle, I told myself that soon enough, we'd be back at the hotel where I could hold my little girl. That would make me feel better.

I felt Everett shift on the seat beside me but didn't turn to look at him until he reached for my left hand, inspected it, then said, "Aye, Dunn!"

"Yeah, Boss?"

"I need to holla' at you once we get back to the hotel."

"All right."

Then Everett turned to me. "You got my phone?"

I frowned a little and nodded, digging his phone out of my purse and handing it to him.

"Thanks," he said, dropping my hand and giving his full attention to the phone.

I wasn't sure what to think at first when he began returning phone calls, then I realized this was Business Everett and knew when he was in this mode to leave him alone. So I pulled my own phone out and decided to check Instagram. My number of followers had exploded shortly after Everett and I became a thing and my identity was discovered by the masses, continuing to grow by the second despite the fact that I hadn't posted anything in weeks and had never posted a picture of me and Everett at all. I was up to sixty thousand followers, a lot for me but nothing compared to Everett, who had close to ten million followers. He had posted tons of pictures of us, but none of Nat at my request. I could deal with people talking shit about me. She didn't deserve to be the target of people's vitriol.

As expected, Instagram was buzzing over the fight. All of the blogs had posted about it, with loads of people clogging up their comments section with speculation. Most people agreed that Sid earned the ass-whooping he got, a few decided Everett and I must've been seeing each other when I was still married to Sid, and there were tons of other theories and many insults directed at me, as usual. When I saw a comment suggesting that my daughter was Everett's instead of Sid's, I closed the app.

Relief flooded me once we made it to the hotel. All I could think of was getting to Ms. Sherry's room and cuddling with my Nat. At this point, she was the only sure thing in my life, the one thing Sid was too disinterested in to ruin for me, because even though Evil Jo talked all that shit, clapping back at Dunn, Regular Jo knew he had a point. I was no good to Everett because of my connection to Sidney. Sidney wasn't going to let go. He wasn't going to stop antagonizing Everett, and it was probably only a matter of time before Everett got sick of it all.

Everett said something to Dunn that I missed because I was too busy opening the car door and hopping out. Everett caught up with me before I made it all the way through the lobby, clutching my arm, and asking, "You in a hurry or something?"

As we stepped onto the elevator, I shrugged. "I'm tired. It's late...or early." As I said the words, I realized it was too late to disturb Ms. Sherry and Nat, and a sadness hit me.

"Yeah, I hear you," he replied.

"I-I know you're tired, too. I didn't mean—"

"I know what you meant. Just chill, Jo."

He walked me to our suite, which had been vacated by Sage and Bridgette, and said, "Let me go talk to Dunn and I'll be right back."

"You want me to stay up and wait for you?"

"Yeah."

I nodded. "Okay."

Then he left. No kiss. His touchy-feely ass had barely laid a finger on me since getting out of jail. Try as I did to stay awake and wait for him, I ended up crying myself to sleep.

*****

I woke up in the middle of the night, but I wasn't sure why. He was all over me, leg over mine, heavy arm on my waist, his big body against the back of mine. I sighed as I tried to relax against him. He was here. He hadn't left me.

"I thought you were gonna wait up for me." His voice was gravelly and laden with sleep.

"I tried. Told you I was tired."

He pulled me closer. "Yeah."

"Ev?"

"Hmm?"

"I'm sorry about Sidney and you getting arrested and—"

"Not your place to apologize, wasn't your fault. Besides, I'm a rapper. This shit probably boosted my record sales, gave me some street cred."

I fell silent, not sure what to say next.

"You're not leaving me, Jo. Not over this."

"I wasn't going to leave you. I thought you would want to leave me."

"I love you. I ain't going nowhere."

"I love you, too."

"Then we're good."

"Yeah…did you call Ella?"

"Uh-huh, told her I was fine. Called my sister and brothers, my management, my publicist, fired Dunn. All business is taken care of."

I flipped over to face him in the dark. "You fired—why?"

"Because he let you get out of that truck alone at the police station wearing a one-point-four million-dollar ring. And even if he didn't think he had a duty to protect *you*, *I* had to walk through the paparazzi alone to get to the truck. Plus, he's been too preoccupied lately. It was time for him to go."

I shook my head. "He's gonna blame me."

"Why would he do that?"

I didn't answer.

A lamp popped on, and Everett searched my eyes. "What's going on, Jo?"

"Uh…" I told him about the things Dunn had said to me in the truck on the way to pick him up. "He tried to get with me before we became official, so I don't know if he really liked me or what it is, but he has a problem with us being together."

Everett scrubbed his hand down his face. "I knew something was up with him lately and I figured it had something to do with you. Wish I'd known he said all that shit to you before I fired him. I gave his ass too much severance pay for him to have disrespected you like that, and he tried to say I been fucking someone else, too? Man, I wish he *would* make good on that threat to do something to you. Motherfucker…"

I rolled over onto my back and stared at the ceiling. "When are you going to hire someone else?"

"As soon as I can. Got Tommy getting in touch with some guys that might be looking for work."

"Good, you don't need to be short on security with Sid out here acting like he is."

"It was just Dunn fucking with you, right? Not Tommy?"

"No, Tommy's always been nice to me."

"All right. Get some sleep. I gotta be in court in the morning and I need you there with me."

"Court?!" I shrieked.

"Yeah, my lawyer worked a miracle calling in all kinds of favors to get me ROR'd, but I still gotta face a judge."

The tears came before I could stop them. He grabbed me, squeezed me tight, and said, "I know this is all messed up, but I need something from you right now."

"W-what?"

"To be my rock and have my back no matter what. You think you can do that? I need to know you're not gonna fold on me, Jo, that you can be strong for me. That's the only way we gonna make it through this or anything else people try to throw at us."

"I'm sorry for crying. I cry too much, don't I?"

"No, baby. That's not what I'm saying. Shit is fucked up, all the way fucked up. Bugz is a fool that ain't going away. Dunn said some stupid shit. I fucked up by staying at that show after the proposal, knowing Bugz wasn't going to come shake my hand and congratulate me. You supposed to be upset. If you need to cry, then cry. I'm asking that you be upset and cry and still let me love you. Don't use this as a chance to forget what I've been trying to show you all this time."

"What's that?" I asked, as I wiped my face.

"Your worth. You deserve the world, Jo, and I'ma give it to you. I just need you to let me."

"I can be strong. I *will* be strong…for us." I held up my hand, gazing at my ring.

"You think I spent too much on it, don't you?"

"Yes, but you ain't getting it back."

He laughed. "You could try to give it back, but I wouldn't take it. You're mine and I'm yours, Jo. Forever and always."

"And I'm thankful for that."

28

Everett

The next morning, a trial date was set and I was allowed to leave New York under the condition that I only travel to LA or Houston, where I owned homes. Any work-related travel would have to be approved by the court on a case by case basis, including the European leg of my tour, which was scheduled to begin after the holidays. Luckily, any other business could be handled via phone or Skype.

I chartered a plane to take us all home, including Jo's friends, knowing she'd be more comfortable that way. I was trying my best to keep her calm, because I could tell her ex knew which of her buttons to push to get what he wanted out of her. Not that I was worried about her going back to him. I was worried about the guilt she felt over his crazy-ass antics running her away from me. See, I knew he didn't really want Jo. He might have still loved her, but if he wanted her, he would've stayed with her. Shit is really that black and white for us men. The truth was: he just didn't want her with anyone else, and evidently didn't expect her to ever move on. Why, I don't know, but now that she had, he was losing it. Would he marry her again if given the chance? I believed he would, but would he treat her any better? Behave like a man who truly regretted his actions? Hell, no. Bugz was the type of nigga who'd woo a woman back, dog her out worse than he did before, and convince her she deserved it. And so many good women fell for that shit over and over again. But like I said, I didn't think Jo would go back to him, she'd just be alone, and she didn't deserve that either.

I watched as Nat stared out the window at the clouds and Jo stared at nothing. At first, I thought she was looking at me but could tell her eyes weren't really focused on anything in particular. So I left my seat, picked up Nat, who was next to her, and sat down beside Jo, placing Nat in my lap.

"What you thinking about, Jo Lena?"

Her startled eyes met mine. "Oh...just wondering if you ever furnished your new house."

"You mean *our* new house? The one I bought for *us*?"

She gave me a slow smile. "Yeah, that one."

"Yeah, mostly. Why?"

"Um, after we get to LA, I'll need to drop by my place and grab some things so we can move into *our* new house. All three of us."

"Word? For real, Jo?" I had planned on convincing her to move in since all the shit that had gone down, but never expected her to make the decision on her own. Jo didn't want to take anything from me, no matter how willing I was to give it, and I knew she saw the house as a gift, too.

She nodded. "For real. I can't expect you to stay in that house now with all that's happened and knowing Sid still thinks it belongs to him and might pop up starting mess at any moment, and I don't wanna be there anymore or apart from you, so we're moving. I already talked to Nat about it over breakfast while you were making phone calls. Not sure if she really understands, but hopefully, she'll adjust okay."

As Nat laid her little head on my chest, a sure sign she was about to fall asleep, I said, "You're her constant. As long as she's with you, she'll be good."

"And you. The first thing she asked when I told her about the new house was, 'Is Ebbwitt coming?'"

I smiled and kissed Nat's forehead. "I'm crazy about y'all, you know that?"

"Gotta be to be willing to deal with Sid to be with us."

"He ain't nothing. Just a gnat. I swatted his ass once. Don't mind doing it again."

"Ass," Nat mumbled in her sleep. How she managed to home in

on curse words like that was just strange and kind of ingenious. I gave Jo a guilty look, telling myself I was really going to have to start watching my language around Nat-Nat.

*****

I smiled at the look on Jo's face when we pulled through the gate onto the property. Jo was used to money and nice stuff. Bugz might've been a fool, but he wasn't stingy or cheap when it came to her and Nat with the exception of that baby-ass car he got her. He had been paying good child support, gave her a huge settlement when they split, and didn't really fight her on anything during their divorce. So to see the look of awe on her face as we approached the house made me feel like I'd really done something. Jo wasn't easily impressed, and even when she *was* impressed, she was uncomfortable with what she deemed inflated prices. We often argued over my spending habits, especially when the money was spent on her. But at this moment as she turned to me with her mouth hung open, I could tell she was speechless, possibly too awestruck to fuss over a house with an obviously hefty price tag attached to it.

"Ohhhhh, pwetty!" Nat squealed from her car seat, pointing toward the house.

"It sure is, Nat-Nat. It sure is," Jo said softly.

"I'm glad you two like it. Thought I was gonna have to buy another one," I said, trying not to appear as geeked as I felt as I ran down the stats for Jo—over seven thousand square feet situated on one-and-a-half acres of land. Six bedrooms, eight baths, a family room, formal living and dining rooms, an office, and a theater. It was an Italian villa-style house with tons of windows and high ceilings, including a twenty-one-foot entryway.

Tommy pulled the SUV around the circular motor court, stopping in front of the house. I hopped out and opened Jo's door while she pulled Nat out of her car seat. Nat beat us to the front door, excited to see the inside.

I showed her around downstairs first and grinned when she gasped at the sliding wall in the kitchen that opened up to the backyard for entertaining purposes. Most of the house was furnished and decorated with the exception of the theater and four of the bedrooms.

We took the elevator to the second floor to Nat's pure delight, and the first room I showed Jo was the master suite, which was decorated in shades of blue, because I knew that was her favorite color, and had his and hers bathrooms and closets, plus a huge sitting area. Our last stop was Nat's room, which had a lion theme from the jungle painted on the walls to the lion print comforter on the little twin bed.

Nat climbed onto the low bed, jumping and squealing loudly. Then she let out a "Rawr!"

"Stop jumping on that bed, Nat," Jo fussed, then turned to me before letting her eyes sweep over the room, stopping at the open bathroom door. "She has her own bathroom, too?"

I nodded. "All the bedrooms have en suite bathrooms, except ours, of course, which has two."

"We'll have to, uh, put a lock on that door or she'll be playing in the toilet all the time. She does that, you know?"

"Most kids her age do. That's why it already has a safety lock on it. Key's in our room. And I had the toilet in there replaced with a toddler-height one, so she can easily get on and off it."

"Wow, you thought of everything," she said softly, her voice wavering.

I reached for her, pulling her close to me. "I know this is a big change, a lot of big changes, but we'll be okay. I promise. Nat seems to like it, and—"

"That's not it. I just—you told me you bought a house for us and I didn't even ask to see it. You've been having it furnished and decorated for us, all of us, even Nat. You did this for us, and I just dismissed it trying to hold on to something I knew I needed to let go of. I'm so sorry, Everett."

"It's all right, baby."

"No, it's not, and I promise to stop fighting you on stuff and just accept your kindness."

"Thank God, because you were wearing me out."

She laughed into my chest. "Ev?"

"Hmm?"

"How much did this house cost?"

"Nope. Not telling you. Come on. I'm hungry, and I think Courtney had the fridge stocked."

"I'm hungry, too. I really gotta learn to cook now with that kitchen. It's gorgeous!"

"You can if you want to, but that ain't why I'm marrying you." I wiggled my eyebrows at her.

After she rolled her eyes at me, she said, "Come on, Nat. Let's go eat-eat."

"Eat-eat!" Nat replied.

29

I'd thought my home was a secure one, but living in a gated property with a state-of-the-art alarm system inside a gated community was a whole other type of security. It'd been a week or so since we moved into the new house, and in that short time, I understood the sacrifices Everett made when he lived with me in my old house. There was a guest house where his security—Tommy and the new guys he'd hired—could stay when they were on duty and be available when he needed them. There wasn't enough space for that at my old house. There was much more room at the new house, and he had an office where he could conduct his business instead of holing up in my guest room hoping Nat wouldn't disturb him. Plus, he seemed more at ease now, much more comfortable. His siblings, who all lived in LA, too, would drop by pretty often, and that was always fun for both of us because they were all some nuts. And to be honest, I loved being there with him. It just felt like ours, something we were both new to. When he asked me if I wanted to finish decorating or pick out the furniture for the guest rooms and the theater, I told him the decorator was doing a great job, so why mess with that sister's money?

Sid had called twice since the awards show debacle. The conversations were mercifully abbreviated with him only calling to check on Nat...and me, of course. He acted as if he hadn't cut a fool and provoked Everett into kicking his ass on national TV, causing him to get arrested. Sid had avoided arrest since he never even got a shot in on Everett. I probably should've filed charges against him for feeling on my ass in front of millions, but much rather preferred not to even have to think about the whole situation. Besides, that ass-whooping Everett put on him was more than enough punishment. I'd seen a TMZ video of him in New York after the show, and the entire left side of his face was swollen. He couldn't even open his left eye. Yeah, he'd been punished enough. Plus, Everett said to let it go, because he was confident Sid would back off now. I wasn't so sure about that.

A little over a week before we were to travel to Houston to have Thanksgiving with his family, Everett insisted I sit in on a meeting with Courtney, and as we sat in the sitting room portion of our bedroom, I had to wonder why. Maybe he wanted me to really feel like I was a part of his world? I already did. Not that it wasn't interesting to hear about all the working parts of his life, the commitments and all that stuff, but we'd been in there for nearly two hours and I was getting sleepy from just sitting there contributing nothing.

"Jo, I have a couple of things I need to go over with you," Courtney said.

I frowned slightly as I turned to look at Everett beside me on the love seat, then gave Courtney my attention. "Me?"

She nodded. "First, Everett is scheduled to do an interview and photo spread for *Essence*. It's something he agreed to awhile back, but now they're asking that you be included."

"Me?" I repeated, as if that was the only word in my vocabulary.

"Yes, they initially wanted to talk to Everett about his career, longevity, future goals. Now they want to include your love story. How you met. All that jazz."

"Wow, *Essence*? That was my mom's favorite magazine. Hands down. If she couldn't afford to buy a copy, she'd steal it. She loved that magazine," I rambled.

"You wanna do it?" Everett asked, skepticism in his voice. He knew I wasn't a spotlight whore. But this was *Essence* we were talking about.

"I—what would I say? I'm probably the least impressive woman on Earth. No education, no job, not enough ambition to get one. I'm just a mom who's in a relationship with a famous man."

"You're more than that to me. You give me balance, make me smile, give me a reason to look forward to the future in addition to watching Ella grow up."

My eyes misted almost instantly. "Everett..."

He smiled at me. "You do, baby, and you do some other stuff you probably don't want me to bring up in front of Court."

"You better not!"

Chuckling as he leaned in to kiss my cheek, he said, "I won't. Look, this'll be my chance to tell the world all that you do for me, but I can do that whether you're a part of the interview or not. It's up to you. I'll understand if you don't—"

"I do. I mean, I'll do it. I think my mom would like that if she was here. It'd probably make her smile to see me in *Essence*. She would be...she'd be proud of me."

"You'll be in it *and* on it. They guaranteed us the cover. That would've really made her proud, huh?"

My mouth dropped open. "The cover?! Wait until I tell Bridgette. I gotta call her now!"

Courtney held her hand up, her iPad still balanced on her lap. "Hold up, Jo. I've also been getting all kinds of requests for you to contact different companies that are wanting to do business with you."

"Seriously?"

She nodded. "There are designers wanting to dress you for future awards shows. S.H.E. Athletics is talking a sneaker line. Pink Vodka wants you to be their spokeswoman. Glam On It Cosmetics wants to collaborate with you on a lip gloss line. They say your lips are perfect for one."

"What?! But...why?"

"You're hot right now, baby," Everett said. "They know you were with Bugz, now you're with me, and plus, I kicked his ass over you. They're fascinated by you. And besides all that, you've got this...*thing*, the same thing that drew me to you and has damn near driven Bugz's ass crazy. You're special."

I shook my head. "No, they're just tryna figure out why y'all want my funny-looking ass."

"You know how I feel about you saying shit like that, Jo. You're beautiful, inside and out."

"In your eyes, yes, and I appreciate that, but I'm not model pretty. I'm just a regular chick with lots of flaws."

"And that's who these companies sell their products to. Regular chicks, and right now, you're 'hashtag goals' for all of them," Courtney stated.

I'll be damned if she wasn't right.

Everett rested a huge hand on my thigh "Jo, it bothers you that you don't have a career, right? That's why you took that shit off Park? Well, here's your chance to be an entrepreneur if you want it. But again, it's your choice."

He was right, too. These opportunities were just dropping in my lap. Maybe this was all meant to be. But— "Isn't this kind of like me riding off your success, though?" I asked, as the thought hit me. "I'll really look like a gold digger if I take these folks up on their offers."

Everett shrugged. "They calling you one anyway, ain't they? Shit, may as well make you some paper, baby. I mean, I got you. You know that, but I know you women like to make your own money, and I'm good with that, too."

I nodded and realized some women prayed for opportunities like these, and none of this even seemed like work. It seemed...fun. I needed fun. "I think I wanna do it."

"You sure?" Everett asked.

"Yeah. I mean, I can at least see what the companies are talking about."

Courtney smiled. "Great! I'll give them your email address. And if it's okay, I'll give it to anyone who contacts me regarding you in the future, too."

"But before you agree to meet with anyone, I'll need to get you a meeting with my lawyer unless you have one in mind who can negotiate contracts and stuff like that," Everett offered.

"No, your lawyer will be fine."

Everett walked his play cousin-slash-assistant to the front door and I remained in my spot, glued to the loveseat. I felt scared, terrified about all of this, but also excited, more excited than I ever felt about a job before.

Just as I picked my phone up to call Bridgette and give her the news, it began to buzz. I stared at it for a moment as Sidney's name flashed on the screen, not because I didn't want to talk to him, but because I just felt dazed about the impending changes in my life. So I missed the call, but he quickly called back.

This time, I answered. "Hello?"

"Where you at?"

"Home. Why?"

"Why you ain't answering the door, then?"

Damn. I hadn't told him I moved. It hadn't even crossed my mind to tell him. "Oh, we moved. Meant to tell you that."

"Moved? Where? Your car is still here. I'm standing here looking at it."

"Uh, we moved to Calabasas, and I got a new car, too."

"You moved with South?"

"Yeah."

"How the fuck I'm supposed to see my daughter, Jo? You got her in the motherfucker's house?"

"It's my house, too, and I think we should work out a real visitation schedule. No more pop-ups. Nat deserves stability."

"Stability like moving her to some nigga's house?!"

"Everett is not just some nigga, Sid. Nat knows him. Come on, if we're both mature about this, we can work it out, but you can't keep trying to start stuff with my fiancé. He's more than willing to forget the whole hip hop awards mess if you agree to stop doing stuff like that."

"Fian—you know what? Fuck this shit!" He shouted the words into the phone and then hung up on me.

A second later, a text from him came through: *I'm sorry, Jo. I'm tryna deal with this shit but I can't get with u marrying that nigga. I still love u.*

If this negro wasn't a total and complete lunatic.

I shook my head as I finally got up and headed to Nat's room, where she was napping. As I stood there deciding whether or not to go ahead and wake her up and get her ready for dinner since we had plans to go out to eat, I felt him behind me.

Wrapping his long arms around me, he leaned in and nuzzled my neck before whispering directly in my ear, "You wanna do a little something before she wakes up?"

I grinned. "Naw."

He lifted me from my feet, making me giggle. "Oh, you don't?"

"Ev, stop! You're gonna make me wake her up and you damn sure won't get none then."

As he carried me from her room to ours, he said, "But I'm the loud one?" He laid me on my back and settled over me.

"You are! And you better be quiet, or she'll be at the door knocking before you can finish."

"You know what you gotta do, then."

"Man, your fans would never believe your freaky ass likes panty gags."

He grinned down at me before covering my mouth with his.

Everett

Call me.

Why are you ignoring me?

We need to talk!

How could you get engaged without discussing it with me?!

I thought you weren't ever going to get married again.

You're a liar!

Why are you acting like this?

Call me.

Call me.

Call me.

Everett, call me!

As I scrolled through the messages from Esther, I sighed. Her ass was really losing it. Since when did I need to consult her before I made a decision? And did she forget the whole me not getting married again thing was said right after I caught her ass having a damn orgy in my house? She was upset, maybe even hurt, because I guess she was comfortable as long as I was alone and miserable, fucking chicks just to have something close to a connection with someone, but she was going to have to stay mad, because I was not letting Jo go. Not if I could help it. I didn't give a shit how Esther or Bugz or the world at large felt about it. Being with her made me happy, complete, and that was all that mattered to me.

This was my favorite time of day, bedtime, when everything was quiet. I turned my head and watched her sleep for a minute, eyes closed, mouth slightly open, freckles in full effect, hair everywhere, and I smiled. Then I deleted all of Esther's stupid-ass messages and took a picture of Jo, uploading it to Instagram with the caption: *My sleeping beauty.* The picture already had like a thousand likes a few seconds later when I kissed her nose and pulled her to me.

She frowned, eyes still shut as she mumbled, "Unh-uh. I can't take anymore. You—my coochie is tired, baby. Go to sleep. I'll give you some in the morning. You can have all of it in the morning. I promise."

I smiled, kissed her forehead, and was soon fast asleep myself.

30

Everett, Nat, and I arrived in Houston the Monday of Thanksgiving week. Bridgette came with us since she had no family to spend the holiday with. Tommy was our only security and he was only with us for a day as Everett usually paid a couple of his cousins to be his bodyguards when he was in his hometown. As soon as the chartered plane landed, we hit the ground running, heading straight to a huge food giveaway Everett sponsored every year. He had told me to dress comfortably because he knew that would be our first stop and I had relayed this information to Bridgette, but she was determined to look cute. She helped us out and didn't complain, but I knew her feet had to be killing her in the heels she wore.

After we finished assisting the volunteers with giving out turkeys, bags of stuffing mix, cans of vegetables, frozen pies, and department store gift cards, we made our way to Everett's house, which was actually located in a small town a few miles west of Houston on a plot of land that also included a cottage he had built for his mother that was now his aunt's home.

Everett's Houston home was beautiful, a red brick house with five bedrooms and six full baths, structurally much smaller than our LA home but with more privacy since Everett owned several acres of land surrounding it.

Once inside and exhausted from the flight and the work we'd engaged in, we all headed upstairs where I fell into bed with Nat for a nap. I was too tired to wonder what Bridgette and Everett planned to do. When I woke up a couple of hours later to an empty bed, I smiled. A wonderful aroma had wafted all the way from the kitchen straight into my nose. Everett had told me his Aunt Everlina, whom he was named after, would be staying with us and cooking for us all week, including the bulk of Thanksgiving dinner. Since she was, as he put it, more like a mother to him than an aunt, I couldn't wait to meet her or taste what smelled like greens and porkchops. It was Aunt Everlina who raised Leland and Kathryn after their mother's death, since they were eleven and sixteen at the time. Everett, Nolan, and Neil were all young adults back then.

I was looking forward to meeting all of his aunts and uncles and cousins and getting acquainted with them like I had his siblings since we'd moved into the new house. The only person I wasn't looking forward to seeing was Ella, who was flying in on Wednesday night. I know that sounds bad, but it's the truth. As hard as I tried to be kind and cordial to her when she'd visit Everett, all I got was rolled eyes and sucked teeth in response. She had enough sense to act like she was trying to get along with me in her father's presence, but as soon as his back was turned or he left the room for even a second, Miss Attitude returned. I knew the root of it was jealousy. Her dad was building a family, and as hard as he tried to include her in it, she saw herself being phased out. I dealt with it, with her, didn't bother telling him, because I didn't want to make him feel like he had to choose between us. Hell, I wasn't dumb. I knew that would be a losing battle for me, and I didn't want to lose Everett. Not ever. So I made sure to take Nat to Ms. Sherry's whenever I knew Ella was coming over, because I didn't want her little feelings hurt by the teenager, and then I took Ella's meanness and tried to return it with kindness. I just hoped and prayed there never came a time when something would necessitate her living with us, because that shit was never going to work.

After a quick stop in the bathroom, I made my way through the second floor, down the stairs, and to the kitchen where I found a hefty older woman stirring something in a huge bowl—a closer look told me it was potato salad—and Nat sitting at the kitchen table eating applesauce. I kissed her little forehead and then moved toward the woman.

"Hi," I said softly. "Aunt Everlina?"

She looked up, the smooth brown skin of her face that matched Everett's spreading into a bright smile. "Jo?"

I returned her smile, moved closer, and proffered my hand to her. "Yes, ma'am."

She shook her head and opened her arms. "Girl, you about to marry my favorite nephew and you think you can get away with just shaking my hand? I'ma need a hug!"

With a gigantic grin on my face, I walked into her open arms and was soon enveloped in the warmth of this woman who was nearly a foot taller than me.

When she backed out of the hug, she took my face in her hands and smiled. "Mm-hmm, I see it."

My brow furrowed a bit. "See what?"

"What *he* sees, what had him fighting over you on TV. It's in your spirit. It's not dark like that heifer he married before. I knew she wasn't nothing but trouble. So did his mama. We tried to tell him, but he always been hard-headed. But you? He got it right this time."

I heard his voice before I felt him lay his hand on my shoulder. "So she passes your test?" he asked.

"Ebbwitt!" Nat squealed. "I got applesauce!"

"Did Auntie Everlina give that to you?" he asked.

She showed him all of her short teeth as she nodded.

"Did you say thank you?" I asked.

She nodded again.

"She sure did. This sweet baby got good manners. Someone been raising her right." Aunt Everlina went back to her bowl, and then said, "You did good, Tick. Picked you a good woman this time."

Tick?

"Come on, Auntie. Don't nobody call me that no more," Everett groaned.

"Everybody here in Millstone does." She looked up from the bowl with raised brows. "Oh, you didn't tell her about your nickname, did you?"

I glanced over my shoulder at his towering frame. "No, ma'am. He didn't."

"Shit. Here we go," Everett muttered.

"Well, for the longest time, this boy would eat anybody out of house and home. His daddy—God rest Randy's soul—used to always say if this boy didn't stop eating so much, he was gonna swell up and pop like a tick!" Aunt Everlina grabbed her jiggly stomach and laughed. "That Randy was sho' nuff a mess! Anyway, he said it so much, everybody started calling Everett Tick."

Everett sighed. "Auntie, come on!"

"What? Didn't nobody tell you to come in here anyway. Go on in there and watch TV while I get to know Jo."

"Naw, I ain't gonna let you keep telling her stuff to run her away."

I shook my head as I turned to face him. "Is Bridgette down here somewhere?"

"She's out back sitting on the patio talking to Tommy," Everett replied.

"She is?" I knew she had been on a penis-finding mission for a while that had gone into overdrive after I got with Everett, but Tommy? He wasn't bad-looking, but he was so…huge and well, a bodyguard. I'd always known Bridgette to date metrosexual, manicured fingernail-type men. Maybe they were just having a friendly chat.

Nah, I knew her better than that. She was scoping out some dick.

"Yeah…" Everett said, and then slipped his chiming phone from his pocket, accepting a call. The conversation lasted less than a full minute, and as he hung up, he turned to me, and said, "That was Courtney reminding me about my interview tomorrow with Latisha Grandy from KCHT. She's good people. We go way back. She'll be here at five in the morning. My interview will be part of their morning show. You wanna sit in on it? She requested that you be a part of it if you were available."

I frowned a little. Poor Everett was always working in some form, shape, or fashion, even when he was supposed to be *not* working. "But I didn't bring Sage to do my makeup."

"I'm sure Latisha can bring a makeup artist, baby."

"Ev, I can't use just any makeup on my skin."

"Maybe Bridgette can help you out. You got something to wear? If not, we can go get something."

"Uh…" I was about to panic, feeling like he'd sprung this on me when I was sure he'd mentioned it before. There was just always so much going on in his world. Would I ever get used to his lifestyle?

"Latisha Grandy? Didn't that used to be your girlfriend?" Aunt Everlina asked.

Girlfriend?

"Way back in high school, yeah," Everett replied.

"She still like you, don't she?" Everlina returned.

Everett shrugged. "I don't know about all that, Auntie."

Giving me a pointed look, she said, "That's what I heard. That girl still wants you."

"Uh, I have something to wear and Bridgette can help me with hair and makeup. She can keep Nat occupied for us, too. I'll be ready in the morning," I said.

He leaned in and softly kissed my lips. "Good. I think you'll like Tish."

Tish, huh? "I'm sure I will."

Everett

I knew shit was going too well.

Monday night after we put Nat down in the bedroom that connected to the master, I managed to convince Jo to give me some, despite her being weirded out about doing it with my aunt sleeping down the hall. So I was in a great mood for the interview the next morning, which, by the way, went really well. Tish had always been cool, and while she did still want me, she showed nothing but respect to Jo, who rocked the interview even though she was nervous as hell before we started. Jo always managed to pull it together for stuff like that, a fact that told me she'd be good at working with those companies that were courting her. Jo was intelligent and extremely well-spoken, made for the public eye whether she realized it or not. She just needed someone to put her where she belonged. She fit into my world more than she knew.

That evening, I took her to the Calming Waters Rest Home where my Uncle Tisdale, my dad's only living sibling, resided. He was confused as hell, but always recognized me. We sat with him for a few minutes before having lunch in the city at one of my favorite little hole-in-the-wall chicken joints with my twin cousins Tadd and Toot—yeah, twins run mean in our family—serving as our security since Tommy was supposed to head back to LA to spend the holidays with his family. His ass was so wrapped up in Jo's girl, Bridgette, that he decided to stay, but I kept him off the clock to give my cousins a chance to make some money. After that, we returned to my house and to Nat. That was one of the things I loved most about Jo: she didn't like being away from her baby girl for long, even though Nat was crazy about Bridgette and didn't mind hanging with her.

Later that Tuesday night, Aunt Ever, as I called her, solicited Jo's and Bridgette's help in the kitchen. It had slipped over breakfast that morning that neither of them could cook, and I thought my auntie was going to have a damn stroke at the revelation. I tried to tell her it didn't matter to me. It wasn't like I couldn't afford to hire someone to cook for us, but for a woman who loved food and loved cooking like Aunt Ever, a woman who couldn't cook wasn't really a woman at all. She just didn't get it.

So, like I said, things were good. Everyone was getting along. Bridgette and Jo even seemed to enjoy the cooking lessons Aunt Ever was giving them. Nat was as happy as she always was. My dozens of cousins had been dropping in all day that Wednesday, just to see me and meet Jo. Leland and the twins had arrived. Leland was staying with me and the twins plus Nolan's latest foreign girlfriend—a different one from the one I'd met at the benefit—were bunking at my mom's place on the property. The only hiccup was that I couldn't reach Ella. I had been calling and texting her for two days to see when her flight was to arrive, since she'd decided to take a later one than the one Courtney originally booked for her, and had gotten no answer. Shit, I was getting worried that something had happened to her. I was contemplating calling Esther when she finally called me back, informing me that she had arrived in Houston and was taking an Uber to my place.

"Why the hell would you do that?" I barked into the phone. "That ain't safe! I was gonna have your cousin, Toot, pick you up."

"I didn't feel like waiting for a ride to get to the airport," she whined into the phone.

"If you'd texted me back or answered your phone and told me what time you were getting in, your ride woulda been there waiting on you!"

"I'm sorry! My phone's been acting up. Can you stop yelling at me?"

I sighed as I clutched my forehead and glanced up at Leland, who was frowning at me. We had been watching a football game despite my worry over her radio silence, and while I was relieved to hear from her, my daughter could be just as frustrating as every other woman I'd ever known. "Look, just be safe...and next time, stay in contact with me."

"Okay. Sorry, Daddy. See you in a little bit."

"All right."

"You good, bro?" Leland asked, as I ended the call and rested the phone on my thigh.

I shook my head as I dragged my hand down my face. "Shit, I don't know. Kids, man."

He chuckled. "And you gon' have another one to deal with. Little Nat. You a glutton for punishment, man!"

"Nah, the good outweighs the bad when it comes to being a father. You'll see."

"Shiiiit, I ain't having no kids. That's why I like the older women. They got that baby fever shit out of their system. All they want is some Leland." He popped the collar of his polo shirt.

I gave him a smirk. "The way you always volunteering at them youth programs? You love kids."

"I *like* kids, but I don't want any. I'm too selfish for that shit."

"Whatever, nigga. You young. You got time to change your mind."

"I bet I won't. But you do you. I can see why you'd be willing to go down that road again with Jo, though. She's good for you. Real sweet, too. Nothing like that damn Esther. I couldn't never stand her."

"Shit, nobody that shared my blood could. I just couldn't see her for what she was."

He shrugged. "Hell, I'da probably been just as blind to her if I was you. She still turning heads."

"Don't you get no ideas over there."

"Naw, man. I like 'em older, but I also like for them to have a heart. Esther ain't got no soul."

"You ain't never lied. Let me go see what Jo is up to."

"Yeah, I'ma go in here and see if I can sneak me a piece of Aunt Ever's sweet potato pie."

"Cool. Just leave that pineapple upside down cake alone. I had her make that special for Jo."

"Damn, you done told me that ten times! I ain't gon' mess with your woman's cake, man!"

"Nigga, you better not."

Me and my little brother both left the theater room, him heading to the kitchen and me to the great room where I knew Jo and Nat were. Bridgette and Tommy had left early that morning to do some sight-seeing, so they said. Jo was convinced they were in some hotel room fucking. That was probably closer to the truth, but shit, whatever.

The music met me before I made it to the room, Diana Ross's *Upside Down*. While Jo was a true hip hop head, her musical tastes where still greatly influenced by her mother, a fact I found endearing. As hard as her upbringing had been, she still held a profound respect for her mom. Rounding the corner, I entered the room, leaning against the wall undetected as I watched her and Nat dance to the music. I loved seeing this, the two of them cutting loose, little Nat, who was too young to know the lyrics, belting them out at the top of her lungs nonetheless. Jo holding her tiny hands, leading her in the dance. But at the same time, I knew these little dance parties coincided with her having something heavy on her mind. She and Nat danced and sang to the clean versions of damn near every Outkast song in existence for a week after my arrest. And what made my heart sink was that I knew what was on her mind today—Ella.

And I wished there was something I could do about her discomfort and Ella's funky attitude. Sure, she'd been playing the part of a respectful teenager in my face, but that morning when I suggested an outing with both Ella and Nat, Jo broke down and told me about Ella's behavior when I wasn't paying attention and said she wanted to shelter Nat from it. I understood, figured that was why she made a point to take Nat to Ms. Sherry whenever she knew Ella was going to be around, and despite that, Jo still agreed to come here with me knowing it was tradition for Ella to come, too, because she believed having so much family around would buffer things. Now it seemed she wasn't so sure.

As I stood there watching her rock her hips to the song, I wondered why this all had to be so hard, why everyone—Ella, Esther, Bugz, the fucking world at large—couldn't just get with the damn program. All I wanted to do was love this woman and make a life with her. Shit, was that really too much to ask?

Closing my eyes, I sighed, and opened them when I heard a sound that felt like velvet to my ears. Jo's back was still to me as she sang along with Diana Ross, and Jo's ass could sing. No, bump that. She could *sang*. She could sang like a motherfucker.

Shit!

My mouth hung open as she continued belting out the lyrics, out-singing the hell out of The Boss on her own song. She hit the chorus and spun around, clutching her chest and shrieking when she saw me, "You scared the hell outta me!"

"Scared! Scared! Scared!" Nat echoed. I smiled at her, wondering why she didn't pick out her mama's curse word like she did all the time with me.

"My bad, baby. Why you ain't tell me you can sing?" I asked, as the music faded out.

She frowned a little. "I don't know. I mean, you think I can sing?"

"You don't *know* you can sing? No one ever told you that?"

"My mom, but she wasn't a reliable source."

"Bridgette? Bugz?"

"Bridgette's heard me before. Look, I don't sing around people, Ev. I don't like singing around people," she said, dropping her eyes.

"I don't know why the he—why not. Baby—" *Missing You* began to play, and I cut myself off.

"What?" she asked. "Something wrong?"

"Sing this one."

"Huh? Ev, I just told you I don't sing in front of people. If I knew you were in here, I wouldn't have been singing before."

"Okay, but sing this one."

She sighed and shook her head as Nat toddled over to me and tugged on my pant leg.

Picking Nat up, I said, "Please, Jo Lena?"

"Pweeeeease," Nat sang.

Jo blew out a breath and scratched her forehead. "I don't know this one."

"Stop lying."

"Ev, come on. I'm not even that good."

"Damn, girl, can you do anything I ask without fighting me on it?"

She groaned, "Okaeeeyuh!"

Taking a deep breath, she finally began singing along with Diana Ross, starting out soft and timid at first. I could see her confidence build note by note, and by the bridge, she was belting the words out. She blew me away! When I say my baby could sing, I'm talking about she was on some Ledisi shit, a strong, rich alto voice, and her ass could do runs, too.

When the song ended, light applause could be heard behind me. I couldn't turn to see who it was, because my eyes were locked on this woman with so much heart and talent that she had no idea she possessed. I was in awe, enthralled, and at the same time, my damn heart ached for the little girl inside of her who wasn't given a fair chance or made to understand just how special she was.

"Girl! How that voice come out of that little body of yours?!" Aunt Ever yelled, as she stepped up beside me. "Reminds me of little Stephanie Mills!"

"I been told her she could sing. Won't listen to me," Bridgette said, stepping up behind my aunt.

"Ev, why you ain't tell me she could sing like that, man?" That was Leland.

I shook my head. "Just found out myself."

"She need to be in the studio, like yesterday," Leland said.

Before I could answer, Toot's voice boomed from the hallway. "Hey, Tick! Your little girl is here. Just opened the gate for her."

Jo grabbed Nat from me and headed out the room. "I'm gonna put her down for a nap," she said softly, but abruptly.

I sighed, knowing she was just trying to protect her baby from Ella and feeling like shit because she felt she had to.

Leland gave me a look, and I just shook my head again. "I need to talk to Jo for a second. Let Ella in for me."

"A'ight," he said, still giving me a curious look.

I left everyone downstairs and trotted upstairs in time to see Jo backing out of Nat's room and closing the door.

"I won't let her be mean to her ever again. I told you I won't. I shoulda checked Ella the first time she acted like that with y'all the second she did it."

Jo gave me a weak smile while placing a hand on my chest. "It was her nap time, Ev. Everything's okay. I'll be down to greet Ella in a bit. I'm not running away from her; I just need a few minutes."

"Jo—"

"Ev! Aye, can you come down here?" Leland shouted from downstairs, his voice echoing in the open foyer.

"Hold on a minute!"

Jo squeezed her eyes shut. "Please stop yelling." She pointed toward Nat's room. "She's never gonna go to sleep if you keep yelling."

"My bad," I said softly. "Baby, look, I promise things are going to be okay. I'ma *make* them okay."

"Ev, man, you really need to come down here!"

"Shit!" I groaned.

"Everett!" Jo hissed, stabbing a finger toward the door again.

"My bad!" I whispered. "I'll be right back, okay?"

She shrugged, and I grabbed the back of my head, rubbing it as I made my way down the stairs. Once I reached the foyer, my footsteps faltered as I found myself face to face with Ella and Esther-motherfucking-Reese.

31

Everett

"You dropping her off?" I asked, as my eyes jumped from Ella's guilty face to Esther's fake innocent one.

"What? Why would I fly all the way out here to drop her off? She's not a baby, Everett," Esther said.

I scratched my eyebrow. "You got business in Houston or something?"

"No."

My eyes shifted back to Ella as I lifted a brow. "Then what's going on?" The question was for whichever one of them wanted to answer.

"Uh, if you don't need me for anything, I got some calls to make," Leland said. He was standing by the door, behind Esther and Ella.

I glanced at him. "Can you tell Jo to come down here?"

He nodded and left for the stairs.

I focused on Ella again. She dropped her head, looked up at me, and sighed. "Can I talk to you alone for a minute?" she asked, her eyes pleading with me as much as her voice was.

I nodded, glanced around us, and took her arm, leading her into the formal dining room.

Closing the door behind us, I began, "I know you don't like Jo, but this—"

"Mom was going to have to spend Thanksgiving alone, Daddy, and she was so sad," she whined.

"I get Thanksgiving with you and she gets Christmas. That's the way it's always been. This isn't new for her. What happened to her visiting her mother in London like she's been doing every Thanksgiving for the last ten, eleven years?"

"I-I don't know. They had an argument or something."

"So this was your idea?"

She shrugged, and I knew better anyway. Esther put the bug in her ear and made it seem like Ella made the decision. Now she was manipulating her own child to try and fuck my life up. I'd never hit a woman in my life, but Esther Reese was testing me like a motherfucker.

There was a tap at the door, and then it slowly opened to reveal Jo peeping in with wide eyes. "Uh...hi, Ella. Everett, your brother said you needed to see me?"

After Ella mumbled a halfhearted greeting to Jo, I nodded. "Yeah. Come in."

"Can she stay?" Ella asked, as Jo eased into the room, eyes darting from me to Ella and back.

"Let me talk to Jo. I'll be out in a second," was my answer.

Ella hung her head and left, shutting the door behind her. Jo hadn't moved, was still a few inches from the door.

"Esther's here," I said.

Jo's eyes were fixed on me. "I know."

"Baby, I don't know what to say. I knew she was tripping over us, but this?" I blew out a breath and peered over at her.

Jo inched closer to me. "She wants to stay? Here? With us?"

I nodded.

"Ella wants her to stay? This was her idea?"

"I think she believes it's her idea, but I know Esther had to plant it."

"What are you going to do?"

I frowned. "The hell you think I'ma do? I'ma tell her ass she can't stay!"

"Ella's going to think I told you to make her leave."

"I'ont give a shit!"

"I do! It's worse than I thought. For her to agree to bringing her mother? She really must dislike me, and if you leave this room and go out there and make her mother leave after she knows you were in here talking to me, she's going to blame me and hate me for it."

I shook my head. "No, she won't."

"Yes, she will! If we're going to be together—"

"If?!"

She closed her eyes and released a breath. "*If we are going to be together,* I would like to, at some point, have a decent relationship with her. I'd like for us to be able to coexist on some level. That'll never happen if she thinks I told you to kick her mother out."

"We ain't got enough room."

"She'll have to share with Ella."

I stood there for a moment, grabbed the back of my head, and said, "I can't do it. I don't even like the fact that I gotta walk the same planet as her ass does. She ain't sleeping in my house. Fuck that, Jo. For real. Fuck that."

She nodded. "Okay, okay. Compromise. She can't stay here, but she can come to dinner tomorrow."

I sighed.

"Ev, I'm trying to make this work for us. This is your child we're talking about."

"Ella ain't no baby, Jo."

"She's *your* baby."

"Shit! Okay, okay. Come on."

She looked confused and a little wary as I grabbed her hand and led her out the room. My daughter and her mother were still in the foyer. This time, I noticed the Louis Vuitton luggage behind them.

"Ella, your room is ready for you. I'll bring your bags up in a little bit. Esther, you can have dinner with us tomorrow, but uh, you can't stay here, if that's what you thought was gonna happen."

Esther's eyes widened as she swung them over to Ella, who moved closer to me. "Daddy—"

I shook my head. "She can come tomorrow for dinner, and that's it. I love you, Ella, and I wanna share tomorrow with you, but your mom can't stay here. It wouldn't be appropriate or comfortable."

"Comfortable for who?" Ella asked.

I cocked my head to the side. "Excuse me?"

Ella's eyes darted to Jo and back to me. "Nothing."

"Yeah, that's what I thought. You can go to your room. We gon' talk some more later."

Ella dropped her head and slowly walked toward the stairs. When I was sure she was out of earshot, I fixed my eyes on my ex-wife, and said, "And your conniving ass can get your shit and go. *Now.*"

Jo grabbed my arm. "Ev—"

"Everett, I doubt there are any rooms available this close to the holiday," Esther softly said.

With raised eyebrows, I asked, "Do I look like I give a shit?"

"She can stay at my place with Neil and Nolan. Plenty of food in the ice box," Aunt Ever offered. She was somewhere behind me. I didn't turn to see where.

"That's okay, Auntie. She won't appreciate your hospitality, and she can find a room. Toot!"

My cousin appeared in a matter of seconds. "Yeah, cuz?"

"Would you drive Esther into the city? She needs to find a room."

"Yeah, no problem."

Esther glared at me before grabbing her rolling suitcase and following Toot out the front door.

I couldn't stand this woman. I couldn't stand the way she pronounced Ella as "Eller" in that thick accent that it made no sense for her to still have seeing as her ass had been in the US longer than I'd been alive, or the way she smiled with her perfectly white, perfectly straight, gapless teeth, or how graceful she moved, or how flawless her makeup and hair were, but most of all, I couldn't stand the way she kept eyeing my damn man. Even in a house full of Amersons—members of Everett's mother's side of the family—my attention kept making its way back to this woman, this intruder, with her irritating ass.

But you encouraged him to invite her to dinner.

I was so damn stupid.

Esther translated dinner as "all day," arriving at the house that morning before either Everett or I woke up. Ella let her in before the damn sun rose, so when I hopped down the stairs in a t-shirt and sweat pants with a scarf covering my head and without the benefit of having washed my ass to see if Aunt Everlina needed any help with breakfast, Esther was already in the kitchen dressed like she was about to be shot for a spread in fucking *Marie Claire* magazine. After Everett's aunt assured me she had it covered, I gave Esther a little nod that she didn't bother returning and rushed back upstairs to make myself presentable.

I was a ball of nerves when I made it back to our bedroom. Everett was finally up, his attention on his phone when I returned and headed straight to the shower without even tossing him a "good morning." I was almost done with my shower when he joined me and screwed me into a better mood, a mood her presence ruined when Everett, Nat, and I made it to the kitchen to have breakfast with everyone—Aunt Everlina, Bridgett, Tommy, Ella, Leland, and Esther—although she barely uttered a word in Everett's unwelcoming company.

By ten that morning, I was putting Nat's coat on her and heading outside to take a walk on the property. It was about fifty degrees out, downright frigid compared to what I'd grown accustomed to. Everett was so engrossed in watching a football game with his brothers that he barely noticed me leaving.

I was nearing the basketball court about fifty feet from the back patio when I heard her voice. "Jo?!"

I stopped in my tracks, causing Nat to look up at me with big, curious eyes. Turning my head slightly, I saw her moving toward us in her tight jeans, a navy pea coat, and gorgeous camel-colored riding boots. I cocked my head to the side and watched as she approached us.

Bending over and clasping her manicured hands between her knees, she smiled at Nat. "Well, hello there. I don't think we've been properly introduced. I'm Esther. What's your name?"

"Nat!" my baby answered her with her signature toothy smile.

"Natalie," I amended.

"Oh, how pretty!" Esther gushed.

"Thank you!" Nat replied without prompting.

Esther stood erect, her eyes on me now. "Do you mind if I walk with you? I'd like to have a chat."

"Actually, I *do* mind."

"Oh? Well, I simply wanted to tell you that I'm happy for you and Everett, and I hope we can all get along for the sake of my Ella."

I studied her for a moment before saying, "Okay. Thanks."

As I turned to resume our walk, she said, "I'm glad you agree, because as the mother of his only child and the only child he'll *ever* have, I will be in his life for a very long time."

I chuckled lightly as I picked a restless Nat up. "Okay. Well, nice talking to you."

"What's funny?" She sounded…disappointed.

"*You* are, trying to ruffle my feathers, intimidate me, scare me, make me believe you are this huge presence in Everett's life when every move you make has announced the fact that you are actually *not* a part of his life. You had to connive your way into spending Thanksgiving with him, he doesn't answer your calls, and it's almost embarrassing the way he dismisses you. You reek of desperation. You do not scare me. And that little dig about Ella being the only child he'll ever have? Um, okay…if you say so, but I'm young. Like, a lot younger than you. I mean, you could be my mom and my little girl's grandmother. Isn't that crazy?!" I threw in a giggle, but continued speaking before she could answer me. "Your eggs and stuff might be out of commission, but mine are in prime condition, just waiting to be fertilized by Everett. We've been practicing really hard for that. You know? And I've been enjoying every second of it!"

Before she could offer a rebuttal, the patio doors burst open and six feet, six inches of pure rage approached us. Instinctually, I laid Nat's head against my shoulder and covered her ear, because he just looked like he was about to curse Esther out.

He stood between us, facing her as he said, "You must be out your muthafuckin' mind out here talking to her!"

I peeked around his imposing frame to see her slanted eyes expand to twice their size. "We were just chatting since we'll soon be family."

"I don't know what language I need to say this shit in for you to get it, but I don't want nothing to do with you. *Ever.* You wanted to spend the holiday with Ella? Go do it! She's in the house, not out here. You stay the hell away from Jo!"

"W-what makes her so special?" There were tears in her eyes, but I just couldn't muster up any sympathy for her. She was a shit-starter. That was painfully obvious. And she was using her own child as a pawn in this game she was trying to play with Everett. I had no respect for that.

"Maybe because she didn't ruin my fuckin' life!"

When I saw Ella watching the action from the patio doors, I turned and continued my walk with Nat on my hip, knowing this family drama was about to boil out of control.

Fifteen minutes later, I was holding Nat's hand, letting her walk alongside me, when I heard the crunch of gravel behind me—the rapid footsteps of someone approaching us—and without turning around, I knew it was him. He fell in step beside us, reaching down and picking Nat up, much to her delight. He tossed her in the air and caught her, causing her to giggle loudly. "You got her walking all this way? Her legs are too short for that."

"She's too heavy to carry."

"No, she's not."

"I'm not a big tall man, so yes she is."

He nodded toward the two-story, white frame house we were now passing by. "This land is the first piece of real estate I ever bought.

Had this house built for my mom when I was just nineteen. My house here came later, after Esther and I broke up. Before I had this built for my mom, she was renting a duplex up the road, same duplex she raised me in. Five kids, two bedrooms." He shook his head. "We had a house before my dad passed. Lost it a year or so after that. He didn't have any life insurance and she didn't have any education, so she struggled, but she was a good mother. She was tall, big, and beautiful with the biggest heart. A good woman."

"It's a lovely house, and I know she had to be a good mother to have raised a man as good as you." As we passed the house, moving toward the tree line of a wooded area, I asked, "What happened to your father?"

"You mean how'd he die?"

I nodded.

"He was a truck driver. Fell asleep at the wheel and hit another semi. They say he died on impact. He was younger than I am now. Leland was just a baby when it happened. Kat was like in kindergarten. The twins were seven, I think, and I became the man of the house at eleven."

"That had to be a lot of pressure for a little boy to endure."

He shrugged. "I guess, but I didn't see it that way. My father was a good man, the best. I was honored to step into his shoes."

"And then you went on to take care of your whole family financially once you were able to, right? I read somewhere that you put all your siblings through college."

"I did what I could, tried to be there for everyone. Especially Leland, because we've just always been close. I always felt like I needed to take care of him."

"Is that why Leland hangs up under you?"

He glanced at me with a slight frown. "What do you mean?"

"Well, I've barely seen your other brothers since we've been here, and I know Kat's been visiting her husband's family this week, but Leland's been kicking it with you since he got in town, and I can tell he admires you."

"Yeah, well, I'm his big brother."

"Yeah, no point of reference here."

"Did you want siblings?"

"I just wanted a family."

He wrapped his free arm around my shoulders, pulling me close. "You got one now, and they're all back at our house. Albeit, they're dysfunctional as all get out."

I laughed. "How?"

"Leland don't want a woman unless her uterus is out of commission, and yeah, that might be him trying to be like me since I made the fatal mistake of marrying Esther. Nolan won't date anyone unless they need a green card, and Neil won't stop drinking and gambling long enough to date at all. Kat, she's good, I guess, but I don't think she and Wayne are as happy as they want folks to believe. Aunt Ever been shacking up with Uncle Lindell forever, because he didn't ever divorce his first wife from years ago. You won't get to meet him today, because he always spends the holidays with the kids he had before getting with Aunt Ever. And you ain't even met Aunt Wyvetta or Uncle Lee Chester, my mom's other sister and her brother, or my cousins Lunch Meat and Barbie. They all a trip."

"You didn't mention Esther. She seems to think she's your family, too."

"Jo—"

"I'm just messing with you, Tick."

"Don't do that."

"Man, you got like fifty names, but I think I like Tick the best!"

"Stop before you have Nat calling me that shi—stuff."

I giggled, and we continued walking the gravel road, now surrounded by nothing but trees.

"We good, baby?" he asked.

"Yeah. I mean, I'm not gonna lie. This situation is awkward, and it makes me feel like things with Ella are hopeless, and I really, really wanna pack my stuff and get my baby out of here."

"You do that, and I'll be right behind you. I don't wanna be around Esther's ass either, and you're the one who said she could come to dinner."

"Dinner! Not the whole day!"

He hung his head. "I know. She and Ella are—"

"Conspiring against me."

We were silent for a moment, then he stopped and turned around. Nat was limp in his arms, having been lulled to sleep by the extended time in nature. "I don't know what to do about Ella," he admitted.

My eyes were fixed on his. "I can imagine you don't. You've never been in this situation before."

"I want her to like you, but I'm not letting you go even if she never does. I wish I could *make* her like you, but she'll always have her mother in her ear. I—might have to have separate relationships with her and you, which will make days like this impossible. I just don't know…"

"I could, we could—"

"If you say that shit again, I'ma start to wonder if you're really just looking for a way out. Do you want me, Jo?"

My mouth dropped open. "You know I do! I love you!"

"Then stop tryna fucking leave me!" he thundered.

I jumped, my eyes scanning the woods around us for, shit, I don't know. He'd never raised his voice at me before. He had to be on edge. "I'm not trying to leave you. That's not what I want. I'm just trying to be practical and let you know I don't expect you to choose me over your child," I said softly. "And you don't have to yell at me."

Nat's little head had popped up, so he was bouncing her up and down, gently trying to get her back to sleep. "I'm sorry," he said, lowering his voice. "I'm frustrated. I want Esther to go. I want this day to be over."

"Me, too. We better head back. It'll be time for lunch soon."

He nodded and took my hand, leading us back to the house.

32

Everett

"Sis, I'ma let you know right now, you put your foot in this dressing! Ooowee!" Uncle Lee Chester boomed from across the table.

"Thank you," Aunt Wyvetta said, with a huge grin on her face. She was shorter than Aunt Ever, but just as wide and almost as good a cook. Aunt Ever's cooking repertoire was more comprehensive than her sister's, but Aunt Wyvetta was a dressing master.

"It really is good," Jo agreed. We were at the big table in the dining room along with my aunts, Everlina and Wyvetta, my uncle, Bridgette, and Leland. Nolan and Neil, Nolan's date, a bunch of my cousins, Ella, and Esther, plus Tommy were either in the kitchen or the great room. Toot's wife, Miko, had Nat in the great room feeding her. Miko was sweet, quiet, and loved kids. Nat took to her almost instantly.

That's the way we always handled holidays in my family, informal, but we made it a point to spend them together. I was glad Jo could be a part of it since she wasn't close to her family. I was also glad Esther wasn't in there with us. I was almost willing to pay folks to fill up the dining room table to keep her ass away from me.

"So, this is the one you was on TV fighting over?" Uncle Lee Chester's uncouth ass asked me.

"Lee, why you gotta put it like that?" Aunt Ever scolded.

"Hell, ain't that what happened? I saw it on that BET station. That damn channel ain't been the same since they got rid of Donnie 'Tight Eyes' Simpson. Anyway, you put a hurting on that man over this little girl, nephew!"

I shrugged. "Did what I had to do, Unc. That's all."

"Always could fight, though. Stayed in trouble for fighting in school. Was whooping everybody's ass," Uncle Lee said, following it up with his signature wheezing laugh.

Jo's head snapped in my direction. "You did?"

I nodded. "Bullies. They would mess with me about being fat. So I'd beat 'em up. They eventually got the message."

She gave me a sad look, like she was hurting for young me, and I gave her a smile before leaning in and kissing her cheek.

Uncle Lee reclined in his chair, patting his beer gut. "Well, she cute. Little old bitty thang. And light-skinned. Light-skinned women usually mean as a damn python."

"She sure in the hell is," I said through a chuckle.

Out of the corner of my eye, I saw Jo roll hers.

"Can't be too mean to allow your ex woman to spend the whoooole day here," Aunt Ever noted.

Bridgette slapped her hand over her mouth, her eyes inflated.

"It's okay. Ella wanted to spend the holiday with her," Jo said, sounding almost believable.

"Shit, wish I was a part of this new generation. Y'all men get away with anything now. Women willing to share…" Uncle Lee shook his head and sucked his teeth. "Must be nice."

Jo leaned across the table a little, her eyebrows damn near in her hairline. "I don't believe in sharing nothing, especially not Everett. I'm a mother, a divorced one, and I get wanting to be with your child during the holidays, but that's as far as it goes. This big man right here, the one y'all call Tick? I ain't got no sense when it comes to him. Trust and believe."

Aunt Ever fell out laughing, Aunt Wyvetta's eyebrows rose, Bridgette high-fived Jo, Leland chuckled, my ass was grinning from ear to ear, and Uncle Lee gave me an amused look. "Mean as a striped spider, ain't she? I told you," he said.

"I know, and I love it," I replied.

"I bet you do. Oh, got a call." He hit the button on his Bluetooth earpiece that had to be at least fifteen years old, and loudly answered the call with, "What-up-there-now?!" When he said it, it all ran together like one long word.

Bridgette sputtered to keep from laughing.

Jo looked up at me, and whispered, "I can't believe he has a Bluetooth earpiece. I haven't seen one of those in forever."

I leaned in close to her ear. "Shiiiiit, tell him he ain't fly."

She giggled.

"I'ma be there when I get there! You coulda come! Shit! Don't wanna do nothing but sit up in that house and watch *Family Feud*. I told you Steve Harvey don't want your ass...woman, I said I'll be there when I get there! Yeah!" Uncle Lee tapped the button again, shaking his head. For as long as I could remember, he and his wife, Aunt Lou, fought like cats and dogs.

"Ever, Lou crazy ass want me to bring her a plate," he said to his sister.

Aunt Ever nodded. "I'll fix her up a good one. Wish she'd have come to see us."

Uncle Lee shook his head. "Lou crazy as hell. Don't never wanna go nowhere. Nephew! Where you find little Jo at? How y'all meet?"

"Through her job. She worked for a jeweler, delivered a necklace I bought for Ella to me one day, and that was it. Couldn't get her off my mind."

"That's so sweet! You still work there, honey?" Aunt Wyvetta asked.

"No, ma'am. Too busy letting Everett drag me all over the country."

"On tour? I loved accompanying Everett on tour." I groaned inwardly at the sound of Esther's voice coming from behind me and Jo. I didn't even know she'd come into the room, but assumed she'd slid in through the door that led into the foyer.

Neil stepped inside the dining room holding a plate, surveyed the room, shook his head, said, "I ain't about to be in this shit," and backed into the kitchen where he'd entered the dining room from.

A second later, Nolan walked in from the kitchen, plate in hand, and leaned against a wall. He took a bite of something, his eyes shifting from me to Esther, then to Jo as if he was watching a damn tennis match.

Aunt Wyvetta, who never liked Esther anyway, said, "Where you from, Jo? I can tell you were raised in the south."

Jo smiled at my aunt. "Born and raised in Reola, Alabama, a little town not too far from Huntsville."

"Sho' nuff? We got people in Alabama. Who your people? What's your last name again?"

"Walker, but before I married my little girl's father, I was a Curry. My mom's name was April Curry, her parents are Leon and Oradean Curry. My aunt's name is Audrey Curry."

Damn, I'd just learned more about Jo's family than she'd shared in all the time I'd known her. Then again, I never pried about her family, figuring it was a touchy subject for her like Esther was for me.

"Who your daddy's folks?" Aunt Ever asked, taking over Aunt Wyvetta's interrogation.

"Um, well...I really don't know them, but his name is James Bright."

Damn, I was learning all kinds of stuff.

"Bright? Odd name," Aunt Wyvetta observed.

"Oh, not really. I know several Brights both here and in the UK. I think I'm related to some. Wouldn't it be funny if we were related?" Esther chimed in.

"Hilarious," Bridgette muttered.

"Have we met?" Esther asked.

"Nope. I try not to acquaint myself with desperate hoes. Sorry," Bridgette replied.

"Aww, yeah! That's what I'm talking about. This what I been waiting for. Some damn action!" Uncle Lee piped up. "Aw, shit! Got a call." He hit the Bluetooth button again. "What-up-there-now? Earl? Y'all playing cards? Slack leg-ass Willy there? Shit, I *keep* money! Got fifteen dollars on me right now! Yeah...yeah...uh-huh...I'll come through and kick some ass after I drop a plate off to Lou...Okay." He tapped the button again and fixed his eyes expectantly on Esther.

But I spoke up before she could. "Hey, Esther, Ella ain't in here."

"I know," she responded.

"Your little girl is so cute, Jo. Just a doll," Aunt Wyvetta cut in.

"Thank you," Jo replied.

I turned to face Esther, who was standing there holding a plate and a fork. Every time I looked up, this motherfucker was eating some of Jo's pineapple upside down cake. "You need to go find her so you can get in that quality time you crashed my holiday for."

I turned back around at the same time Aunt Wyvetta asked Jo, "So what you plan on doing with yourself after you two get married?"

"Um, besides raising my baby, I got some business opportunities I'm looking into."

"Really?" Aunt Wyvetta asked.

Jo nodded.

"She need to be in a studio. Jo got a voice you wouldn't believe," I interjected.

"Sho' nuff?" That was Aunt Wyvetta again.

"Evvv," Jo whined.

There was a gasp behind me—Esther. Her ass had not moved. "Is that what this arrangement is about? Music? You want to start producing or managing people and she's your first artist? Well, now I understand…it's business!"

Before I could respond, Jo twisted all the way around in her chair. "Arrangement? What this is about? What this is about is Everett running my ass down, relentlessly pursuing me, wooing me, and eventually loving me. It's about me loving him back. I don't care about singing. I care about being with him and raising my daughter, and you need to get over him. Goodness!"

"Oh. come on! You were with Bugz and now Everett? You sing? It's obvious what your angle is!" Esther said excitedly, like she'd just figured out the solution to some elusive problem.

"Shit! What-up-there-now? Hell, I said I'd bring you a plate! Damn! You worrying the shit out of me!"

While Uncle Lee argued with his wife, I said, "I tell you what, let me read some bullshit like that on one of them blogs, Esther. You don't want the shit you gonna get if I do."

"Are you threatening me?"

"No, I'm *promising* you."

"For you to be this angry, I must be right. She's using you and you're using her. I knew this couldn't be real. You with *her*? Willing to raise her child? Deal with her ex? Now I know why."

"You are as crazy as you look, you know that? You fly your ass all the way here to Texas to try to disrupt my life. Can't you see how pathetic it is that your ass hasn't let go in all these years? Let me make this clear: I. Don't. Want. You. I never will. I got who I want, and all your stupid ass plotting ain't gonna change that. Shit! Get a clue, Esther!"

The room fell silent, and Esther just stood there staring at me.

Jo turned to me. "I'ma go check on Nat. I'm sorry I talked you into letting her have dinner here. She's just..." She shook her head as she stood from the table.

"Mom, what's going on?" Ella asked timidly. I wasn't sure when she walked in the room.

Jo froze, her eyes on Esther. I guess she was waiting to see how she'd answer.

"Ella, say goodbye to your mom. If y'all wanna spend any more time together, you'll have to do it somewhere else," I said.

"Um..." Ella's eyes went from me to her mother.

"I just wanted answers. I needed to know why she was so special, special enough for you to break your promise to me," Esther said.

Seeing Jo make her move, I grabbed her wrist before she could leave the table. "I didn't promise you anything, Esther. Look, you're going down a road you don't wanna travel in front of Ella. You *know* you don't. But we can if you insist. I can handle it. Can you?"

She hesitated before turning to leave the room.

"Daddy—"

I shook my head. "You staying or going?"

"Uh-um, staying...but I think I should go check on her."

I nodded.

I stood, taking Jo's hand. "Let's go check on Nat."

As we left the dining room, I heard Uncle Lee Chester say, "Another damn call...what-up-there-now?!"

I tore my eyes from the door that joined our room to Nat's and squeezed them shut, trying to clear my head of the anxiety.

"Jo, you gotta relax. You gon' kill me down here."

My thighs were clenching his head, but it was hard to be in the moment with a house full of people. "I'm trying."

His tongue slid across my pearl and I jerked, letting my thighs fall open.

"Yeah, baby. Let me get in here," he murmured, his hot breath tickling my sensitive flesh.

"Oh!" I whispered as he slid a finger inside me. "Everett..."

"Uh-huh...."

His big tongue flattened and swiped up and down my treasure while he added another finger to my wetness. I bucked, thrusting my yoni in his face as he reached up and grasped my left nipple, twisting it gently. Now my mind was devoid of thoughts, full of static as the whirring between my legs increased. My heart was speeding out of control as his tongue lashed me and his fingers explored me. My back bowed from the bed as pure bliss hit me, sliding over me like hot water from a shower. I stiffened, holding my breath as the waves of pleasure washed over me, my fingers gripping my man's hair. Then I dropped my arms to my sides as my senses began returning to normal.

I felt him move, and seconds later, felt his breath on my face. The scent of my essence hit my nose, and his lips were on mine. He slid his tongue in my mouth, then slid his shaft inside me, causing me to gasp.

His eyes were closed, his mouth open as he glided out of me and slid back in. He whispered, "You got any idea how much I love you?"

I blinked, trying to figure out how I could answer him when he felt so damn good. "No...how much?" I whimpered.

"I love you so much," he said, his voice strained, "there's nothing I wouldn't do for you."

"Y-you'd die for me?"

"Today."

"Lie for me?"

"Right now."

"Kill for me?"

"In a heartbeat."

"Ohhhh, I'd do the same f-for youuuuu."

He kept with the relaxed pace, making me feel every inch of him. "Jo..."

"I wanna ride it," I murmured.

He stopped, no questions asked, and laid on his back beside me. I straddled him, taking him into my hand to guide him inside of me.

"Take your time, baby," he croaked. "I'll help you if you need me to. Just say the word."

I nodded, biting my bottom lip as I slowly sank down on him with a low moan. Squeezing my thighs to anchor myself, I lifted before sliding down on him again. I managed to control the pace and the depth of him, and it felt good, but I can't lie, I was breaking a sweat.

He reached up and grabbed the back of my head, pulling my face close to his. "You working too hard, baby. Relax. You ready for me to help?"

I nodded as he grabbed my ass and orchestrated my movements. I closed my eyes as I clutched his chest, leaning forward to suckle on his neck. This...this was different, a type of goodness I'd never felt before as his erection massaged me at different angles, varying depths. I moaned as pleasure galvanized my core and the building orgasm peaked, causing me to throw my head back with my mouth open. My breathing stalled as sensations rolled over me and abated. Then I collapsed on his chest. A second later, I was being rolled over onto my stomach and he was entering me from behind, easily sliding inside the drenched walls of my treasure. I buried my face in the mattress and whined almost uncontrollably as he increased the pace of his thrusts, softly groaning and grunting as the weight of his huge body hovered over mine. "Jo! Jo! Jo! Oooooo shiiiiiiit!" He shouted before I felt him expand inside me and stiffen before collapsing onto my back, his ragged breaths on the back of my neck. We lay there with me bearing his weight for a few minutes before he lifted off me, pulled out of my core while sucking air through his teeth, and fell onto his back, pulling me to him.

"You all right?" he asked.

I nodded. "Better than all right. I can still feel you, and you still feel good."

"Damn, baby. Really?"

"Mm-hmm, I'm no good for any other man now."

"That was the goal."

"Well, you met it."

"Shit, good."

"Hey, you didn't scream until the end. I don't know whether to be proud of you or concerned."

He chuckled. "Why would you be concerned?"

"I don't know. Maybe it ain't good to you no more."

"Nah, it's still nuclear as a mug. I was just trying to show you I could restrain myself. I almost made it."

"I'm surprised you didn't wake the house up."

"Aunt Ever went home. Ain't no one here but Tommy and Bridgette—who're probably somewhere screwing, themselves— Ella, who sleeps like a damn corpse, and Nat. And Nat ain't as light a sleeper as you think she is."

"Whatever. I'm gagging you next time."

"Why you ain't gag me this time?" He actually sounded

disappointed.

"Because you caught me off guard, waking me up licking me and stuff."

"Like that's the first time I've done it."

"But you have to add that to the fact that I'm not used to this house and there are other people here."

"We'll have to come visit more often, then. I mean, did you enjoy this trip at all?"

"Yeah."

"Esther being here just fucked it up, right?"

"Yeah, but that was my fault."

"Naw, I coulda said no anyway. Won't let that shit happen again."

"Ev?"

"Yeah, baby?"

"What exactly did you promise her? Why is she so convinced what we have can't be real?"

"For the same reason Bugz's ass won't get with the program. She's crazy. I didn't promise her a damn thing. In the heat of me catching her in her shit, I said I wouldn't do this love stuff again. Think I said fuck marriage, too. Didn't know she would see that as a pledge of fidelity. Esther is nuts and a sore-ass loser because I guess she thought there was a chance in hell of me taking her back. Everybody around me tried to tell me she wasn't shit. Wish I'd listened. Hell, she's the reason me and my friend, Keith, fell out. He tried to tell me about her and I wouldn't listen. Been too damn ashamed to reconnect with him since the divorce."

"I'm sorry, Everett."

"It's my fuck up, not yours."

"I know the feeling, though. So you never told her there was a chance you two would get back together?"

"Hell, no! You ever told Bugz you would wait for him?"

"Shit, no! What I look like?"

"Exactly. Man, I gotta talk to Ella. This mess cannot happen again. Ever."

"Yeah."

"Thanks for sticking with me through this bullshit over the last couple of days, baby."

"Where was I supposed to go? I only wanna be where you are."

"Got-*damn* I love you."

"I love you, too."

A few minutes later, I was almost asleep when I heard him say, "You hear that?"

"What?" I answered him groggily. "My coochie reverting back to its regular size?"

Laughter rumbled in his chest. "No. I heard a thud or something. You didn't hear it?"

"No."

We lay there for a moment before he shifted to leave the bed.

"Where you going?" I asked.

"To see what that was. Be right back."

"What could it be? No one can get through the gate or the security system."

He ignored me, turning a lamp on and searching the floor for his underwear. I sat up and grabbed his t-shirt, handing it to him as I slipped into my robe.

"Stay here, Jo."

"No, I'm checking on Nat."

"I'll check on h—"

This time, I did hear the thud and we both froze. It could've been anything or anyone, since we weren't in the house alone, but something felt off. Very off.

I couldn't tell where the sound came from, but watched as Everett turned toward the closet in the room, eyeing it briefly and then moving toward it. He stood there for a moment before snatching the door open. When I saw her, I almost screamed.

Everett's words echoed my thoughts. "What the fuck?!"

She shrank away from him, her eyes wild, mouth hung open. I could hear movement outside our door, then a knock. "Boss Man! Y'all good in there?"

"Hell, no!" Everett answered.

The doorknob jiggled, and the door opened. It was unlocked, because who was going to come in there but Nat? She was allowed to bust in there on us but she never did, because as paranoid as I was about her catching us in the middle of something, Everett was right. Once Nat went down, a tornado couldn't wake her up.

"What's going—you have got to be kidding me!" Tommy shouted. Bridgette was right behind him.

"What are you doing in my damn closet?!" Everett roared, sounding angrier than I'd ever seen him. "You left. How'd you get back in the house?!"

"Daddy?" Ella appeared in the doorway now as Tommy moved closer to Everett. Bridgette opened the connecting door to Nat's room and peeked at her before returning her attention to the melee in our room.

"Mom?!" Ella shrieked, upon seeing Esther still crouched in the damn closet.

"Did you record us?!" Everett shouted, ignoring his daughter. Not giving Esther time to respond, he snatched a cell phone from her hand, threw it against a wall, picked it up, and slammed it on the hard, mahogany floor. Then he kicked it somewhere and inched closer to Esther. "How the fuck did you get back in my house?!"

"I-I-I just needed to see for myself that this was real. I—"

"Mom...Daddy—"

"Ella, get out of here!" Everett screamed without turning around.

"I let her in!" Ella divulged, her voice trembling.

Everett spun around, deep grooves in his forehead. "What?!"

"She was so sad and...she called me crying, saying she didn't want to be alone in that hotel room, and after everyone went to bed, I let her in the gate and the house. She was sleeping in my room and was supposed to leave before anyone got up. Mom, what are you doing in here?"

Esther shook her head. "I—I still love your father. Everett, I can't help it."

Everett hung his head before gripping the back of his neck. "Ella...I don't even know what to say. I don't...just go back to bed right now."

"Daddy—"

"Go. Back. To. Bed."

With tears in her eyes, Ella hurried from the room, and everyone's attention returned to Esther.

"Tommy, can you go get whatever luggage or purse or whatever this motherfucker brought back in here and throw it outside?"

"Yeah, Boss."

"And call a damn cab."

"Got it." Tommy left.

Bridgette was still standing there, but I had a feeling she needed to leave, too, so I asked her to stay in Nat's room with her until things calmed down. She quickly agreed.

Once only the three of us were in the room, Everett said, "I knew you were a little off, but for you to connive your way back into my house, sneak in my room, hide in my closet, and watch me fuck my woman? Your ass needs to be institutionalized."

Esther shook her head. "She doesn't even know how to handle you. I saw—"

"Hear me, and hear me good! I don't want you! I only want her! What I got to say to make you understand this shit?!"

Esther and I both jumped.

"I'm getting a fucking restraining order against you. You come near me or Jo ever again and your ass is going to jail."

"We have a child together!"

"Who is a teenager! Like you said, she ain't a baby. I don't have to go through you to get to her. Esther, you are in my home without my permission. If I had a gun here, I'd be justified in shooting you. I could call the police. I got witnesses to you stalking me. But what I'm going to do, because of Ella, is let you leave. If any shit, if *anything* at all pops up on a blog about me and Jo, I'm going to make your life a living hell, spill all your shit. And don't forget, I got receipts. I don't give a fuck anymore!"

"I'm sorry," she whimpered.

"Get your sorry ass out my house!"

"My phone—I need a phone. How will I contact anyone like a car service when I get back to LA?"

"I look like I give a shit? Figure it out!"

He backed away from her enough for her to scurry out of the room. Tommy was outside the door with her things, and I watched as he followed her down the hall. I don't know what hit me, the invasion of my privacy or the fact that she was lurking around the house while my baby was there, innocent and asleep, but my skin began to burn and my eyes stung, and as Everett approached me asking if I was okay, all I could do was shake my head as the tears fell.

Everett

We took a private jet home the next day, two days earlier than planned. Jo was quiet, holding Nat in her lap as Bridgette sat beside her engrossed in her cell phone. I sat across from them trying to figure out how to fix this mess. Nolan, Neil, and Leland, who had a game in LA the next day and would've had to leave anyway, were on board, too, but I had no desire to talk to them, couldn't even laugh about Neil messing with Nolan about sending his girl home on a commercial flight. He kept calling her Svetlana when I don't even think that was anymore her name that it was that chick at the benefit's. Shit was all twisted up, and probably the only thing good about the situation was that Ella was so remorseful about letting her mom into the house, she'd been nice to Jo and Nat ever since we woke up this morning. She was on the plane, too, off to herself, staring out a window. I tore into her before the sun was up, but she obviously saw the wrong in what she did anyway.

When Bridgette left her seat, I quickly claimed it, leaning in close to Jo, and asking, "You all right?"

She looked at me with red-rimmed eyes and nodded. "You okay?"

"Honestly, no. It's my job to protect you and Nat. I'm doing a poor job of it, huh?"

She shook her head. "If what she did is your fault, then all the crap Sid has done is my fault."

"I guess you got a point."

She sighed. "How is it that we both have these insane exes that won't let go?"

"Yours is more talk than anything. Mine? I don't even know what to say. She's fuc—freakin' psychotic."

"Yeah. I just…I feel dirty knowing she was watching us, listening to our pillow talk. And she saw me struggling to ri—"

"Fuck-forget what she said. She was trying to get under your skin. What she saw was us enjoying each other, us doing something she evidently misses. I'm serious, fu—dam—forget her, and please don't let this change us. You got every right to run from this, but I'm begging you not to." My eyes fell to Nat, who was thankfully engrossed in something on Jo's iPad.

"I love you, Ev. I can't just up and leave you, but I'm not gonna act like I'm not weirded completely out. I-I feel violated."

"So do I. I'm getting that restraining order, though. I meant that."

Jo nodded, and then closed her eyes, effectively ending the conversation. I wasn't sure if she believed me. I'd just have to show her how serious I was.

33

So I guess this negro really forgot.

From the time we climbed out of bed until now, I'd been waiting for his black ass to say it. He'd said, "Good morning," "You sleep well?" "You hungry?" "You sore?" And his all-time favorite, "Can I have some pussy?" Yeah, I gave him some, but anyway, he had not once uttered the words, "Happy birthday." I was so mad, I couldn't think straight. He could remember everything else, including the lyrics to his million and one songs, but remembering my birthday was just too much.

I'd been pouting—yes, pouting—the whole day. Sure, Bridgette had called, and so had Shirl despite the fact that I hadn't kept in touch with her like I should've, but no one had come to visit or brought me a gift, and with the man who declared his love for me damn near every hour of the day not mentioning it, this was turning out to be an especially sucky birthday.

He was at his studio right now, had spent most of the day in his office at the house, and I'd just been sitting around watching Nat play and staring at my Instagram feed. I was still news, or rather the subject of much speculation, but nothing was being posted along the lines of what Esther witnessed while her insane ass was holed up in that closet. I guess she had sense enough to adhere to the restraining order. Yeah, Everett actually got one. I'm telling you, that lawyer of his was no joke. The restraining order covered me and Nat as well as Everett, and I wasn't even present in the courtroom when it was issued. She was forbidden from contacting any of us. If she wanted to talk to Everett about Ella, she had to do it through their lawyers. I was glad about it, because I still felt some kind of way about her watching us have sex. That was just beyond sick.

Everett asked if I wanted to get one against Sid, but I declined. Sid talked a lot of shit but had proven he wouldn't and *couldn't* bust a grape. Plus, I held on to hope that he'd one day be a decent father to Nat. We'd have to be able to communicate freely for that to happen. I had come to realize that Sid was essentially a harmless shit-talker who liked to get under people's skin. Esther was unhinged.

But when my phone buzzed and Sid's name appeared on the screen, that restraining order started sounding really sweet, because I was in no mood to deal with his crazy. "Hello." My voice was deadpan. I was just over *everything*.

"Aye, just wanted to wish you a happy birthday."

I took the phone from my ear and stared at it. He remembered?

"Jo? You there?"

"Yeah...um, thank you?"

"You're welcome, baby. Hey, I miss you."

I sighed. "Sid, don't—"

"It's all good. Just wanted you to know. Nat okay?"

He said her name and there wasn't an audience present? "Uh, yeah. She's good. I'm in her room watching her play right now."

"She like it there? At the new house?"

"She does."

"You like it?"

"Yes, I do."

"That's good. Hey, send me a picture of her playing."

"Uh...okay."

We talked for a few more minutes with him asking a bunch of questions about Nat, like what kind of toys she liked, because he wanted to get her some stuff for Christmas. He even apologized for not getting her anything before now. I hung up the phone feeling hopeful that this was his first step in the right direction and spent the next few minutes snapping pictures of Nat.

"Hey."

I looked up to find Everett in Nat's doorway. As usual, she abandoned what she was doing and ran to him. As he picked her up and tossed her in the air, I finished selecting a picture from the ten or so I'd just taken of Nat and sent it to her father. Then I looked up and gave him a halfhearted, "Hey."

"What's wrong with you?" his clueless ass asked.

"Nothing, Ev. Absolutely nothing."

"Good. Call Ms. Young and see if she can watch Nat-Nat for us tonight. I wanna go out." Ms. Young was our new backup sitter, the once-ill friend of Ms. Sherry's that Nat had visited several times. She was no Ms. Sherry, but she was just as kind and caring when it came to Nat. Before I could ask, he added, "I already talked to Ms. Sherry. She's busy."

Hope blossomed in my heart. If he wanted to go out, maybe he remembered. "What's the occasion?" I asked.

"I gotta have a reason to take my lady out?"

"No. I just thought there was one."

He walked over to where I sat at the foot of Nat's bed and kissed my forehead. "Nope. Call her."

I sighed. "What if I don't wanna go out?"

"You don't?"

Shit, I wanted to. I was tired of sitting around the house, no matter that it was a mansion, and feeling sorry for myself. "I'll call Ms. Young."

We had dinner at Ilbert's in the same private room where we had our first date. I was quiet as I enjoyed my lobster bisque, memories of me arriving late and absolutely inundated with nervousness at having a date with *Big South* filling my mind. Then, I didn't understand his attraction to me. I still didn't to a large degree, but I knew what he felt for me was genuine.

He did most of the talking and I tried to engage with him, telling myself that he had been good to me and he loved me like no one had before. Yes, he forgot my damn birthday, but it wasn't the end of the world. Shit, I was sure my biological father had forgotten I even existed. Everett could get a pass this one time.

He held my hand as we left the restaurant and climbed into the back of his SUV with Tommy behind the wheel. I was ready to go home and get it on, because forgetful or not, Everett looked fine as hell in his jeans and white t-shirt.

When Tommy stopped at the back entrance of Everett's club, Second Avenue, I frowned. "What are we doing here? I thought we were going home."

"I didn't say we were going home, did I?" He was staring at his phone as he answered me.

"No, but I thought that's where we were going."

"You in a hurry to get home? Something you need to do?" he asked, glancing up at me.

Yeah, you. "I don't know...why are we here?"

"I need to check on something. You wanna come in?"

I fell against the back of the seat, crossing my arms over my chest. "No."

"The hell wrong with you?"

"Absolutely nothing, Everett. Nothing at all. Not a damn thing is wrong with me."

He chuckled lightly. "I'll be right back. You and your funky little attitude can wait here."

I turned and stared out the window. "Whatever."

He leaned in and kissed my cheek. "Be right back, mean ass."

I wiped my cheek with my shoulder, refusing to look at him as he opened the door, laughing while telling Chink—one of our new bodyguards, a Puerto Rican giant—to follow him. I watched as Chink slid out the front passenger seat. Tommy remained behind the wheel. I wanted to cry but didn't let myself. He actually forgot my birthday...like, for real.

Damn.

I'm not sure how long I sat there fighting tears before hearing Tommy say, "Aye, Boss Man wants us in there."

I blinked a couple of times before checking my phone. "He texted you?"

"Yup."

"Why didn't he text me?"

"I'ont know. I just know what he sent me."

I blew out a breath, then sent Everett a text: *You can't text me? Why you sending messages through Tommy like you don't know my number?*

Everett: *My bad. U coming in? I'ma be a minute. Don't want u sitting out there too long.*

I sat there for a minute before snatching the door open, and mumbling, "This motherfucker…"

"Whoa, whoa, whoa!" Tommy said. "You tryna get me fired? You know you can't get out this car without me shadowing you. Boss don't play that shit."

Yeah, well, fuck your boss.

Even as the thought echoed in my mind, I waited for Tommy to come around the truck. As we stepped inside through the back door, Tommy told me we were going to the office, where we found Chink standing guard. Once inside, I gave Nolan a feeble greeting before settling my eyes on Everett.

"I'm here," I said.

He grinned at me, then turned to his brother, and said, "She so damn mean."

"Man, what'd you do?" Nolan asked. "She looks like she wants to slap the shit outta you."

Tilting my head to the side, I asked, "Yeah, what did you do, *Everett?*"

He stood from his seat on the edge of Nolan's desk and approached me. "I'm sure you'll let me know. Come on. I wanna show you something."

As he grabbed my elbow and led me away from the office, I asked, "And then can we go home?"

He moved in close to my ear as we continued walking. "You tryna fuck, ain't you?"

Before I could answer, a bright light hit my face and a mixture of voices screamed, "Surprise!"

I jumped, my eyes adjusting to the light enough to see the floor of the club filled with people, then shifting to a smiling Everett. We were on the stage. I was so mad at him, I didn't realize that was where he was leading me.

"Happy birthday, Jo!" he said, laughter in his eyes. "Your little ass thought I forgot, didn't you?"

I turned back to the crowd, and that's when the tears fell. I'd never had a real birthday party. *Ever.* Covering my face with my hands, I sobbed like a baby. Then I felt Everett's arms around me and heard the crowd's "Awwwww."

"Hey, hey, it's all right," Everett soothed.

Wrapping my arms around him, I whimpered, "Thank you."

"Come on. Let's go sit down," he said, before grabbing the mic from the stand in front of us, and announcing, "I'ma get the overwhelmed birthday girl to our table. Come wish her happy birthday."

Amid cheers and applause, we made it to a booth and sat down. Everett ordered me a Blue Hawaiian, and I didn't object to drinking alcohol, gulping it down as soon as it arrived to settle my nerves from the impact of this surprise.

"Your ass was thirty-eight hot at South!" Bridgette teased, as she slid into the booth and hugged me. "I could tell on the phone earlier."

I rolled my eyes. "So you were in on this?"

"Of course! I'm the one who invited everybody."

"Who all is here?"

"Viv, Hera, Sage, Ms. Shirl from Bijou Park, Teki and Meek from the donut shop you used to work at. Our old roommate, Debbie, Marie from that cell phone store you worked at a few years back. Carmen from back home. I meant to tell you she moved out here. Um, and Ms. Sherry, but South invited her."

"Wow! No wonder she couldn't babysit. But hey, this place is packed. Who are all these other people?"

Bridgette shrugged. "Friends of your man, I think."

"And my brothers and sister, plus their dates," Everett added.

G-Eazy's *No Limit* began to play, and I automatically started twerking in my seat because that's what that song evokes—involuntary twerking. Leaning in close to Everett, who was talking to some dude I didn't recognize, I asked, "You mind if I hit the dancefloor with Bridge?"

"Naw, it's your party, baby. Do you."

We left the booth and were stopped by several well-wishers, including Nolan, who stopped me to introduce me to his Russian date—a different one from the one I met at the benefit and the other one I met at Thanksgiving—Kat and her husband, who both looked unhappy, Leland, who was there with a woman that looked like the president of someone's PTA, a drunk Neil, and a bunch of folks I didn't even know before we finally made it to the dancefloor in time for Cardi B's verse. I danced so hard, I bumped into Kendrick Lamar. Yeah, motherfucking Kendrick Lamar was at my party. I played it cool, though, apologizing and turning around to see Bridgette's eyes wide with shock.

As we continued dancing, she leaned in, and said, "I will never get used to this shit."

"Me either," was my response.

After the song ended, I headed back to my booth while Bridgette went on a mission to, in her words, "bag one of South's rich-ass friends." She didn't get far before Tommy's supposed-to-be-bodyguarding-ass caught up with her. I didn't know what they were supposed to have going on, and she wouldn't speak on it, but he was feeling her. That was plain to see.

There was a piece of birthday cake waiting on the table for me—pineapple cake. Taking a bite, I scooted close to Everett, who wrapped his arm around my shoulder and kissed me.

"Hey, I have a confession," I yelled over the music.

He lifted his eyebrows. "What's that?"

I pressed my mouth to his ear. "The only reason I eat pineapples all the time is because Bridgette told me they make your coochie taste good."

"You think I haven't figured that out?"

My mouth fell open.

He nodded. "Uh-huh...why you think I keep feeding 'em to you? Now, eat up so I can do some birthday pussy-eating when we get home."

I shook my head and took another bite of cake. "You're silly."

"Mm-hmm. I see your ass is eating that cake, though."

"You just forgot about me, huh?!" a familiar voice shouted.

I scooted out of the booth and wrapped Shirl in a hug. "I'm so glad to see you!"

"Mm-hmm. You look good, happy."

"I am!"

"Well, I miss you at work, but I'm glad you left. And I'm glad about *that*." She nodded toward Everett. "Girl..."

I giggled. "Let me introduce you to *that*."

"Finally!"

And that was how the night went, tons of people wishing me a happy birthday, me introducing them to Everett, and him introducing me to his friends. There were so many people there, famous people and their bodyguards mixing with my common friends and my common self. It was surreal.

I was feeling nice, having downed three of those Blue Hawaiians, when Everett asked me, "You ready for your gifts?"

"This party isn't my gift?"

He shook his head, pulling a gift box I hadn't noticed from under the table. A small crowd gathered in front of our booth as I untied the big red bow that held the gold box together and lifted the lid. Inside were several open-ended airline tickets with various departure dates, tickets to Bora Bora, Venezuela, Rio, Bali, Maui, and Venice. My misting eyes crawled up to meet his. "Ev..."

"I made a plea deal for that charge in New York. Gotta go back before the judge to seal it, but I got some community service to do, probation for a few months, and as soon as that's over, we're taking these trips after the European leg of my tour if the judge okays me traveling overseas for it. I didn't put tickets to England or Germany or France in there, because those are tour stops and you'll be with me anyway. I told you I was gonna show you the world, and I will…starting with these." He gestured toward the tickets.

I was crying again as I thanked him. He pulled me to him, and said, "Hold on. I got you something else."

I nodded, wiping my eyes. He pulled his phone from his pocket, tapped on the screen a few times, and held it in front of my face. On it was a picture of a headstone with my mom's name on it.

"You gotta give them the dates to put on it, but it's paid for. Bought it at a place close to your hometown. The guy at the monument shop said he knew your mom, knows where her grave is—"

I covered his mouth with mine, kissing him long and hard before grabbing his face, and saying, "Thank you! Thank you! Thank you!"

After that, I was all over him, my hormones having revved up from his beautiful gifts. And from what I felt when I placed my hand on his thigh, he was revved up, too. He'd told me we could go to VIP if at any time I wanted some privacy, so once I reached my boiling point, I told him I wanted to go upstairs. Once inside the only room up there since the other part of VIP in his club consisted of open, roped-off areas, I had Everett lock the door and I attacked him before he could sit down good, sucked his dick like I was trying to detach it from his body, had him screaming like a twelve-year-old white girl named Molly. Then I rode him—something I had gotten good at, because practice makes perfect—until we were both howling like maniacs. After we got ourselves together, I was ready to hit the dancefloor again.

It was a good night, the best night. A *perfect* night. And I owed it all to one Everett "Big South" McClain.

34

Sid was on his way to drop off Nat's Christmas gifts. Plus, we'd been texting back and forth for a week or so, and surprisingly, he hadn't said anything stupid, so of course I was happy, but cautiously so. With him, you never knew when he was going to switch up on you.

Standing in the foyer staring out one of the huge windows, I wrung my hands and bit my bottom lip. I was taking a chance letting him come to our house, had to convince Everett it was a safe choice, and really hoped Sid didn't make me regret the decision.

"Damn, you act like you waiting on a date or something."

I turned to face Everett, rolling my eyes. "Don't do that. I'm just...nervous. He's been acting like he has some sense, but you never know. Seeing the house, my car? I'm afraid that might trigger his crazy side or something."

"Well, if it does, we got armed security on the property. I'ma have them outside watching this whole gift delivery thing. His ass makes one wrong move and it's over."

"Well, damn...I'm glad I took Nat to Ms. Sherry's. I did it because I didn't want her to see the gifts in case Sid brings them unwrapped, but I'd also hate for her to see him get gunned down for smiling at me."

With a smirk on his face, he said, "Whatever. His ass just better come correct, 'cause I'll be out there with you." He gave me a look that said he expected me to protest.

Instead, I said, "Okay."

He stumbled backward and grabbed his chest. "You ain't gonna fight me on it?" Moving closer, he placed a hand on my forehead. "You a'ight? Sick?"

I slapped his hand away. "You're an asshole."

"So I've been told."

"Look, I don't wanna be alone with him any more than you want me to. I don't have time for him to get the wrong idea and think this is a date or something since he likes to act like we are still in a relationship sometimes."

His phone dinged with a text, and after staring down at it for a second, he looked up at me, and said, "Tommy just buzzed him in the gate. Let's go."

We stepped outside onto the driveway and watched as Sid's Range Rover stopped in front of us. Everett moved behind me as Sid hopped out and walked to the back of his truck to get the gifts.

From the sides of us, I noticed Tommy and Chink approaching. Oba—yes, *that* Oba—who Everett had stolen from Peter Park because I was familiar with him, stood behind us on the front steps. All eyes were on Sid, who was now approaching me with a couple of beautifully-wrapped boxes.

"Damn," he said. "Y'all got an army in this bitch, huh? All these big motherfuckers out here…"

I took the boxes from him. "Thanks so much. Nat is going to be thrilled," I said, ignoring his statement. Yes, the security was excessive, but what did he expect after the show he put on at the National Hip Hop Awards?

"'Sup, South?" Sid said, giving Everett a backwards nod.

"'Sup? Hey, Chink! Come get these boxes. Got anymore, Bugz?" Everett asked.

"Yeah, 'bout five more. Shit, dude can just come get 'em out my truck if that's cool with you."

"Yeah, that'll work," Everett replied, probably wanting to limit Sid's contact with me as much as possible.

I was watching Chink unload Sid's truck, aware that Sid's eyes were on me and praying that he didn't have some kind of relapse and try something dumb in front of Everett. When he moved closer to me, I held my breath. As soon as he placed a hand on my arm, I heard movement and voices.

"Aye, man! Get your got-damn hands off her!" That, of course, was Everett.

"Yo! Back up!" came from Tommy.

Chink dropped the boxes he was carrying and grabbed his gun.

Oba's gigantic ass had made it down the steps and was in between me and Sid.

Sid stumbled backward with his hands raised in the air. "Damn! Shit! Can I talk to her for a second? I just wanna talk! The fuck?!"

My eyes danced all over the place before I turned and looked at Everett, waiting for him to respond.

"The hell you got to talk to her about that you need to be that close?" Everett asked.

"Ev—" I tried.

"Natalie! I need to talk to her about Natalie!" Sid shouted. "Just a second. That's it. Right over here." He pointed toward the hood of his vehicle.

I reached up and kissed Everett. "It's okay. You can still see us."

He sighed and nodded.

Once we were at his truck, Sid nearly whispered, "Hey, I just wanted to tell you I realized I went about this the wrong way with you. I ain't never tell you I'm sorry for what I did with Sonya and everything. You know, leaving you and shit. I shouldn't have called you a bitch at South's party, either. All of that was my bad, Jo. I just—you was a good wife. I wanted you to know that."

"Oh…thank you, but I thought you wanted to talk about Nat?"

"I obviously couldn't tell that big muh-fucker the truth, could I? Hey, if this don't work out with him, I hope you'll give us another try."

"Uh, that would be a no. Even if I wasn't in love with Everett, there are just some things I can't forget, you know? But thanks for the apology and for stepping up where Nat is concerned."

"Yeah, yeah, no problem. Hey, what if I leave Sonya? I mean, I stay with her because she lets me do what I want. Hell, I could fuck you on top of her and she wouldn't flinch, but I'll leave her for you, if I can have you back. Say the word."

"You can leave her, but you still won't get me back. I'm getting married, Sid."

He hung his head a little. "Shit, okay. Look, I'ma be on the road Christmas day, but I'ma Skype Nat or something, a'ight?"

"That sounds good."

"I love you, Jo. I mean that. I'm glad you're happy, even if it ain't with me."

"Thanks, Sid. That means a lot."

*****

I might have been nervous as hell about this meeting, but I don't think anyone could tell. Sitting next to Everett's lawyer, who was now also my lawyer, I felt like a boss and tried to look like I belonged at the table with these people. My lawyer, Adam Henderson, a handsome piece of dark chocolate in a tailored suit, had negotiated a sweet licensing deal for me with Glam On It Cosmetics. There would be a line of seven long-lasting, no-smear lip glosses to be known as the Mrs. South collection despite the fact that one, I wasn't even married to Everett yet, and two, South wasn't Everett's real last name. I had to admit the name was cute, though, and they let me pick and name my lip gloss shades, including a gorgeous peach color that I named Audacious April after my mom. I named the other colors in my small collection Reola Red, Natalie Nutmeg, Bridgette Bronze, Just Like Candy Coral, Sienna Sage, and Mrs. South Magenta.

Excitement does not describe what it felt like to be there, giving my input about packaging and everything else surrounding this line of lip gloss. Photo shoots were scheduled, as well as follow-up meetings with their marketing department. The line was launching in a month or so, and I couldn't wait. Maybe Everett was right. Maybe this was what I was made for, being a damn boss!

I thanked Mr. Henderson profusely as we left the building with Bridgette and Oba following closely behind us. Everett had offered to come, too, but I asked him not to. He had plenty of his own business ventures to deal with, and I didn't want to burden him with mine, too. I had to work hard not to feel bad about him being the only reason these opportunities were afforded to me, and him being there would be a constant reminder of that fact and throw me off my game. I definitely didn't need that.

"Don't forget about our meeting with S.H.E. Athletics next week," Mr. Henderson reminded me. "The Lady South sneakers."

"Oh, I won't let her forget," Bridgette chirped. I had never seen her so giddy and not only because I'd named a lip gloss after her. When I asked her to be my assistant a few days earlier, I was scared she'd curse me out for even thinking about asking her to do it, that she'd think I thought I was above her or something. But she saw it in the spirit that I meant it—me moving up in the world and wanting to take her with me. When I told her what I was willing to pay her every month and presented her with the first check, she pulled out her phone and quit her job on the spot. I promised her she would still have time to pursue her acting career. I wasn't trying to step on her dreams, I just needed someone to help me keep everything straight now that I was a mother, an entrepreneur, *and* Big South's woman. Shoot, being his woman alone required an assistant to help me keep track of the events I had to attend with him.

"Girl, that was fun! Thank you for bringing me along!" Bridgette gushed, once we were in my truck.

"Girl, that's your job now, to follow my ass around."

She giggled. "Right! And I took a ton of notes for you."

"Good. My head was spinning in there. I'm sure I forgot something that was said."

One thing I figured out really quickly after Everett started insisting that I always have security with me when I leave the house is that it's easier to just let the bodyguard drive, so we were in the back and Oba was at the wheel. Now I got why Everett always had Tommy driving him around. Made more sense than taking more than one vehicle everywhere or chauffeuring your own bodyguard.

"You know what? Oba, let's head to Rodeo. I feel like some celebratory shopping."

"Got you, Boss Lady," he replied. Wow, I was really Oba's boss, or at least my man was. Life was crazy!

"Yes, bish! You better spend that Mrs. South shmoney!" Bridgette squealed. "Girl, you've got the best life now and my ass is taking notes on that, too! One, find a fine, sexy rapper who can't take his eyes off you. Two, put that kitty cat on him real good. Three—"

I could see Oba smirking in the rearview mirror, so I turned to Bridgette, and said, "If you shut up, I'll buy you some Loubs."

She raised her eyebrows and fell against the back of the seat. "Hell, just call my ass Helen Keller, then."

Everett

I was heading down the stairs when my phone started buzzing in my hand. I'd slept through most of the morning after spending a late night in the studio, and Jo was still gone. I would've dragged myself out of bed and gone to that meeting with her, but she wanted this to be her thing and didn't want to trouble me with it. I was proud of her, of how she was coming into her own, becoming a boss, and a sexy-ass one at that.

"Hello?" I answered, activating the speakerphone so I could answer Jo's *Your woman is officially a boss* text.

"Ev! Man, I been trying to get you all morning!" Leland shouted into the phone.

"My bad, man. Slept in. Long night in the studio."

Me to Jo: *Shit, u was always bossy as hell anyway.*

"What you working on? Didn't you just put an album out?" Leland asked.

"That's like me asking you why you still practice. Don't you already play for the NBA? This is what I do. It's my job and it keeps me sane."

Jo: *Whatever. You like my bossiness.*

"Yeah, I guess I can see that. How's the wife?" Leland asked.

I chuckled. He'd been calling Jo my wife since he met her at the benefit. "She's good. She had that meeting with Glam On It today. Just texted me to let me know she signed on the dotted line."

Me to Jo: *I do. Hey, congrats baby. I'm proud of u.*

"That's what's up! Tell her congrats for me. Can't believe you ain't with her. I didn't think you ever let her out of your sight, the way you are about her."

Jo: *Thank you. What you doing there without me and Nat? Miss us?*

Me: *Hell no.*

Jo: *Lmao!! Lying ass. Be home after I do a little shopping with Bridgette. Love you.*

That text was followed up with about ten heart emojis and some water droplets.

Me: *Love ur freaky ass 2. Hurry up and come home.*

"Ev! You still there?"

"Yeah, I'm here. What you tryna say? I'm sprung or something?"

"No, I'm saying you sprung like a motherfucker!" He laughed into the phone.

"Man, shut your ass up. You called me to mess with me about my woman because you ain't got one? What happened to old Bertha I met at Jo's party? She break her hip or something? They won't let you sign her out the nursing home anymore?"

"First of all, you dumb motherfucker, her name is Janet, and we decided to take a break. She was getting too damn clingy, asked if I wanted kids. Shit, she's forty-five! The hell she want more kids for?"

"She already got kids?" I was in the kitchen now, trying to find something to eat. Jo didn't want a cook, but we were gonna have to do something. Ordering food all the time was messing with my diet. I wasn't trying to go back to being Tick.

"One. A girl. I think she's my age."

"And you don't see a problem with that?"

"Nope."

"Man, you a trip with them old women." I grabbed some grapes and sat at the kitchen table. "Hey, what happened at that game last week? Been meaning to ask you about that. Was that shit with Armand Daniels for real?"

"Yeah. He's a hot head. Always wants to fight someone when we lose. I guess he chose me last Thursday. To be honest, I'm tired of his ass, but the owners love him."

"The kid's got talent. You can't dispute that."

"Yeah, but he's a ball hog and an asshole. Got no respect for anyone. You know, I'll be a free agent at the end of this season. I'm seriously weighing my options."

"For real? You thinking about leaving Miami? You love that team, man."

"I loved the Clippers, too, and I left them. I always know when it's time to move on. Feels like it's that time again."

"Word? You thinking about St. Louis? I know they been looking at you."

"I don't know. Maybe. I just know it's either make a move or get fined and shit for beating Daniels' ass on the court. Dude irks the shit outta me."

"Yeah...I feel you. Well, you know I got your back. Wherever you go, they gonna get a new fan in me."

"'Preciate it, Ev. Aye, but here's what I called you for. Neil."

I sighed, chewed a grape, and said, "He at it again?"

"Yep, tried to hit me up for five G's, man. Talking about some investment. But I didn't fall for it. Just giving you a heads-up."

I shook my head. "The last time he came to me with that weak shit, I shut him down. He probably won't be calling me. What'd you say to him?"

"I told him to stop that damn gambling."

"But you ain't give him anything?"

"Didn't I say I didn't?"

"But you wanted to?"

Leland sighed into the phone. "Man, Ev. Shit, it's hard. I mean, I didn't give him anything, but what if he owes some crazy muh-fucker? I don't know...he ain't been right since he and Emery broke up. Her leaving him really messed his head up."

"Yeah, I know. Look, Leland, you do what you feel is right and I'ma do the same thing. I love Neil just like I love all y'all, and I know he's still getting over his girl, but I've done enough. I put him through college, bought his first, second, and third cars, bought him a house, even gave his ass a business, just like I gave Kat one, and—"

"And me one, too, huh?"

"Nah, you made it into the NBA all on your own. I ain't have nothing to do with that."

"Yeah, you did. You paid for all my gear from the time I was like seven or eight, paid for me to go to the best basketball camps and private high schools, paid for my tutors so my test scores would be good enough to take advantage of the scholarships they were throwing at me, encouraged me, believed in me. You definitely gave me a career, Ev."

I shrugged. "Just did what was right, what Daddy would've done if he'd been there. He was a good man, Leland. One of the best. Wasn't nothing he wouldn't do for us."

"Yeah, wish I'd known him."

"Me, too." I paused for a second and then continued, "But look, like I was saying, I gave him that business, one of the few independent book stores that are still in the black, and I offered to get his ass some counseling and pay for rehab, but he refused. I just can't do no more. I'm tryna build a family, here. I can't keep bailing Neil's grown ass out of trouble forever."

"I hear you, and I know you're right. He gotta stop this shit."

"Yeah, man." I glanced down at the notifications filling the screen of my phone—IG, Twitter, Facebook. Several were popping up every second.

"So, you ready for this game tonight? Y'all in Memphis, right? You think y'all gonna win?"

"Man, it's always my goal to win, and I *stay* ready."

Before I could respond, a text from Tommy popped up on my phone: *Boss man, you seen that video yet?*

I frowned. "Good to hear, man. Hey, let me hit you back."

"A'ight. I'll holla' at you later."

I texted Tommy back: *What video?*

I'd basically destroyed Esther's phone that night, but the video she made could've been on her cloud. If she released that shit, her ass was mine. Then again, it couldn't have been much more than voices. It was too dark in the bedroom for her to capture a decent image, but my voice was recognizable. If that motherf—

Tommy: *Of Jo and old dude.*

I froze in my seat. Jo and what dude?

Me: *What dude? What they doing?*

While I waited for Tommy to reply, I went to my IG notifications. Tons of folks had tagged me. I clicked on like ten of the notifications but kept getting a message that the content had been removed and wondered what the hell was going on. Then I decided to check my DMs, and that's when I saw it.

I picked the phone up and brought it closer to my face, hoping that maybe I was just seeing things, but it was her. Freckles, sandy red hair, and eventually, I saw the gap in her teeth.

I dropped the phone like it was boiling hot and stood from my seat, grabbing the back of my head. I could see texts pop up from Leland, Nolan, and Kathryn, all asking if I'd seen the video. I ignored the calls from Courtney and Neil. I'm not sure how long I stood there and stared at the phone before picking it up and watching the video again. Then I wondered if there was more, maybe another video? My damn head started feeling tight and shit as I checked other DMs to find stills of the video and a bunch of other pictures that I didn't click on. Then I went back to the video, her mouth on some nigga, giving him what I was used to receiving from her.

Jo's eyes kept flickering open and closed as she gave some guy head, smiling every now and then and showing that gap. I could hear him moaning and mumbling something. The video was long as hell, or maybe it wasn't. Maybe it felt long because I was watching the woman I loved suck another man's dick. I clicked off the video and went back to the pics. Nudes, all of them with her legs wide open. She was playing with herself in a couple of them. Upon close inspection, I could tell they were old, taken before Nat was born because her breasts were perky in them and she didn't have that little stomach pouch she had now. Was the video old, too? I couldn't tell, because all you could see was her mouth, her hand, and his...dick.

Shit.

I fell back into the chair and kind of just stared into space, watched the video one more time, focused on the mumbling voice, and realized I recognized it.

Tommy: *Jo outside. Oba and Bridgette can't get her out the truck. She won't move.*

All kinds of shit was filling my brain. I needed a timeline for the video. I needed to know it was made before us. It had to be, right? I mean, she hadn't been messing with him, had she?

I blew out a breath and told myself to stop tripping. Jo wasn't a cheater or a ho'.

That's what you thought about Esther, too.

I quickly shook that thought off. Jo was no damn Esther. Not by a mile.

Leaving my phone on the table, I headed outside to find Jo's truck sitting in front of the house. Oba was standing by the open back door with his head lowered, and as I moved closer, I could see Bridgette beside Jo, softly talking to her.

"Jo...baby? Uh, what's going on?" I tried to play it cool, but I know I was sounding crazy.

She lifted her head as she rubbed her own arms, probably to ward off one of her itching fits. That's when I saw the tears. "You don't know? You didn't see?"

I glanced around the backseat of the truck. There weren't any sacks and Oba wasn't holding any, either. So I guessed this shit had hit before she had a chance to buy anything. Fixing my eyes on her again, I asked, "S-see what?"

"The video of me and Sidney. He-we were married back then. I-I trusted him. I'm his daughter's mother. How could he do this to me?"

Relief hit my ass like a ton of bricks, followed quickly by guilt for even thinking she'd cheated on me with him. And then I was pissed the hell off. Why would he do this to her?

"Everyone has seen that video. It-it's everywhere! Someone tweeted that it's on a porn site! A porn site, Everett! Your daughter has probably seen it! Nat will see it one day! What am I supposed to do now?" She buried her face in her hands, scratched her nails down her face, and sobbed while Bridgette looked helplessly at me.

"Jo, baby. Let's—"

Jo's head popped up. "And the pictures...they're all over the place, too. Strangers know how I look naked! Oh, God!" she whimpered, covering her face again.

"Jo..." I looked at Bridgette, who nodded and slid out the truck. Climbing inside, I pulled Jo into my arms, and said, "I got it," dismissing Oba and letting Bridgette off the hook. "Hey," I whispered to Jo. "I got you. It's gonna be okay."

"How? I mean, I dealt with the whole Esther watching us have sex thing as well as I could. It still bothers me that she did that, but I was moving past it. But this? I can't deal with this, Everett. I just wanna crawl in a hole and die."

"Don't say shit like that, Jo. What about Natalie?"

"She'd be better off without a porn star for a mother!"

"No-the-hell she wouldn't! Look, this is fucked up, but it's not the end of the world. Shit, Kim Kardashian built a whole career off a sex tape. My album sales are probably through the roof off this shit. I bet you're gonna get even more business offers, too."

"I don't care about that! The whole world has seen me suck

Sidney's dick! The whole world has seen me naked! Don't you get it? I have been exposed and humiliated! Fuck a career! I want my damn dignity back! Can't you see how messed up this is?!"

I could. I just didn't know what to say or how to handle this. It hurt me, too, to know she was exposed like that. It made me want to throw up knowing all these people got to see what was supposed to be exclusively mine. It made me want to split Bugz's skull open. But I couldn't find the right words to articulate all of that to her, so I just held her and let her cry before carrying her into the house.

*****

She wouldn't eat.

She wouldn't leave our bed, either. The first night after the video came out, I asked Ms. Sherry, who'd been watching Nat during Jo's meeting, to keep her overnight. Two days later, I decided maybe Nat being home would motivate Jo to return to the land of the living. So I picked her up and brought her home. I was wrong. She gave Nat a weak smile, kissed her forehead, and rolled over in the bed. Nat didn't seem bothered and bounced to her room, but that's when I realized just how bad things were. Jo would do anything for Nat, had never been neglectful toward her. This video thing had really messed her head up. At one point, I came in the room to check on her to find her phone on the floor right by the door, screen cracked, and I realized her notifications probably were even more active than mine.

Bridgette dropped by on the third day, but Jo refused to see her. Same thing for the fourth day. Essentially, it was like Jo wasn't there. All that was left was a shell of the woman I knew and loved.

I took care of Nat, tried to keep her from feeling deserted, but what I wanted to do more than anything was to kill Bugz. Not that it would fix anything, but shit, it would make me feel better. Tommy offered to have some of his cousins beat Bugz's ass, with a promise that it wouldn't be traced back to me. All I would have to do was buy some weed. It was a tempting offer, but I knew I'd automatically be under suspicion at this point. I wasn't trying to go to jail for real.

The only thing that made me believe all hope wasn't lost was that despite having basically checked out, Jo let me hold her at night, let me dry her tears, even let me make love to her. But she wouldn't talk, only left the bed to pee, and after I begged her to, she took a shower. I managed to get her to eat some oatmeal on day five. But this shit was so bad, I wasn't sure how we were going to survive it.

35

Everett

I remembered what she said about her mom, about her falling into a depression and Jo having to go to a group home, about her having to take medicine and never being the same again after that, about her committing suicide. I couldn't make it if that happened to Jo, and I didn't want that for Nat. I had to do something to pull Jo out of this damn hole, but what?

A whole damn week had passed with her barely talking, barely eating, and only walking the few steps from our bed to her bathroom. Now Nat was starting to ask questions, wanting to know what was wrong with her mother. I told her she was sick, because I didn't know what else to say. Plus, it was the truth. She *was* sick, depressed.

Nat liked fried rice, so I had Tommy pick some up and was sitting at the kitchen table watching her chew a mouthful while holding another spoonful. "It's good, Nat?"

She nodded, then grinned, showing me teeth and rice. "Mmmmmm! Yummy!"

I smiled at her. It was hard to be sad around Nat. That's why I knew this shit with Jo was serious. If Nat climbing in bed with her, kissing her and saying good morning couldn't bring her out of her funk, what the hell was I supposed to do?

After Nat finished her rice, I cleaned her, the table, and the floor up, and we went to the family room to watch *The Lion King* for the tenth time in two days. She climbed in my lap, giving me a big grin and a sloppy kiss on the cheek. All I could do was smile at her and kiss her little forehead. Yeah, Nat was special. She rested her head against my chest and gave the movie her attention while I perused her mom's phone since it still worked despite the screen being cracked. I don't know why I was checking it other than to make myself mad as hell at all the dumb-ass DMs and shit she was getting. Stupid people saying stupid stuff, and besides making me angry, it made me feel like this was all my fault.

I couldn't help but think about how Jo was worried about being on the gossip blogs when we first started talking. No one knew who Jo was before me. Bugz's dumb ass had inadvertently protected her from this mess when they were together. I flung her into a spotlight she wasn't ready for by making her mine, and he was so damn jealous, he exposed her.

And I still wanted to kill his ass for it. Just had to figure out a way to do it that wouldn't put *my* ass in jail.

As I stared at Jo's phone, my own phone dinged with a text from Tommy: *Yo check this out. Wonder if he had anything to do with the video getting out?*

I looked at the attached picture of Bugz and his security, including Dunn. That put a bad taste in my mouth. Dunn knew a lot about me, a lot of information he could pass on to Bugz. Luckily, he didn't know shit about the new house or the gate codes. But still…his shady ass was working for Bugz?

I was typing out my answer to Tommy when Jo's phone began to ring. Bugz.

I stood from my seat and sat Nat in it, kissing her forehead before I headed to the kitchen with both phones. By the time I made it in there, I'd missed the call, so I called him back.

He answered with, "Look, baby, I ain't put that video out. I wouldn't do no shit like that to you. Somebody got my phone. I lost it in my car or something. Just found it or I woulda called you before now. I promise on my dead Uncle Jimmy I ain't do this shit! I wouldn't put you out there like that, baby!"

Every time this nigga said *baby*, I wanted to reach through the phone and choke his ass completely out. "Motherfucker, you gonna get yours! Just wait for it!" I replied.

"South? Put Jo on!"

"Fuck you! I ain't letting you talk to my damn woman! Just get ready to get fucked up!"

"I didn't—"

I hung up on his ass and pulled out my phone, ready to give Tommy the okay to put his cousins on the job when I heard Nat squeal, "Mama!"

I almost ran out the kitchen. Jo was out of bed? I found her sitting on the sofa with Nat's little arms around her neck. Jo's eyes were closed, a single tear rolling down her cheek. I stood and watched, relieved but still ready to kill Bugz. "You all right?" I asked.

Eyes still closed, she shook her head. "No, but I'm hungry. Weak."

"We got fwied wice!" Nat announced.

"Fried rice? Wow! Is it good?" Jo asked, as Nat crawled out of her lap, returning to my seat.

"Mm-hmm!" Nat hummed.

"Stay there. I'll bring you some," I said.

A few minutes later, I was back in my seat with a knocked-out Nat in my lap, trying not to stare at Jo. I was so glad to see her out of bed.

"I did it for his birthday," she said softly.

I frowned a little. "Huh?"

"The video and the pictures. They were birthday gifts. He begged me to let him record us and take those pictures. I didn't want to at first, but I was just...I loved him, we'd just gotten married, and I figured if anyone hacked into his phone or his cloud, it was me and my husband, not me and some random dude. So I let him do it." Her eyes were on her plate as she spoke.

"Jo, I-uh...I understand."

"There are more. He took more pictures, a couple more videos, but what he put out there exposed me more than him." She looked up at me. "He released the ones that would and did humiliate me the most. There are other pictures and videos where you can see his face, too."

"Baby—"

"Ev, after he left, I never let him touch me again. I know some divorced couples still get together sometimes, and he tried, but I wasn't going to lower myself to becoming a side chick to a man I was once married to. I want you to be clear that the video and the pictures are years old. I didn't let him touch me after he left. Not before us or after us."

"I know that, Jo. I believe you."

She nodded, put her plate of half-eaten food on the coffee table, and left the family room. A few minutes later, she was back in the bed.

*****

You shouldn't dread talking to your child, but when Ella's name flashed on my phone's screen a little more than a week after the video and photos were first circulated, that was what I felt plus apprehension, and shit, irritation. Jo was still out of commission, I was trying hard to keep Nat from feeling neglected, and I was just *fucking exhausted*. I was running on empty like a motherfucker. I loved my daughter but didn't feel like discussing this shit with anyone, especially not her.

I prepared myself to answer it, hoping she still had the compassion she developed for Jo after the Thanksgiving mess. The couple of times she visited us after that, she'd been on her best behavior. And then there was always the possibility of it being Esther calling me on Ella's phone, but surely her ass wasn't crazy enough to violate the no-contact order.

Actually, she was *exactly* that crazy.

"Hello?" I answered, my eyes on little Nat on the floor of the family room, playing with the huge stuffed lion I got her. Christmas was right around the corner and we didn't even have a tree. I was thinking about hiring this lady I'd heard about who specialized in holiday decorating so Nat could have a real Christmas. Ella, too, if she decided to visit. Christmas was officially Esther's holiday with her, though. I hadn't even done any shopping up until that point.

"Hey, Daddy," she replied. "Everything okay?"

I sighed as I dragged my hand down my face. "Uh…" I couldn't lie. Didn't have the energy to. "No, baby girl. Things are definitely not okay."

"I'm sorry. How is Jo?"

"Not good."

"I know she's upset."

"Very," I replied.

The fact that I was having this conversation with my kid, knowing she'd probably seen that video and those pictures or at the very least heard about them, made my stomach turn. I hadn't been eating much better than Jo. Shit was just all messed up.

"I hate this happened to her. Is she gonna sue Bugz-NYC for revenge porn?" Ella asked.

"What?"

"That's what Blac Chyna did when Rob Kardashian posted those pics on IG, sued him for revenge porn."

"Yeah, I forgot about that. It's a good idea. I'll run it by Jo." Hell, it was a *great* idea. Maybe the possibility of some justice would pull Jo out of the hole she was in.

"I hope she does it, and I hope she wins. He was wrong to do that to her. She doesn't deserve this or…anything else she's had to deal with." She sounded sincere, which surprised me. Sincere and sad.

"You talking about that stuff with your mom? It's all right. Don't sweat it." It really wasn't all right, but I didn't want her to be sad. I was still her father, always wanted her to be happy even if it was at my expense.

"No, I was wrong, and Mom was *really* wrong. That was just…insane. I'm so sorry, Daddy. I didn't know she'd take it that far. But she promised to calm down and leave you guys alone."

"She doesn't really have a choice anymore, Ella."

"I know. Well, tell Jo I said hi. I hope things get better. People can be so cruel."

"They sure can, baby. Thanks for calling."

"No problem, Daddy."

I ended the call and actually felt better. Maybe I could turn this situation around, after all.

36

My eyes were glued to my bathroom door as my mind turned over the absurdity of there being his and hers bathrooms and closets in our master suite, the size of our bed with its high tufted headboard, and the fully furnished sitting area. Everything about this bedroom was over the top, just like the entire house and this life with Everett. This shared life with him was almost as overwhelming as his love for me, which he demonstrated by taking care of me while I couldn't find the strength to and by taking care of Nat, a child he had no biological ties to. I'd spent so much time wishing Sid would be a father to her when Everett stepped into that role with ease and without any prodding from me. I was done bending over backwards and trying to accommodate Sid so he could be the father to her he obviously didn't want to be and never would be.

Yeah, I was over that shit.

The room also reminded me of the Teema Jane Smith Community Youth Home, a facility built to address the overflow of entrants into the foster care system, kids like me who had no place else to go when those registered to foster children in their homes had no more room. It reminded me of the dorm-style room in which I slept those four months because of its striking contrast to it and any other home I'd claimed as mine, whether permanent or temporary. To be honest, this place felt more like home than any other place ever had. It also reminded me of how far I'd come, of who I was, and of what made me…*me*.

It had been almost two weeks since I'd retreated to this bedroom in an attempt to hide from the world, and well, I was over *that* shit, too. I didn't lie down and die when Sid shat on me. I went through the end of my pregnancy alone, pushed Nat out with only Bridgette by my side, and had been raising her solo like a G. I was tougher than this! I was a damn beast! Being in a group home didn't break me. Tragically losing my mother didn't break me. Divorcing Sid didn't break me, and I wasn't going to let that video and those pictures or anything else he decided to release break me, either.

Screw that.

And *fuck* Sidney "Bugz-NYC" Walker.

For real.

Seriously...FUCK HIM.

Yeah, he sucker-punched me by releasing that footage after giving me the impression that he had two or three percent common sense left in his brain, but screw that and screw him.

Majorly.

This shouldn't have come as a surprise anyway. Sid was nothing if not a flip-flopping fool.

I rolled over in bed and faced the ceiling, my mind meandering to thoughts of my mother and how I hated her, like actually despised her, when she ended up being committed. I hated her for being a fool for my father and for being too weak to get over him and move on. The emotion was misplaced, but all I knew at the time was that I needed her and she was unavailable to me and that made me angry. I didn't want Nat to hate me for the same reason. I also didn't want to lose Everett but had common sense enough to know I was wearing him out. My depression was real—painfully, paralyzingly real. But so was my resolve, my strength, and my determination. My current situation gave me a newfound understanding of my mom's plight, but lying in that bed with nothing to do but think and think some more, showed me how greatly my situation differed from hers.

Unlike my mother, I had friends and I had a man who'd walk through fire for me. I was fortunate, *blessed,* and it was time for me to return to the land of the living. I'd spent enough time feeling sorry for myself. More than enough, and no matter how long I stayed buried beneath these covers, this wasn't going away.

I wasn't the first woman something like this ever happened to, and I undoubtedly wouldn't be the last. Like old Frank Sinatra once said, "The best revenge is massive success." I was going to take this mess and flip it, build one hell of a career out of it like Everett said. If that video and those pictures were going to keep circulating the internet, I was going to find a way to benefit from it. I was going to become more famous than Sid. Yeah, that was how I was going to handle this cluster fuck. I was going to turn these nasty-ass lemons into some bomb-ass lemonade.

Game. On.

I'd kicked the covers off my legs and was about to head to the shower and wash my ass when Everett burst through the bedroom door.

"Baby, listen," he began, "shit is fucked up. I get that. You're embarrassed, worried about folks seeing you in the most compromising position. But fuck people! Seeing those pictures doesn't mean they know you. *I* know you, your friends know you, and we gonna love you regardless. That's all that matters. Fuck the rest. And Nat? She knows her mom. When she's old enough to know about this shit, she'll have lived with you being her mother for years and there's nothing you won't be able to explain to her. Bugz is the damn villain here, not you! You ain't got a damn thing to be ashamed of. You were doing what comes natural when you love someone. She'll understand that."

I sat up on the side of the bed. "Ev—"

"It's time to fight. You're tougher than this, been through worse shit before. You gotta pull yourself out of that damn pit and fight! Fight for Nat! Shit, fight for us because I feel like I'm losing you, like you're slipping through my fingers right before my eyes and ain't nothing I can do about it. I love you, Jo, and I miss you. I miss the fuck out of your mean ass. I need my Jo back."

"Baby—"

"We gonna sue that motherfucker and we're gonna go on with our life together. I ain't letting you lay up in here no more even if I have to carry your ass around the house all day. I mean that shit!"

"Okay."

He shook his head. "I ain't tryna hear that shit, Jo. You need a counselor or therapist to help you get past this? Fine. I'll pay a motherfucker to live in here and talk to you twenty-four-seven. Whatever it takes! I need my damn woman back!"

"All right."

"See, you still on that bullshit! Look! You need to get up out that bed and come downstairs and get something to eat. Your pineapple levels probably all low and shit..."

"Pineapple levels?"

He nodded, staring at me with the most serious look on his face. "Yeah."

I stood on weak legs and ambled over to him, leaning against his big body. "Baby, I said *okay*. You're right. I have to get out of this bed and live again. I'm ready, and I'm sorry for checking out on you. I just...couldn't deal. But I know not dealing isn't an option when you have a child to take care of and a man who needs your attention. I'm still upset and sad, but you're right. It's time to fight. I'm *ready* to fight."

He wrapped his arms around me. "Shit, for real?"

"Yep."

"Thank you," he breathed, as he rested his chin atop my head.

"Thank *you* for not killing Sid and getting taken away from me. Wait, you didn't kill him or have him killed, did you?"

"No."

"But I know you wanted to."

"Still do."

"Please don't. If I lose you to jail or whatever, I won't recover. I know I won't."

"Baby, that mother—"

"We'll sue him, like you said. If he loses his money, that's the same as killing him. He loves money more than anything."

Rubbing his hand up and down my back, he mumbled. "I'll try not to kill him."

"Try real hard for Nat."

"You're wrong for bringing her up. That was low. You know she's my heart, just like Ella is."

"Mm-hmm. That's why I brought her up. Uh…where is she right now?"

"I just put her down for a nap."

"Oh, okay."

"Well, since you being all agreeable and shit, I'ma hire a cook. Can't keep eating out like this."

"All right," I assented.

"Word? Okay, and you're gonna come to the studio and sing on this track I been working on."

"Nope. Not gonna happen."

"Damn, I had to try."

"Uh-huh…hey, would you be mad if I never gave you head again?"

His body stiffened. "Huh?"

"After all that's happened, that video—I just don't feel comfortable sucking dick anymore. You understand, right?"

"Um…what?"

I placed my hand on his groin and felt him instantly harden. "I can't suck your penis, *this* penis, anymore, baby. I can't put it in my mouth and lick that one vein that runs up the back of it or twirl my tongue around it or scrape my teeth over it real gently or get all sloppy with it like you love for me to do. I can't do any of that anymore. It would just be too hard, bring back painful memories, you know? You're okay with that, aren't you?"

He backed away from me with a look of horror on his face. "Damn…um, I ain't gonna record it or nothing, baby, if that's what you're worried about. I mean…I mean, are you serious, Jo?"

I dropped to my knees, tugged on the waistband of his jogging pants, and said, "Nope."

As I pulled his super erection out of his pants and watched it bounce in front of my face, he said, "Your ass need to stop playing so damn much."

"Oh, wait," I said, standing and walking over to the nightstand on my side of the bed.

"Wait? I just told you to stop playing. How I'ma wait and you got me all hard?"

I ignored him, digging in the drawer and quickly finding what I was looking for. Turning around, I held it by one end of its wrapper and dangled it between my fingers as I made my way back to him.

"A cough drop? You 'bout to do the cough drop thing? Shit!" he said. Then he snatched his t-shirt off and stuffed it in his mouth.

Everett

"Love at first sight?" I repeated part of the interviewer, Dev's, question. "I wouldn't say that, exactly. I'd say for me, it was fascination at first sight. From the moment I met Jo, she intrigued me because she clearly wasn't impressed by me. I don't think she liked me at all."

Dev shifted her amused eyes to Jo. "Really?"

Jo shrugged. "He was kind of douchy at first. I won't go into how, but he was on his Big South stuff and I wasn't feeling it. He changed my mind, though."

I smiled, not just at her words, but because during this *Essence* interview, Jo once again proved what I already knew about her—she was a boss. She never belonged under Peter Park's thumb or in Bugz-NYC's background. Despite all the bullshit that came with being in the public eye, that was where she belonged.

"So you worked some magic on her, Big South?"

I shook my head as I squeezed Jo's hand. "I just showed her who I am, introduced her to Everett McClain. She seems to like him."

Jo leaned in and kissed me. "Correction, I *love* Everett McClain."

"You know I love Jo Lena Walker."

"Aww, you two really are the cutest thing, but I know things have not been easy. I've read the blogs. Jo, from day one you were pegged a gold digger because of your association with two high profile men. And most recently, you've been dealing with the revenge porn scandal. I know there's a pending law suit, so you can't say much about the video of you and your ex-husband, Bugz-NYC, but I want to give you a chance to address all the things that have been reported about you, to set the record straight."

Jo blew out a breath, bit her bottom lip, and sighed. We were in our formal living room, studio lights glaring at us as the interview was being recorded and snippets of it would be posted on the *Essence* website. We had done our photo shoot for the cover and spread days earlier, and now, with Christmas fast approaching, we were sitting down to tell our story.

"Well," Jo finally said, "I'm not sure anything I say will make that much of a difference. If I have learned anything since being in this relationship, it's that people will believe what they want to believe, no matter the evidence staring them in the face. I could sit here and try to convince you and the world at large that I'm not a gold digger, that I love the man sitting next to me, that I'm just a regular girl who somehow attracts who I attract, but what I'm going to do instead is address the everyday girl who suffers from the impact of rumors and conjecture. I want to tell her to do what I have decided to do: Hold your head up and live your life to the fullest in spite of what anyone thinks they know about you. You prove people wrong with actions, not with words. Sure, what people say about you will hurt, but it won't kill you unless you let it. In my case, while they're saying what they're saying and thinking what they're thinking, I'm still gonna be wearing this ring, living in this house, sleeping in bed beside this man, making money moves, being a boss and a mother. They ain't stopping nothing. I won't let them."

I wrapped my arm around her shoulder and squeezed her to me. I was proud as hell of my Jo Lena. Proud as hell.

37

"I can't believe I'm here! Girl, this place is packed with famous folks!" Bridgette whisper-yelled.

I frowned at her. "It's my engagement party, where else you think your ass was supposed to be?"

"I know, but still…"

"And anyway, you deserve a night of fun. We've been working hard the last month or so."

"Shit, don't I know it! Who knew a sex tape and some nudes could drum up this much business for a person? I mean, damn!"

I nodded. "It's nuts." It really was crazy how many folks wanted to do business with me as a result of me being exposed. It was almost disturbing to think about it. In addition to the Glam On It deal, which hadn't missed a beat despite the video mess, I'd signed on to rep the "Melanated and Unbothered" t-shirt line, had negotiated a partnership with Coily-Q hair care, and was working on my sneaker line with S.H.E. The best part about it was that I was having fun making these moves. It didn't really feel like work. The added bonus was I was earning my own money, too. Of course Everett had my back, actually loved taking care of me, I still had a chunk of money saved up from my divorce settlement, and Sid never missed a child support payment, but Everett was right—there's nothing like a woman who makes her own money.

"Hey, you been working on your passport? Ms. Sherry got hers."

Bridgette nodded. "Yes! I should have it in time for the tour. This assistant shit is lit! I get to follow you and South around the damn world!"

"When he works, I work. But when we play, your ass is gonna have to find something to do."

"Don't nobody wanna be around y'all freaky asses no way. I can't wait to hop on your Christmas gift, though, and finally get out of the states!"

"Yeah, Everett was extra as hell for buying that jet."

"*And* putting it in your name. Girrrrllll, I like that kinda extra!"

"I guess, but it made that Patek watch I got him look like a Timex."

"You complaining?"

"Hell, no!"

Bridgette laughed. "Hey, I'm glad you're good now. You had me scared there for a while. I was so afraid I was gonna lose you over Sid's bullshit."

"Yeah, I know. I'm fine, though." I pointed my champagne flute toward Everett who was standing across the ballroom talking to his brother Nolan—or it could've been Neil since I had trouble telling them apart—and Michael B. Jordan, of all people. "How could I *not* be fine when I get to lay up under that every night."

"Bay-bee! And now that I've seen that extra shmedium dick Sid got, I know your ass is more than fine with that monstrosity you say Everett is working with!"

I loudly guffawed like we weren't in the elegant ballroom of a high-end hotel. "You are a fool, Bridgette! Extra shmedium?! Monstrosity?!"

"Yeah! And I can't believe Sid had the audacity to cheat with that starter dick!"

I fell out laughing at that, gathered my composure, and said, "Speaking of dicks…"

"Nope. Not going there. There's nothing to tell."

"You and Tommy were joined at the hip during Thanksgiving. It's damn January! Are you ever gonna tell me what's going on with you two?"

"No."

"Ho'."

"Whatever."

"Okay, I see how it is. That's cool, Bridgette. Be that way."

"Ughhhh! Stop with the guilt-tripping! Look, we had fun in Texas, a lot of fun, but I don't have time for anything serious right now between pursuing my career and being your assistant."

"Then you're fired."

"Shidddd, where?"

I rolled my eyes. "So you two are over? You haven't talked or anything since Houston?" Tommy was sweet and actually really cute. Humongous, but cute. In my opinion, Bridgette was straight tripping.

"Oh, I didn't say that. We still screwing, just with no strings attached. Girl, he got it going on!"

"Wow."

"Good, your man's coming this way, so you can leave me alone."

"You still owe me details, considering I share everything about me and Everett with you."

"Hell, he's *Big South*. The whole world knows everything about y'all."

"You know what I meant. Petty ass."

"Just call me Petty Davis. Anyway, since your man is coming over here, I'ma go peel Sage off Ice Cube's fine-ass son." Bridgette slid away from me, greeting Everett as he approached.

He grinned at me, reaching for my hand. "They're playing our song. Let's dance."

"Since when did *The Weekend* become our song? What you tryna tell me? You bet-not have a ho' on the side."

"I ain't got no woman on the side. Bring your crazy ass on out here so we can dance," he said, grasping my hand.

I followed him, because he had on white pants and a white dress shirt and he was looking like three whole snacks, but I still asked, "How is this our song, Everett James McClain?"

As he pulled me into his arms on the dance floor, he replied, "Hell, I was just saying something. I didn't even recognize the song;

I just heard something we could slow dance to and came for you. Now stop tripping. I'm up under your little-mean-sexy-ass all the time. Ain't fucked up about nobody else." His hand slid from my back to my butt. "Can't wait to get you home and test your pineapple levels."

"You been testing them for over a month now. I think they're good."

"They sure in the hell are."

We did so much bumping and grinding and rubbing to the song that by the time it ended, my cookie was completely water-logged, so as we left the dancefloor, I asked, "Why don't you get us a room upstairs?"

His eyebrows peaked. "You ready like that?"

I nodded. "I'm wet as the Pacific Ocean right now."

"Be right back."

"Where you going?"

"To get a room."

I mingled with people, sipped the Matador Everett had ordered for me, and was laughing at Shirl's report of Peter Park's latest beat down—in the lobby of Bijou Park—at the hands of one of his side chicks this time, not his wife, when I realized it was taking Everett way longer than it should've to get a room. Then I noticed Ella sitting alone at a table and decided to see how she was since she was looking a little forlorn. We'd been kind of sort of getting along since the Houston debacle, so I felt okay approaching her.

"Hey," I said, "you having a good time?"

She nodded, giving me a smile. "Yeah, just texted Tommy. He's pulling the truck around and then he's gonna come in here and get me."

"Leaving?"

She nodded again, took a sip of something I hoped was non-alcoholic, and replied, "Yes. I have this brunch thing me and M-Mom have to go to. We're shooting it for the show. Gotta be up early for hair and makeup."

"Oh, okay. Well, I'm glad you came. Hope you enjoyed yourself.

Your dad said you liked your Christmas gift." She'd spent Christmas with her mother, but Everett had given her our joint gift a few days early—the newest iPhone.

She picked the phone up and smiled. "I love it. Thanks."

"Good. You're welcome."

"Um, Jo? I wanna say I'm sorry again, for acting like I used to act around you and for my mom. You didn't deserve any of that. I just felt—"

"Like I was taking your dad away from you? I never had a relationship with my father, so I value the closeness you have with yours. I would leave him before I'd come between the two of you. It would hurt, but I'd do it."

She stared at me for a second. "Wow, really?"

"Yeah, I want him to be happy above anything else."

"Well, you obviously make him happy."

"So do you, Ella."

She dropped her eyes for a moment, then looked back up at me. "I saw Ms. Sherry earlier. Where's little Nat?"

That was a surprising question. I didn't realize she even knew Nat's name. "With the other sitter."

"Oh...how's she doing?"

"Good, still always happy no matter what's going on. We're thinking about putting her in preschool after the overseas leg of your dad's tour is over, so she can be around other kids, work on her speech."

"I love how she talks. It's cute, especially the way she says Daddy's name." She glanced at her phone, then toward the doorway to the ballroom. "There's Tommy. Gotta go. Talk to you later?"

"Sure."

I sat and watched as she ran into her dad and they hugged. Then he came to me, reaching for my hand. "Sorry, I got held up. Ran into a fan in the lobby. Let's go upstairs."

I smiled. "Lead the way."

*****

After two solid months of me ignoring his calls and texts, Sid had common sense enough to schedule a meeting with me through our lawyers. I was done with his ass, to the point that I paid Ms. Sherry to handle his Christmas FaceTime call to Nat. I'd never keep him out of his daughter's life, but he had no place in mine. If he ever decided to be a real father to Nat, we'd have to arrange everything through a third party. And if he never stepped up and spent time with her, she had Everett. I honestly wished Sid would do both Nat and me the courtesy of disappearing. Neither of us needed his stupid ass.

There in the conference room in his lawyer's office, he looked tired, harried as he sat across from me, his lawyer leaning in close, telling him something. His eyes were on me, then on Everett who sat at my side, having refused my request to do this alone. My lawyer—who was actually Everett's lawyer—sat on the other side of me.

"On behalf of my client, I first want to thank Ms. Walker for agreeing to meet with us."

I just stared at Sid's lawyer. What was I supposed to say to that? "You're welcome?"

Nope.

"Okay," his lawyer continued, turning to Sid. "Mr. Walker?"

"Yeah...Uh, South? Man, can you give us a minute?" Sid's eyes were trained on me as he spoke.

"No," Everett replied matter-of-factly.

Silence and tension populated the room as the two men in my life—former and current—stared each other down. Sid was the first to break, narrowing his eyes at Everett before sliding them to me. Without a word, he pulled his cell phone out, the same one he'd had nearly since I met him because, while he loved spending money, he refused to upgrade his phone, tapped on the screen a few times, and placed it on the table between us. Soon, voices flowed from the device's tiny speakers.

"Hey, thanks again for all your help. I really appreciate it. I got industry connects, but not like you. The people you know? Like...wow! They were really able to get this stuff out there fast."

I didn't recognize that first voice, but the second one was distinct.

"Oh, the pleasure was all mine!" the second voice gushed. "She deserves everything she gets."

Everett dropped my hand, the one he had been clutching under the table. His brows knitted as he peered down at the phone.

"Yeah. I don't get what they see in her ass, but maybe the world will now. Nasty bitch."

I straightened in my seat. Now, I recognized the first voice, Sid's side piece turned second wife, ugly-ass Sonya. The hell?

"I can't believe he left his phone lying around knowing that footage was on it," the crisply accented voice returned.

"Uh...yeah. Me either." Sonya's voice was strained, as if she suddenly wanted the conversation to end.

"Well, let me know if you need me to leak any of the other pictures or videos. I'll gladly get them to the right people."

"I will. Thanks, Esther."

"You're welcome."

The recording ended, filling the rectangular room with thick, almost tangible silence until Sid said, "This what I been calling trying to tell you. I didn't leak that shit, Jo. I've done a lot of stuff, but I wouldn't do nothing like that to my little girl's mom. Or to the only woman I've ever loved."

Out of the corner of my eye, I could see Everett shake his head. "Motherfucker—" he began.

"Man, I don't mean no disrespect. I know she don't want my ass no more. I know she with you now. You got her. You won. I'm just stating facts. I love her, was dumb as fuck for leaving her and my little girl. Now I gotta divorce Sonya's ass. Done already left her."

My eyes shot over to Sid. "What?"

He nodded. "Yeah, I left her stupid, jealous ass. She knew how we got together, knew I still wanted you from jump because I told her that shit, more than once. She knew me and her was a business arrangement, just tried to act like she didn't care at first when she really did. Sat there and acted like me wanting you didn't bother her, then she pulled this shit. So her ass had to go."

"Dunn didn't have nothing to do with this?" Everett asked.

Dunn? I shot a curious glance at Everett, but his eyes were on Sid, who shook his head.

"Nah. I don't think so. Can't be sure though, because I had to fire his ass a couple of weeks ago for thinking he could talk shit about Jo to me." He turned to me. "You done made some enemies, bab—Jo."

"And I have no idea why. How—how'd you get this recording?"

"When I figured this shit out, realized she was the only somebody who coulda got ahold of my phone like that, I asked her. She tried to deny it but finally admitted it and spilled all the damn beans, told me she sneaked my phone, found them videos and shit, and asked that England ho' to help her. Said they been talking for a while behind my back, hating on you. Sonya in the industry pretty deep, so I didn't believe her when she said ole girl helped her, made her call her right in front of me and taped that shit. Almost messed up and let that pip-pip-cheerio muh-fucker know I was listening when Sonya started tryna talk shit about you during that call."

I just sat there. I mean, what was I supposed to say or do in the face of something like this? This was pure insanity! On one side, you have Sonya who screwed my damn husband, then moved in with him after he left me alone and pregnant, and she had the nerve to hate me? What kind of shit is that? Then there was Esther, a woman who lost her man because she couldn't keep her legs closed to any and everybody, a woman with a sick obsession with said man, a woman who couldn't fathom how and why he could move on after more than ten years of being divorced from her to the point that she would be a part of this mess. She hated me, literally hated me, and why? Because he loved me? So, that was my fault?

These fools were seriously touched in the head.

As Sid's lawyer explained that they were taking the recording to the DA—who was considering charging Sid with revenge porn, AKA nonconsensual pornography—and anticipated the investigation shifting to Sonya and Esther, I watched Everett. His eyes were glued to the silent cell phone resting on the table, and I could almost see the gears shifting in his mind as he clenched and unclenched his jaw.

"…and we hope this evidence is also sufficient enough for you to consider dropping your civil suit against my client." Sid's lawyer said.

I had opened my mouth to agree when Everett shot to his feet.

"Ev?" I asked, getting to my feet next to him.

"Man, don't do it. I see that look in your eyes. You do that shit, and I'm moving in on your territory. I want Jo back and I'm about to be a free man again. Just saying," Sid said. I never thought I'd appreciate anything this fool ever let leave his mouth, and while he made it sound like I had no choice in the matter, his words did make Everett take pause.

He stared down at Sid, who was still seated. "Look, nigga, don't make me fuck—"

Sid held up both hands. "South, man…I'm tryna help you. I know you wanna go kick that fish and chips ho's ass right now, just like I wanna kick Sonya's, but I already almost lost my record deal off this revenge porn shit and I ain't tryna get locked up, either. And ain't your ass already on probation?"

"You mean for kicking your ass, the same ass I'm about to come across this table and kick again because it ain't shit for me to fuck you up?"

Sid shrugged. "Man, I'm just saying…chill on ole girl. You can't come back from beating a woman's ass. Well, unless you're a light-skinned R&B singer. And Sonya wanna get back in with me so bad, she willing to roll on her Big Ben ass in court. She gonna get hers. So…chill."

"Yeah, I'ma chill all right," Everett said. Then he was moving toward the door, making strides I could barely keep up with.

38

Everett

I ducked into the first restroom I could find to try and get myself together, because I needed to get myself together before I started randomly kicking asses. I hadn't used the word bitch when referring to a woman in a long time, not since I overheard Ella rapping along with one of my songs when she was eleven or twelve and I realized I didn't ever want her to think it was okay for a man to call her that, but for the life of me, I couldn't think of another word to call Esther. She was the damn definition of the word—a female dog, a pit bull with a bone clenched in her jaws that she refused to let go of. I was the bone, a big meaty one she was holding in her mouth like it was a fucking steak.

And if I never hated her before, I despised her ass now.

Fuck the restraining order; fuck waiting on a prosecutor to take care of her. I needed to do what I should've done years ago—*show* her I was not playing with her, because evidently, my words weren't making enough of an impact.

I had moved to leave the restroom when the door flew open and Jo walked in. "You can't be in here, baby," I said, trying not to sound homicidal.

"I can be wherever you are and what you *not* gonna do ever again, is ignore me when I'm talking to you!"

I frowned. "When did I ignore you?"

"When you left that boardroom and I followed you, asking you what you were getting ready to do. You ignored me, ran up in here, and I want to know what you been in here doing!"

"Using the got-damn restroom! What else?!"

She crossed her arms over her chest, making her tiny Chanel bag swing back and forth on her wrist. "Oh, I don't know...maybe violating your own restraining order by calling that miserable bitch of an ex-wife of yours."

I shook my head and slid my hand down my face. "Nah, I ain't called her yet."

"Yet? You're not calling her at all! You're not going to see her, either! You ain't doing shit that involves her! Sid is stupid as hell, but he has a point. She is not worth you getting locked up for."

"Uh-huh," I said, as I eased past her and out the restroom door.

She flew out of the restroom and grabbed my arm. "Nigga, I know you are *not* dismissing me!"

"No, I'm not, but I'm also not having a conversation with you in the damn men's restroom anymore!"

She closed her eyes and sighed. "We're arguing. I don't want to argue. I just wanna pick Nat up from Ms. Sherry's and go home and be with you. I don't care about Esther or what she's trying to do to us. This? Us fighting? That's giving her what she wants!"

"What she wants is us apart. You leaving me, Jo?"

"For the ten-millionth time, no!"

"Then that motherfucker ain't getting what she wants. You can't talk me out of doing what I know I gotta do, baby. Not after this. She went too far. If it had been me she exposed, I'd let it ride, but it was you, and I'd be less than a man to let this slide."

"Ev, please! Leave it alone!"

"I can't!" My voice echoed so loudly against the slick floors and white walls of the hallway, it almost startled *me*.

Jo's eyes darted around us before she finally stepped forward and wrapped her arms around me. "Please..."

I closed my eyes and rested a hand on her back. She wasn't playing fair. She never played fair. "Jo..."

"Just sleep on it. Let's leave and go get Nat and go home, and you sleep on it. If you wake up in the morning and still wanna do whatever it is you feel you need to do, I won't stop you."

"Jo—"

"Please, Everett. I am *begging* you. Please!"

I sighed as I pulled her closer to me. "All right."

I couldn't sleep, so I knew when he lifted from the bed. I kept my eyes shut as he quietly moved around our bedroom and eased into his bathroom, softly closing the door behind him. Climbing out of bed, I tipped next door to check on Nat, because that's what mothers do, returning to our room and quickly slipping out of my nightie into a romper and a pair of flip-flops.

When he finally emerged from the bathroom, he jumped at the sight of me sitting on his side of the bed waiting for him. "Where you going?" he asked, eyeing me.

"Wherever you're going."

He shook his head. "You can't go with me."

"I bet the hell I can. You were supposed to sleep on this."

"I couldn't. I can never sleep when I know I got unfinished business."

"Okay, then let's finish it."

"Who's gonna watch Nat?"

"I was just about to get her up so she can go with us."

"You know how crazy you sound right now?"

"You know how crazy you look right now? What're you planning on doing? Killing Esther?"

"Don't worry about that. Just stay here."

"Nope."

He sighed. "Whatever."

I was on his heels when he left the bedroom, but took a detour into Nat's room. I was almost to her bed when I heard him behind me. "Jo, don't you wake that baby up."

"But we're leaving, aren't we? Can't leave her alone, and it's too late to call a sitter—"

"That's why your ass is staying here."

"No, I am fucking not."

Everett grabbed his head and groaned. "Fine! Fuck it! Let's go back to bed, Jo. Come on!" He wasn't yelling, but he wasn't whispering either. So I gave him the eye.

In response, he lifted his eyebrows, and said, "Come the hell on, then, before I mess around and wake her up!"

We climbed back into bed fully clothed, lying there in silence. I could feel his rage seeping from his pores. It was eating him up, and that broke my heart.

"Ev, I understand—"

"No, you don't. You can't. There's no way you'll ever understand what I'm feeling right now."

"I think I have an idea since it's me out here sucking dick for the world to see and not you."

He tore his eyes from the ceiling and rolled over to face me. "That motherfucker has done everything in her power to ruin my life, and I have sat back and let her. I can't let this shit go anymore! I'm tired of her making a damn fool of me! I gotta show her I'm not playing with her ass anymore!"

"And you don't care if they cancel the restraining order for you contacting her? You don't care if you do something that gets you arrested? You don't care if you get put in jail? Away from Ella and me and Nat?"

"I love you, don't want to spend a second away from you or the girls, but this is something I've *got* to do. If I don't *make* her leave us the fuck alone, she'll never stop."

Silence surrounded us as I let his words and the desperation in his voice sink in. He was angry, but more than that, he was hurting—badly. It had to stop, *she* had to stop, and maybe he was right. Maybe his words would never be enough.

"Did you call her when you were in the bathroom?"

I turned to face him completely, watched as he nodded, his eyes on me.

"You're supposed to go to her house? What'd you tell her? That you wanted to talk?"

He nodded again.

"She ask about me?"

"Yeah...I lied, told her you weren't an issue. Not anymore."

I bit my bottom lip for a moment. "Call her back. Tell her to come over here."

I watched his serious expression morph into a confused one. "What?"

"Call her, tell her you need her to come over here instead."

"Jo, I—"

"You're not skipping out of here in the middle of the night, alone. I mean, you weren't planning to take Chink or Oba, were you?" I asked, referring to the two members of our security team that were spending the night in the guest house.

"N-no?"

"Yeah, so...no, that's not happening. Esther's a nut. Whatever you need to do, you do it here. I'll be your witness."

"She thinks—I made her think we broke up, remember?"

"So? Don't tell her I'm here. Let her in, and I'll pop up. Call her, Everett."

"Jo..."

"I love you. I don't want to lose you over some bullshit. I *won't* lose you over some bullshit. You wanna confront this fool? You do it here. Call her."

Ten minutes later, we were sitting in the family room staring at each other, waiting for Esther's arrival. We were quiet, tense, and I could tell Everett wanted to back out of this, but not enough to use the phone in his hand to call and cancel with her.

"You not itching?" he asked.

"Nope. Not anxious, actually looking forward to this."

He nodded, his eyes on the floor. "Me, too."

My mind rewound to the phone call he made on speakerphone,

the excitement I could hear in Esther's voice at the prospect of coming here, probably in anticipation of screwing my man. I had added her to a very short list of people I hated, right behind my father. I was tired, exhausted from the mere thought of the shit she'd pulled in the time me and Everett had been together, and to be brutally honest, didn't care if Everett kicked her ass all up and down our house. I just wanted this nut to cease to exist. And if she did, I was prepared to help hide the body. As messed up as it sounds, those were the thoughts swirling in my mind when the gate intercom buzzed in the noiseless house. Everett cut his eyes at me as he pressed the button on the gate remote control, allowing her entry onto the property. At that point, I could only hope she hadn't brought her security so we could get this over and done with.

"You can still go back to bed," he said, as he stood to answer the door.

"No, I can't," I replied.

He left, returning moments later with a very chatty Esther Reese waltzing in behind him.

"I'm so glad you called and invited me over. I've been waiting for this for so long. I've missed you so—" She cut herself off once she spotted me sitting on the sofa, then she turned to face Everett. "I thought—"

"You thought you got rid of me?" I spoke up with one eyebrow cocked, making her turn to face me. "I bet you did."

"Everett?" She was still facing me as he stepped around her.

I shook my head, and before he could speak, I said, "No, you talk to me, not him, since I'm the one you seem to have an issue with."

"The only issue I have with you is you being a thorn in my side," she countered, eyes narrowed.

"Look—" Everett tried, but I cut him off.

"And why is that? Because he loves me and not you? That's why you helped Sonya Lugo leak that video and those pictures? Because you thought it would make him stop loving me?"

The shock registered on her face for a few seconds before she wiped it off. "I-I don't know what you're talking about."

Everett damn near jumped in her face. "Sonya taped your conversation. We heard you offer to leak more shit, you motherfucking—"

Esther jumped at his thundering voice. "What?! You're lying! I didn't—"

"You know, Esther, I didn't get you and Everett's relationship for a long time. I struggled to understand why you wouldn't let go, why you felt so comfortable making demands of him, calling him to get in his personal business, expecting him to still want you after you two being divorced for all these years."

"We were in love. Real love, love that created a child. That kind of love never dies," she declared.

"Uh-huh," I said. "And then him? Him hating you so much? I mean, yeah, I know you hurt him, but I was like, he should be over that by now. For a while there, I thought he was still hung up on you."

"He still loves me, I know it," she said, lifting her chin a bit.

"Hell-no I don't! I can't stand your ass!" Everett shouted. At this point, even as huge as the house was, I half-expected Nat to take the elevator down there if she could reach the buttons.

"I thought so, too, but that's not it. I *know* he loves me. No doubt about that. So that's when it hit me. I realized hate like he has for you is much deeper than you cheating on him, even though he caught you with *two* people. He should've been over that. Plus, why would you keep letting him threaten to tell people what you did? Hell, if folks found out about your freaky-deaky ways, it'd probably boost that pathetic reality show career of yours. Shoot, you leaking that tape put me on the map. Who knew people would appreciate my fellatio skills so greatly? Thanks, by the way. That shit you did backfired like a motherfucker." I laughed for effect. Yeah, Evil Jo was in the building and in rare form.

Esther was visibly pissed. "Look, you—"

"Don't worry, I'm almost finished. So I've figured it out. The reason he hates you, the only thing that could make a man despise a woman he once loved the way Everett does you is there's a constant reminder of what you did present, a physical manifestation of your infidelity and disrespect for him—Ella."

The air seemed to leave the room as they both wore shocked expressions. Everett even stumbled a bit before sitting down beside me, speechless.

"What are you...Everett?" Esther stammered.

"Oh, he didn't tell me, didn't have to," I said. "I just put two and two together, placed myself in his shoes, and realized he probably started having doubts after he caught you in your mess, had a DNA test done, and found out she wasn't his. The problem was, he loved her, and he was the only father she knew. It's just like him to keep this secret for her sake. And because he did, because he agreed to be a father to her despite her not being his, you took that to mean he still loved you. The fact that he never had a serious relationship with another woman after you two split only fueled that delusion." I smiled at her. "Until I came along."

"You don't know what you're talking about!" she hissed.

"Oh, but I do. Ella isn't any more his than my Nat is, but he loves her. He cares about her wellbeing, and he would never hurt her by revealing the truth." I stood from the couch. "But bitch, *I will*."

"Jo!" Everett sounded panicked, but I ignored him.

"Here's what you're gonna do. You're gonna go about your life, let them prosecute you for distributing nonconsensual porn or whatever, do your probation, and leave us the fuck alone or I will spill all the beans about EVERYTHING."

"Jo—" Everett began.

"You don't want Ella to hate you, do you? No mother wants that, not even you. But she will, because she actually loves him more than she loves you. You know I'm right. She already thinks you're crazy for that mess you pulled in Houston, and rightfully so, and when the truth about the video comes out, that's only going to make things worse. Don't add to it by making me reveal the truth about her father."

"He'll never forgive you if you do it. You'll lose him."

I shrugged, my eyes on the tall, beautiful, stupid-ass woman before me. "Maybe, or maybe he's tired of lying to her. Maybe he knows she should know the truth. Who's the daddy? A bodyguard, your trainer, the mailman, a male prostitute, some crackhead, crying-ass Tyrese Gibson? I mean, how you gonna not make sure the baby was his? That's Hoenomics 101. If you were gonna fuck around on him, the very least you could've done was make sure he was the daddy."

"Fuck you!"

"No thank you. I prefer penis. Got enough dick to keep me occupied. You remember what he's packing, right? Girl! I ain't walked straight in months! It's like ground beef down there!"

She gave me half a smirk. "You can't even handle him." Damn, this heifer just would not lie down.

So Evil Jo said, "Oh, I can handle him now. I can handle the *shit* outta him. Wanna see? I know you like watching us...or listening to us...or whatever you were doing in that closet."

I heard Everett behind me. "Jo, baby—"

"I'm done, but so is she if she wants her daughter to keep loving her. I'm not playing. I'm not gonna be her victim anymore, and neither are you."

Everett stood, placing a hand on my shoulder. "Um, Esther...you should go."

She stood there for a moment, her pouty lips trembling like her big bad ass wanted to cry. Then she said, "I can't believe this."

"Believe it, and heed it, ho'. Don't think for a minute I won't do it. After what you did to me, it would be a pleasure. I'm even willing to pay for Ella's counseling afterwards. I do care about her, you know?"

She shook her head as she glared at me.

"Oh, and you better not tell anyone about tonight. You were never here, and if you say otherwise, you know what I'm gonna do."

"You bitch," she gritted.

"Awww, thanks," I replied.

A few seconds later, she stormed out of the house, burning rubber as she left our property.

I turned to a still-stunned Everett, and said, "I was bluffing. I'd never do that to Ella, but I had to make her believe I would. I just wanted her to know I knew, to take some of her power away. That secret was like Kryptonite to you, and well, I'm over people treating me like shit and me just taking it. I—"

"How long have you known?"

"I figured it out when I was stuck in my depression, lying in bed with nothing to do but think."

He nodded. "Why didn't you say something before now? Why didn't you mention it to me first?"

"I...I didn't think it was something you wanted to discuss, figured you'd tell me when you were ready."

"But you changed your mind?"

"No, I wanted to keep you out of it and confront her alone, but I couldn't figure out how to do that."

"I wasn't gonna tell you. I don't think I could've. My family doesn't even know."

"They don't?"

"No. I know that's fucked up, but I just didn't want *anyone* to know. I-it's...I don't know how to deal with you knowing this."

"Ev, I think it's beautiful that you put Ella's needs and wellbeing before your own. It's nothing to be ashamed of. You are a good man, the best I've ever known, and I'm proud to call you mine. I'm sorry if what I said to her hurt you. That wasn't my intention. I just wanted to shake her up. She was too bold with her shit and—"

"Jo, I hear you. I just..." He sighed.

My heart fell as I watched him struggle internally. I knew I was running a risk when I decided to confront her, but I honestly wasn't ready for losing him to be the consequence I'd have to face. "You can't be with me now that I know, or because I threatened her?"

"I didn't say that. I'm just...embarrassed as hell about how she fucking played me like that from day one. She was already pregnant when we got married. The baby was the main reason I rushed to marry her, and everything...everything went just like you said. I didn't have even one doubt until after I caught her cheating, had the test done, and my whole world fell apart. Ella's been my heart since she came into this world, and to find out she wasn't mine? That just, it broke me. For real. And it made me look like a sucker, a fool. I still feel like a damn fool. And if anyone else finds out—this shit is embarrassing, Jo. Yeah, Esther's the one in the wrong, but still…"

"I would never, *ever* tell anyone, Ev. I wouldn't do that to you. I just had to make her believe I was as low as she is, but I wouldn't do that to you or Ella. I promise you. I won't tell *anyone*."

"But *you* know."

"And like I said, I think it's beautiful that you decided to still be a father to Ella."

"But…how can you respect me after this? Knowing this?"

"I respect you more for your sacrifice, for your big heart. I—I'm sorry. If I could take it back, I would. I just didn't know any other way to stop her. I…"

We stood there for a moment, both of us mute. I didn't know what else to do or say, and evidently, neither did he. So I just said, "Let's go to bed, talk about it in the morning?"

"No."

I stared at him, my heart thrashing in my chest. This was it. I'd overstepped and messed everything up. It was over. "W-why?"

"Nothing left to talk about. You did what you felt you had to do. I appreciate that, because I was ready to go to jail. Didn't want to, but I was willing to. You probably saved my ass."

"I *know* I did."

He chuckled and shook his head. "Same old Jo."

"There's only one old person in this room, Everett."

With raised brows, he countered, "You don't be calling me old when I—"

"You still love me? You still want me after what I said to her? You believe I was just bluffing?"

He pulled me to him. "I know your heart. I know you'd never do anything to hurt me, and you know that would hurt me."

"I really wouldn't."

"And to see you go that hard for me makes me want you even

more, love you even deeper. Shit, the way you fired those shots at Esther? You a rider for real."

"Only for you, Big South. Only for you."

39

Everett

Two months later...

My heart was full as I watched her standing there. She'd changed out of her cream gown into a short white dress covered in crystals and some stilettos that made it hard for me to keep from attacking her right there in that room where we waited to be escorted out to the receiving line in the grand ballroom. She was my wife now, and I couldn't get the image of her floating down the aisle toward me to OutKast's *Prototype* out of my mind. Jo almost tripped over her feet when she saw Andre 3000 standing on the other side of Leland, my best man, serenading everyone. I was glad I was able to pull that surprise off.

And now, as she turned to face me, excitement in her eyes, I couldn't help but smile. I loved this woman so much, more than I even knew I was capable of.

She returned my smile as she inched closer to where I sat on a chair observing her in the small room. Standing between my legs, she asked, "What are you looking at?"

I placed my hands on her hips. "You, Mrs. McClain."

She pulled her bottom lip between her teeth, grinning down at me. "That's Mrs. South to you."

I slid my hands around to her ass. "You know what I've never done before, Mrs. South?"

She shook her head. "No, what?"

Sliding my hand under her short dress to grip her bare ass in her thong underwear, I answered, "Made love to my new wife."

Closing her eyes as I slid my hand from her ass to her mound, she murmured, "Uh...isn't that what the honeymoon is for?"

As I found my way into her panties and slid a finger inside her, I said, "Traditionally, but I say, fuck tradition. I want you right here, *right now.*"

She grabbed my shoulders as I used my thumb to massage her clit. "But-But we have to greet people, do the dance, and I don't wanna be—ohhh, shit! I don't wanna be leaking you from me while I do that stuff."

I reached up with my free hand and tilted her head so that I could kiss her, sliding my tongue into her mouth.

A minute later, she pulled her mouth from mine. "Ev, for real. I don't wanna be all juicy and stuff out there."

I slid my fingers out of her and licked them. "You can stop in a restroom before we go to the ballroom, clean yourself up. I saw one close by when they were leading us in here. Shit, I'll wash you up myself, but I need it, baby. Right now."

Her eyes narrowed with what was undeniable desire as she reached down and began unbuttoning my pants. I stood, slid them down my legs, and was pushed back onto the chair by Jo, who pulled her dress up and was about to pull her underwear off when I stopped her.

"I'ma just slide them motherfuckers to the side," I said in a voice so full of lust, I barely recognized it myself.

Without another word, she straddled me, giving me room to slide her panties to the side and line my dick up with her treasure. She clamped her hand to my mouth as she sank down on me.

"Shit!" I yelled into her hand, then grabbed her hips to help her move, but she shook her head.

"I got it. Let me do the work, baby," she said.

That shit was so sexy, I almost busted right then, but managed to hold it because I knew the longer I held it, the better the explosion would feel. She slid up and down me, coating me with her juices as she looked into my eyes with heavy lids, moaning softly, her face in a pretty frown. I slid one of her dress straps down her shoulder, and reached inside the strapless bra to grab and twist her nipple, making her lose her rhythm for a second as she rode the hell out of me.

"Damn, baby!" I mumbled, her hand still muzzling me. She felt so damn good and hot and shit, I closed my eyes and just felt it all, felt her clenching and pulling at me each time she lifted from my lap, as if her pussy was trying to take possession of something it already owned—me. I would hop in a damn volcano just for a taste of it.

When she stiffened and I heard a soft, tortured-sounding grunt, I opened my eyes and grabbed her hips, moving her up and down me at a hectic pace as she vibrated around my dick, contracting, jerking, milking me. Then I felt it coming, the sensation so strong there was no holding out this time. I reached around and clutched her ass tightly as my ass lifted from the chair and I emptied inside her. Just as my eyesight returned, I saw the door ease open then slam shut. It was the wedding coordinator, a really kind older black lady who'd just gotten an eyeful of Jo's ass and a nose full of our sex. Jo's hand was still covering my mouth, and I was still half high off her pussy. Neither of us had thought to lock the door.

"Who was that?" Jo asked with big, panicked eyes.

"The wedding planner," I said into her hand.

"Shit," Jo mumbled, as she removed her hand from my mouth and lifted from my lap, sucking in air as I slipped out of her. "I can't believe we just sort of got caught. She must think we are the nastiest people..."

"Much as I'm paying her? She ain't got room to think shit. Come on. Let's find that restroom."

Jo shook her head. "You just couldn't wait. Had to have some right now..."

"Sure did, and don't act like you didn't enjoy it."

"Did I say that?"

"Then what's the problem?"

"The problem is I'm sure she's livid to have seen that...*us*."

"I'll give her a fat-ass bonus. That should fix it."

She rolled her eyes at me, and I grinned as I guided her out of the room.

*****

"Thanks for coming," I said for probably the thousandth time, but I didn't mind. I didn't mind any of it, not the money we spent on the wedding, the millions of pictures we took, or having to stand in this receiving line. It was all part of the best day of my life.

I glanced at Jo as she graciously shook hands with the head of my record label, accepting his congratulatory wishes with a bright smile. I knew she had to be tired, but what I had planned for her once we left and boarded her jet was really going to wear her out. Yeah, I stayed horny around her, and I ain't ashamed to admit it.

"You actually look the same. I was wondering if I'd even recognize you after all these years. Been seeing you on TV and YouTube and stuff, but thought maybe they were photoshopping your big ass or something."

My head jerked around to find my boy, Keith, standing in front of me. "Nigga!" I shouted, as we slapped hands and pulled each other into half a hug. "What you doing here, man?!"

"Damn, you don't want me here, Ev?"

"Naw, not that. Just surprised to see you. Glad to see you, too. Been meaning to call."

He nodded toward Jo. "Well, your new wife took the initiative, called and invited me. See, that's how I know you got the right one this time."

I looked at her and smiled, before returning my attention to Keith. "I sure do. Hey, thanks for coming, man. For real. It's good to see you."

"We gotta keep in touch, bruh. Seriously."

"We will. I promise."

As he shook Jo's hand and moved along, I asked her, "How in the world did you get in touch with him?"

"Stole his number from your phone. It's been the same all these years. Isn't that crazy?"

"It really is."

A few minutes later, I heard Jo say, "Just a few more people." She was leaning forward, checking out the folks lined up to the left of us. "Thank God, because I'm about to starve."

"You and me both," I replied. About ten more minutes had passed, and we were down to the last five or six guests when I nodded at the older lady standing before me in a pink dress suit. "Thanks for coming. We appreciate it."

She gave me a wink. "Thank you, honey."

Once she was in front of Jo, I heard a soft gasp, and tried to concentrate on shaking the woman's husband's hand, but needed to gauge Jo's reaction.

"Oh, my...I saw you standing in line, but didn't recognize you from a distance, and there are so many people here, and how—what are you doing here?" Her eyes shifted to the gentleman as he left me and joined his wife, standing at her side.

"I invited them," I offered. "And her," I added, pointing to a lady who resembled the older woman greatly.

Jo raised her hand to cover her mouth, then dropped it. "Um...thank you all for coming?" She sounded both surprised and skeptical. I couldn't blame her, knowing her history with her grandparents and aunt. They hadn't exactly been a positive presence in her life. Hell, they hadn't been present at all. I could only hope she didn't hate me for reaching out to them.

"You're welcome. When you get time, maybe after your honeymoon, we'd like to sit down and talk to you. Get to know you?"

Jo's eyes swept over to me, then slid back over to her mother's kin. "Uh, I'll have to think about it."

Her aunt nodded. "We understand." Then they left, clearing the way for the last of our well-wishers to approach us.

Closing my eyes, I leaned into Everett as The Whispers performed *Just Gets Better with Time*. I smiled, remembering how he said them performing at our reception felt like having his mother there. The entire day was magical, from the exchanging of our vows, to that little treat in the holding room, to the receiving line where I was shocked to see my mother's parents and sister—who Everett contacted and flew in to surprise me—to this moment, in his arms.

"You gonna get up there and sing with them?" he asked, breaking into my thoughts.

"I only sing for you, in private. That was our deal."

"Yeah, but I'ma pull you out of that shell, make sure the world hears that voice."

"Never gonna happen. Hey, thanks again for my surprise."

"You're welcome. I know you ain't really got nothing for them, but I wanted you to have some family here today."

"I appreciate it. They seemed different, nicer, but that's probably because I just married a very rich man."

"Maybe not."

"Yeah, right, but it doesn't matter. It's the thought behind your gesture that counts."

"Yeah. I'm glad you're not mad at me."

"Never. Hey, did you try to contact my father, too? You located him?"

"Uh, yeah."

"Let me guess. He wouldn't come?"

"No. I'm sorry, Jo."

"Nah, it's his loss. I'm good."

He backed away a little and peered down at me. "You sure?"

"I got you and a whole new family, including another daughter. How could I not be good?"

He pulled me closer. "I'm so damn glad Ella fell in line. Shit!"

My eyes roamed the room, finding her dancing with her Uncle

Leland. "Me, too. And I'm glad her mother's been quiet."

"Hope she stays that way, her *and* Bugz's ass."

"I think they will."

"Thanks for inviting my boy, Keith, baby."

"You're welcome. Hey, Ev?"

"Yeah?"

"Happy birthday."

He abruptly released me, and I noticed him looking down at something. I smiled when I saw Nat tugging at his tuxedo pant leg. She looked so adorable in her little cream-colored, satin and tulle dress. Picking her up, he used his free hand to pull me closer as he danced with both of us. "Thank you for being my birthday gift, Jo Lena. I love your little ass, you know that?"

With a huge smile on her face, Nat chirped, "Little ass!"

A southern girl at heart, Alexandria House has an affinity for a good banana pudding, Neo Soul music, and tall black men in suits. When this fashionista is not shopping, she's writing steamy stories about real black love.

Connect with Alexandria!
Email: **msalexhouse@gmail.com**
Website: **http://www.msalexhouse.com/**
Newsletter: **http://eepurl.com/cOUVg5**
Blog: **http://msalexhouse.blogspot.com/**
Facebook: **Alexandria House**
Instagram: **@msalexhouse**
Twitter: **@mzalexhouse**

Also by Alexandria House:

The Strickland Sisters Series:
Stay with Me
Believe in Me
Be with Me

The Love After Series:
Higher Love
Made to Love
Real Love

Short Stories
Merry Christmas, Baby
Baby, Be Mine